Copyright © 2022 by Jordyn A Moretti

All rights reserved.

No portion of this book may be reproduced in any form without written permission from the publisher or author, except as permitted by U.S. copyright law.

Any references to historical events, real people, or real places are used fictitiously. Names, characters, and places are products of the author's imagination.

First printing edition 2022

Front cover image by Chris Moretti

Book design by Pandora_halk

Map design by Jordyn A Moretti courtesy of features found on Inkarnate

Cursed Is The Blood

A Dark Divinity Novel

Jordyn A Moretti

Contents

Dedication	VII
Intro	1
1. The World Keeps Spinning Without You	3
2. A Fresh Hell	12
3. Another Day, Another Nightmare	36
4. Haunting Encounters	60
5. Peace Is The For Lucky	75
6. Adjustment Pains	88
7. The Nature Of Monsters	109
8. Hidden Desires	138
9. The Past, Present, & Future Of Pain	158
10. To Hurt & Heal	174
11. Loved & Lost	190
12. Thoughts Of A Villain	209
13. What Could Be Worse	228
14. Fateful Inclinations	252
15. Famous Last Words	278
16. The Hardest Goodbyes	300
17. Going Through The Motions	317
18. Passageway	337
19. Consequences In Lust	356

20.	What Lies In Wait	378
21.	The Final Straw	397
22.	Chasing Retribution	413
23.	A Court Of Gods & Vampires	432
24.	Cursed Royalty	449
25.	With The Setting Sun	473
26.	Look To The Sky & See The Stars	489
27.	Hereafter We Wander	506
28.	Poorly Mistaken Maygen	524
Acknowledgments		544
About the Author		550

In memory of Kenneth Latin Steele
My beloved big brother
9/21/1983 - 8/24/2016

"I wish you could see the ways we remember you
In dreams, memories, song lyrics, and dancing flames
We find you in deafening silence and rainy days
We see you in the shadows
And in between the lines on a page
You weigh heavily on our hearts
All these years apart
Our love for you remains the same"

I love you and will continue missing you immensely for as long as I live.

If you or a loved one are struggling, know you are not alone and help is available. The National Suicide Prevention Lifeline is now: 988 Suicide and Crisis Lifeline.

988 has been designated as the new three-digit dialing code that will route callers to the National Suicide Prevention Lifeline.

1-800-273-8255

Intro

Flickers are all I get, if I'm lucky. The rest is darkness.

I don't know how long it's been. I don't know if I've moved, where I am, or what has changed around me. It doesn't feel like it has been as long as the whispers have said. Although, considering my predicament, I shouldn't be surprised. How often does a Dark Mage make idle threats? Why waste their time on anything at all, with the powers they possess? I made my bed long ago, and I'm paying dearly for it.

At this moment, I have only silence and darkness. Alone with my feeble consciousness is my usual state. Sometimes memories will play in my mind like a dream. I have this awareness, but I never leave the sleep, I cannot open my eyes. Rarely, there are whispers, but I cannot speak back to them. The last thing I saw was the cloud of darkness spiraling toward me, helpless as it enveloped my entire being. The last thing I truly heard was my own desperate scream, reminiscent of the screams of my loved ones as my Fate befell me. That kind of fear warps one's mind, the trauma of losing everything all at once. If I ever was to escape this purgatory, this personal hell, I could not be who I once was; even if I wanted to.

I'd been cursed.

Consciousness craves freedom, and being aware of entrapment births a terror that crawls up your throat and chokes you. It swallows and drowns like the treacherous depths of the Ende Sea. It freezes your bones as if you were adrift in the tundra. A death by drowning or freezing would be a welcomed gift; anything to put an end to this lifeless floating, the suffering that I've endured.

I wonder what I might've done differently to avoid this Fate. Perhaps if I'd left home when the High Court had inquired for me, I never would have crossed paths with a villain. Perhaps if I had not been a hopeless fool, giving my warmth to those around me despite their intentions, I would not have been ensnared by a deceiver. Had I not been so desperate for love, I would not have been searching for it in all the wrong places. Yet, the thought that plagues me the most: what if I had just given him what he'd wanted from me? What if I had said yes?

Every fiber of my being told me to say no, to never give in to the likes of him. I said no, unknowingly evoking the wrath of a man who was corrupted by dark magic, who was swayed by potent forces beyond my understanding.

A futile effort had been made on my part to fight back, and I failed to save myself.

I was lost.

Chapter One

The World Keeps Spinning Without You

Obscured images began forming in my mind. Memories of a courtyard that once grew the daisies I'd braid into my younger sister's delicate hair, and an old willow with a rope swing, where I'd sing melodies into the open air; wondering if the breeze might carry the tunes to the Nymphs of the meadows. As a child I had always dreamed of befriending a Nymph, one of those rare and magical beings of the meadows, mountains, shadows, and water of the seas and rivers.

I was lucky enough to meet one once, by chance, while I drank water from the brook near my family's estate. Her hair looked as though it was made of sweetgrass, with skin a tinted sage green. She had eyes so shockingly clear, as though they mirrored the sky when it was without a single cloud, ever changing.

She took shape before me, appearing just as she'd been the morning I met her. I could see her extended hand, beckoning me, friendly and welcoming. I felt a smile pulling up the corners of my lips, swelling the skin of my cheeks to reveal a toothy grin. I lifted my gaze from our slowly approaching hands to meet her own stare and suddenly she was changing, distorting — becoming something else, someone else.

The blurred shapes and shadowed features took form, and it was him... The Mage. Panic gripped me like a vice. I tried to rip my hand away. I wanted to disappear; I had to run. I was frozen, unable to flee, and I stared hopelessly into his eyes. Hollow eyes, unfeeling and unyielding. Merciless.

Please don't, please let me go. Let me go, let me go, let me go.

A soundless plea screamed from my unmoving lips. My cries were in my mind, I could not give them sound.

"Give me what I desire."

The voice that came forth was not of this world. Deeper than the void, as unnerving as if a demon was calling upon you.

No. No. No. I won't.

Perhaps yielding could grant me the peace I desired? It might grant me freedom. What if I could have my life back? What if I could escape?

Wishful thinking... don't be naive. I know better.

If I yielded to this monster, it would spell a Fate much worse than this, something worse than death. I would never be released. I have to remain strong, but I've been strong for so long. Every passing moment was taxing, draining me.

This was the game that he played. I was allowed to see things I loved, if only for a moment, to weaken my resolve. The memories were carefully selected to break me, so that I might give him what he wanted. Although I noticed something was different this time, it happened faster, he seemed more desperate, more demanding. The usual patience he utilized to methodically tear down my walls was gone; an urgency had replaced it. These moments were typically elaborate and tedious enough that I would begin to relent without realizing. I had never fully given up, but it seemed as though he was now out of time.

An unearthly shriek ripped through the air. It did not belong to me, even in the midst of terror replacing every ounce of reason I had left. The illusion became black and twisted, a true horror to behold. The screaming made my head feel like it was going to burst, with the pressure against my eardrums excruciating. This must finally be my end; at long last, he must've lost his patience with me and moved on. I think perhaps I am ready to be at peace, to become nothing at all. It would be better than this.

I braced myself.

My body was upright and the world around me made little sense.

What was I seeing? How was I seeing? My ears rang so painfully that I needed to grip my head to find relief. I felt my elbows bend, felt my fingers entwining with locks of hair, felt my palms against my ears. I was moving. How was I moving? That was not possible, he had frozen me.

I lowered my arms down to my lap.

How strange it was to feel my chest expand as air filled my lungs, to feel how cold my skin was, to be chilled all the way to my bones. I ran my fingers across the tattered fabric of the shift that covered my body. I was awake, and this was real. I did not even want to blink, as I couldn't allow this to be taken from me, and I feared the darkness would claim me again.

My eyes burned; tears streamed down my cheeks. The hot, damp streaks began to dry, tightening the pores on my face. A muffled sound left me, a terrified whimper. It had slithered its way up my dry, hoarse throat. My lips parted, granting a full escape to the pathetic cry. My gaze did not leave my hands, hands that I could see and feel. They were so stiff and frigid, so pale.

A pressure formed against my shoulder, there was warmth in the touch that gripped me, causing panic to set in once again. Whirling, my body was propelled from where I had been lying, crashing to the stone floor. Pain sliced through my senses, radiating from the points of impact. From the ground, I looked up to the ledge I'd fallen from, a stone table that looked as though it had been carved specifically for sacrifices. Rushed breaths heaved my chest as I watched booted feet move against the stone. I was starting to hyperventilate, my senses urged me to flee, to escape.

I decided on a whim that I did not want to die, and apparently, I wasn't truly ready as I had thought. My mortal instincts insisted that I fight to live. I nearly begged for mercy, until gentle fingers lifted my chin to look into the eyes of... a woman?

This was not the Mage, nor the creatures that terrorized me in my cursed sleep, just a woman. A stranger.

"We need to leave now."

She forced me upright, but my weak legs buckled under my body. The woman was petite in stature, but shouldered herself beneath me, heaving my weight up into her arms. A pungent scent invaded the air I inhaled, lodging deep in my nose, foul and metallic. Slowly, I became more aware of my surroundings.

Blood was everywhere.

That much blood couldn't possibly have come from a single source. There was no consistency to the madness, pools and splatters, with smears and streams of it painted on the floors and the walls. Amidst the crimson display, there were various shapes of matter... Body parts.

Nausea took further hold as the woman began to run. I was being jostled and handled like a small child, wrapped tightly in her arms; at a closer examination of myself, I was comparable to just that. Frail and sickly, my bones were poking through my skin. I looked up at the woman's face, trying to sort out who now held me in their grasp. She had high cheekbones with a round face, and an upturned nose, thin brows that matched her ashy blonde hair.

I was blinded by the intensity of bright rays of sunlight. I could hardly bear to look, but my fear of returning to the magic sleep kept my eyes open. Without warning, I was stuffed into a small carriage, where the woman hastily covered me in blankets.

"Please understand that you must remain still, and you must remain silent. The magic that is leaving your system will take a severe toll on you, expending any unnecessary energy will only make it more difficult for you to recover. We may be riding for some time."

I was not given a moment to nod my understanding before the door latched shut. Everything was dark again, but it felt as though it might be peaceful. Despite my desire to live, I gave in, and I let it take me.

"Wake up, damn it! I did not endure all of this for you to die in your sleep!"

The voice was a distant echo, disturbing my blissful unawareness.

I was sure everything that had happened, my escape, was just a new and even crueler illusion used by *him* to get what he wanted. Giving me such convincing false hope would be an ingenious plan to force my submission; only to be crushed again when he snatched it away. I wouldn't give in.

Opening my eyes, I found myself looking directly at the strange woman. She appeared irate, not the panicked face I had seen when she had lifted me from the cold floor in that prison. When would she become something else? Would his face take hold, leaving me to fight against his will once more?

She kept staring at me, impatient.

This cannot be real.

"You put me in a panic. It's been a full day since I pulled you out of that hellhole, and you have not opened your eyes once, no matter how much I tried to rouse you. You looked dead, you're freezing, and your breathing was shallow. The black magic should've left your system by now. Drink this."

She held a cup in her hands and began to lift it to my mouth. I flinched.

The woman snorted and rolled her eyes, "It's water. You've been out of the magic's grip for too long without any sustenance, and unless you want to actually die, you need to drink water and eat food."

I tried to speak, my lips parted slightly, but my body failed in its frail state. Looking into her eyes, an overwhelming sense of relief erupted inside my chest and tears rolled down my cheeks.

Thoughtfully taking in my reaction, the woman sighed and lifted the cup once more, this time placing it against my cracked lips. Cold, life-giving liquid streamed down my throat. Drinking greedily, I drained the cup in just a few deep gulps. She offered two more until I was gasping.

"You'll make yourself sick. Breathe. Do you think you can speak? Do you remember anything? Do you know who you are?"

Do I know who I am? Yes, of course I did.

Except, I didn't.

When did that leave me? My sense of awareness was fully intact, surely I knew who I was? No, I couldn't have had it all taken away. Yet for all the searching I did in my brain, I found nothing. The few memories available to me had been warped and manipulated by the illusions of my slumber.

"No," I croaked, speaking felt foreign and unnatural.

"I'm sorry that this happened to you. It wouldn't be this severe if someone had located you sooner. I can tell you what you need to know, if you're ready."

My voice was hoarse as I spoke, "Sooner?"

Processing exactly what that meant, unease formed a heavy weight in the pit of my stomach.

"How long?"

Hyperventilating was incredibly undignified, yet here I was, losing control.

"Calm down. Nothing I'm about to tell you is going to make you feel any better. I need you to come to terms with that now because this hysteria will attract unwanted attention, and we cannot risk that. Do you understand?"

Swallowing my hiccups and ragged breaths, I nodded my head.

"Your name is Celessa Umbraeon, you are the third daughter of Lord Altan Umbraeon. Your family were among the last noble mortals to be descended from the divine God Syades, and you possess a unique power. The Dark Mage Asuras stole you to harness your magic because you were the first in the family line to display exceptional abilities and any bearing of divinity. An anomaly unheard of in a mortal being."

None of that sounded right. In fact, it sounded like nonsense. Yet it *felt* like the truth. I could remember what the Mage asked me for, my gift, a dark and ancient power. He wanted it for himself. Vaguely, I remembered the incident where it reared its ugly head for the first time. Summoned by intense emotion, it quickly became uncontrollable and dangerous.

Deadly.

I hadn't suspected ill intentions when I'd met the handsome, charming man for the first time. The onslaught of unexpected memories birthed a splitting headache along the top of my skull.

"You and I are the last."

"The last?" I whispered.

"I'm sorry, your family was murdered when you were taken. Every distant relative, every trace of blood erased. Except for you, stolen and imprisoned, and your youngest sister Ephyra. She was rescued from the massacre by one of the Mage's acolytes who had allegedly fallen in love with her, so the story goes. She lived under a false name, and they had children."

Processing everything she said was difficult. It sounded as though generations of my family had sought me out. For what? A gift that could not offer them salvation? That much time couldn't have passed.

"How long?"

How many days, months, years had I been imprisoned? Tormented? Surely she was taking my time held captive to extreme exaggerations. I couldn't fathom how I might react otherwise.

"I am the seventh generation that came after the Umbraeon name was wiped away."

"Seven generations..." My voice hollowed, barely above a whisper.

"The Mage held you for one hundred and forty-two years."

The silence became deafening, the sound of pulsating blood roared in my ears.

"How?"

"He's a Dark Mage, he uses black magic. What do you think? If I had to guess, I'd say he probably stopped the flow of time in the chamber you were kept in. It seems as though you've only aged a few weeks to maybe a few months, considering how scrawny you are."

My loved ones were long dead, and I was alone.

"Who are you?"

"Ephyra was my 'quite-a-few-greats' grandmother. Which makes you my rather distant aunt, I suppose."

"I can't remember," I could barely form the faces of my family in my mind, and I struggled to summon their names.

"The memories should return soon; your mind needs time to reacclimate to reality. We need to get on the road to Lysenna's Keep, just outside of Autumnmoor in Euros. We'll find refuge there. Lysenna is my Godmother, so she will help keep you safe and hidden."

"I'm not safe... from Asuras."

"You could kill him?" A rather nonchalant suggestion in regards to an impossible feat. "Which is what I expect you would want to do. Avenge your family, and put an end to his madness."

"Impossible," I whispered; I knew that to be true in my heart. I was no match for ancient, evil magic.

"Your name?"

"Maygen," she answered.

"Leave, Maygen," I swallowed roughly, "You're not safe."

She chuckled, "I'm sure he knows who I am now, I won't be safe anymore, whether I keep you with me or not. I slayed several acolytes inside the keep when I retrieved you, but I know some of those who fled saw my face."

Very slowly, I consumed the dried meat and boiled vegetables Maygen prepared, hoping it would return some of the strength I had lost. It was as painful as it was relieving for food to stretch my empty stomach. With the fullness came an unshakable drowsiness.

"Sleep, recover your strength. You are safe, I promise. The more you rest, the faster you'll regain that which you have lost."

She smiled tightly and left the carriage, leaving me to slumber.

Chapter Two

A Fresh Hell

The carriage lurched forward abruptly before halting to a sudden stop.

Maygen had said this morning that we'd traveled through the Barren Mountains Pass and Tamaa Forest, geography I knew only from maps: fleeting memories. The carriage was without windows, and I had not stepped out since I'd entered it, with the woman only appearing to provide me food and water.

A shout drew me from my stupor, and I heaved myself up on weak legs. I was alarmed because Maygen usually remained quiet on the road, so the urgency of the sound sent me into a frenzy. I drew the blade that I suspected the woman had used to slay the acolytes from its sheath, and shoved the door open. It was dusk, and our carriage was exposed in the open valley that lies before Grim's Peak.

As fast as my legs could carry me, I rushed around the carriage to meet a horrific sight. Maygen was pinned to the ground by what appeared to be a large man with antlers and a rotten face. The creature sported elongated canine fangs and a disgustingly long tongue that hung limply from its mouth. An ear-splitting cry left her as it gnashed salivating jaws near the woman's exposed neck. My heartbeat thundered in my head. Instinct took over, and I leapt forward, enforcing the short sword with every ounce of strength I could muster from my frail body.

A terrified scream escaped my chest as I drove the blade into its back, unleashing a horrific howl from the beast as it registered the assault. A gangly arm collided with my body, propelling me through the air.

The breath was forced violently from my lungs. Gasping and trying to blink through the white that had overtaken my vision, I attempted to piece together my surroundings. A clawed hand met my throat and hoisted my body into the air. I thrashed wildly. The creature's gaze met mine for only a second before my eyes darted around seeking an escape. I noticed the blade remained where I'd impaled it; it had done nothing. The creature's crooked, sharp grin parted and an otherworldly sound spewed from the depths of its being. Black eyes locked onto my face, unblinking.

A strangled scream was cut short by the talons gripping my neck. Pure terror threatened to freeze me, and I desperately grasped at whatever I had left. Reaching in vain for something, anything to save myself.

I lashed out, grabbing the beast's arms with my hands, a feeble attempt to claw my way to freedom. It felt like the world around me shuddered, blackening my vision, making my very bones groan. I swear I felt my soul leaving my body as I faced this unnatural horror. It appeared I would meet my death after all, and it would be gruesome.

What appeared to be red fog began to emerge from and melt between my fingers, snaking tendrils up the body of the monster; sinking into its flesh. It began screaming again, but this time it was pained. It released me from its grasp. My body dropped limply to the ground; the mist still bellowed from my hands, across the ground and up the length of the creature's body.

I was killing it with my curse. A presence of death and destruction, dark and twisted.

Its skin melted from its bones. The monster was shrieking and battering what remained of its body against the ground, until there was nothing left to fight and silence fell. Blood red mist retreated, painfully filling up my body, stretching my skin and wrapping around my lungs. Groaning, I prayed for it to end quickly. It felt like it was struggling to fit in where it did not belong, where it was not wanted.

My guts twisted. I heaved myself over the best I could manage and vomited violently into the dirt, choking and sputtering. Hair fell into my face, becoming tainted with my stomach's contents, and I sobbed. Violent spasms rattled my ribcage and tore at my abdominal muscles as I lay in my own mess, floating somewhere between being thankful I survived and wishing I had died to end this cursed existence.

I lingered in silence, watching the world around me give way to the creeping shadows of evening.

"Celessa?" I could hear Maygen's call past the ringing in my ears; I'd forgotten that creature had thrown me far from where she'd been assaulted.

"Here," I choked, pulling at tiny shreds of strength.

"How are you alive?"

Her head turned, taking notice of the simmering pile of blood and gore that coated the ground.

"Is this your gift? Is this what you can do?"

Wide eyes met mine, having nothing else to offer, I only nodded slowly. Maygen shuddered as she attempted to lift me from the ground.

"You saved us."

"What the fuck was that?" I demanded.

She appeared surprised by my cursing. Ladies were not meant to use inappropriate language; one of many rules I'd broken throughout my life. There were no nobles lording over me to enforce what they deemed proper anymore. I had endured so much... I felt I had earned the right to speak as I please.

"A Wyndiga. They dwell in the Tamaa Forest, that's why you can typically only make it out of Sanctuary by ship, through the bay. The

Mage cursed the folk who lived in these lands when he claimed the fortress," she rasped hoarsely, "I was prepared in the thick of the trees, but when we made it out with no trouble, I let my guard down. I assumed we'd gotten lucky."

Inhaling roughly, she coughed and spat blood on the ground.

"The curse he cast was for them to become gnarled, forced to hunt any beings who dare travel the forest. Typically *people*. However, this one killed our horse."

Defeat resonated in her shaky voice as we neared the carriage, lowering our bodies into the small doorway.

"Are there any settlements nearby?"

"There's a village not far from here, but I'm sure word has already spread about you. Everyone will be on the lookout for unfamiliar women."

She continued after catching my questioning gaze, "Teskaria was falling backwards before you were taken, and the way the laws were rewritten a few decades ago made things worse. Women aren't allowed to travel alone without a man accompanying them. If we are caught, we're done for."

Watching her rub the tears and blood away from her face, I placed a hand on her shoulder.

"We can't stay here," Maygen whispered.

It took several grueling hours on foot to reach the settlement on the coast of Serpent's Bay, when Maygen informed me that it was overseen by a man called Tobian. Not many people still lived here due to the Wyndiga affliction, and those that remained didn't have the means to leave. Small homes were reinforced with steel and wood, sporting boarded windows and high fences topped with long spikes.

We had the advantage of night's shadows, but we were weak from the attack, further battered by the seemingly endless trek to arrive here. Maygen signaled for me to stop, and we ducked into a shadowed alley. Three large men strode past, blissfully unaware of our presence. Once they cleared our field of vision, we began to move toward a building that appeared to be stables.

I was watching her back, following her step for step, when I heard a noise behind me. The hair on my body rose as the realization sunk in that we were being followed. Turning slowly to assess my surroundings, I found myself restrained, unable to fight against the unexpected assailant. A hand slipped over my mouth to muffle my effort to alert Maygen.

Struggling was futile, as my body was succumbing to its compromised state. I was forced against a stone wall, and the hand remained clamped over my mouth. A strong body pressed against my own, wrapping a thick arm around my chest, pinning my arms to my body to force my submission.

"Don't make a sound. They've been keeping an eye out for Sanctuary's lost lady," a man whispered.

A voice in my head battled against my instinct to fight, telling me to hold fast. The minutes seemed to drag, making me feel as though I'd been held captive for hours. Maygen hadn't returned to seek me out. I hoped she made it to the stables and I prayed she would not try to return the way we'd come.

The men that previously passed by made a return, and I could see now that they were a patrol of some sort.

"A woman was spotted making for the stables, one of the locals just reported it. Grab her and take her to Tobian. The Sentinels are a few days out," I heard someone say.

As one of the men ordered the other two in the direction Maygen had run, an urgency to reach her overtook my senses and I resumed my struggle.

"They don't want her; she isn't worth anything to them. She'll be questioned and held until the Sentinel patrol comes through. I need you to stop fighting and come quietly, I'll keep you safe," he breathed against my neck.

I didn't have a choice or an opportunity to object; the man lifted my body and began to sprint, carrying me off into the night. His hand never left my mouth, despite my continuing efforts to escape, until exhaustion finally subdued me and I had no strength left. My mind shuffled through what possible outcomes awaited me. I found myself imagining my demise often, yet I kept fighting to live. As much as I considered giving up, Fate urged me on.

We crept up to a cottage at the edge of the settlement. The mysterious man kicked open the door, rushing inside and forcing it shut with his back, keeping me locked in his grip.

"I'm going to let you go, but if you scream, they will come for you. Nowhere else is safe for you, I can promise you that," he threatened.

Hesitantly, I nodded and was gently lowered onto what felt like a bed. His palm left my mouth, and I sucked in a breath of cool air. I collapsed to the floor as quickly as I tried to stand, my being entirely bereft of energy, while bursts of light filled my vision. My brain felt like it was tumbling around the walls of my skull, bouncing helplessly against its bone cage. It was dark, no fire nor candles lit.

"Who are you, what do you want with me? Why am I here?" I demanded into the blackened room.

A snap sounded to my left, and a flicker of light appeared as kindling was placed into the silhouette of a hearth. As it dimly illuminated the surroundings, I was able to make out the man's figure. His back remained to me as flames licked dry branches, spreading timidly.

"Please do not be upset with me for my manner of retrieving you, I've been watching for you ever since word arrived that you escaped.

I couldn't believe you were still alive until I heard the name in the report. I can save you, Celessa."

The way this man spoke my name made me shudder, as if a dead winter's breeze kissed my skin.

"Who are you?" I demanded once more.

He turned slowly, cautiously.

His hair was copper and looked as though it had been kissed by fire itself, with unnaturally deep green eyes. Vague memories passed through my mind, of a boy older than me with fiery locks, and a farm where he'd kissed my cheek by the brook. He'd held my hand through a grove of trees and sang me songs that my mother said were only meant for peasants, songs of fun and folklore.

Suddenly came a memory of a young man being lashed in the courtyard, with my cries of desperation the only sound to be heard over the horrific cracking of a whip. Being commanded to let him go made my gift appear for the first time, wringing life from the man who delivered punishment upon a boy whose only crime was loving someone he knew he should not.

My brow furrowed as I scanned the long, deep scar that ran from his cheekbone to his chin, crossing plump lips and creating a deep ravine in once perfect skin. A peasant boy, from a mixed bloodline, that was kind and brave. My parents had him sent away for fear that I would not take my place in court due to the infatuation we shared.

Evidence of my disbelief trickled along the curves of my cheeks, a wave of astonishment washed over me as precious memories were unlocked, allowing me to remember a boy whom I had loved fiercely.

"Thibault?" My core began to tighten at the recognition, "You're alive?"

"My mother was Fae, remember? When I reached maturity, my aging slowed as the Fae blood took hold. It hasn't stopped, but I only have the body of a mortal in his early thirties," he chuckled lightheartedly, "Do you know how much time has passed?"

I had nearly forgotten about his immortal blood, as he resembled his father and the only indication he had any trace of Fae in him was the slightly elongated point to his ears. I was rattled by disbelief and awe. Thibault was here all these years later, and he was saving me, as unworthy as I was.

"Impossible," I whispered, reaching a weak hand toward him, fingers grazing his lips.

This man whom I hardly recognized yet knew with all my heart, who outlasted the ages and the dangers of this world, who showed me the affections of a lover the only time I had ever truly known it… knelt before me. The reality of my fortune sank in, and I felt myself smile. He took my hand in his, placing a gentle kiss onto my palm. Thibault lifted my body again, settling me into the bed, pulling up warm blankets until I felt as though I had been hidden within a nesting burrow.

"Rest. I'll find out what is happening to the woman you were with. I have a tincture to bring back your strength and help you heal quickly. You're safe."

Sleep overcame me in no time at all, and I welcomed it.

Thibault roused me early in the morning with the promised remedy, and as it worked its way into my system, I began to feel more alive. My legs were able to readily support my weight, my arms did not shake as I lifted myself from the bed. Deep breaths that expanded my lungs were pleasant and relieving, rather than painful and troublesome. I nearly felt like myself again, aside from the mental and emotional turmoil, as well as the general chaos that surrounded my existence.

"Thyme, raw honey from Tamaa forest, spring water, and Evelian root," he said over a mouthful of the porridge he'd mixed for a quick breakfast.

I was surprised at the contents, because Evelian root was hard to come by. Trade to Evelia had been cut off hundreds of years ago when it became a frozen wasteland, having incurred the wrath of a few deities. It seemed as though the tincture was also aiding in the restoration of my mind, as my memories pieced together to reveal what had been my life and who I truly was.

The simple fact that he possessed something that barely existed outside of lore amazed me. It had magical properties to return health to a body long bereft of strength, with only a small amount I could be nearly as healthy as I'd been before the sleep.

"Thank you," I managed to whisper.

"There is no need to thank me; you know I would do anything for you."

I had always known Thibault to be true to his word.

I never forgave my father for banishing the boy I loved. I was left so vulnerable, so heartbroken. When I met Asuras just weeks after Thibault's exile, I found myself completely at his mercy. He had whispered to me spells of desire, laid charmed flowers at my feet, planted poisonous kisses upon my hands. With every act, he would tell me the truth in them, that he was enchanting me to fall completely under his power. There was nothing I could do to stop it.

He had snared me with a kind smile and promising words; spinning me lies of a better future, lands untold, purpose, and happiness. He bewitched me. He'd asked me to give up my power to him; my reason barely broke through every carefully constructed layer of magic he'd caged me in, and I refused.

A sharp pang struck my chest, as I realized I had betrayed Thibault's love for me in such little time after he'd been exiled. I'd readily lent my affections to another man in my disparaged and traumatized state. I'd paid for it by sealing my Fate, trusting the strange man with an alluring aura and a voice that swaddled my fragile mind in fine silk. I told him my secrets and within moments of his demands, my refusal; he imprisoned me in darkness.

Perhaps I deserved all I had endured? I betrayed the boy I loved, and I hated my parents and cursed them many times over. I had taken a mortal life — there was blood on my hands, that of a man who was only doing what his lord commanded. We were all prisoners of some sort, it seemed.

"Have you found Maygen?" I asked, as an anxious wave of needles settled into me; a sharp awareness took hold, fearing for her safety.

A dark look spread over Thibault's face.

"They're holding her in Tobian's keep, as they do with anyone who is taken into custody. The laws that govern much of Teskaria are not enforced here; we exist far enough out of reach that we're mostly overlooked by the courts. Tobian does what he wants with these people, and they have no choice but to obey."

I shuddered at the thought.

"He came here with a small force of men with whom he provided lodging and income, in exchange for abusing the citizens. Sentinels only come every so often, the patrol leader for these parts is paid off and draws up false reports in Tobian's favor so he can go on tormenting innocents. This time they're coming to look for you."

"When? What are they going to do to her while she waits? They'll know she isn't me, because she doesn't look anything like me. Asuras would've given a description to anyone dispatched to hunt me down."

Thibault flinched at the mention of the Mage's name. I frowned, overcome with disappointment in myself.

"Do you know what happened?" I asked, "He courted me with magic, but I let him. I let him in entirely, blinded by my pain and desperation."

He nodded slowly, "I don't blame you. You never would've seen me again if you'd lived out your mortal life. I only returned to Teskaria fifteen years ago; they had sent me across the strait to Adristan."

I never would have seen him again. The thought made my chest ache. If I had eluded the Fate I'd endured, would I have gone looking for him? Would we have found each other by chance? Would I have ever moved on from him, truly?

"What will they do to Maygen, Thibault?" My voice shook, wary of the answer.

I turned my gaze down to my fingers, locked together and resting in my lap. A heavy sigh drained from his lungs, a sound of defeat and sadness.

"People that are taken into custody are more often than not abused by the guards and by Tobian to extract information. Their methods are barbaric, and because she's a woman..." he trailed off, "They're not going to *just* hurt her because she's a woman; they're going to ruin her."

I had suffered illusions of being assaulted in my slumber; my imprisoned consciousness was subjected to all manner of torture, the kind that evil men inflict, more often than not upon women. Such an act used as a weapon of control was despicable and unforgivable, not to mention traumatizing beyond measure. I couldn't allow this to happen to her.

Power thrummed in my veins, readying itself to lay waste to anyone who dared stop me from my immediate resolution.

"I'm getting her out," I stated flatly.

"No! If you're caught, you will suffer similar punishments until the Sentinels arrive and take you away from here."

The color in his eyes roiled and twisted, a deep and foresty green, the likeness of evergreen trees bellowing in the winter winds.

"You expect me to lose you again?" Exasperation filled his voice.

"Playing on my guilt won't stop me. You don't know what that manner of abuse does to someone!" I cringed at my own words.

He was silent for a long while, letting my proclamation resonate within him. Mentally, I prepared to leave and attempt to free her myself, in this settlement that was entirely foreign to me. I lingered on baited breath, quietly praying he would understand, that he would be willing to aid me in this daunting endeavor.

When he finally spoke again, sympathy replaced the previous reluctance, "I do know what it does to a person."

Our gazes locked and my heart cracked wide open. I knew only of the suffering inflicted upon him that I had witnessed firsthand, but I had not considered what over a century in this world could've been like for him. I hadn't had time to think about what exile entailed for the banished, or what it's like to be tossed away as if you're nothing more than rubbish. How many times had he been at the mercy of those with ill intentions and no regard for his life?

"The keep is guarded regularly by Tobian's lackeys. I know their rotations; I know the layout. Tonight, we'll use the cover of darkness to retrieve her if we can," he conceded.

"It's only morning! They've had her all through the night, so who knows what they may have subjected her to already? We can't keep waiting and allow her to be at the mercy of tyrants!" My voice began to rise, and my curse pushed against my skin like a rapid river's current against the wall of a compromised dam, threatening to burst as my pulse hastened in frustration.

I moved towards the door, but a gentle hand tugged at my arm, desperately beckoning me to stop.

"It's the safest option and our best chance of freeing her. We need a plan, and we need to have a way for you to escape immediately following her release. There are also the Sentinels to worry about, they said they were only a few days out. If they arrive before then, or if you cross them on your way out, who knows what might happen?"

Relenting, "You're right. I'm being irrational," I sighed, pondering for a moment before continuing, "I would do anything to prevent someone from experiencing something so horrific."

"We will do what we can, Celessa. She will have her freedom again, and you will make it far away from this cursed place."

His words hinted that he intended to stay, as if he did not plan on seeing us through.

"You will come with us, won't you?" I asked, "You can't expect me to let you remain here when you have already stayed my impulsivity with your insistence to not part again."

He hesitated before admitting, "Celessa, this is most unexpected. I never would have imagined I'd have this opportunity, because I never thought I would see you again. You were thought to be long dead or worse, corrupted by Asuras' magic. I came back here to see if anyone was left, to find out what truly happened to your family."

Thibault frowned.

"I sailed straight through the bay when I finally had the means to leave Adristan, meaning to make for Briobar, but I couldn't escape. It's been years, and in my waiting, I met a woman whom I've grown to care for deeply."

His words struck me like an axe to the chest.

"A woman?"

I struggled to rationalize the chaotic emotions that bubbled to the surface, threatening to spew incoherent thoughts born of jealousy. I knew to myself, physically, that it had only been weeks. Mentally, though, it had been an endless unknowing of the time that had passed. I had no opportunity to live to make up for all my time trapped in suffering. My love for him lingered on, as there had never been a man to take his place after I'd seen through the Mage's glamour.

Thibault had lived, all these years he had experienced a life I knew nothing about. He had become a different man, and the one I knew only existed in my memory.

"If you're involved with someone, then I cannot remain here to disrupt your life, Thibault. That is not right."

"I only wish to ensure her safety before making any moves! If they connect me to your escape, her safety becomes compromised, because Tobian knows we are involved. My disappearance will endanger her, and she doesn't deserve that. Please, just allow me some time to figure this out!" He insisted, sliding his fingers between my own.

"It may prove difficult, but I will try to sacrifice my infatuation to claim a love that I have been missing for several lifetimes."

I did not allow myself to move as he threaded the fingers of his free hand into loose strands of my hair, leading me gently to close the space between us.

"I'll try," he whispered.

It was wrong to feel this way, to steal these moments I did not deserve while others suffered. It was wrong to covet a man who was entangled with another. Another woman would face betrayal because a ghost of the past has returned to a lost lover. Yet, I could not stop myself from yearning for more. I did not remember what it felt like to be touched tenderly, spoken to softly, or treated with kindness. I only knew pain and suffering.

I was being selfish as I inhaled his earthy scent, letting it fill my lungs with the seconds that passed between us, trapped in a whirlwind of ageless emotion. I grazed my palm along his chest, upward until I could curl my fingers slightly to mold against the nape of his neck.

"Despite the circumstances, I do believe we have some catching up to do," I sighed as I drew his head down.

My mind melted as soft lips met mine, pressing them together in a tender union that sent shockwaves through my body.

A sigh of relief left him, followed by the slightest desperate whimper as I allowed his tongue to part my moistened lips, heat filling my mouth. A hand slid along my scalp, and his gentle grip tightened in the locks of my chestnut brown hair. The hand that had been holding mine untangled from my fingers to wrap around my hip. He pulled me close, the slightest sense of restraint still lingering between us.

An unfamiliar throbbing sensation ignited my senses, insisting that I press myself further into the man I had always desired so furiously. I realized I had an opportunity to experience what I had been unable to in the past, something we had attempted once before, something that was forbidden to an unwed lady. I was no longer a lady, my name had no bearing left in this world, and I was free from the chains of expectation.

Despite the horrific experiences I'd endured and the violence that had tainted this kind of intimacy, I wanted this. Every feeling I'd suppressed in our time together before had begun rushing against the floodgates of my self control. I could allow myself a few moments after long years of nightmares, and he could bring me back to a state of comfortability, one where I did not loathe my own existence. His presence meant there was hope for me still.

He released me suddenly, sending my senses into a frenzy. Taking a step back, Thibault drew a shaky breath and cleared his throat. I stared at him, disappointed.

"This isn't right. Your friend may be experiencing literal hell at this very moment. There's also my own predicament to consider, I'm hurting another with every second I spend desiring you, Celessa," he croaked, visibly struggling.

"Thibault, you said yourself there is nothing we can do until we are protected by the cover of night. I suffered through my own personal hell for over a century. I want this, I have never stopped wanting you. If you want me too, little else matters."

I advanced toward him, and his hands flexed with anticipation. Hesitantly, I reached for him again, using the tips of my toes to lift myself back toward his gradually parting lips.

"You don't have to deny yourself what we have waited several lifetimes for. I know every reason why we shouldn't, and yet I want to anyway," I whispered against his jaw.

I could not fight the urge to relish this moment or to claim something I wanted. A small voice in the back of my mind whispered that it was only a distraction, a too small bandage I was attempting to stretch over many deep wounds... I didn't care.

His hands returned to my waist, encircling me. He carried us to the bed, capturing my mouth with his own. Thibault gripped the bottom of my tattered tunic. His green eyes met mine, silently requesting permission to go further. I nodded breathlessly, and he began removing my clothes.

Seeing my exposed body for the first time since I'd awoken, the full shock of how emaciated and threadlike my figure had become overtook me. I gasped at my image, distressed and embarrassed, missing my full figure. Thibault took my chin into his hand, lifting my gaze toward him once more and away from my jutting rib cage, and shook his head.

"You are as beautiful as you have always been. Grace yourself the opportunity to heal, you will be as you were."

His smile was as beautiful as the first time I'd seen it, beneath an apple tree as the morning sunlight filtered through the branches, turning his perfect skin an entrancing shade of gold. We had been so young and full of life, unaware of the cruelty that awaited us.

I had no words to convey my gratitude for his reassurance. He was always so kind. I brought my lips to his with more insistence than before; he met my effort and covered my small body with his own tall and sculpted one. He was built now like he had seen many trials during his time in this world, decorated in discolored markings and reinforced with strong muscles.

As my hands explored, my fingertips grazed scars engraved up and down his back, from the lashing. Intense emotion began to roil within my stomach, filling me up and threatening to spill out. I fought to swallow it down, desperate to not let anything interfere with these stolen moments.

A strong leg slid between my thighs, urging them to part. He trailed a hand from my neck down to my breast, long fingers circling delicately. A calloused thumb gently rolled over the sensitive peak. I was losing myself in his predatory gaze and the intrusive thoughts melted away. The corner of his mouth kicked up in a smirk, before leaning down and taking my bottom lip between his teeth.

My pelvis ground against the hard length that had been hovering just out of reach, held back by fabric, and Thibault let out a breathy moan. The sensation of his body against my most sensitive parts left me breathless. He reached down and began to tug away the breeches Maygen had given me, and a strange feeling began coiling deep within my body: anticipation. I pulled at his waistband with my own hands.

A warm hand caressed my leg, making a slow climb toward my aching pelvis. His fingers made contact with the sensitive bundle that lay nestled between my thighs, and I couldn't suppress the whimper that arose from the gratification of him stroking me so intimately.

"I've waited so long to experience you, Celessa. I spent a lifetime dreaming of you, yearning for you. I'm trying to remain patient but the urge to completely lose myself in you is making my mouth water. It feels as though I might burst at any moment." Thibault was nearly panting above me, his breaths shaky and uneven.

I had no reassurance to offer him because I shared the desire to be completely undone by this man. My gasps caught in my throat as his fingers left the throbbing bud, and my pelvis rose in a silent plea for his touch to return.

I watched him drag his bottom lip between his teeth as he took in the sight of my exposure.

"I could not imagine you being any more perfect," he whispered.

I wanted to touch him in the way he had touched me, so I lowered my hand to the hard length that pressed against my thigh. I had never done this before and felt nervous, cautiously wrapping my fingers around the velvety skin. Without realizing, I had guided him down to the entrance of my body, feeling the tip of him nudging my delicate opening made my muscles tense. He lent his hand to replace my own, bracing himself to enter me. Mild fear mixed with excitement flooded over as I placed my hands on his shoulders, gripping tightly.

"I'll be gentle."

I trusted him; I was ready this time. He pushed into me, the stretching of my body burned slightly, but it was not unbearable. I breathed in deeply and relaxed against him, allowing him to take complete control. Thibault was scanning my face, checking for any unpleasant reactions or any indication to stop.

"I want this," I gasped, "I want you."

He groaned quietly, allowing himself to slide his length back out of my body, before gently pushing in again. With every stroke of him the burning lessened, slowly but surely being replaced with pleasure. My nails dug into his skin as I felt myself creeping toward release with every gentle pump into my body. My legs trembled and I moaned against his mouth as my climax built, desperately urging him to increase his pace to bring me over the edge. He drove deep inside of my body as I began to tighten around him.

A loud banging at the door froze me, panic rising into my chest. Thibault leapt from the bed, and I pulled a heavy quilt up over my body. Of every inconvenience I've ever experienced, this one currently felt as though it was the worst. A frustrating throbbing sensation had settled between my legs, irritation taking hold as the ache from the unfulfilled arousal made me swell uncomfortably.

He slipped his trousers back on and attempted to tidy himself up in a handful of seconds, still looking out of sorts as he prepared to handle the summons. I hid under the cover. Breathing shallow, I quieted myself as much as physically possible to go unnoticed.

He did not answer the door at first, only speaking through the barrier, "Who's there?"

"Thibault, it's Aloise. Please, I must speak with you, may I come in?"

A woman. The woman he'd been involved with? Jealousy soured my mouth, my jaw clenched in irritation. I had just given myself to him, and here *she* was disintegrating the moments of passion.

Thibault breathed out a quiet sigh before whispering toward me, "Stay still, I'll do my best to make this quick."

The latch popped, and the weight of the wood groaned on weak hinges as it opened. I could hear footsteps shuffle into the living space as the door closed behind. It was becoming increasingly difficult to lie still as the sensation of my thighs pressing together made the throbbing more intense, my body still lusting for Thibault despite the unfavorable circumstances.

"I hadn't seen you this morning, I was so worried that Tobian had called you to the keep."

Her voice was higher pitched than I would've expected, and I found it irritating. Whether that was a rational reaction to the tone or my jealousy, I didn't know nor did I care.

"He has no reason to call upon me, Aloise. I only had a rough night and meant to rest a bit longer," he lied.

"Are you ill?"

The concerned tone made my skin crawl, she must've taken notice of his disheveled appearance. I silently wished for her to disappear.

"No, I am not ill. Why did you think that Tobian had called for me?"

"A woman was taken into custody, people are being called in for questioning. I learned in passing that this woman had meant to steal horses and supplies, and she has an accomplice who is still missing."

They know I'm here. My heart twisted as I began to wonder what methods they had used on Maygen to extract information about me. Anything that happened to her was my fault. I had been holed up here, selfishly enjoying myself. I was ashamed.

"Have you been called in?" he asked quietly, his voice shaking.

"No, but the homes on our drive will be rounded up soon. Thibault, I am afraid to go alone. Please accompany me, since you know how they treat the women here. I risked being spotted already coming here without an escort," she begged.

My irritation surged, and I began wrestling with thoughts of revealing myself. I would either damn us all, or I could fast track getting the hell out of here. I've always been labeled as impulsive, and that accusation truly wasn't wrong.

I stirred beneath the sheets.

"Thibault? Is there someone else here?"

Aloise's voice grew fearful more than anything, as if she expected a monster to leap from the shadows and claim her at any moment. Although, that's likely a predisposition she had to live with, taking the Wyndiga issue into account as well as Tobian's tyranny. I felt slightly less sure of my decision to kick start this engagement.

"Aloise, please don't be alarmed, there is no danger!" He spoke fervently, attempting to calm her while subtly alerting me to stop what I was doing. He should know better. I should've known better.

Too late.

"Tell me you don't have the fugitive here. Oh, Gods. What are you thinking? They'll kill you! You've damned us!"

She began weeping, I heard Thibault's feet shuffle toward the door, pinning his back to it so she could not flee.

I sat up then, suddenly realizing I was still naked, my bare body entirely exposed. Aloise's eyes bulged at the sight, her face heating up to a bright shade of red, but she didn't look away. Her skin was sun kissed as though she had grown up in Adristan's deserts, with dark eyes and a slightly arched nose. Long black hair tumbled around her small body in waves. Her lip quivered, and she turned back to Thibault.

"Is that *her*?" she whispered.

"There is no need to act as if I do not exist. I can answer your questions," I snapped, but she did not move to acknowledge me.

"Aloise, please, I need you to understand!"

Thibault's face looked pained. He was upset, but I couldn't bring myself to care about his feelings toward this woman.

"Understand?" she exclaimed, "You want me to understand what? That the fugitive woman who had escaped from *Sanctuary*, your love from another life, is exposed in your bed?"

She whirled toward me again, disgust twisting her features.

"She was in desperate need of aid, Aloise."

He touched her shoulder, gently beckoning her to meet his gaze.

"I never intended this. We have something else, and I care for you deeply; I have love for you," he hesitated, "Celessa has never left me — not when I feared her dead, not for all of the years that have passed me by. You knew this when we met, you knew it when we learned she had been in Sanctuary all this time."

"I did not think it could be true that she lived; she is *mortal*!" Aloise spat, "There is no excuse for this, Thibault. Justify it as you will, but you promised yourself to me, and you shared my bed!"

A hollow pit yawned open inside of me; all of my rationality was fleeing. Jealousy, envy, and anger swelled, pulsing under the surface of my being. My renewed strength awakened something in me, and I paced forward.

"Well," I grimaced, "What a situation we've found ourselves in."

Delicate flesh burned, and I was cracking open, with an ugly presence making itself known. Thibault's eyes widened in shock and fear; fear of me. I looked down to see that the skin on my arms had, in fact, broken open. An otherworldly red hue glowed, emanating from the gashes, with a red mist that began to curl around my palms.

My attention flickered to Aloise, whose face looked several shades paler as she beheld me now. The horror that lit up her eyes alerted me to exactly how I appeared to her: a dangerous creature that had been held in Sanctuary for a reason. It was a despicable power, contained for fear of what it might unleash.

"Celessa?"

I hear the lovely, sultry voice. It was Thibault's voice, trying to reach me. Instinct driven senses had taken over, giving into every horrible emotion I felt. Losing control meant bringing death. It meant I would hurt those around me, like the day I killed the man delivering lashes to the boy I loved.

Panic gripped my heart as I realized I could kill them both, and I propelled myself backwards, stumbling to the floor — trying and failing to beckon the deadly fog back into my skin. Instead it spread, enveloping my body, bellowing over the floor.

"Leave," I gasped, wild eyes flicking between the two helpless bodies pressed against the wall.

"LEAVE!" a voice that did not quite belong to me thundered through the home.

The man swept the cowering woman up into his arms before escaping through the entrance of the small space.

Searing hot pain exploded through my limbs, and the mist seemed like it had its own sentience, its own will; it was far from my control. Magic spasmed and lashed out in every direction of the room, as my body convulsed violently. I was writhing in pain, unable to scream, while horrible experiences and painful memories plagued my consciousness, fueling the weaponized essence. I fought desperately to regain control. The thought of letting go and allowing this curse to take over drifted through my thoughts.

A voice whispered to me, *be the monster they fear you are.*

Was I a monster? Had I become nothing more than a calamity? Had everything I'd been through shaped me into something only capable of death and destruction? Was I becoming the evil I feared, the kind of evil that would kill and torment simply because its desires were not met? Does it lash out simply because it is jealous or inconvenienced?

As I fought back against the force, reality began to fade out. I relented to the surges, feeling myself falling into nothing. For a few moments, I let myself drift into the blackness of unconsciousness. Floating away, I retreated into a vast expanse of endlessness.

I was aware, but there was nothing here. It was a familiar kind of imprisonment within my own mind, but something was different this time. I was not being forced or held; I was here by choice. This was somewhere else entirely, not my former prison, as there were no malicious forces here. I could feel a presence within the depths of the unknown, unfamiliar and powerful, but I felt no fear.

"You get to choose," a soft voice echoed in the distance of the void.

Confusion flooded my senses, but I was not afraid.

"Choose what?" I asked.

"What you become."

"I don't even know who I really am," I confessed.

I felt like I could trust this far away presence, that it bore no ill will against me. It felt as though it was not good or evil... it just *was*.

"What are you?"

A strange question for it to ask.

"I am mortal. I was born with a gift of chaos, and I am dangerous," I answered.

"These are not things you know."

"I don't understand, I do know that much," I argued.

"You think you are mortal; you think you are born of chaos; you think you are dangerous."

The voice was growing faint, further out of reach.

"My knowledge of myself is not the truth?" I asked.

"You get to choose," it whispered again.

Suddenly I was falling, falling into something, but nothing all at once. It was an endless sensation of dropping, as if I was being returned to myself, with my soul searching for its physical being.

Chapter Three

Another Day, Another Nightmare

My eyes opened to a different kind of dark, with trickles of faint yellow light filtered between cracks around a splintered window frame. The pounding in my head stirred intense nausea. I remembered I had used my gift, uncontrollably so. It takes a toll on my body, leaving me sick and weak for a short time after it returns to dormancy. My throat was being scalded by every breath I took, too dry for me to speak or attempt to call out for someone, for anyone.

Fingers brushed my cheek. Weakly lifting my head, I rotated to look for the source.

"I'm so sorry," I rasped.

"It's my fault, Celessa." Aloise spoke timidly, "I let my jealousy cloud my judgment. I villainized you. You were acting on instinct, and I would have done the same. Meeting this way was not my intention. Making you feel threatened wasn't either. You've been through enough; you're a victim caught in a bad situation."

The crushing acknowledgement of that statement settled on me with the weight of a mountain. I was a victim. I had been traumatized: stolen, tormented, imprisoned. I was abused for a century, then awakened to learn everyone I'd known had long since perished and that I was alone. Violent sobs shook my body, and Thibault scooped me up into his arms to cradle me like a wailing infant.

Aloise's entire demeanor had shifted. She now looked at me with pity and a hint of curiosity. She sat silently as I melted deep into my self despair. She watched him comfort me, even draping a thin blanket over my bare body. I wonder what they had discussed while I'd slept. What had Thibault said to her?

When I regained composure, she brewed an herbal tea for us and offered me a simple, but clean, dress to clothe myself. The warm liquid soothed my throat and relaxed the taut muscles that were still been tense with shock from my earlier explosion. I paced over to the barricaded window after dressing, peering through the small spaces between the boards. As pinks and oranges colored the dusk sky, I realized it was nearly nightfall.

"Is your power the reason you were taken, because it's dangerous?" Aloise blurted.

Thibault shot her a surprised look.

"As far as I know, only my family and the staff were aware of it, and that was only after my outburst. Until I met the Mage... I'd confided in him under the compulsion of his charms. He'd wanted my powers for himself, but I refused him. Then he took me," I confessed. "I was born of a mortal bloodline, so my ancestors did not have the ability to use magic. We were just an average family of nobility. No one ever expected that something like this would ever occur. Even magic wielding lines don't possess things like *this*."

I looked up from my cup to meet her gaze. She was, admittedly, a beautiful woman. I envied her, but not in a hateful way. It was in a way that when you admire someone and wish you possessed some of their traits. Her sultry brown eyes were like a hot brew of cocoa on a frigid winter's day, her full lips were as smooth as silk, and her tumbling waves of dark hair framed a delicate jawline.

"I am sorry for what happened," I mumbled.

Embarrassment clouded my mind as I thought of how my power had reached for her, how badly I'd wanted to end her simply because I was jealous of her involvement with Thibault.

"I wanted to hurt you. I love him."

It was an age of unending love for a man who had moved on without me.

How could I blame him?

"I love him too. Believe me when I say the feeling was mutual. Although, I do not think I would stand much of a chance," she smiled warily. "Thibault explained a few things to me, he told me what happened this morning."

Swallowing loudly, she continued, "We can figure out how to move forward with this *predicament* the three of us have found ourselves in at a later time. More important things need our attention at the moment. Thibault and I were taken in for questioning while you were unconscious."

I had almost forgotten about Tobian's inquiry, about Maygen. Shame cloaked me in its unforgiving and suffocating embrace.

Thibault and Aloise must've returned to find me asleep on the floor after they'd visited the keep, I wondered how long they'd been watching over me as I recovered.

I crushed down my jealousy and somewhat petty dislike of this woman so that I could focus on the looming problems, heavy like rain clouds and threatening to erupt into a storm at any moment.

"Did you see Maygen?"

We could save her soon, Thibault had assured me this morning we would get her out at nightfall. We were so close, but they exchanged a glance that made my stomach twist into a painful knot.

"We didn't see her, but we heard screaming," Thibault said softly. My heart sank.

"Were they her screams..." I couldn't stop my voice from shaking.

"We don't know. Tobian takes people into custody for any reason, and has several people at a time detained in the cells."

"What did they ask you?"

Aloise spoke up again, "Basic questions; we lied about everything, they don't know the truth and should believe us. Tobian is a suspicious man; he plans on doing rounds himself to search the settlement. If he finds you here..." she trailed off.

"When can we leave?"

"And not get caught? We'll have to go separately." She huffed, frustrated.

"Too risky," Thibault chimed in. "If either of you gets spotted without an escort that's enough justification in itself for them to take you into custody with no questions asked."

Silently weighing our options, I drew a deep breath.

I sighed, "We could dress as men?"

It seemed like a good idea until I said it out loud. Aloise was the epitome of petite, and my once full body was emaciated due to neglect.

Thibault snorted, "Young boys, maybe."

Aloise nodded fervently, "That could work."

"I'm bigger than both of you combined, nothing I have will fit you well enough to not make you appear completely out of sorts."

"My brother's clothes," she murmured. "We still have his things."

"I'll escort you to your home to retrieve the clothes; we'll need to disguise them among some produce to not arouse any suspicion."

Aloise mumbled her agreement, and they rose to leave.

"Please hurry," I urged. "We need to get her out."

The too familiar weight formed on my shoulders once again as I imagined Maygen injured and desperate, locked away in a cell.

Hours had passed.

Black of night lay like a thick blanket on the outside world. The moon's light shone faintly, only a sliver of its full form visible. The night sky was bereft of stars, beautiful twinkling lights only known through stories and paintings. It was said the stars would not return until Astera, Goddess of the Stars, returned from her exile.

If I paced these floors anymore, I'd carve trenches into the wooden planks with my feet. Impatience was gripping me like a vice as more and more time passed since Thibault's departure. Uncomfortable silence had fallen over the settlement, save for the low crackling of torches decorating the door frames of neighboring homes.

Peering through the narrow openings of the boarded window, I surveyed the area around the front of the house, looking for any sign of my companions. Several moments passed before I noticed the shadowy figure of a man passing through dim light glowing amidst the line of houses, and there was no woman. Unease tingled my nerves, my senses reverting to alert survival settings. I watched him intently for only a few seconds before I realized he was walking in my direction.

I need to hide.

Grabbing a bread knife from the small wooden table in the center of the room, I forced myself into the narrow space under Thibault's bed. Taking a few slow breaths to steady myself, I waited.

Seconds passed, with my heartbeat thundering in my ears, as the anticipation of facing a potential adversary built. I peeked below where a blanket was dangling over the side of my hiding place, locking my gaze on the bottom of the entryway. My field of vision was limited to just the floor.

The door knob snapped off, dropping with a loud thud. I stifled a shocked gasp as the door was then kicked open. All I could see were booted feet, with the mystery person halting to survey the home for any sign of occupation. My thoughts flitted around, attempting to reassure myself that there was no indication of my presence in the home.

My blood chilled as I remembered the clothes Maygen had given me.

Thibault had removed them during our heated moments that morning, and I was wearing the clean dress Aloise had provided to me after I had awoken from my incident. The tattered and bloodied tunic and leggings were lying at the bedside. I silently prayed the intruder wouldn't notice, though I suspected luck would not be on my side.

Heavy steps began to make their way through the home, stopping inches from where I was barely concealed. I could smell the mud from the settlement pathways that coated the leather footwear. My palms began to sweat against the planks of the wooden floors, every splinter and grain scratching against my sensitive skin. The air seemed to thicken, with every breath more painful than the last as I tried to control the flow into my lungs slowly, silently.

The deep throaty hum the person exhaled revealed that the intruder was, in fact, a man. He began shuffling the blankets around, searching the bed. He must've noticed my garments because he stopped fumbling with the layers and leaned towards the small nightstand. Hearing him inhale deeply, I instantly became nauseated.

He was *smelling* my dirty clothes.

There would only be two reasons he was doing that. One, he was a disgusting pervert with a smelly shirt fetish... Or two, he was a vampire committing my scent to memory to track me. My sense told me which of my assumptions were correct.

If I didn't act fast, I was doomed.

Gripping the knife tightly, I lashed out from under the bed, driving the serrated blade deep into his ankle. I withdrew it back, unwilling to lose my only weapon by leaving it in his body. A startled scream bounced off the walls of the home, reverberating around the small space and filling me with adrenaline as I watched the falling body collide with the floor. As the man fell, I struggled to get myself free of the bed as quickly as possible to gain the upper hand before he recovered. Vampires had a rapid healing time, so I had only a few moments to secure my safety.

As swiftly as I could manage, I stacked my body upright, bloodied blade in hand.

I locked eyes with the intruder, who was nearly bursting at the seams with rage.

"Evil, hateful creature," he hissed.

"That's no way to speak to a lady," I growled.

I squeezed the knife handle once again, bracing myself to end yet another life. My pulse thrummed wildly, and I could feel every vein stretching in anticipation as the muscles in my arm clenched to maintain full control of my weapon.

Realizing I was hesitating too long, I made my move to drive the blade into any vulnerable part in which I could deliver a fatal wound. I aimed for his head, but I was out of time. He anticipated my sloppy maneuver and dodged the blow, grabbing my knife wielding hand in his own and wrapping his free arm around my body to restrain me. I thrashed violently, attempting to free myself, to no avail. He wrenched the weapon from my hand. Denial of my defeat surged through me, and my power swelled beneath my skin.

I willed it to release, *desiring* to use it, but it seemed trapped beneath the surface, refusing to act against the assailant. It will happily kill mortals and monsters, but vampires are off limits? Impossible.

A scream climbed up my throat as I struggled. He twisted my body around and pushed us to the floor to trap me with his full weight. With the man on my back and my face pressed against the ground, my hands were pinned above my head, and I was rendered immobilized, left staring across the floor.

"Now that you've gotten that out of your system, you and I should get acquainted," he whispered into my ear, sending chills down the length of my body.

"I'm going to assume that you either know who I am, or you're looking for Thibault, otherwise you wouldn't be here," I spat.

"Oh, I know who you are, and I know *what* you are, Celessa."

The words made my skin crawl, with the weight of him growing increasingly heavy.

"What I'm going to be in a moment is crushed to death, so get the fuck off of me!"

The man let out a low chuckle, lifting his body just enough to release some pressure while still pinning me. I didn't spare a moment as he compromised his position and reared my head back, headbutting the man in the mouth. His hold faltered just enough for me to tug one of my hands loose from his grip, and I used my elbow to strike him in the ribs as hard as I could manage.

He folded slightly, breathing out a curse. It was just enough for me to roll my body, though I remained beneath him. I had aimed a knee to strike him in the unmentionables, but his weight fell down on me before I could deliver the blow. He reacted too quickly and caught my arms again.

"Stop!" He shouted, flattening himself against me, and lowering his head to my neck.

I froze, feeling two *very* sharp pin pricks against the tender, vulnerable flesh. I dared not to draw even a single breath as I assessed my situation. I was completely caught by a vampire, a deadly creature, capable of snuffing out mortal lives as simply as one would blow away the flame from a candlewick.

As I stilled, he slowly drew back, relieving my skin of the discomfort. The fact that I still breathed meant his intention was not to kill me. I looked my attacker in the face, observing his features entirely for the first time.

Vampires were equipped with lethal good looks. He was no exception. His eyes were a glowing hazel, colored like the dying fields in autumn, when the grasses die at different times and are a peppered mix of greens and browns. His face was framed by unruly dark hair, with the locks thick and slightly wavy, cut just below his ears.

"Like what you see, milady?"

A playful glint shone in his eyes, containing a reflection of the low burning fire just a few feet away from our entanglement.

"When does anyone *like* to see a vampire?" I hissed, "And I am no lady."

"You just said you were when I cursed you. Isn't your family name Umbraeon?" A thick brow raised inquisitively.

"I have no family left, so it makes little difference, but I'm guessing you knew that already."

I squirmed again, searching for a way out of his grip.

"Gently. My ankle is still sore."

The teeth lining his grin were perfectly straight, armed with the deadly fangs that had just threatened to pierce my flesh, shining between full lips.

"What do you want?" I demanded. "I'm still alive, so you're not assassinating me, but you have me pinned to the floor rather than bound and heading toward the keep."

I shifted under his weight, the curves of his body becoming too noticeable as I struggled.

"This is inappropriate."

His eyebrows raised slightly, amusement lightening his eyes.

"I don't think you know much about being inappropriate."

"We just met," I said flatly, with no hint of care in my tone as I wrestled with the thoughts of Thibault from just this morning.

Unfulfilled desires and complicated attachments were lined with jealousy and bitterness, that I was not the only one to have earned his affections, that I was not the only one to have experienced his body and the intimacy he offered.

"I feel like I've known you forever," he purred, "You remind me of someone."

"It appears you have the wrong person, as I haven't exactly been around meeting people for quite some time... especially not vampires," I said, wriggling again.

"You're the right person. You have the eyes," he whispered, "and the same cunning look on your face when you're mulling over the dark thoughts that plague your mind. The same frustration etches into your features when things don't go your way."

His breath was warm on my face, metallic and tangy. He smelled like blood.

"Can you do your reminiscing somewhere that isn't on top of my body?"

"Oh, but you're so warm."

He sighed deeply, lowering his face closer to my own. His lips were nearly touching mine as he murmured against them.

"I can help you if you let me but you'll have to behave."

"How did you know I was here?" I ground out through clenched teeth.

His head lifted slightly away, the limited space between us full of heat.

"A friend told me."

"I didn't know vampires had friends."

"I'm sensing a bit of animosity here; one could almost surmise that you are not a fan of my kind."

"You didn't exactly make a good first impression," I snapped.

He *'tsked'*, "You *stabbed* me," he justified.

"You didn't knock."

My eyes began to burn from returning his unwavering gaze. *Doesn't he ever blink?*

The man continued smirking for a few moments, with no sound in the small home aside from our shallow breaths and the crackling firewood.

"I like you," he decided, "I'm going to let you up, but if you try to stab me again or run away, I'll actually use these fangs rather than just teasing you with them. Although, I have a feeling you'd like it."

My muscles tensed at the threat, both frightened and intrigued by the thought of my flesh being pierced.

After what seemed like an eternity, he released me. I felt light as a feather, as the weight lifted from my chest. He stood up remarkably fast, then reached down with both hands to scoop me up, planting me firmly on my feet. His hands did not leave my arms, and I eyed them suspiciously before giving him an irritated look.

"What a lovely creature you are, and not what I expected. No more fighting, hmm? Let's talk."

He motioned for me to sit down. Cautiously, I sat on the bedside, eyes never leaving the vampire. Attempting to act casual, I crossed my legs and leaned back gently on my palms.

"Go on then," I urged, "I'm dying to hear your reasons for breaking in to a stranger's home and attacking me."

"Thibault is hardly a stranger," he laughed. "We're friends."

That smile was poisonous. The kind of poison that sinks deep into the veins, slowly crawling its way through your body, infecting and overwhelming every inch of your being.

"Thibault hasn't told me about any *friends* in the area."

I paused, thinking of Aloise, irritation scalding my throat.

"I've been out of town."

"Who are you? You know my name, it's only fair to exchange. Especially since you attacked me."

As I reiterated my offense to the altercation, I hoped to cause him even the slightest bit of the irritation that I'd been feeling a moment ago.

His grin only widened, as he explained, "My name is Aklys, milady."

"How do you know Thibault?" I challenged.

"I was on duty in the keep the day he showed up requesting a plot of land in the settlement."

My body chilled.

"You work for Tobian?"

"I do what I want," Aklys snickered.

I took notice of him eyeing me like I was a piece of meat. I suppose to a vampire, any mortal being was thought of as little more than a blood source or a toy. I watched him bite down on his lip, smiling as he watched me become aware of his indecency. A lump formed in my throat that I couldn't seem to swallow down, thoughts returning to the sharp warning that had been on my neck just minutes ago.

Growing tired of waiting for a response from me, he sighed.

"I returned for my own reasons; I come and go as I wish. Tobian happens to pay well for my services, and there is no shortage of... *entertainment.*"

Nausea roiled in my gut. He was surely referring to the prisoners they abuse in the keep, people they take into custody for any reason too far from the laws governing the rest of Teskaria.

"You're here to take me to Tobian? Which friend told you I was here?" I snarled.

Aklys shook his head, looking rather amused as he spoke, "Now why would I want to give Tobian the opportunity to torment such a lovely lady?"

"Having too much fun doing that yourself?"

"I don't usually mind sharing," he chuckled, "but perhaps not this time."

He leaned closer, now only an arm's length away. Reaching out with long fingers, Aklys touched my hair, twisting the locks between them playfully.

"Maygen sent me."

His proclamation sent my head whirling. A wave of hot anger spread across my cheeks: *why would she tell a vampire anything?*

"I don't believe you."

"I know."

He moistened his lips with his tongue before running it across the length of his smile, toying with sharp canines.

"Would you stop that?" I glowered, "Let's get on with whatever it is you have planned; I'm growing bored of your games. You break in here like you own the place, hold me down on the floor, then proceed to play mind games with *me*? What do *you* want?"

Aklys was nose to nose with me in less than a blink, his speed taking me off guard, and I gasped. He planted his hands firmly on the bed, one on each side of my hips.

"I require your assistance," the vampire murmured.

"I ask for you to be forthcoming, and yet you're still incredibly vague. Help with what?"

"I really do like you," he breathed, "feisty."

I grunted in frustration. If this is how every vampire acts, I pray I never meet another.

He extended a hand, beckoning me to stand. I ignored the gesture and rose on my own, never breaking his stare. I've never found a smirk so irritating before meeting this man.

"I want you to help me kill Tobian."

That was probably the very last thing I'd expected him to say. A vampire shouldn't need the help of a mortal to kill anything at all. Only two species rivaled vampires in combat and social standing, so did that mean Tobian was Fae or Elvish?

"I know what you're thinking: he is Fae, and one of the worst. He's a castaway of the Crassus family of Osceau, bereaved of his title when they exiled him. He doesn't use the noble name. I do believe that only his inner circle knows who he truly is... aside from me, of course."

I sucked in a breath.

The Crassus family had been one of many noble families that had shown interest in my sisters and I as we reached adulthood. It wasn't often that immortal lines sought after mortal families for unions, due to the taboo nature of races mixing. However, my family had been the last of Syades' mortal line and held a respected, high standing within the noble families and courts of the Three Kingdoms. I didn't remember the name Tobian Crassus. The men that we were introduced to as potential suitors had been Luther Crassus and Kilian Crassus, but I had been gone a long time.

My older sister, Arecelle, had engaged in a torrid affair with Kilian Crassus against my father's wishes. When he uncovered her indiscretions, she was forced into an arranged marriage with a mortal nobleman from one of Teskaria's sister cities, Ofror; Elias Whitlock turned out to be an awful, abusive man. After some months at Elias' mercy, my sister fled back to Kilian, who'd harbored her until her husband came searching.

Kilian killed him and several others in a vengeful rage, and was imprisoned for adultery and murder. My sister had been sent home after her lover's sentencing; rejected by her late husband's family.

"Tobian knows who you are, he suspects you're somewhere in the settlement. He means to make a bounty on turning you over to the Sentinels."

"That doesn't explain why you would want me to kill him, nor does it explain how you even expect me to kill him, considering I'm a mortal and he is *Fae*."

Aklys snorted, "No need to act poor and defenseless. I know all about your power. I would surmise just about every immortal in the Three Kingdoms knows all about what you can do."

I glared at him, awaiting more information. He turned toward the window, and I huffed out an exasperated sigh. It shouldn't matter to him that I have power when it was apparent I couldn't use it against him. Vampires wouldn't need to pay me any mind at all.

Unless that made me the perfect weapon for them to utilize.

Vampires had ruled for centuries after they overthrew the first reign, until they were unseated by Fae armies and forced from the Three Kingdoms. If I couldn't harm vampires, then they had no reason to fear me, but everyone else did. I had never used my power against anyone of Fae blood, so I didn't know if it would work the same way it had against mortals and monsters. It had wanted to harm Thibault, but he was half mortal.

He whispered, "The people here need your help."

"I thought you said *you* needed my help, now it's the people? Why should I believe that you care about anyone but yourself, considering what you are? You work for Tobian, and you just enlightened me to the fact that you hang around for the *entertainment!*" I snarled.

"Clearly, you know every truth of the world after being asleep for over a century, huh? You're so wise, you can uncover the meaning of every word spoken to you without any further elaboration? How bold of you to assume anything at all!" He snapped, anger flaring in the bright hazel eyes.

"I have no reason to help you."

"You have every reason to help me," he retorted.

"Helping me liberates the people of this settlement from being tormented, starved, and abused. Helping me saves your friend Maygen," he paused to study my reaction, "Helping me saves Aloise and Thibault."

My heart dropped into an empty pit at the very center of my being.

"What are you talking about? They went to retrieve clothing, you have no idea what they might be doing."

Unwelcome thoughts of Thibault and Aloise engaging in the same activities he had indulged in with me took shape in my mind.

"Tobian's lackeys grabbed them as I was on my way over here. I came here to assure your safety and offer you my aid, but then you stabbed me. So, here we are. You have some decisions to make."

Strong arms folded over his chest as he stared down at me.

Taking Thibault and Aloise meant that Tobian figured out that they had been lying during their inquiry. Surely, they'd be punished not only for lying to the tyrant, but for harboring a fugitive as well. They'd be punished because of me.

"There is no decision to be made – I have to get them out."

Panic began to flood my senses, an all-too-common occurrence lately, one that I needed to gain control over. Aklys must have sensed my fear and began approaching me. The instinct to cower away from the tall man made my knees want to tremble, but I held fast, allowing him to come close.

"Then let's be on our way."

Lifting a hand, he trailed a finger along my collarbone, up the side of my neck to my cheek and brushed the soft skin with his thumb reassuringly.

"You and I will be unstoppable."

I flinched away, irritated.

"If you're lying to me, you'll regret it. My power may refuse to kill you, but the rest of me will find a way."

"I don't doubt you, milady. Shall we?" Aklys gestured toward the door, and we stepped out into the crisp, salty bay air.

In the distance, I could see a large keep silhouetted against a background of gray waves and a dark shoreline dimly illuminated by moonlight. My feet propelled me forward, but they left the ground as I was scooped up in an unexpected embrace. Aklys pulled me close to his chest without warning, and the breath was pushed from my lungs as he utilized his vampiric speed to dart through the settlement unseen.

We ended up along the bay's shore beneath the towering walls of the keep. Aklys lowered me from his hold, placing my feet into the cool sand. Upon first glance, I didn't see any way to enter the building from our location.

"Did you just bring me down here to drown me? I could've walked," I huffed.

The winds rolling in from the water were frigid and sent me shivering. I didn't have anything to cover myself with and donned only the thin white dress Aloise had provided.

Aklys chuckled, a deep throaty sound.

"I enjoy your company far too much."

He began walking up the shoreline, heading away from the keep.

"In case you forgot, we're supposed to be breaking in; we aren't here for a beach trip," I groaned as my frustration bubbled over; he wasn't giving me any details or enlightening me to any plan that may be in the works.

Far off in the gray expanse, lightning struck the water. The wind was picking up its speed, heavy clouds rolled over the moon, sending us further into darkness. Tiny droplets of rain began to patter against the sand, dampening my skin and clothes.

I trailed after Aklys, awaiting instruction as the rain picked up, drenching us. We reached an opening several meters off from the keep, hidden amidst roots in the side of the drop between the land to the shore. I was examining the concealed entryway as the vampire shuffled in front of me, pushing the heavy metal door open with little effort.

He turned to speak to me, his mouth opening and then remaining so, as he looked in my direction. I suddenly felt very aware of the fact that vampires had incredibly keen eyesight, able to see much better in the dark than mortals. My gaze shifted down to my body, and it became glaringly obvious that the thin white dress had become see-through as it absorbed the rain water.

My breasts were firmly peaked from being assaulted by the cold air, the fabric of the wet dress clung to my skin, leaving little to the imagination. I glared back at Aklys.

"Not that I would be surprised, but have you never seen a woman's body before?" I snapped.

Grumbling, he turned his head back to the entrance.

"It's too dark for you to see in here, so you can either hold my hand to guide you, or I can carry you again."

"Where does this lead? What is our plan? You've told me nothing."

"It leads to the lowest level, a room that only holds dust covered nonsense. If we can make it up the stairs to the holding cells, we can spring the doors and free your friends. Easy."

"And if it's not easy?"

Folding my arms impatiently, I stepped toward his outstretched hand.

"Then I guess we'll have to figure something else out, milady. No time like the present," he insisted.

I reached to accept his hand, so he could lead me through the black tunnel. He ignored my outstretched palm and swept me up into his arms again. I made a disgusted sound, prompting another amused laugh from the vampire.

"You said I could hold your hand!"

"I changed my mind."

Tucking me close to his chest, the heat radiating from him slightly warmed my chilled skin. Breathing a sigh of relief, I decided I would allow him to hold me, if only for the warmth. The quality of the air changed as we moved forward through the narrow passageway, and it became thicker and damp, with the lingering moisture clinging to me as relentlessly as the rain. My hair and dress would never dry in these conditions.

Eventually, we came into a room dimly lit by a lone torch. I became worried that someone would find us here, as the room hadn't been untouched like I'd assumed, and I tensed in Aklys' arms. He looked down at my frail figure in his arms, our gazes locking for a brief moment before he loosened his hold, gently lowering me to stand on my own.

"If the torch is lit, doesn't that mean everyone is aware of this room and the tunnel? Wouldn't they be keeping an eye on everything since a person of interest is loose in their village?" I whispered.

He shook his head.

"The fires in the keep stay lit with magic. Tobian and his brood are entirely too lazy to actually maintain anything in this shithole. They have a Mage that they keep locked up who tends to their demands for things like medical treatments, fire maintenance, and abusing innocents."

Aklys slowly cracked open the door, peering out into a stairwell and checking the area before opening it wide enough for us to slip through. The vampire motioned me forward so I'd be ahead of him, and a deep sound that resembled a growl emanated from his throat.

"What? Do you see something?"

"No, just you. Literally all of you."

He was staring at my indecently exposed figure again, still damp and even more visible in the torch light. I stood as still as a statue, unsure of what to do next. On one hand, I didn't want him looking at me that way. He was a stranger that I'd just met, someone who could have very bad intentions for me, and I'd made that mistake before. On another hand, I secretly enjoyed the attention.

My mind flitted back to Thibault, and I was conflicted. I had given myself over to him so freely, having loved him most of my life, only to find out he'd been with another; likely recently as they were in such close proximity. I felt slighted, used. I was not interested in being in competition with other women.

The vampire was still observing my body with lusting eyes. Based on what I knew about his kind, they had extremely heightened senses, prone to act on any and all desires simply because they could. I could use this to my advantage.

I stepped toward Aklys' body, taking him by surprise as I pressed against his chest. He let out a shocked gasp, stilling entirely, not daring to move. This was a game, and I would be sure I had the upper hand.

"We don't have time for games, we have a job to do," I whispered, my lips only a few inches from his as I stood on the tips of my toes in an attempt to reach him.

"Ah, but if we did, the games I'd play with you," he grinned.

"I hope you enjoy whatever fantasies you're conjuring in your mind because that is the only place where they'll come to fruition."

Aklys didn't look convinced, arching a brow as he watched me return to my place by the door.

"Let's go," I demanded.

We crept silently up the corridor, careful to ensure our steps didn't make a sound. Aklys kept a hand on my lower back as he followed behind, ready to snatch me at a moment's notice if I stumbled or if he sensed danger. At the top of the long and winding stairwell, an opening gave us a view into a long room lined with iron barred cells that were carved into the rock walls of the underground. The air in the space was musty – you could practically taste the dust particles that floated about.

I peered into the cells one by one, half of them contained bones and dried remains: remains of people. A cruel Fate, being left to suffer and rot in a cage far beneath the earth, forgotten to those above. In a handful of cells, people cowered as I approached the bars, hiding their faces and scrambling toward the shadows. My heart ached for them.

At long last, in a cell close to the stairwell that leads up to the next level, I found Aloise. She didn't stir as I approached, her body sitting still against the wall, head turned away.

"Aloise?" I whispered.

She didn't move.

Aklys nudged me out of the way and shoved a long metal pick into the cell lock, and after some persuasion, it quietly clicked open. I pushed past him, opening the creaking door and rushing over to the woman. Her skin was cold to the touch, and I reached my hand out to rotate her head toward me. What I beheld caused the blood to drain from my face and sent my brain spinning.

Her eyes were blackened and swollen shut, her face bloodied beyond recognition. A section of hair on the side of her head had been ripped from the scalp, hanging by strands and leaving behind an oozing wound. Blood had crusted around her nose and mouth, I fought to swallow down the bile that crept up my throat as the severity of her condition dawned on me.

She was nearly dead.

I felt strong hands on my shoulders, squeezing gently.

"There's nothing you can do. She's too far gone," Aklys whispered.

Every nasty thought I'd had about the woman passed through my mind. I felt so guilty. I was responsible for this. She had lied to protect Thibault, who had lied to protect me. Now, here she was, dying for a love that betrayed her the very same day. She didn't deserve this. I had to do something. I had to save her.

I took her face in my hands and begged, "Don't die! Don't you fucking die!"

"You have to be quiet!" Aklys hissed.

"Don't die. Don't die. Don't die." I cried, pulling her limp body into my arms and across my lap. "This is my fault. She's dying because of me."

"No, she's dying because of Tobian. You didn't do this," he insisted.

I refused to accept that. I knew I was responsible. If she had told the truth, exposed me, perhaps she would be home safe right now.

Her body twitched, choking on the blood that pooled in her mouth. I held her tightly, the woman I'd both envied and felt so much animosity toward. My power hummed under the surface of my skin. I ignored it, trying to gently wipe away the blood from her delicate face.

I didn't want anyone to die... not for me, nor because of me.

Red mist snaked out in thin tendrils, invading the openings of her face; seeping into her eyes, her nostrils and her mouth. Horrified, I tried to pull away, disgusted that any part of me could attack someone so compromised and defenseless. Aklys backed into the cell bars.

"What are you doing to her?" He exclaimed quietly.

"I-I don't k-know. I'm not trying to do a-anything." I whimpered, stuttering between my sobs.

I pulled my gaze away from him and back toward the atrocity I was committing.

Something was different.

The mist was pulling back toward me, and as it returned to my body, I noticed the color changing. A black essence was being tugged from the body and into my own. As the mysterious substance entered me, it felt as though I'd been lit on fire.

I dropped her from my arms and slammed my body backwards helplessly against the ground. I couldn't even scream as I burned from the inside, writhing in silent pain. I briefly made eye contact with Aklys, who had frozen in horror as he beheld whatever was happening to the two bodies now lying on the floor.

A handful of minutes passed before I was able to move again. When the pain finally stopped, I sucked in a deep breath and groaned.

Aklys rushed over, lifting me into a sitting position and examining me thoroughly, using his hand to lift and turn my head and limbs.

"I'm okay," I whispered and closed my eyes, just for a moment.

"Milady?"

Slowly opening up to the world around me, I looked up at his face. He was no longer staring at me but at something else in the room. Panicked, I shot upright, thinking we'd been discovered. When I realized there was nothing amiss, I followed the direction of his gaze. He was looking at Aloise.

Her face remained bruised, but only slightly, and there was blood crusted along now closed wounds. I didn't understand what I was seeing. Her chest rose and fell gently; she was very much alive.

Aklys stood quickly, yanking me upright and spinning me to face him.

"What do you know about your power?" he demanded.

Stunned, I fumbled my words, "I... It, it kills things! It just kills things!"

"It absorbed the black magic from her body! It sucked it right out and healed it along the way. You siphoned it into your body and somehow neutralized it!"

He was still shaking me slightly, and I couldn't make sense of what he was saying.

"You absorbed the essence. You can absorb life force and kill things, yes, but you can absorb magic. *You just absorbed magic.* They must've used cursed objects on her or had the Mage do their dirty work for magic to have inflicted that damage. You pulled it out." He drew a shaky breath, "You just saved her life."

The shock of what had just happened was too much for me to bear, and I bolted from the cell, feet carrying me toward the stairs. Thibault and Maygen were not here. Rounding the wall of the curved stairwell, I collided with something solid. I tumbled backwards, unable to catch myself, falling down towards the treacherous steps. A large hand reached out and gripped my throat, catching me and squeezing. I was lifted off my feet and brought face to face with a man: a Fae man.

I lingered only inches away from a cold, familiar stare. Dark eyes that held no light looked familiar, with even darker hair that dusted his forehead. I struggled against the grip on my neck, grabbing the man's wrist in a desperate attempt to force him away from me.

"Hello, Celessa. It's so nice to see you again," a low voice growled.

Kilian?

Chapter Four

Haunting Encounters

B right white exploded throughout my vision, and a sharp pain split my skull. The next few moments were a daze, with only brief and blurry scenes passing me by. The sounds around me were muffled, like I was listening to people speaking from behind a closed door. The movement of the shapes, along with the painful scratching and digging along my skin, rendered a faint awareness that I was being dragged across the ground.

I found myself restrained and kneeling on cold, stone tile. A cloth was wrapped around my head, pulled tightly between my lips. I wriggled my hands, which had been tied with chains behind my back, an uncomfortable sensation around my ankles alerted me that my feet were also bound. I struggled, grunting in an attempt to fight off the gag reflex that was causing my mouth to water and my stomach to turn.

The more aware I became, the more the throbbing pain in my head took over. Someone had struck and immobilized me. Looking around, I found myself staring directly at a man, the Fae man. Kilian Crassus. He was sitting quietly on an oversized wooden dais that was perched atop a large, cracked, stone platform.

Only the sounds of breath being drawn filled the corridor, and a few men stood a small distance away, watching as intently as the person in the chair before me. The slow realization that Kilian was *actually* present dawned on me. My sister's lover was here in Tobian's settlement.

Surely, that could not be a coincidence? Why was he not doing anything to help me? He *knew* me.

Who had struck me? The only people in that stairwell besides me were Kilian and Aklys.

Aklys... Where was he?

I turned my head to examine the room, searching the faces. As I scanned the group of onlookers, I met the vampire's gaze. He was standing there with these strange men, watching as I knelt helplessly on the floor. He betrayed me. I huffed a disgusted sound through the fabric between my teeth. I glared at him, unblinking; if looks could kill, I would have murdered him a thousand times over.

A man cleared his throat, and I swiveled my attention back to where Kilian sat, his eyes now flicking lazily between Aklys and myself.

"Lady Celessa. The stolen daughter and great demise of the Umbraeon family. How could it be after all this time you've shown up on my doorstep?" Kilian crooned, "Such luck. What a prize you are."

There was no point in trying to speak or move. I was still processing exactly the mess in which my already unfavorable situation had evolved into. The way Kilian spoke gave me no indication that he was pleased with my presence or interested in helping me. He rose from the makeshift throne, stepping down to stand directly before my quivering figure. The familiar man reached out to stroke my cheek, running his fingertips along my jawline and up into my hair, taking a fistful in his grasp.

Pain erupted where the strands were pulled against my most recent injury, making my eyes water uncontrollably. Kilian smiled, and a low growl rumbled in his ribcage.

"So submissive," he spoke through gritted teeth, lowering himself to meet me face to face. "You pale in comparison to your sister."

Hot anger exploded in my chest as I thought about how my sister had suffered so severely at the hands of men. He was supposed to love her. He murdered for her, and yet he stood here abusing me. Confusion replaced the rage, and I struggled against the fist knotted in my hair.

Kilian wrapped his free hand around my neck and lifted me by my throat, causing me to cough and gasp around the choking hold. He then released me onto my feet and pulled the gag from my mouth. With the fabric gone, I ran my tongue over dry lips, tasting blood that had crept between cracks in the delicate flesh.

"Why are you doing this?" I squeaked, "I'm Arecelle's sister! You loved her! Please!"

Burning shocks of pain exploded in my face, as Kilian backhanded me. My body crashed to the floor, unable to catch myself due to the restraints. I cried out in agony, the force of the fall cracking through my paper-thin resolve.

How could he be doing this, why was he doing this? Why did Aklys hand me over to him, and why had he lured me here under the guise of offering his aid? Why go through all the trouble of sneaking me into the keep instead of bringing me through the front door? Why help me enter Aloise's cell where she lay dying?

I was a damn fool. I'd put my trust in men yet again. I never learned.

"Don't you fucking speak of her. You're the reason she died!" Kilian hissed.

My body went rigid. He was right; I was the reason she died.

Asuras had taken me, and then my family had been murdered, only my youngest sister escaped. Arecelle and Necilia were slain simply because I refused to give up my curse to the Mage. The tears I had been struggling against flowed freely now. I hadn't had the opportunity to mourn my sisters, and he was wounding me with the truth of their Fate. Wielding my guilt as the sharpest of weapons, he utilized the most effective way to break me.

"If it wasn't for you, I would've been able to take her away after I escaped my sentencing."

Escaped? He had eluded imprisonment and come for her?

"By the time I got to the grounds, everyone was dead... except you, nowhere to be found, and sweet Ephyra. She and I crossed paths sometime later, what an experience she was. She told me all about how everything was *your fault*."

A booted foot collided with my stomach, and I screamed at the impact.

"I held her dead body in my arms! I cradled her corpse, Celessa. I see her lifeless face in my dreams, still, after all this time." Kilian had crouched down to whisper in my ear, "You deserve everything you're going to get."

His hand returned to my hair, forcing my head back to face him again.

"You're going to pay for every day I have had to spend without her, for every stolen moment I should've been with her. These long years have left me cruel, Celessa. I feel nothing but hatred. I was branded a monster when I killed those men, when I killed for love. I wasn't a monster then."

His hot tongue licked my bloodied lips, and my reflexes jerked me backwards, horrified.

"I'm a monster now."

He watched me for a long moment before speaking again.

"The name Kilian Crassus died when he was stripped of his titles, cast from his home, and left only to find the woman he'd sacrificed it all for *dead*. He'd sacrificed it all for nothing, simply because her little bitch of a sister *exists*."

Understanding what he meant, choked words left me, "You're Tobian?"

Kilian was the tyrant. A twisted smile formed on his face as he lifted his hands into the air dramatically, signaling to himself.

"Lord Tobian, bereaved yet beloved by all who dwell within my little slice of hell!"

He laughed, signaling to the group of men lingering nearby to approach. I was hoisted back to a standing position by strangers, trembling uncontrollably. Kilian darted forward as the men held me and lashed out, tearing my dress down the front to expose my body.

"You lot can have some fun before the patrol picks her up tomorrow. Just make sure she's still breathing so I get paid. I'll be retiring to my chambers; I've got a long night ahead of me."

The words were tossed nonchalantly over his shoulder as he strolled from the room.

My knees buckled in fear and the two men, who were now laughing amongst themselves, drug me across the floor toward an entryway on the far side of the room.

"Just kill me. Kill me, instead," I begged, thrashing as they hauled me away.

My cries were ignored as the men continued on their way, up a flight of stone stairs to reveal a corridor, where we entered a barely furnished bedroom. They tossed me onto the bed, turning away and exiting the room. My eyes darted rapidly, searching for anything I could use to wield as a weapon or use to free myself. I wiggled my hands aggressively, praying I could slip from the binding chains. When I found the struggle futile, violent sobs shook my body.

Why wouldn't my power come out? Why wouldn't it protect me?

The pair returned, wearing nothing but their breeches, telltale to the abuse that awaited me. I screamed. The bigger of the two placed a large hand over my mouth, squeezing my face roughly and making it difficult to breathe.

"If you keep screaming, I'll bust your teeth out. Won't be so pretty then, will ya?" he sneered.

Still, I cried, hoping death would release me.

They tore away the rest of the fabric that clung to my skin, leaving me entirely exposed and quaking in fear. Loud clacking of a belt buckle echoed through the room as one of the men began to fully undress. I thrashed wildly as the brute struggled to effectively pin me beneath him. He halted his efforts when a loud knock sounded on the door.

"Go tell those bastards to wait for their bloody turn... I haven't had my go yet," he grumbled at his companion.

Huffing a sigh, the observing man exited the room, leaving the door slightly cracked as the aggressor returned his focus to me.

"Now hold still, and it'll be easier on everyone – what do you say?"

Decayed teeth lined his disgusting smile, and my head shook wildly, attempting to elude him as he tried to press his mouth against me.

Suddenly, the man stopped moving and made not a sound more than a single strained grunt.

Hot liquid sprayed my face, filling my mouth and obscuring my vision. I heard a squelching sound, but couldn't see what was happening past the substance seeping between my eyelids. Without warning, the weight of the man no longer pressed down on my body, and a garbled cry resonated throughout the space.

Panicking, I rolled away from the commotion. The air was forced from my chest as I landed on the floor, having fallen from the bed. Completely blinded, I wriggled to where I assumed was underneath the bed frame, wiping my face frantically against the ground.

A loud thud sent vibrations rippling through the floor.

Stilling, I listened to my surroundings.

Silence.

A hand wrapped around my ankle, yanking me out from my pathetic hiding place. Bucking frantically, I screamed as loud as I could manage, even as a gentle hand covered my mouth. I wouldn't survive this assault. Even if I did physically, I would not mentally. I'd endured too much already, and I was grasping at mere threads to preserve myself.

Someone was wrestling me down, not to subdue, but to calm me. Rough fabric wiped across my face, trying to remove the sticky substance from my eyes. A useless effort, as it felt like it was just smearing deeper into my skin.

"Lie still, and don't make a sound," a male voice demanded.

Was that... *Oh, hell no.* Traitor.

That bastard handed me right over to Kilian, watched him beat and humiliate me. I'd rather suffer alone and struggle to find a way out of this than accept his aid.

Cold liquid rushed over my face. I hadn't been prepared and accidentally inhaled it, choking and gasping, as he wrangled me still to clean my face further. My blurry vision slowly pieced back together, until I could clearly make out the features of Aklys' face. I realized now that my head had been in his lap while he'd tried to remedy the mess. His clothes were soaked, but not with the water... He looked down at me thoughtfully, drenched in blood.

Shifting my gaze, I realized my naked body had been splattered with sticky redness. Through my peripheral vision, I caught sight of a dead body on the floor just a short distance away.

"You killed him," I whispered.

"I killed all of them," he snapped. "I ripped the throats out of every single one of those bastards."

Aklys began undoing the chains around my wrists, freeing me. My skin was stinging from the friction burns that I inflicted upon myself as I fought to escape, the tender flesh colored pink. The joints of my wrists ached, as I flexed and rotated them in an effort to loosen the distressed muscles. Aklys' hands were gentle as he went to work on my bound feet. I noticed he wasn't ogling me the way he'd done on the way into the keep, even though now I was entirely nude.

In fact, it was beyond noticeable just how much he was trying to avoid looking at me. Either he respected my position after what had happened, or the former interest he'd displayed earlier was merely a ploy to get me to lower my guard.

"Do you have any spare clothes?" I asked.

"No."

Aklys removed his own bloodied shirt and handed it to me. It was better than nothing, and I slipped it on without thanking him.

We sat in silence for what felt like an eternity, looking at one another and overly wary of engaging in conversation after all that had just transpired. I wanted to know why he'd done it, why he handed me over to people who would hurt me in every way imaginable.

I was a stranger to him, I remembered. He owed me nothing. I hadn't given him any reason to consider defending me. I was nothing to this man, this vampire. My thoughts finally got the best of me; I moved my lips to speak, still making eye contact with Aklys.

"I'm sorry," he said, cutting me off.

My mouth snapped back shut, and I exhaled slowly through my nostrils, waiting for him to justify his actions. Aklys pondered thoughtfully, his eyes scanned my face as though he was committing every detail to memory. Sharp fangs pressed the delicate skin of his bottom lip as he chose his next words.

"You aren't what I expected," he said finally. "I want to help you."

"I'm pretty sure you've already fed me that lie once tonight," I snarled.

Aklys flinched.

"Our position was compromised. It wasn't my intention for you to get hurt."

"It wasn't your intention to let Kilian blindside me? Was it your intention to sit idly by as he beat me, or to let him expose me in front of strange men? How about when he offered me up like a brood mare to be abused until it was time to send me off to the next monster?"

"They were never supposed to get their hands on you, but they did and my incompetence is to blame. Your gifts on display in the cells threw me off. While that's not an excuse, I think anyone who hasn't seen what you can do would be awestruck at that kind of power. I couldn't allow my true intentions to be exposed until they were vulnerable. I hadn't planned to commit a mass murder; I only wanted Tobian to die."

"Then why throw your plans out the window?" I sneered.

"They hurt you."

Shadowed, brooding eyes locked onto my own. I let him keep waiting for me to swoon over his lies, as any normal mortal woman with a weak mind would at the feet of a handsome, charming vampire.

"You hurt me," I returned.

Aklys frowned, his gaze moving to the floor.

"You killed them all?" I asked, as I fought to keep the tone of my voice flat and unfeeling.

"Yes."

"Where is Kilian?"

"I can't dispatch him on my own. He has the Mage in his bed; she protects him. That's why I need you."

"I'm flattered to know that you desperately require my help, but before anything else happens I need to find Thibault and Maygen to make sure they're safe."

They hadn't been in the cells. Not knowing their whereabouts, after having been through the dungeon and in the main corridor with no sign of them, made my stomach twist. Was I too late for them? I'd nearly been too late for Aloise, but it seems Fate had been on her side.

"Thibault is chained up in the stables. Tobian had said it was the best place to store a half-breed. They didn't beat him too terribly, so he'll recover soon."

Aklys spoke carelessly, as if Thibault's mistreatment didn't matter.

"You knew where he was the entire time, and you said nothing?" I exclaimed.

I stalked over to the smug vampire and pushed him as hard as I could, to my surprise he faltered, but only slightly. Anger surged, and I raised my hand to threaten him. In a mere second, I was pinned to the bloodied bed, with strong hands restraining my own above my head. Aklys hovered mere inches from my face.

"I knew your feelings for him would cloud your judgment. It was in your best interest to have the women become your priority."

"You don't know anything about my feelings for him!"

"I could *smell* you all over his quaint little cottage," he growled, inhaling deeply, and the sound made my lip quiver. He continued, "Unless you indulge freely, which I doubt, I would surmise that you think you love him."

What an incredibly bold statement to make of someone you've just met. I considered for a brief moment what punishment he would have faced if he'd said such things to me when I was a lady. As a noble lady, I wasn't to be touched, and I was never insulted for fear of my father. My status of nobility was exactly why he'd assumed I would not offer myself up freely, but I was no longer a person of high standing.

Indulging was my right, at this point. Was I meant only to suffer? Fate was cruel and twisted, but ever changing. I will shape mine how I see fit; I'll grant myself the small pleasures to break up the monotony of my tormented, hellish reality.

"Apparently, I lack common sense and have poor judgment, seeing as I trusted him, and he's in love with another woman. I trusted you, and then you coerced me into a torture chamber."

An exasperated sound left him.

"I feel guilty, alright? I am capable of remorse. Being a vampire doesn't make me devoid of emotion. I know that doesn't right the damage that's been done, and it doesn't excuse my actions," Aklys sighed heavily. "If I would've acted when I wanted to, the moment he touched you, I'd be dead right now, and you would be suffering at the hands of those men."

He nodded to the bloody corpses.

"The only reason you care is so I can carry out your plans. I don't want or need your apologies, so get away from me," I bit out angrily.

Wordlessly, the vampire stood, looming over the bed, as I continued to lie there staring up at him. The color seemed to swirl in his eyes, more golden than hazel now. Blood still coated his face; it had started drying and flaking against his skin. As I brought my body into a sitting position, he moved further away from me, granting me the space I had requested.

I eyed him suspiciously.

Aklys had quickly proven that he was unpredictable at best, either completely violating every boundary that should exist between two acquaintances or fully withdrawing to respect them. It seemed almost as though he gravitated towards me, only displaying restraint when it has been assertively requested.

"Does every vampire act the way that you do?"

"I'm not the kind of vampire with whom you're familiar," the tone of his voice was cooler than before, as if I'd offended him.

I was only familiar with vampires in stories, as not many dwelled in the Three Kingdoms after they were driven out in the Blood Wars.

"Surprise, you're my first," I jeered. "My familiarity comes from the scary tales nursemaids read to the little ladies of the manor. Please, enlighten me."

My hands folded thoughtfully in my lap, and I stuck a pouty bottom lip out, mocking the man.

"As I said, I'm not the kind of vampire with whom you're familiar. I'm not the uncontrollable monster that can think of nothing more than draining every living thing of its blood. I don't even originate from the same curse."

How incredibly vague.

"We don't have time for this right now. We need to eliminate Tobian and leave the settlement. He's banking on the Sentinel patrol to show up tomorrow to procure you, so we need to be gone before that happens."

"I'm sorry, 'we'?"

"Do you actually think you'll make it through the Ashen Lands alone? Do you know what's out there?"

I did know what was out there, and I hadn't considered we would have to go that route. Without a reinforced ship, sailing Serpent's Bay was a death sentence, and the only other way out was over Grim's Peak and through the barren wasteland into northern Teskaria.

Where would I even go?

The families that ruled the major cities were mostly tyrannical Fae lords, with the exception of a few Elvish households. I had no family left. Maygen had wanted to travel to Euros, but the courts in the neighboring country were likely just as treacherous as the ones we faced in my homeland. The slow realization that there was no place for me in this world was swallowing me up in a black wave of defeat.

What am I fighting for?

In this moment, I was fighting for Maygen, Thibault, and even Aloise. After that? After they were safe? I had no interest in my presence continuing to endanger them. I should leave; it was a mercy for us all.. but would I survive on my own?

"Hey?" Aklys' voice snapped me out of my downward emotional spiral.

I swallowed the lump in my throat, "Do you have a plan?"

He scoffed, "We go to his chambers and kill him?"

"You said he had a Mage?" I countered.

"You absorb magic, so why should we be worried?"

"I can't control my power, Aklys. It does what it wants, it explodes beyond control, and it apparently can heal magical wounds. I tried to summon it against you earlier, and it wouldn't work."

The vampire snickered, "Yeah, I caught that."

I shot him a glare in response.

"Show up at his door then. Distract him, engage the Mage, and then I'll kill him," he spoke carelessly, as if it'd be easy.

"I think you're overconfident in your abilities," I scoffed, "and mine."

Aklys reached out his hand — accepting his offer, I gingerly slid my fingers across his palm and allowed him to guide me up from the bed.

I sucked in a shaky breath to brace myself, and we left the room.

Nothing could've prepared me for the gruesome scene lining the corridor. My mind flickered back to my escape from Sanctuary, after Maygen had fought the acolytes to retrieve me from the prison.

Acolytes were merely mortals at the service of a Mage, not much different from household help, but the title gave them some sense of ominous purpose.

A few bodies lay strewn across the floor, necks gaping and painted with crimson. Aklys hadn't lied, he'd ripped their throats out. The power display, the absolute carnage before me, had me rethinking my snarky attitude towards the vampire.

Unable to stop myself, I asked, "Did you drink their blood?"

"No, not really. I was more concerned at that moment with killing them all before they could call for help."

He shrugged carelessly.

"How often do you need blood?"

He arched a brow at me, looking more intrigued than offended, but answered, "That's a bit of a personal question, isn't it?"

"Well, if I'm going to be in your presence, I'd like to know that I don't have to worry about ending up as your personal blood source if you haven't *eaten* anything."

Aklys threw his head back and laughed.

Folding my arms across my chest, I huffed and looked away to observe the bloody mess once more. As I turned back, he was in my face quicker than my eyes could register, and the unexpected presence made me stumble. The vampire caught my arm, pulling my body close to his.

"Don't you want me to bite you?" Aklys purred, revealing his fangs in a broad smile.

He was doing it again, violating boundaries.

"Keep your affliction to yourself," I commanded, brushing away his hold. "Your hands, too."

"As you wish, milady," he chuckled.

"Stop calling me that."

"Not going to happen."

Groaning, I stepped away from him and began making my way down the long hallway. He followed closely behind, and each time I glanced back at him his grin grew wider.

"You're in an awfully good mood for someone who is about to commit murder," I paused for a moment, "again."

"I've been waiting for this for a long time. He's a stain that needs to be wiped from the world. It'll be a better place without him."

He was right. If how I was treated had been any allusion to the horrors Kilian inflicted upon other innocents, someone should've wrung the life from him long ago. I prayed my power was up to the task of ending a full-blooded Fae's life. My steps faltered as I doubted myself, delaying my advance. Aklys had been following so closely that he collided with my body.

I shot him an irritated look in an attempt to get him to fall back, putting space between us. He stood fast, unwavering, and only continued to smile at me. I'd never met someone so infuriating in my life.

"Where is his room? Or are you going to let me wander aimlessly into a trap again?" I hissed.

"No traps. I could carry you to our destination if you'd like?"

He bit his bottom lip with those sharp teeth, making me cringe, it looked as though he might puncture the delicate skin.

"That will never happen again, since I know better than to trust you now."

Without sparing another glance at him, I continued on my way. Aklys followed again, this time at a greater distance.

"We're almost there. Are you ready to end this?" The vampire asked.

I was ready.

Chapter Five

Peace Is The For Lucky

The long, winding hallway was nearing its end, with a final door coming into view. I turned back to Aklys, unspeaking as I questioned him with my eyes. Stretching out his muscles, he stepped around me and kicked the large wooden door open in one fluid movement. Had the circumstances been less dire, the dramatic flair would've made me giggle.

Kilian leapt from the bed, snarling, and to the misfortune of my stomach, he was stark naked. The sight was more nauseating than the brutalized bodies that lined the hallways. He squinted his eyes, studying the pair of us looming in the entryway.

"It seems the only bait you need to lure out a snake is a squealing little bitch."

Kilian's words felt like daggers in my gut.

His smile was taunting, twisted and evil. He wasn't paying me much mind as he glared down his adversary, the vampire to my left. The two were evenly matched in height and stature, two immortal beings with exceptional strength and agility. The deciding factors in the impending bloodbath boiled down to Kilian's Mage... and me.

A woman cowered under the bed sheets, only the top of her head visible, locks of curly copper hair peeking out from behind the cover. I scanned the room, spotting a small iron cage draped with chains in a dark corner. A wounded woman was crammed inside, the smell of her blood lingering in the air.

The woman was Maygen.

Every nerve in my body urged me to go to her, to set her free and take her far away from this cursed place. I only stared in horror, frozen in place.

"What's the matter little lady, would you like a turn?"

Kilian's taunt drew my gaze away from the horrific display.

He stripped away the bedsheets, revealing a tiny woman in a see-through shift. She'd been thoroughly corrupted by black magic, but I doubted it had been her choice. Blackened veins crept up around her arms all the way to her neck, twisting along her skin like a poisonous tattoo. Her eyes were black, nearly lifeless, and she would've looked completely devoid of awareness if it weren't for the fearful expression painting her features. I felt my power swelling below the surface, awakening and answering my subconscious call. Anger roared to life in my chest amidst the fear and disbelief I felt.

I was angry for Aloise, who had been lingering at death's doorstep. I was angry for Thibault, chained up in a pen like an animal. I was angry for Maygen, rendered helpless and tortured mercilessly. I was angry for Aklys, who had been left with no choice but to play along with the cruel whims of the Fae lord. I was angry for the cowering Mage, who was likely being used against her will. I was angry for myself. He'd put his hands on me and had relished in inflicting that pain. He'd offered me up to be used by his lackeys. I was angry for the nameless people he terrorized now and before I'd come to this place.

Painfully, my skin began to pull apart, deadly crimson tendrils crept forth from my body. I welcomed the agony that came with the use of my gift, knowing it meant the demise of the tyrant. I watched his expression pale as he beheld my wrath revealing itself, as he anticipated what was to come.

Kilian reached back, grabbing the trembling Mage by her thin arm, and flung her forward. She landed at the end of the bed, her head hanging low, with hair draped in front of her face.

"It's time to play, Neina."

My power had already begun to withdraw at the sight of the frail girl. I would not hurt an innocent, but perhaps I could save her from Kilian.

As quickly as she had landed, the woman was springing to life, her expression twisting into something awful. Black liquid dripped from her lips and the dark veins were stark against luminescent skin; writhing with the life of forbidden magic. She shot forth from her hand what appeared to be a shadow, but when it collided with my body, explosive pain erupted inside of my ribs.

I screamed, thrashing and wailing as I tried to free myself from the malevolent force. Through my peripheral vision, I could see Aklys lunging for Kilian. The two locked in violent hand to hand combat, wrestling and striking the other, each trying to gain the upper hand against their adversary.

As my gift pushed free from my body, despite the unexpectedly powerful attack, I began drawing in and absorbing the Mage's power within my own. Realizing that her magic was being depleted, rendered ineffective, her head tipped back, and she parted her jaws to unleash an ear-splitting scream. The sound instantly caused everyone to drop to the floor, nearly paralyzed. Aklys and Kilian continued kicking at each other as they attempted to cover their ears against the assault.

Squeezing my head between my palms, trying to protect myself from the damaging sound, I lunged toward the woman. I released my head to grab her by the throat, squeezing tightly to cut off the hellish wail. I threw her to the ground, landing on top of her, still grasping the woman's neck.

"Let me help you! If you stop, I can help you!" I screamed at her.

Deep, black eyes stared back at me. I was desperate to break through to her, but the hollowness of the pits revealed just how far gone she was. This girl was nothing more than a puppet for Kilian, and she would kill me if I gave her the chance. Sorrow washed over as I held her, still struggling beneath me. She was trying to force the deadly scream past my hold on her throat. I used one of my hands to cover her mouth, smearing the dark, inky fluid across her face; the texture under my fingers made me feel sick.

A burning pain tore through the flesh of my hand, and I howled as I withdrew, sitting up and losing my hold on the woman. Blood ran down my wrist; she'd bitten me, hard. The slime was seeping into the wound, black veins crawled up the length of my arm as her poison assaulted me. My eyes bulged; I didn't know how to stop it. The woman bucked me off, rolling to pin me against the ground. The oozing substance dripped from her mouth, falling on to my face as I struggled beneath her.

I had never found myself in a position like this: the only time I'd been in a situation where I'd *needed* to kill was against a true monster, the Wyndiga. This was a girl, and despite the corruption she was still *someone*. Her jaw separated again, only this time a shadowy essence crept forth from the depths of her body, coiling to strike like a viper. I thrashed violently to no avail, parting my jaws to scream for Aklys.

The twisted magic forced its way down my throat the moment I opened myself up. It slithered down into my lungs, choking me, draining the life from my body. Helplessly, I bucked against the woman as I felt myself begin to die.

My eyes fluttered shut, unable to breathe, and I started to slip away.

You have a gift, Celessa, become the weapon you were meant to be.

A renewed energy pushed forward at the command of this foreign voice inside my head. I reached out my hand, grabbing the woman's lower jaw and yanking her towards my face. I used my legs to force my pelvis up against her, sending her tumbling overhead. The shadowy force ripped away from my body as I escaped her hold, leaving me gasping for breath. As quickly as I could manage, I whirled and grabbed her by the hair, dragging her deeper into my reach. Her body was writhing like a snake, instinctual but not aware.

"I don't want to kill you!" I screamed. "Show me that I won't have to, please!"

The woman spat the poisonous fluid at me.

"*Die.*" The voice she produced was guttural and unsettling... She was beyond saving.

My power erupted, and crept along the woman's skin, forcing itself into the openings of her face. It invaded her mouth, her nose, her ears; reaching into her skull. The mist emanating from me turned black as it absorbed the tainted magic from deep inside the mage. As it reached my veins, the painful scorching took hold.

I fought against it, not allowing it to subdue me as it had done before. I battled for control, forcing it to submit to my will and harmonize with my body rather than siphoning anything it could from me. The woman screamed, and it became a girl's scream again, not the evil presence that had possessed her before. There was life and awareness in her eyes as she watched me drain the magic from her with my curse.

Panicking, I tried to withdraw the blood mist, willing it back to me. I'd absorbed the black magic that plagued her, and she was in there; I couldn't kill this girl. Frantically, I fought, physically trying to pull it away. I yanked my arms, backing my body away from the assault. Her screams began to falter, with her life ending right before my eyes.

The surrounding world eluded me for a few moments as I succumbed to darkness. Violence whirled in my mind; my gift combatted the black magic I'd absorbed, fighting for control over my being. A struggle of red and black twisted and roiled inside. The pain surpassed the point of agony, and I was left numb.

My eyes focused slowly, a blur of shapes and colors appearing around me. I drew a breath as my heartbeat thundered in my head, and I rolled my body to search for the Mage. A mangled pile of bone and gore lay close by, the horror of the sight shocked me back into reality. That was what was left of the girl. This was the carnage I was capable of. I'd murdered her.

"Celessa!" A male voice screamed.

Aklys had tried to lunge for me, to help me, and now Kilian had him captured in a deadly position. I watched him struggle against the tyrant's hold around his head and neck, with his desperate expression begging me for help. He was going to die, and all I could do was lie here, watching.

Kilian smiled at me with his mouth bloodied, staining once white teeth red. An open gash along his forehead was leaking, leaving streams of crimson glistening on his skin. The subdued Aklys was bleeding as severely as if you'd turned on a faucet, draining from his nose and mouth. I shook my head weakly.

"Let him go," I begged.

"Why would I do that?" Kilian taunted, squeezing Aklys tighter.

Aklys sputtered blood from his mouth onto the arm that choked him.

"Please."

"Celessa, come on," Kilian laughed, "He watched me hurt you, don't you want to return the favor?"

No, I didn't. Truly, I didn't want Aklys to be hurt. I wanted him to live. I couldn't allow another person to die because of me. However, I wanted to kill the evil Fae standing before me.

Clenching my jaw, "Let go," I ground out.

Kilian made a mocking, thoughtful face at me.

"I don't think I will," he sneered.

Aklys had begun to fall limp in his grasp.

My power surged with a type of ferocity it hadn't displayed before. It felt as though it had broken the bonds I'd placed on it, my once feeble attempts to stifle and contain it for fear of hurting others.

It was fully awake now. I held the power to consume and decimate magic and life itself.

It lashed out at Kilian. I felt no fear for Aklys because, for reasons unknown, it would not work against the vampire; he was safe from me. A primal, ferocious sound emerged from my chest, expanding my ribcage and tearing its way up my throat. The power within me flexed like a muscle and took Kilian in its clutches, wrenching him away from Aklys' body. The vampire dropped to the ground, gasping and barely clinging to consciousness.

The red mist acted as an extension of my being, and my rage consumed me. I watched Kilian writhe helplessly, ensnared several feet above the ground. A twisted grin lifted my face.

I was enjoying this.

"Oh, come on, Kilian, don't you like being helpless? Don't you like being at the mercy of someone much, *much* more powerful than you?" My voice didn't sound like my own at the moment, but I couldn't bring myself to feel concerned.

"No wonder you do this, I bet you love watching people squirm," I growled, mocking him, "I love watching you squirm."

He still fought against my power's hold, with the realization that he was going to die birthing an uncontrollable panic in the man.

"Wait! Wait!"

He screamed as my power tugged at his limbs, creeping toward his face to decimate him from the inside out as it had done to the Mage.

"I know what you are! No one else knows, Celessa! I can help you!" He wailed.

"He doesn't know anything," Aklys sputtered, "end it."

My head cocked to the side slightly as I viewed the life before me, the life I was going to end.

"You're not mortal!" he screamed.

Lies.

"You could've done better than that, Kilian," I hissed, inching the tendrils closer to his face; savoring every second of his despair.

"Amalgam!" He screamed.

Stopping for a moment, I stared at him in disbelief.

An Amalgam was a child that was the product of a God or Goddesses' forbidden union with a being that wasn't of divine blood: a Demi-God... Something twisted, deadly, and wrong. The legends say they wreaked havoc in the early world, forcing deities to forbid their creation and wipe out those that had been made.

"Every moment he draws breath, he poisons the world around him," Aklys insisted, and I listened.

Kilian's screams grew in terror, as the mist found its way into his mouth and began filling his body. I used the new control I'd found to tear his limbs from the sockets of his body, blood painted the floors and furniture, and sprayed the walls. The tendrils dropped body parts around the stump that was left of the man, with all the pieces splayed out on the ground. He was dying quickly, but I wanted to watch the light leave his eyes.

I crawled over to him, climbing on top of what was left of his body, smearing his blood between my fingers. My hand twisted in his hair, to turn his head to look me in the eyes. I wanted to be the last face he saw as he died.

"Don't," he choked, the word garbled in blood.

"Don't what, Kilian? It's too late to beg for your life, it's over."

"Don't," he tried again, "trust any... vampires."

Hell of a choice of last words.

The reflection in his eyes glassed over, stilling and becoming lifeless. I could see a small picture of myself in them, covered in my blood, his blood, and the Mage woman's blood. It was a true horror to behold, a monstrous scene. My power had taken its place back inside my body, and I hadn't even felt it return.

I glared at the vampire who lingered nearby.

"Don't you think it would've been easier coming in here with, I don't know, some weapons?" I growled at Aklys.

"I am the weapon, milady." He laughed, spitting red fluid from his mouth. He was lucky his affliction granted him rapid healing, or he likely wouldn't be speaking to me now.

"It's become pretty clear that *I* am the weapon," I shot back.

The full realization of what lay beneath my hands dawned on me, with the horror of my actions clawing through the bloodlust that had clouded my mind. I scrambled away from the mess, slipping on the crimson coated floor, with panic overwhelming me. Strong arms captured my retreat, gripping me tightly.

In a matter of minutes, I had brutalized and ended two lives.

"Breathe. It's over." Aklys' voice sang in my ear.

My body fell limp, the weight and strain of it all crashing down like a landslide, covering me in the rubble of shock and shame.

I fainted in his embrace.

∞

Swimming.

I was swimming, and the water was warm. It cleansed the skin and refreshed the soul. Blissfully unaware, I floated. Splashes caressed my skin. Gentle currents swept by, holding me lovingly, kissing away my aches and pains. It was peaceful, comfortable, and I could linger here forever. Simply existing.

"Wake up," a whisper echoed.

No, I'm happy here, I thought.

"Please, wake up."

Please just let me stay, I'm so warm. I'm so tired.

"Come back, milady."

Slowly, my eyelids parted, squinting against the light of a small room. Liquid sloshed around my stirring body, and I realized that someone had put me in a bathtub. I searched for the source of the voice; a handsome man sat by the basin, pouring water over my hair as I soaked.

"There you are," he sighed as he smiled at me.

The air I inhaled burned my lungs, my skin was sore and my muscles were rigid. I felt as if I'd been carried and dropped like a ragdoll, one that had been swept up by a whirlwind. Trying to sit up, I winced and gasped as pain sang throughout my body.

"Just relax," Aklys crooned.

He brought a rag to my face, gently wiping away the blood that had dried to my cheeks. Relaxing my head, I allowed him to clean me without a single word of protest.

"Are you injured?" I managed to ask.

"I'm a vampire, I heal exceptionally well. Remember how quickly I was back on my feet after you stabbed me?" He mused.

I attempted to assess the damage done to my body. My legs were already bruised, mostly my knees during the scuffle with the Mage. I felt the wound of the bitemark she'd left when she caught me with her teeth. Black veins still polluted my skin, and the sight of them made me gasp.

"I can fix that," Aklys offered.

"How?" I whispered.

"I can drain it, draw the poison out."

"How?" I repeated.

Meeting his eyes, he smiled at me with glistening fangs, using his tongue to toy with the sharp points of the elongated teeth.

"Oh," was the only word I could manage.

"Or we can leave it, and your body will absorb it over time. It would be deadly for a normal mortal, but you aren't normal, are you?"

No, I wasn't. I possessed a power that absorbed and neutralized black magic, but why hadn't it fixed this yet?

The thought of Aklys biting me made my stomach twist into a knot, but how badly would it hurt? It couldn't possibly be worse than anything I've already endured.

"Will it take the pain away?" I asked.

"Yes."

"Will it harm you?"

"No, milady, I won't swallow it." Aklys winked.

I offered him the damaged hand, and he took it in his own, tenderly inspecting it. Gliding the tip of his tongue down my wrist, the vampire carefully pricked the thin skin with his fangs. Startled, I whimpered, and swore I heard a growl rumble from the man's chest as he drew my infected blood into his mouth.

After each draw, he would spit the tainted liquid into a towel, and the darkened veins grew lesser as he pulled. It was slightly uncomfortable, but not unbearable. I pressed my thighs together tightly, tensing my body as I waited for him to finish. Finally, he looked up at me, clean blood painted on his lips, red and glistening. He ran a long tongue over his bottom lip, lapping up the leftover drops.

"What does it taste like?" I blurted.

"All blood tastes different; every person and every *thing* has its own flavor, the same as any food or drink." He ran his tongue along the two tiny holes he left in my wrist as he said, "Yours is like citrus and honey."

"Does everyone's blood taste *good*?"

"Not as good as yours," the vampire purred.

I cleared my throat, noticing that my body was clean and the water was cooling, and I'm naked. Oh Gods, I'm naked in front of Aklys, *again*. I've just met the man, and he's seen me indecently exposed more than any other person I'd ever known.

"Is there a towel nearby?" I muttered.

I attempted to rise from the tub, but my legs betrayed me, sending my full weight tumbling back down into the water. Aklys caught me around the waist to lift me from the tub. I clung to him as he supported me with one arm, offering a large towel with the other. I lifted my hands to take it from him, but instead he wrapped it around my body and scooped me up without warning.

"You're entirely too comfortable doing that," I grumbled.

"You don't seem to mind."

"Just because it's occasionally convenient, doesn't make it any less annoying."

The vampire laughed.

I wanted to hate him, blame him for all I'd endured since meeting him. Logically, I knew it wasn't his fault, and rational thinking understood his position, but I was still angry. He carried me to a bed on the other side of the cozy room, setting me down gently.

"Are we still in the keep?" I asked.

"Yes," Aklys said as he sat down beside me.

"Maygen? Thibault and Aloise?"

"All safe and resting, which is what you should be doing. We need to get out of here in the morning to avoid a run in with the Sentinel patrol."

Sentinels are special units of the Teskarian army who are regularly dispatched by the noble families to 'maintain order' throughout the kingdom. I had never met a Sentinel soldier who wasn't a complete bastard. Speaking of bastards, I turned toward Aklys with a glare and slapped him hard.

The vampire was visibly stunned, although he'd hardly flinched at the unexpected strike. Wide eyes met mine, and I clenched my jaw tightly.

"That was for... all of the bullshit," I grumbled, "and I'm still pissed off!"

Aklys leaned in close, so close that the tips of our noses were nearly touching.

"Milady, I think what you just did had quite the opposite effect of what you'd intended," he murmured.

My face caught fire. Turning away from the vampire, I slid toward the pillows to lie down. Aklys covered me with a heavy blanket before plopping down in the bed himself.

"What are you doing?" I exclaimed.

"Getting comfortable," he chirped.

"There are other rooms, other beds!"

"Actually, this keep is mostly empty aside from the few rooms that were occupied by Tobian and his favorite lackeys. Two of those are covered in blood and the other two are occupied by your friends."

Only two other rooms. That meant Thibault was with Aloise. He was with her, and I was left with a man I'd just met. My heart sank.

"Goodnight, milady," Aklys sighed.

I squeezed my eyes shut and prayed to the Gods for a peaceful sleep.

Chapter Six

Adjustment Pains

The prospect of a new day offered no comfort.

Today we would leave the settlement to make for Grim's Peak. The barren mountain was not of much concern, for nothing grew or lingered there. My troubled mind could only think about the expanse beyond; The Ashen Lands. Our first choice would have been to travel by ship through the bay, but Kilian had not kept ships docked near the settlement, therefore trapping the people who dwelled there.

Aklys had insisted we leave at dawn. The bleak haze of night still lingered in the dimly lit gray sky, slowly giving way to the light of the rising sun. I exhaled a shaky breath, as I was not sure I was ready to face further hardship.

What choice did I have?

I shifted my toes in the sand, looking out across the dark waters of Serpent's Bay. The gritty particles were cold from the night, but I didn't mind. The coolness of the salty air and the ground underfoot helped to free me from the unrelenting drowsiness that weighed down my eyelids. I stifled a yawn and stretched sleepy muscles, reaching my hands far above my head.

Footsteps approached, prompting me to turn to greet whichever of my companions had come to retrieve me. To my surprise, my eyes met the deep emerald gaze of Thibault. For a moment, happiness had bubbled up at the sight of him. Then, my heart twisted, and I turned away to refocus on the horizon beyond the gloomy bay. He audibly sighed behind me, a defeated and sad sound.

"Thank you."

"For what?" I did not return my gaze to him as I spoke.

"For saving us all, for ending Tobian or... Kilian."

"No problem."

Fingers grazed my arm, silently requesting my attention. I flinched away from the touch, imagining how he may have touched Aloise during the night when he left me alone with Aklys. He'd never even come to see if I was alright, and knowing that he had chosen her weighed on me heavily.

"Celessa, I don't expect you to understand..." he started, "I know you're probably feeling betrayed."

"Probably?" I snapped.

A startled look settled on his features as I finally turned to face him.

"You profess your enduring love to me, make me think that you'd *choose* me!" Voice cracking, my stern demeanor was faltering. "You *fucked* me! Then you left with your other woman with promises to return!"

I laughed wickedly and continued, "I risked my life saving you, saving her; I saved her life with my power. Did you know that? She'd be dead right now if I hadn't unleashed and discovered that part of myself!"

"I know, and I'm so grateful..."

"Shut up! Do not speak until I finish." I pointed an angry finger at the man as I said, "I didn't mean to save her life; I hadn't thought I could, and now I don't know that I truly wanted to save her."

Thibault frowned.

"I could have died saving all of you. Yet, when I lie unconscious, teetering on the brink – scared and confused; where were you?"

He didn't answer, pressing his lips together in frustration.

"Where were you?" I shouted, pushing against his chest with both hands.

"I was with Aloise," he said flatly.

Tauntingly, I said, "You were with Aloise. You didn't care whether or not I lived because she was back in your arms. You left me with a man I had just met, not knowing his intentions or what might happen to me."

His eyes lowered to the ground, heavy with shame.

"You used me," I whispered, feeling the break in my voice all the way down into my core.

I was devastated at everything that had transpired the past few days, but somehow, in this moment, losing Thibault to another woman hurt me the most. I prayed it would pass quickly.

"I meant it when I told you I still have love for you, Celessa, and I would never lie about that."

"Let me guess, you're *in love* with her?"

"Yes."

Yes, of course he was. I was a fool to hope for anything less. Never again would I be used and left broken, full of sorrow and disdain. Never again would I leave myself at the mercy of *love*. The very word felt poisonous.

"I hope your reunion was everything you two could've wished for. Thank you, Thibault, for reminding me what happens when I trust anyone. Thank you for reinforcing what I've learned, that I'm only an object to be used. Perhaps you would get on well with Asuras."

Swiveling away from him, I grunted my dismissal. I bared my shoulders, my body taut with anger. He waited for a few moments, and my muscles tensed as I anticipated more painful confessions. As I braced myself, the only sound to leave him was yet another sad sigh.

To my relief, he left me alone without another word. I allowed tears to spill as I lingered in solitude, watching rays of sunlight break over the rise. Warmth kissed my skin as the sun set the world aglow. I basked in the rays, savoring the peaceful moments, and allowed myself to mourn the death of yet another piece of my heart.

"Milady?" A soft voice spoke from somewhere behind.

It was the vampire. His voice was melodic, gently calling to me. Reluctantly, I moved to look at him.

His features were etched with awe, beholding me as I stood in the morning light. A breeze sent the waves of my chestnut brown hair tumbling around my shoulders. The dress I wore was a deep shade of forest green, and I wished now that I had chosen something that didn't resemble the eyes of the man who had wounded my heart.

I made no attempt to wipe away the dampness on my cheeks, knowing full well that Aklys could see it. He extended his arm toward me, with silent understanding passing between us. I accepted the gesture, placing my hand on his own. He wordlessly led me away from the moments of sorrow. I decided to try to leave them behind, buried in the sand.

Several horses were burdened with the baggage that carried our provisions and soon they would bear our weight as well. I felt sympathy for the creatures, carrying so much because they were expected to; they had no choice. They were serving their purpose, being used for what they could offer. I could relate to the tame beasts, as I too kept finding myself used for the gain of others. The thought soured my mouth as I stroked the dark brown pelt of the mare I'd been drawn to.

Tilting my head slightly, I was startled by a figure lingering too close to my side, and flinched away from the intrusion.

"Was that necessary?" I grumbled.

"I'm a vampire, so you should be on your guard at all times," Aklys chuckled, "What if I decide to bite you some more, to taste that sweet blood again?"

Thibault stalked forward to where we stood.

"You bit her?" He growled, now eye to eye with the vampire.

A disgusted sound left me as I witnessed the altercation. Without giving Aklys a chance to respond, I wedged myself between the two men, shoving my wrist into Thibault's face to show him the puncture wounds indented in my skin.

"He did, right here, to get the black magic out of my body," I hissed, "not that you would've known about that, since you were too busy to check on me. Remember?"

Thibault's brow furrowed, and he stood down, backing away a step.

"As long as he didn't do it to hurt you or *feed* on you, then fine."

"You don't get a say in who does what to me. Do you really care if someone else uses me for their own selfish reasons? You did!"

Aklys cleared his throat, a strong hand clamping down on my shoulder to turn me away from the confrontation. Thibault grimaced and stalked off toward where Aloise and Maygen busied themselves, readying their own horses and obviously pretending that they couldn't hear the squabble.

I turned my hard glare toward the vampire, challenging him to say something sarcastic or inappropriate. He only looked down at me, remaining quiet. I moved around him to begin mounting my horse, which proved more difficult than I'd expected. Strong hands wrapped around my waist, hoisting me into the air.

"I can do it myself!" I hissed.

"Of course you can, milady."

His hands slid along my thigh after placing me on the mare, and my cheeks heated as a result.

"I don't need your help."

"I know, but you're going to get it anyway," he smiled as he spoke.

"Why?"

"I like you."

Fanged teeth pulled at the delicate skin of his bottom lip; exasperated, I urged my horse onward to get away from the man.

I heard a rumble of laughter behind me as the mare trotted away, irritation pricking my skin.

The road from the keep first weaved through the small homes that made up the settlement. Nervous people peeked out from doorways, some stepping out to watch us make our way along the path. People began thanking us as we passed, and the attention made me uncomfortable. My mind had been busy milling over my intrusive thoughts when an older man leapt out in front of my horse, startling me.

"Please," the man cried, "my daughter."

I looked down at him, confused and unsure of what to say.

"My daughter was in the keep, a prisoner."

My stomach dropped. I hoped she had been one of several people in the cells, still alive and lingering within the keep. Aklys had broken the locks on the iron cages, releasing the wrongfully imprisoned citizens.

"She was a young woman, like you, with red hair. Please, where is she?"

"Did your daughter have gifts of magic?" Aklys asked him.

"Yes! Yes, her mother was from one of those magical lines. We didn't even know that Neina had any until they took her."

Neina. The name rang in my head... Kilian had unleashed the girl upon me. She was an innocent girl he'd forced into corruption. The girl I'd fought and eventually murdered.

Words eluded me, and I only stared back at the desperate man with my mouth agape.

"Your daughter did not survive," Aklys spoke for me.

The poor man wailed, "How? What happened to her?"

Aklys clenched his jaw and answered, "She was corrupted by black magic beyond saving, so I killed her."

The vampire grabbed my horse's reins, pulling me along to follow after him as he left the scene of the devastated man screaming and cursing at him. Heart strings snapped in my chest, with a combination of shame and guilt pooling bitterly in my eyes. Aklys had spared me from the blame, and he'd lied to protect me from the hatred of a heartbroken stranger.

"Why did you do that?" I choked out.

"I've faced hatred most of my life for what I am. He can hate me, and it will make no difference." He glanced over and said, "It matters to you, so you don't deserve to be hated."

I swallowed loudly, struggling to control my emotions.

"I saw you panic once you absorbed all the magic from that girl, when awareness returned to her. I watched you try to pull your power away and the fight you put up to spare her. You didn't mean to take her life."

"It doesn't matter what I meant to do," I whispered. "She's dead."

The passage into the mountains hadn't been as difficult as I'd expected, but my mind remained troubled, picturing the wailing man's face again and again. I could not imagine that pain, how catastrophic it would be to experience losing a child. It was a parent's worst nightmare. I found myself wondering if my parents had died before my sisters, or if they had been forced to witness the horror of their deaths first.

"How are you feeling?" Maygen asked quietly.

I hadn't found a moment to speak with her since we'd awoken. Her face was swollen and bruised. We all suffered several injuries we would need time to recover from, save for Aklys with his rapid healing.

"I'll be okay... I'm more worried about you."

"I'm alive. We all are, thanks to you. Don't worry about me, I'm tougher than I look," she mused.

"I don't doubt you for a moment, after all you've done and endured."

A declaration tickled my tongue, itching to break free: none of them would've faced this in the first place, if not for me. I thought back to her small body hauling me to safety after fighting her way through Sanctuary; she truly was an incredible woman. She'd survived Kilian's torture, and was now walking around and even riding a damned horse. I didn't know how she fared so well, but I was simply grateful for her safety and her life.

"How are you so strong, Maygen? No mortal could accomplish and endure what you have."

She flashed me an uneasy glance.

"I have a few drops of immortal blood," she mumbled, as if she were embarrassed.

One's origins had never mattered to me as it did to some people. Many people in the Three Kingdoms were against mixing bloodlines, believing the different lines were meant to continue on without 'tainting' their lineage. Mortals, Elves, and Fae kept to their own, as marrying or procreating outside of what was considered 'appropriate' usually bore consequences for those involved.

Thibault's mother had been Fae, his father a mortal; I remembered him telling me, when we were young and I had asked why he only had his father, that his mother had faced the gallows. When her family found out she'd lain with a mortal man, they condemned the poor woman to death by hanging. It was barbaric, and I could never understand how such atrocities were tolerated. For simply loving someone outside of what is 'allowed', you risk your life. It was despicable.

"Maygen, I don't think less of anyone based on heritage. You're still my family either way, and I still care for you regardless of what blood runs in your veins."

She seemed to relax at my words.

"Well, my grandfather was Elvish."

"Elvish? That's unexpected. Elves are the strictest in not straying from their own kind, if I'm not mistaken."

"Yes, that man was an anomaly," she chuckled. "He was the one that took me to Lysenna when my family was discovered. The courts condemned my mother and father when I was three, and my mortal grandmother had passed from illness already."

Sadness flooded over me, understanding how much she had endured.

"Lysenna had known him all her life because her parents and grandparents were his friends," she continued after a moment, "My grandfather was a well-known and well-loved man. Many people kept his secret. Many of them died because of it."

"Lysenna is the one who will keep us safe?" I asked.

"Lysenna's keep is my home. She encouraged me to come after you after I'd learned about the Umbraeon family, my ancestry. She knew I was capable, and she'd known that what was left of the family line had sought you out for..." Maygen trailed off.

"For my power?" I finished for her.

Solemnly, she nodded in agreement. We remained quiet for a long time, riding along the rugged path.

"Celessa, I want you to know: I don't plan to beg you to use your power to avenge our family. I know I had mentioned it before, but I don't wish to wield you as a weapon."

Maygen's eyes were full of sincerity and affection as she looked at me and said, "You deserve to simply be safe."

Two days were spent traveling to reach the summit. I spent much of the time in silence, only thanking my companions when they lent their aid in preparing food or assembling the shelters meant to protect us from the harsh environment. Short conversations were had with Maygen as we attempted to build our friendship.

The land changed from lush and beautiful to desolate and depressed as we made the climb. I relished in the peaceful moments, knowing that the treacherous journey through the Ashen Lands would soon be upon us. Maygen made the plans for our route through Teskaria, deciding we should make the detour to Briobar for provisions once we made it safely through the hellish landscape before us; we knew our rations would not last.

Briobar had been my home once. It was the home I'd been raised in, where I made memories throughout my childhood and lived with my family before my life was snatched away.

We had finished making camp at the summit, and I sat alone a distance away, watching the sunset contentedly, as I allowed memories to take shape in my mind.

Images of my mother and father, of my sisters and our home washed over me with mixed feelings of sorrow and longing. Closing my eyes, I imagined my mother brushing my long hair, humming her favorite melody. I imagined my father in his study, dipping his quill in ink as he busied himself with addressing city matters, as was his duty as a Lord. I pictured my sisters in the courtyard, bickering playfully as they gossiped and picked tiny flowers that dotted the grass.

Kilian's words have plagued me since the fateful events inside the keep; how he'd proclaimed that I was not truly mortal, accusing me of being an Amalgam. I wanted to ignore it, but could not seem to stifle the questions arising in my mind.

I'd been fairer than my three sisters, my complexion pale and my hair a shade of chestnut brown, whereas they had been deep brunette with golden skin. Mother had said it was because the Gods blessed her with one child to favor her likeness, reassuring me that it was their will for my sisters to bear our fathers features.

Mother had always tried to be the most loving and supportive woman that she could be for us. Though, something had seemed amiss many times as I probed the memories. She gravitated towards my sisters, often favoring them, and I had seen her gaze at me many times with a look of subtle fear and suspicion. My mouth dried bitterly as I considered the possibility that perhaps I was another man's child.

Shaking my head, I tried to convince myself that it was nonsense. My father loved and cherished me deeply, with every decision he made meant to be in the best interest of my sisters and I. He'd always been kind; when I would sing for him, he would clap and praise me, calling me his songbird.

I was afraid to see Briobar again. I didn't want to look upon my home knowing my family was gone forever. A single tear escaped my control and slipped down my cheek.

I jumped, startled as a hand reached out to wipe it away. I hadn't even noticed that Aklys had approached me. I did not want kind gestures from the vampire, nor anyone for that matter.

"What troubles you, milady?" he asked, settling next to me.

His fine, sculpted features glowed in the fading sun, as beautiful golden rays kissed his skin. He looked almost ethereal, bathed in evening light; an embodiment of the sunset itself, beautiful and mysterious - a captivating yet daunting promise of the darkness to come.

"Everything troubles me, my existence is nothing but trouble," I grumbled, turning my head away.

"You can still hope for something better than this - it's only the beginning."

I suspect he was attempting to comfort me, but his words did the opposite. My skin prickled, and anger surged inside my chest.

"The beginning of a lifetime of misery." I exhaled before continuing, "I've known nothing but wrath and ruin since I was pulled from a century of equally torturous sleep. I do not hope for anything."

Aklys was quiet for a long while, and he watched me as the sun gave way to the dim emergence of the night sky, decorated only by the ever-growing face of the moon.

"Is there something you want?" I asked bitterly.

"Just to spend time in the company of a beautiful woman," he offered lightheartedly.

"Try your luck elsewhere."

"Would that make you feel better?"

His response caught me off guard. Would I prefer he turned his attention to someone else? Did I want him to leave me alone entirely? My foolish craving for attention did nothing but bring me misery. I was beyond exhausted with hurting myself by longing for the affections of others. When I didn't respond, he pressed further.

"I think I'll keep '*trying my luck*' right here," he whispered, winking when I turned to face him.

My face warmed with embarrassment.

"What do you want from me? You acknowledge my misfortune, my misery, and you respect unspoken boundaries until suddenly you *don't*. You hardly know me, we *just* met; it's been three days. From what you've seen, you should've gathered that my attentions are focused on another man. Foolishly so, considering he doesn't want me. I've been rude to you, and I ignore you, and yet here you are.

"You've watched me murder people. You know I've recently been with another man. I *stabbed* you. Am I forgetting anything?" I snapped.

"No, I think you've just about covered it." The vampire appeared amused, deepening my irritation.

Grunting in frustration, I covered my face with my hands and began focusing on my breathing.

"I find you fascinating," Aklys murmured. "Exquisite, really."

My hands fell, and I found myself glaring at him. He smiled.

"You can keep being mean to me, but it's just going to make me like you more."

"Well, I don't like you," I grumbled.

He laughed, deeply.

"I think you do like me, but you just don't want to admit it."

Aklys stood, offering a hand to help me from my place on the ground. Night had fallen thickly enough that the world danced with shadows, the only light to be seen glowing from the flickering campfire behind us. Reluctantly, I accepted his gesture.

This man was a fool if he truly sought to earn my affections. The men before him had successfully ruined me, and he'd already betrayed me. I had every reason to assume he would do it again the moment it suited him.

Thibault made a disgusted face as we approached the fire where the rest of our companions rested, pointedly staring down the vampire, who only grinned in return. Aklys was using me as a power move to spite Thibault, in an attempt to establish some sort of useless dominance over the other man.

Pathetic. I pulled away angrily, stepping over our small packs to settle beside Maygen.

"Tomorrow, we make the downward descent into the Ashen Lands," she started, "it will take us close to a week to reach the Dead Lake from the mountain's base, and another day or so after that to reach Silenus Forest."

"The closer we remain to the coast, the better chances we'll have at avoiding the monsters that dwell within the waste," Thibault commented.

"It'll add an extra day or longer if we try to make for the coast first, but the danger level is the same no matter where you step in that Gods forsaken desert. We should go straight through to shorten the amount of time it will take to cross," Aklys argued.

"Yes, I'm sure the vampire has made many journeys through the monster infested pit, considering you fit right in," Thibault jeered.

Aklys sneered, taunting him, "Actually, I have."

"I'm sure it will be much easier for you than it will be for us, as we don't have the extra strength and speed that your *affliction* offers you." It was Aloise who countered, speaking up for the first time since we'd departed the settlement.

I considered taking Aklys' side, simply to be at odds with Thibault and Aloise, but in reality, I only knew of the Ashen Lands by reputation. I had never traveled anywhere but the major cities before I was imprisoned in Sanctuary, so I was only familiar with the world by study of maps. My life had never been put in evident danger prior to Asuras, I had no training of any kind, and my survival skills were laughable at best. The only advantage I had was my power.

We were putting a lot at risk by making this journey, still recovering from injuries we'd sustained in the settlement, which took a toll on our strength and endurance.

"Aklys is the only one who isn't injured, and he is the only one with sufficient abilities to see us through this. You should probably be a bit more respectful if you expect him to consider preserving your lives should we face danger."

Thibault's jaw clenched at my words, with his attention fixated on me now.

"You would side with the vampire? He already betrayed you once."

My silence spoke volumes as I merely raised my eyebrows at the man. Aloise shrank under the heavy tension of our quiet exchange, and she began pulling him away, insisting they retire for the night.

He gave Aklys and I each a disdainful look before submitting to her will.

"Your attempt at hurting my feelings is childish," he spat.

I leapt to my feet, with Aklys close behind, his hands encircling my arms as if he meant to restrain me.

"*Hurting* your *feelings*?" I hissed, and my power vibrated subtly under my skin.

Thibault only continued staring at me, as still and solid as a statue.

"She knows you *fucked* me, right? Does she know that's what we were doing before she discovered me in your house?" I gestured angrily toward Aloise.

Her eyes widened as she looked between the two of us, and her rich golden skin deepened, reddened with embarrassment and hurt. I almost felt bad for her, for saying what I did, but he had no right to keep that from her and act like I was a terrible person for merely entertaining conversation with Aklys.

"You were sleeping with her?" Her voice was soft and barely above a whisper.

"It meant nothing and was against my better judgment," he growled.

"Obviously," I laughed.

How easily some men were able to switch up like this, how second nature it was; it was disturbing.

"Why did you even come, Thibault? Why bother to get stuck with me like this?"

"What choice did I have? The Sentinels would've taken us into custody the moment they found out we were tied to you and the murders," he retorted.

My chest felt like it'd been struck by a blade. He wasn't here for anyone other than himself, or maybe the woman at his side. Perhaps his defensiveness was merely a facade, or maybe he was trying to wound me to protect himself. One thing was clear: he was not the same man I'd once known.

"Fuck you!" I spat, pulling free from Aklys' hold to storm off into the empty darkness.

"Celessa!" Maygen called after me.

Aklys stopped her, reaching out an arm to halt her advance.

"Let her go; let her cool off," he insisted.

Maygen relented immediately, knowing full well that if I didn't get a grip I could lose control, putting everyone in danger.

I broke into a run, wanting to get as far away from the group as I could manage. I continued until the light of the fire was only a faint speck in the distance. As I attempted to assess my surroundings, I stumbled, falling to the dirt. I remained on my hands and knees, staring down at the earth beneath me, trembling.

I don't know how long I'd slept on the cold ground; I didn't even remember falling asleep during my sobbing. Looking up, I met the concerned gaze of Aklys.

"What?" I demanded.

"I'm the only one that's safe from your gift, so you should probably get used to me being the one to check on you when you're upset."

"Aren't you lucky?" I sneered. "Why even bother?"

"I care about you."

"You barely know me," I countered.

"I feel like I've known you forever. We're a lot alike, you and I."

I scoffed at the vampire, "How?"

"We're deadly, misunderstood, and incredibly attractive," he teased, "and I'm alone like you," the sincerity in his voice cooled my simmering sarcasm, "I've been alone for a long time."

Without warning, he lifted me from the ground, cradling me in his arms as if I were some damsel in distress.

"Eventually, you'll realize you don't have to be alone if you don't want to be. I hope you accept that faster than I did, because it isn't worth it to be miserable all your life."

Aklys always smelled like he'd been swimming in salt water, I noticed, but not in an unpleasant way. His scent was like the open ocean air, like the refreshing breezes that roll in over the coast, the kind that make you want to savor every breath and melt into the world around you. He smelled like bliss; like home.

We lingered for a while like that, just frozen and drinking each other in. This was something I was forbidding myself from indulging in, deeming it not worth the risk.

The vampire leaned in, delivering the gentlest brush of his lips against my own; it was not quite a kiss, but the contact made me shudder. I pulled away, turning my head in denial of his advance. I wasn't ready for anything remotely close to this, and I hadn't forgiven him.

Aklys sighed.

I let him carry me back to the encampment where three tents had been erected. One had been claimed by Thibault and Aloise, another by Maygen. Only one tent remained. My brow furrowed. I didn't know how long I'd been gone, and I didn't want to disturb Maygen as she slept. She desperately needed her rest after all she'd endured.

I hesitated.

"You can sleep in here with me," Aklys offered, "I won't touch you."

Eyeing him suspiciously, I remained still.

"Unless you decide you want me to," he grinned.

"You could've left me on the ground."

"What kind of man would I be if I'd done that?"

"A less irritating one," I grumbled as I made my way inside the tent.

Aklys settled in behind me. We faced away from each other, with our backs pressed together in the small space. His warmth was a welcome luxury, and I hadn't realized just how cold I was from being at the mercy of the elements. Sighing deeply, I allowed exhaustion to claim me, embracing the peaceful darkness and praying my nightmares would grace a reprieve from their intrusions.

I craved comfort.

Morning light filtered through the thin canopy of the tent, disturbing my once blissful sleep.

The interruption of my relaxation was not well received, and I groaned with irritation before snuggling further into the warm blanket. Sleep hadn't been peaceful recently, and my body sang with newfound refreshment. I wasn't ready to get up yet, as I was comfortably tucked into my covers. I wiggled in, pulling the warmth as close to my body as I could manage. The strong arm tightened around me, meeting my demand.

The arm?

My eyes popped open fully, as I tried to get a grip on reality before making any sudden movements. Adjusting my gaze slightly, I could see the sleeping face of Aklys just inches from my own. His entire body had wrapped around mine in the night, with our legs overlapping, and one of his arms was underneath my head while the other was wrapped tightly around my waist.

A thousand curses sounded in my mind, knowing I had unconsciously sought out his heat as we shared the cramped space, and now I was imprisoned in his embrace. I attempted to shift away from his body, careful not to wake him. The effort was futile; he was like a sleeping statue, frozen in place. I huffed with frustration and struggled further.

"If you keep wiggling like that, you're going to sense the presence of an unexpected surprise," he mumbled lazily.

The blood drained from my face. I knew full well what he was referring to, and I went entirely still, not even daring to breathe. Aklys pressed his face to my hair and inhaled deeply, breathing me in.

"I knew you liked me, milady."

"What are you talking about?" I hissed.

"You'd been asleep for all of ten minutes before you started grabbing at me." He chuckled, and his grip around me remained unfaltering.

Embarrassment burned my tongue; words eluded me entirely. This was not happening.

"Not that I mind at all... you're very warm."

He nuzzled his face further into the mess of hair tumbling around my head.

"Let me up," I demanded.

"Just a few more moments, milady. There's no shame in enjoying simple affections, considering we comforted each other all through the night," he purred happily.

"I do not feel any affection for you!"

"That's a lie, you talk in your sleep."

I could practically hear his smile, and I groaned.

"You mumbled something along the lines of..." In a heartbeat, he rolled me beneath him. "'*Handsome and ocean breezes*'," he finished.

Swallowing roughly, "W-we need to get m-moving," I stammered.

"Pity," Aklys sighed, "I could stay like this all day long."

That poisonous smile was creeping its way into my blood.

Pushing the giggling vampire away with all my might, I crawled hastily from the tent, nearly blinding myself with the beaming sunlight. As I squinted through the onslaught of brightness, my surroundings began to piece themselves together. My eyes met Thibault's, who sat at a freshly started fire, alone.

Fantastic.

He stared at me; his expression unreadable. I wondered what he was thinking as he stared at me, appearing visibly flustered, crawling from Aklys' tent. Secretly hoping he was jealous, I approached the growing flames, lazily seating myself on the ground to stretch out into a comfortable position. At last, I returned his silent gaze.

"I wanted to apologize..." Thibault started.

"Save it. What's done is done. Let's just leave it at that."

"I don't want you to keep doing whatever it is you've been up to with *him*."

I laughed, "Aklys?"

Thibault only stared at me.

"I haven't done anything with him, Thibault. As it stands, you're the only man I've been with. If nothing else, you have successfully traumatized me into never wanting to be with anyone ever again." I spat the bitterness of my words at him, the remnants stinging my mouth.

Before Thibault could speak, Aklys emerged, interrupting the uncomfortable confrontation.

"Now, that would be a shame." Aklys winked at me and continued, "Don't swear off of intimacy until you've been with someone who can show you just how worthwhile it can be. I bet you'd be incredible."

Thibault stood abruptly as if he intended to challenge the vampire. He stalked forward, bringing them face to face. Aklys was bigger than Thibault, taller by just a few inches, but broader. Even if Aklys wasn't a vampire, I suspected Thibault would be no match for him.

"Pity you'll never know," Thibault growled at his adversary.

"If ever I find myself blessed with receiving the affection of such a woman," Aklys' eyes flickered to me for a brief moment, "I'd be sure to give her everything she deserves. Nothing to be ashamed of Thibault, not every man has what it takes to satisfy a powerful woman."

I nearly choked on the air I breathed.

"Alright boys, sit!" Maygen grumbled, finally joining us and alleviating me of the burden of witnessing their nonsense alone.

Thibault stomped off, leaving Aklys smirking in the wake of his imagined victory. I rolled my eyes and began pulling out provisions to feed our caravan before we began to move into dangerous territory. The looming struggle ahead of us had me too nauseated to care for food, but I forced myself knowing I needed the nutrients.

I am not prepared for what lies ahead.

Chapter Seven

The Nature Of Monsters

Traveling down the mountain was less strenuous, with the descent much quicker than the upward journey, and we did not stop to rest until the ground leveled out beneath us. The Ashen Lands were nothing more than wastelands, but were infested with all manners of deadly monsters, like Chimeras and Shades.

I knew that Aklys and I could likely handle Shades, shadow Nymphs that had been cursed by ancient magics. They were very rarely seen, as most had been exterminated after the war, having served their purpose when they were created by corrupted Mages to be used as weapons.

Chimeras posed the real threat, venomous monsters that could breathe fire. The creatures were composed of parts of different beasts, but no one was quite sure where they'd originated from. They possessed the head of a large forest cat, the flightless wings of an overgrown bat, the tail of a scorpion, and the poisonous venom of a basilisk. Chimeras are a true horror to behold and an almost certain death sentence to those who cross their paths. The only place they were known to dwell was in the Ashen Lands, and despite the daunting conditions of the expanse, they were the real reason no one dared travel there.

If not for the Ashen Lands, the people in Tobian's settlement would have been able to escape his clutches. If not for the Wyndigas polluting Tamaa Forest and the Basilisks of Serpent's Bay, I would not have wound up on the Peninsula of Desmoterion. Every beast, all the dangerous conditions, and the isolated location made it the one place in this world I may have remained unreachable. I should be more grateful to be free of it, to be moving further away with each passing day.

Yet, I found myself wary of life, wary of the sun that rises every morning and the moon that follows the night. Danger lurked within every shadow, it lingered on every breath, and it whispered promises of despair on the wind.

I struggled to sleep as we settled for the journey ahead, terrified.

Time crawled by painfully, the sun a vicious adversary, as we made our way through the desert.

It had been four long, quiet days since we'd left the base of the mountain, stepping into treacherous territory. We had been lucky thus far, as there had been no signs of the monsters we feared would pose a threat. The squabbling had lessened between our group to maintain a calm atmosphere. We didn't want to draw any unwanted attention.

Everyone was thoroughly exhausted, having not rested until the sun had fully set and then moving again before it crept back over the horizon to light our way. Shifts were rotated through the night to stand alert and watch for danger. Restful sleep was impossible to come by, as we were nearly out of water and still had at least three days until we reached the forest, based on Maygen's estimations.

One of the horses had died the day after we left the mountain; Thibault suspected it had been suffering illness before we had departed the settlement. Another had been lost during the night, with Aloise having dozed off during her shift and claiming she didn't know how it had escaped.

I was worried we were being followed by Shades and that our horse had been claimed for a meal. We were stuck enduring pairing rotations to lessen the strain on the remaining mares. Aloise and I took turns riding with Maygen, and when we switched around, I would end up with Aklys and she with Thibault. It was frustrating being in such close proximity to the vampire on a daily basis, but I knew we had to give the animals breaks from additional weight. The deadly conditions weighed heavily on them, and we feared they wouldn't last much longer.

Night had fallen. I offered to take the first shift, not yet burdened by the desire to sleep and needing time to myself. I gazed into the night sky, imagining the paintings my parents had kept in our home of when stars sparkled amidst the vast expanse of black. The artwork had been passed down through generations of our families, as the stars had been gone for hundreds of years. I couldn't even fathom what it would be like to gaze upon a midnight sky glimmering with magic.

Footsteps interrupted my fantasies, and I turned to see Aklys approaching. He'd made a habit of disturbing me when I was attempting to be alone with my thoughts these past few days.

The vampire made it no secret that he was more than interested in my company. I fought tooth and nail against it, not giving in to his irritating attempts at charm. I hated myself for being physically attracted to him, and I thought myself to be weak. After all I'd suffered at the hands of men, I found myself yearning after one yet again. My lustful inclinations would be my demise.

"Enjoying the view?" he asked.

"Not much to see," I remarked flatly.

Aklys settled in next to me, nonchalantly placing one of his hands close to my own, teasing my fingers with his touch. I was beginning to enjoy his smile, his presence, and even his distasteful attempts at wooing me, though I would never tell him as much. He was still little more than a stranger to me, but there was something about him that was comforting.

I watched him pop a small piece of dried meat into his mouth, chewing slowly, savoring it. Confusion overtook my train of thought.

"Vampires can eat more than blood?"

My words tumbled out without much forethought.

Aklys chuckled, deep and throaty, genuine amusement.

"We *drink* blood, milady."

I cursed myself internally.

"But yes, we can eat things. However, we need blood to survive, whereas food is more for a vampire like what wine tasting is for mortals. It's fun, like a hobby, and it tastes good. Unfortunately, due to the curse, it doesn't sustain us."

He sighed, brushing against my fingertips again.

I looked back to the sky, the endless darkness, cold and empty.

"Do you know what happened to the stars?" he asked.

I nodded, "The Goddess Astera took them with her into exile."

Aklys half-smiled and continued, "Do you know why she went into exile?"

Rolling my eyes, I said, "Everyone knows the legends."

"Legends don't always equate to truth, milady."

I arched an inquisitive brow at the vampire and waited to see if he would elaborate on his statement. He inched closer, sliding a strong arm around my shoulders.

"Get comfortable, my sweet lady. I'm about to blow your mind."

For the first time since entering my second life, I couldn't stifle a giggle, and the sound startled Aklys.

A wicked grin spread across his face.

"What a lovely sound."

"Your flattery is doing nothing for me. Tell your story," I grumbled, feigning discontent.

Unexpectedly, he pulled me closer and reclined us both to the ground. We were now laying on our backs, gazing at the void above.

"I'm sure you've heard about the vampire curse?" Aklys asked.

"In the beginning, the Primordial Beings birthed existence: one inherently 'light' and the other inherently 'dark'. There must be a balance of existence. Before the beings were at odds with each other, they brought forth the Gods and Goddesses into creation, not by a union as if they were their children, but by a combination of magics. The deities were intended to create life, shape the future, and spin the wheel of Fate itself.

Fate is the beginning and end of all things – all that has passed, all that was, and all that will be. Several bloodlines descended from the Gods and Goddesses of creation. Mortal and immortal beings alike were created through unions between the deities. Together they created Mortals, Mages, Elves, Fae, Nymphs, and other fantastical creatures.

An immortal line known as Spectrals were brought forth by Odric, God of War, and Astera, Goddess of the Stars. The children were pale and fair, as if hewn from the very starlight their mother had created to bless the night skies. They possessed gifts of the mind and speed that was rivaled only by the Fae and the Elves in the mortal realm. In time, they were deceived and infected with corrupt magic by Syades, the God of Chaos, to be bloodthirsty and prone to all manner of violence. They were cursed to become Vampires.

The children were beautiful beyond measure, but lethal and dangerous, twisted by the curse. The legends tell that before Syades sired a blood line with his consort, Calaeya, Goddess of Beauty, he'd been obsessed with Astera, who had refused him. Astera's gifts were pure, but what existed within Syades were all the terrible things to be unleashed upon creation, the chaos that would sway the minds of future generations. When Astera chose his brother in destruction, Syades felt betrayed by the pair. He was madly in love with her and believed Odric's gifts to be just as disdainful as his own, making him unworthy of her. In a secret union, Odric bonded to Astera, and they fled from Syades.

The slighted God waited many years to exact his revenge, hunting them across the realm. After generations of time had passed, he managed to lure a daughter from the Spectral line to accept a gift of peace in the disguise of beautiful red fruit, which she naively accepted. When the daughter offered the fruit to her siblings, they happily feasted on glistening pomegranates, unaware of the Fate that would befall them. They fell cursed as the juices ran red as blood, revealing the poisonous magic and giving birth to a scourge upon the world.

Unable to bear witness to the atrocities her once pure children were committing against the lands, Astera retreated far into exile. She took the stars deep into the void with her and left the night sky as blackened as it had been before her magic graced the realms. Refusing to extinguish the line, Odric went mad as he tried to undo the curse on his children, but it was absolute. Through the gifts and magic of their father, the vampire line siphoned victory in war and succeeded in overthrowing the first kingdoms and those who reigned."

Aklys listened intently as I recited the lore I'd learned as a child.

"What if I told you much of what you know is a lie?"

Confused, I asked, "How would you know?"

Pondering for a moment, I cringed.

"How *old* are you?"

The vampire chuckled, keeping his tone hushed so as to not alert anyone or anything that might be nearby.

"Do you remember when we first started traveling, I said you and I are more alike than you think?"

I met his eyes, and a somber look painted his features.

"I was born *centuries* ago," Aklys confessed.

My eyes widened in surprise. Although I knew vampires were immortal beings like the Elves and the Fae, it was still truly difficult for a mortal to comprehend their life spans.

"But," he continued, "I slept... for a long time."

"How long?" I whispered.

"A very long time, milady."

I was amazed he had shared something so personal with me and wondered if his sleep had been against his will, as it had been for me.

"I know how it feels to wake up and find out that the world kept moving forward without you, to be left wondering how much you've missed. I had many mortal friends that I'll never see again, with their distant descendants hardly bearing resemblance to the people I'd once known."

Unable to stop myself, I asked, "Why were you put to sleep?"

Aklys sighed heavily.

"After my family was afflicted with the curse, the bloodlust began to drive us mad. We made the decision to be put to sleep until our Mages could figure out how to rewrite the magic enough to give us control. It took a lot longer than we thought, as a curse placed by a God is not something to be taken lightly, and it's something that can only be truly undone by the deity who cast it."

The realization that Aklys was one of the original vampires dawned on me. He'd been cursed directly. I shot upright and turned to face him.

"You were one of the first?" I asked, struggling to muffle my voice to prevent the sound from carrying.

Aklys wasn't nearly as pale as I'd imagined a Spectral to be. This meant he was a child of Gods.

"Not in the way you think."

He pondered for a moment, looking as though he didn't wish to reveal more.

"My curse was more of a mimic curse. My family is not descended from the God Odric."

"But only Odric and Astera's line was cursed by Syades?"

The vampire smiled at me, "Legends are legends, milady. I was there. Enough about the curse, I'd like to tell you about the stars."

Disappointment painted a frown on my face. I had so many questions, now deeply curious about the past. The vampire beckoned me down, so I settled next to him, quickly falling into a comfortable position.

I watched contentedly as he traced the sky with his finger, showing me where constellations used to take shape in the night sky. He described the brightest stars and told me their names. He told me about shooting stars and how you were meant to wish upon them, that Astera would answer those who were worthy of her grace.

As fascinated as I was, I had many questions about the mystery behind the curse. I wanted to know about the Gods, what secrets Aklys knew, and all he had seen. I wanted to know the truth.

For once though, I felt happy in this moment I shared with him. It was almost as if I'd seen the lost magic myself by the time he had finished talking. A sadness settled into my heart, knowing I would never experience such wonder.

I didn't remember falling asleep, but Aklys did not disturb me when I did.

I awoke to the dim break of dawn, and the gray sky meant it was time to get moving in hopes of reaching a safer place. I nuzzled into the warmth beside me, realizing in a handful of seconds that it was my vampire companion. This was becoming an entirely too common occurrence. I wished he would just ignore me until we would inevitably part ways; it would make it easier on my already fragile and damaged state.

Maygen's smiling face hovered above me, "You two look cozy."

Squinting a glare in her direction, I sat up, peeking back to check on Aklys. As per usual, he was grinning at me with sharp fangs on display.

"You're getting too comfortable," I remarked.

"You looked pretty comfortable." He shrugged.

The three of us packed up what was left of our provisions, which were dwindling quicker than they should have. We waited impatiently for Thibault and Aloise to emerge from their small shelter, but they did not rouse.

Irritation surging, I ripped open the entryway of the tent to find them slumbering peacefully, nude. Nausea bubbled up from my stomach into my throat, threatening to make my disgust known.

"You're holding us up! Let's go, or we'll leave you here!"

The pair frantically scrambled to cover their bare bodies.

"Aloise isn't feeling well!" Thibault growled after me as I retreated from the opening.

"Not my problem."

I made the decision to ride with Maygen first. Our position in the caravan was at the front to lead the way, with Aloise and Thibault lingering between, and Aklys taking up the rear. We kept a reasonable distance between each horse as we journeyed, as Maygen insisted it was safer than being in direct proximity of one another, in case someone was attacked and the rest of us had no choice but to flee. As much as I couldn't even stand the sight of Thibault and Aloise, I couldn't imagine actually leaving them to fend for themselves if they were attacked.

I had been responsible for too many deaths already, and I didn't want any more blood on my hands. That's exactly what it would be if I abandoned the couple.

"So, Aklys?" Maygen whispered.

"Not up for discussion."

Feigning disinterest, I surveyed the landscape around us for potential threats.

"He's attractive," she persisted.

"He's crude," I grumbled, prompting a giggle from my friend.

I was comfortable with Maygen, and we had quickly fallen into a very trusting and friendly relationship. The immediate bond we formed was more than a few drops of shared blood, as we were alike in attitude and demeanor, and it was one of those things that just felt right.

I had only one bond like this before in my life, with my oldest sister, Necilia. Maygen reminded me of her, and it both warmed and broke my heart. I was grateful for this woman beyond measure.

"Vampires are the most fun," her voice was a light whisper, "I know you're probably not in the best headspace because of Thibault," she paused, "or that bastard Mage, but not every man is the same."

"Aklys isn't any better. He betrayed me the same day I met him, after promising to help me."

"But he did still help you, and he's still here," she murmured.

We rode in silence for a while before she continued.

"Did you know that I saw him the night they caught me? Tobian had beaten me and shoved me in that little cage and locked it up. Aklys came to me when the room was empty, promising they'd pay for their crimes and that he would get me out. I believed him, wholeheartedly, and I told him you were in the settlement," Maygen swallowed roughly before continuing, "I begged him to save you from that kind of torture, since you had been through so much already. When you two showed up and killed that parasite, he kept his promise and freed me from that cage, he ripped it apart."

I hadn't thought much about the events of the keep nor did I want to, as it had been so traumatic for all of us. Maygen was right, that so far Aklys has kept his promises. He helped me, and he rescued her, but I couldn't bring myself to get past my feelings of resentment.

"He gathered you up in his arms when you went unconscious," she relaxed slightly as she spoke, "carried you over to where I was trapped, and pulled me out... Then he took us both out of that room and away from the carnage. He even came back to check on me after he made sure you were safe. I think he might be a good man, Celessa."

"Whose side are you on?" I teased. "I don't doubt that he's a decent man, but he showed me already that he would hurt me if it suited his agenda. Plus, I haven't known him long, that'd be rather foolish on my part."

"My parents had courted only two weeks before getting married. They spent six years together before I was born. From the stories I've been told, they were the happiest couple anyone had ever known." She shrugged half-heartedly. "Men aren't essential, but they can be useful. They aren't always terrible company to keep, especially when they look like him."

I nudged her playfully, unaware of the events unfolding behind us.

A scream tore through the air, ending our lighthearted conversation. The frantic sound had come from Aloise.

A few meters behind Thibault and Aloise lay Aklys' dead horse, mauled by a Chimera. The beast we'd feared from the moment we stepped foot out of the settlement was upon us.

Aklys was running in the opposite direction of our small caravan, in an attempt to lead the creature away. He was shouting and waving his arms at the monster. To our misfortune, Aloise's scream had caught its attention, and it began barreling in her direction. Thibault ordered his horse forward, but it could only run so fast in the loose sand underfoot. Despite my better judgment, I leapt down from my seat behind Maygen.

"Celessa, what the f-", Maygen was cut off as the horse jumped into action, startled to a run at the impact of the hard smack I delivered to its hindquarters.

I ran toward Thibault and Aloise. If I could summon my power against this thing, I could save us all. I didn't know much about my curse, but I knew it had worked on a monster once before. I prayed it would again.

To my dismay, the creature lashed out, severing the hind legs of their horse and sending the two people plummeting to the ground. The creature had focused on dismembering the helpless mare. Thibault didn't waste a second, hoisting Aloise over his shoulder and running as fast as his legs could carry him under her weight, through the tricky sliding of sand.

When my companion was about to sprint past my position, he grabbed me around the chest, tucking me under his arm as he ran from the monster. Thibault was stronger than the average man due to his mixed blood, the Fae were incredibly strong.

I fought against him, searching frantically for Aklys.

"Let go!" I screamed, "I have to help him!"

"You're not fucking dying today; I won't let you! I am not going to lose you for good!" Thibault shouted back, continuing to drag my body as he attempted to escape.

"We can't just let it kill him!"

Thibault let out a sound akin to a roar, dropping Aloise and I to the ground. He pulled the two of us into an embrace and planted a firm kiss on Aloise's forehead.

"Go!" He ordered, releasing us and starting in the direction that we had left Aklys and the Chimera.

In the near distance, Maygen's figure atop our only remaining horse grew closer as she raced toward us. I pulled a screaming Aloise in the direction of her only chance to survive. Maygen reached us, arms outstretched to offer assistance on to the horse. I forced Aloise up and turned back toward the horrific scene.

"Celessa, come on!" Maygen yelled.

"Aloise is the only one here who has no chance of defending herself, you have to protect her!" I commanded, the women's dismayed faces staring back at me.

Maygen shook her head violently, "I'm only here for you, I won't leave you!" she cried.

"I know, it's going to be okay. I'll put an end to this," I reassured her.

"Celessa, please don't let him die. I know you hate us, but please don't let him die," Aloise begged.

This was the first time the woman had spoken directly to me since we'd been in the settlement, and it was a plea for her lover. Meanwhile, her lover was the man who had spurned me in favor of her. Anger surged, but I nodded my acknowledgment of her request and set off toward the battle between a vampire, a half-Fae man, and a Chimera.

Thibault possessed one flimsy blade, which had been strapped to his side since we left the settlement. He was now flailing it wildly in an attempt to stave off the monster. They had to be careful, for a bite from the beast was fatal, with its venom as toxic as that of a Basilisk. Aklys caught sight of me, and a panicked look overtook his expression.

"No! Go ba-" the vampire was cut off by a blow from the monster, its claws slashing deep wounds into his midsection, sending him flying into the dirt.

I screamed, horrified. The foul beast turned its attention toward my outraged cry. My power surged, ripping open the skin on my arms. The Chimera charged me, salivating jaws gnashing. It was terrifying to behold.

I prayed my curse would not fail me and lashed out at the beast with the deadly crimson mist.

The tendrils wrapped around the monster, but it still continued its advance. Panic gripped me as it neared, and I tried to summon the part of my power that had ripped apart Kilian, twisting it around the beast. Still, it came for me, my resolve faltered as I succumbed to fear.

The Chimera landed on top of me, despite my magic still frantically trying to end its life, just barely holding off the rows of sharp teeth from meeting my flesh. I lashed out with my hands in a last-ditch effort to stop the assault, and an explosion erupted between myself and the creature.

White light overtook my vision, and my ears rang loudly. Faintly, I could hear someone yelling my name. The obscured shadow of a man was running toward me, shouting at me. The world around me was in pieces. My arms burned; they felt warm and slick. As my eyes refocused, I realized I was covered in blood. It seemed like some of it belonged to me but there was some that was a darker hue, not human.

Clumps of the creature lay around me like it had been blown apart.

I couldn't move, and I could barely breathe. The blurry man grew closer.

And the one who reached for me was Thibault.

"Celessa, oh Gods, no. No, no, no. I'm so sorry. I'm so sorry for everything, please, please! You'll be okay!" He was crying.

I must look as bad as I feel. I tried to speak to him, but only choked on the blood pooling in my mouth.

Reality was trying to fade to black.

The jostling of being pulled from the sand and into Thibault's arms barely helped me cling to shreds of consciousness, his face hovering above mine as he lifted.

"It's going to be okay, Celessa. There were more Chimera, but the one that you killed was massive compared to the other two. Aklys took care of them. You're safe, everyone is safe now, so please just hold on."

Everyone was safe. Nothing else mattered. I didn't have to fight anymore.

I groaned in pain, my body going rigid before spasming violently.

"Something's wrong, help!" Thibault screamed.

"Give her to me!" A panicked voice demanded. Aklys?

"Fuck off, if we had gone to the coast like I suggested, then this never would've happened!" Thibault growled at him.

"I can save her life if you give her to me, you selfish prick!" Aklys shouted, "She might have venom in her system!"

"How are you going to do that?" Thibault scoffed, squeezing me tighter and moving me away from the vampire's outstretched arms.

"I'll give her my blood."

"You stay away from her, you fucking freak of nature!"

"My blood will heal her, Thibault! If you don't let me, she will die! Look at her!" Aklys screamed.

Let me die, I thought, fading slowly.

"You just want her bonded to you or something messed up, that's all. She's going to be okay; she'll hold on until we reach Briobar and can find a healer," Thibault insisted.

"You're fucking delusional!"

Thibault stumbled and fell to the ground, taking me with him. The force of the impact knocked what little breath I had left from my lungs. Aklys had punched him in the face. He hit him again before wrenching me free of his hold. I could faintly see his bloodied face before I was whisked away. Thibault wouldn't be able to pursue us since vampires were faster on foot than any Fae.

"Aklys," I whined, and it took every ounce of strength in my body to speak his name.

"I'm going to make it better; I've got you."

The vampire stopped suddenly, gently lowering us both to the ground. The pain was giving way to a numb euphoria. I was slipping away.

I was going to die.

A tangy, metallic taste filled my mouth. It didn't taste like the blood that coated my tongue, instead it was bitter like over-steeped black tea; every instinct told me to spit it out.

"I know, but you have to swallow it. I'm sorry, you *have* to."

Aklys pushed his bleeding wrist into my mouth with more force, drowning me in the sour liquid. I struggled against him as it burned my throat, wishing he would just let me go. When he finally pulled away, I gasped and spat at him.

"Let me die," I croaked.

"That's fucking selfish. You are not dying: not today, not next week, not fifty years from now. You'll live a full life, I'm going to make sure of it," he growled.

"You may not value your life, but the people around you do. Fight for them. Fight for Maygen. As much as I don't like the prick, even Thibault cares for you, so fight for him, too. Fight for me," Aklys whispered, squeezing me in his embrace.

"He doesn't care," I groaned. "You don't care."

The vampire scoffed at me, "If you really think that then you obviously haven't been paying attention."

The pain singing through my body ebbed away, slowly being replaced by a kind of hunger that made my skin burn and my muscles throb. The hunger was transforming into something else, something uncontrollable.

Arousal washed over me like a black tidal wave, all consuming, swallowing me whole. I could think of nothing other than how badly my body ached with it. Aklys set me down and backed away a few steps with his hands up.

"Don't be angry with me; it was the only way to heal you."

He swallowed, and I watched intently as his throat bobbed.

"Vampire blood has healing properties, but if you wouldn't have been on death's door, I wouldn't have given it to you. It is also a very, very potent aphrodisiac," he laughed nervously.

The ache between my legs made me groan in frustration, so I shoved my hand beneath the waistband of my pants to relieve the tension. Aklys' eyes bulged as he realized what I was doing, his face lighting up a bright shade of red as I touched myself. He turned his head, flustered by my unexpected indecency.

I found a quick release, but the ache returned with even more ferocity.

"What did you do to me?" I groaned.

"I can fix this!" He swore.

"Then fix it!" I yelled. "It's unbearable!"

Aklys hesitated, and my mind began to whirl. If he was going to fix it how I thought, I changed my mind.

"How?" I ground out through clenched teeth.

"I draw my essence out of your blood."

He smiled sheepishly before clarifying, "I'm going to have to bite you."

I charged at him, ripping my shirt away from my neck.

"Do it, do it now, make it stop!" I screamed.

Without hesitation, he sunk his fangs into me, curling my body into his iron embrace and began drawing the blood into himself. My legs gave out, the sudden loss making me feel faint.

Aklys lowered us to the ground, wrapping my legs around him and holding tightly as he drank from me. My pelvis bucked in his lap, grinding against his thigh. Release came again as I clutched the man, moaning into his neck.

Aklys was rigid against me, growling as he drank. With each pull he took from the wound, the pulsating in my body lessened, and I relaxed into him, relishing in the relief.

He pulled his head away, my blood painting his full lips. The sight of him looking so bloodthirsty with darkened eyes, having given in to his affliction, stirred something within me.

I was intrigued.

"Are you going to let me up?" I asked after a few moments, feigning irritation.

Reluctantly, the vampire released me. I stood, looking around. I didn't see anyone nearby.

"How far did you take me from them?"

Embarrassment was gnawing at me, and I hoped no one had been close enough to hear me or to realize what had happened.

"As far as I had to," he grumbled.

"Take me back; I need to make sure they're okay. I don't really know what happened."

"They're all fine because of you," the vampire muttered, "and me."

"What did I do?"

One moment I was sure I was going to die, and then the next I felt like I *was* dying, but the Chimera was in pieces.

"You concentrated your power, and then set it off in an explosion. I've been around a long time, and I've never seen anything quite like that before. I don't really know how you survived that. The only conclusion I could draw was that your gift doesn't try to harm you directly. The Chimera wounded you badly."

At a loss for words, I only nodded, walking away from Aklys.

Time and time again I hung in the balance, teetering between life and death. Fate taunted me, making me work for my life like I wasn't meant to be here. Maybe I wasn't? Maybe this thing inside me shouldn't exist? The power I possessed was unnatural, like nothing that had ever existed within another being in the mortal realm.

I was a joke, a sick and twisted joke.

Nymphs possess healing magic based within the elements of their creation. Fae with magical gifts were few and far between, usually with nothing more than simple magic over the mind. Elves with magical gifts were more common, but lacked potency, for simple illusions could be conjured. Mages could master any number of magics, but nothing that was ever-changing such as this, nothing that could simply erase life and absorb essence. There was nothing that even came close to the monstrosity I was becoming.

The closest thing to whatever this curse was black magic. Only those too stupid or without a choice succumb to such a force, as it inevitably becomes a death sentence, consuming you entirely.

I shouldn't exist.

Lowering myself to the ground, I placed my hands in the sand, feeling the coarseness of the grains. I pushed my power out gently so that it began to crawl into the earth. The blood red tendrils wrapped around my fingers, swirling and caressing my skin. Its presence felt like what I imagined it would be like to touch a cloud, a soft whisper, or only the promise of a touch.

I hated it.

Pushing, I drove the essence out, trying to send it away from my body. I wanted it to go somewhere else, somewhere far away from me, I didn't want this life. Possessing this power meant I would be looking over my shoulder for as long as I lived; I would never stop running. For the rest of my days, I would be afraid, I would take lives, and I would live in constant fear of losing control. I could never look forward to the future, or find a true home to create a life for myself. I could never have children for fear of them suffering from my affliction. My existence was hell because of this curse.

Grunting, with tears streaming down my face, I pushed harder. The crimson fog leapt and writhed against the ground, responding to the force I was driving into it. The ever-breaking skin on my arms opened once again, allowing the essence to come forth more aggressively. I prayed for it to leave my body, and I didn't care if it took my life with it. I didn't want to fight forever.

Aklys approached, and the deadly mist danced around him, parting as he walked toward me. It never touched him, but rather it allowed him to come to me, to touch me. The vampire placed his strong hands on my cheeks, bringing my face up to meet his gaze. My power began retracting. I noticed the pain and the feelings of sickness lessened each time I used it. My body seemed to grow used to the exposure, like I was building a tolerance to it.

He held my face, wiping away my tears with his thumbs, silently communicating his understanding as I looked into his glowing hazel eyes.

"I can't do this," I sobbed. "It isn't fair!"

Aklys nodded, "You're right, it's not."

"I don't want to live like this."

"I know, but you can."

I shook my head angrily, "I can't."

Steadying me with his grip, our gazes met again, and a fire burned within that enchanting gaze. Passion, understanding, and something *else* simmered inside of the vampire.

His very presence calmed me.

"You will do this because you are selfless. This power is a curse until it's not. Someday you will use it to change the world we live in. I know it doesn't seem like it now," he pressed his forehead to mine as he spoke. "You are allowed to feel like this; you are allowed to be angry. You are allowed to be sad, you're allowed to mourn, and you're allowed to be afraid."

I stilled entirely as I listened to him.

"You are allowed to be broken," he whispered, "but that does not mean that what you rebuild won't be strong."

It was nearly dark by the time we returned to Maygen, Thibault, and Aloise. They'd made camp and had been sitting near a small fire, waiting. Each of them had a different reaction upon our return. Maygen sobbed, throwing her arms around me and thanking the Gods for my safety before turning to Aklys to force the same embrace upon the vampire. She thanked him for saving me, but then smacked him playfully on the arm for running off to do it, for leaving her in wait.

He'd only smiled at her, offering a simple apology for the additional distress.

Thibault's face was red, two washed away streaks visible upon his dirty cheeks, where tears had removed the sand and dust that clung to sweaty skin. He cautiously embraced me and to my own surprise, I allowed it.

Aloise even looked *relieved* to see me in one piece, giving me what almost looked like a smile as I met her gaze.

I decided on the walk back to find them that I would take Aklys' words to heart. I was broken, but I would be strong, and I wanted to heal. To find healing, I knew I would have to confront what hurts and burdens me most.

Mourning my family was a big step I needed to take. I placed it in my mind that I would force myself to visit the estate when we reached Briobar. Another thing on my list was finding closure with Thibault, true closure, and finding common ground with Aloise. I needed to accept that he'd made his choice and that it wasn't her fault he had made certain decisions regarding us both. I was holding her accountable for something that was out of her control. She was as much a victim of his indiscretions as I.

My final resolution, my biggest one, was that someday I would find Asuras.

I would find him, and I would kill him.

The small group had come to an agreement that I would not take a shift tonight, that I had endured too much. Despite my objections, I let them coddle me even though I'd been healed by Aklys, an embarrassment I would not soon be revisiting. No one would hear my complaints.

Maygen estimated that the altercation with the Chimera didn't make much of a delay in our progress, due to the frantic escape that propelled us forward; though it was hard to tell because the landscape looked nearly the same in every direction. We were guided only by the sun and the moon, with no landmarks to be seen until we reached the Dead Lake. The deadly water was the only indication that we were near the forest; once we found it, our trek through the wasteland would be near its end. Only one full day lies between the lake's edge and the forest.

I settled into the makeshift tent, listening to my own breathing, attempting to block out the conversations taking place outside the tent. Aklys had expressed his concern to Maygen about how little concern I had for my own life, prompting outrage from her. The last thing I needed right now.

I pulled the cover up over my head, shielding myself from the world.

At some point during the night Aklys or Maygen had crawled into the shelter to sleep next to me, but I didn't know which one because I felt no desire to look or engage in conversation. I rolled as far away from the body as possible, pressing myself up against the side of the tent.

I spent a long time ignoring the presence until bony fingers touched my shoulder and a coldness settled over me. This wasn't the warm touch of my companions. Sitting up, my vision took in a shadowy figure in the dim light, limited only to visuals from the flickering fire outside. Its face was contorted and unsettling. Long black hair hung limply around a bone thin frame. Hollow eyes stared back at me.

"H-how did you g-get in here?" I stammered.

"What are you?" It whispered.

This was a Shade.

It stared at me, but made no move to attack. Confusion rippled through my thoughts. What I knew of Shades had led me to believe that they had no 'humanity' left within them, that they were twisted monsters who were dangerous to those that crossed paths with them. Yet, here it sat, watching me, *talking* to me.

"What are you?" the creature repeated.

The voice was neither feminine nor masculine, nothing to indicate what or who it may have been before it was cursed.

"I'm a mortal," I whispered back.

"No. You don't smell like a mortal."

I swallowed hard, nervousness trembling my fingers and locking my joints in place.

"You are not Fae or Elven..." It crept closer, sniffing me, "nor a demon. Yet, you are not mortal."

"I am."

"There is something else. I must know what you are, let me see."

The creature outstretched long, clawed fingers toward me.

"What are you doing?" I exclaimed, backing further into the thin fabric I had been pressed against.

"I must see!" It insisted, touching my head.

The contact was sharp and frozen, its fingers reminding me of the icicles my sisters and I would break away from tree branches in the coldest months of the year as children. A searing pain shot through my skull as the creature hissed at me, ripping its hand away. I yelped in pain, likely alerting whoever was on watch, whoever had been careless enough to allow a Shade into my tent.

"I am right," it whispered.

"What am I?" I asked, burning pain still simmered in my skull from whatever it had done.

It inhaled deeply before responding.

"Divine. You are not what you seem."

The hanging flap concealing the inside of the tent was ripped open, with the blade of a sword pointed at the intruder. Thibault's lips peeled back in a snarl.

"Wait!" I shouted as he lunged toward it.

As silent as a shadow, the Shade evaporated into a dark cloud, slipping away under the bottom of the shelter and into the night. That explains how it got in here, and what I thought I knew about Shades was obviously wrong.

Apparently, everything I knew about anything was wrong.

"Did it hurt you?" Thibault asked.

"No."

I grimaced at the dulling ache in my head.

"Well, yes, but I don't think it meant to."

An exasperated huff left the man, "You don't think a *Shade* meant to hurt you?"

I shrugged, rousing myself and pushing past him to leave the tent. Meeting the open air, I looked around, hoping to catch sight of the creature. I had so many questions, but there was nothing. It was gone.

"You scared it away," I growled.

"Excuse me for trying to save you from another monster."

Thibault flopped carelessly next to the fire.

I stood for a long moment, debating on what I wanted to say to the man, or if I even wanted to say anything at all. Aklys' words repeated in my head. I knew I was broken, but I also knew that I was the only one who could try to fix it, even if I hadn't been the one to inflict the damage. Only I could heal myself, and I didn't want to be miserable forever.

Looking around, it was apparent that both Maygen and Aloise were inside of tents sleeping, while Aklys was asleep on the ground a short distance from the fire, with a thin jacket draped over him.

"We should talk," I mumbled, sitting down next to Thibault.

He eyed me suspiciously, surely expecting another one of my verbal assaults, not that he didn't deserve it.

"Maybe if you would explain it to me, I could understand," I started.

"What would you like me to explain, Celessa?"

"Why did you do it? Why did you try to convince me you still wanted me? Why did you insinuate that someone who obviously means everything to you, meant nothing?" I paused. "Why would you take me to bed if your heart belongs to another?"

Thibault sat quietly for a moment.

"Because I'm selfish," he said finally, "I'd spent multiple lifetimes missing you, dreaming of you, longing for you. We'd had potential to be something good, to have a life together, and I held onto that for a long time.

"Then I met Aloise. She was persistent in her affections for me. There had been different women over the years, but I never let them in, not really. I used them.

"Something was different with her. She saw me, and I mean really *saw* me. She was so understanding and accepting when I told her that I was in love with a damned memory."

Thibault sighed, "Aloise helped me move past it, and she showed me that I could be loved, that I could have something good. I don't know when it happened, but she found her way into my heart, and I've been happy with her."

Pausing, he peered nervously to observe my expression.

I struggled to appear indifferent.

He continued, "Then, I saw you in the settlement, and every instinct in my body screamed to protect you, the woman I had loved for so long. When I finally had you in my grasp, when I saw it in your eyes that you still loved me, that you still wanted me..."

He swallowed back his emotion.

"I made a selfish decision because I wanted to claim what I hadn't been able to before. Then, when it came down to you and Aloise, I couldn't take myself away from her. I knew it was her, that she's the one I need. I hate myself for hurting you, for taking advantage of you, and I wouldn't have been able to choose between you both if the circumstances had been different. She almost died, and you could have died."

"But you *did* choose her," I whispered.

Thibault nodded solemnly.

"I forgive you."

The man turned toward me fully, startled.

"What?"

"I forgive you. I've decided to move forward, and do things to fix the broken pieces. You were honest, and with it you gave me closure. This is a different lifetime, and now we're different people. I can't become someone new if I cling to who I was because I'm already beginning to fear she's long gone. It's time to move on."

I shrugged, even though the words hurt.

I could say whatever I wanted, but I knew deep down it would take a long time to rewrite the damage that had been done. To truly forgive those who have wronged me was monumental.

This was only the first step.

"I want you and Aloise to know that I don't blame her. The only reason I don't care for her is because of you, but I'm going to try to change that."

He sighed in understanding.

"I'm sorry," he said.

I felt the sincerity in his words, and I responded, "I know."

We sat quietly for the rest of the night, allowing our conversation to sit in the space between us, giving it time to sink in.

Reaching the Dead Lake should've been a celebration, but at this leg of our journey, the toxic water was merely a torturous obstacle in our way. Our provisions had run out entirely, with no water left, leaving us dehydrated and miserable.

Only one horse remained, and its strength was fading. We did not ride it, it only carried what few supplies we had left as we crept toward the blackened waters. Being forced to travel on foot only exacerbated the unfavorable conditions.

"How do you know it's poisonous?" Aloise croaked, hardly able to speak past the hoarseness in her throat.

It was the same miserable dryness that plagued us all.

"It will kill you," Aklys shot back.

Thibault confirmed the statement and tried to keep Aloise's attention away from the taunting, rippling surface. If one had been stranded here, unaware of the legends surrounding the waters, they would surely meet their demise in an attempt to sate their thirst. It beckons you with promises of refreshment and forces you to imagine the cool liquid pouring down your parched throat.

"We can reach the forest by nightfall if we keep moving," Maygen promised Aloise, "where the water in the streams off the river are safe to drink; they're fresh and cool."

"Do not drink from the river itself," Aklys commanded.

"Why?" I questioned.

The vampire smiled at me.

"The Erotas River is known for powerful enchantment, a magic meant for lovers. It plays on desire, exposing you to powerful lust.

If it finds hidden desires, it makes them known to you and those around you."

He winked at me before continuing, "I'm not sure any of us should risk it. The streams that branch off from the river are filtered out and safe. It won't be much longer now."

We'd been distracted by Aklys' information of what lies ahead and had not noticed that Aloise was making a mad dash for the deadly lake.

"Wait!" I screamed after her, snapping the men's attention toward the fleeing woman.

Thibault pursued her, but Aklys caught her first, his vampiric speed giving him the advantage. The woman thrashed and screamed, clawing at his arms, battering him with her fists. She'd gone mad with thirst, ensnared by the lake's magic.

"Just give her to me, I'll take her!" Thibault yelled at the vampire.

"She's not going to stop now."

Aklys growled, striking the woman in the head, rendering her unconscious. The act made my jaw drop, as it was brutal and heartless, and it left her hanging limply from his arms.

Thibault wailed, charging the vampire. A maddening force had begun to take hold of the man; the closer he got to the water, the worse it became. As he approached them, he began to sprint for the lake instead, forcing Aklys to drop the unconscious Aloise to the sand.

The vampire tackled the man, pressing him firmly to the ground. Thibault howled and fought against the restraint.

I watched Aklys subdue Thibault in the same manner he'd done with Aloise, before he scooped up the two bodies and began approaching us.

"It's either this or let them drink the water and die."

"What the hell happened? They were just fine!"

"Mortals are especially susceptible to dark magic, so the closer they get, the deeper it sinks its claws in. Aloise is mortal, and Thibault is part mortal," The vampire informed me, while thrusting the bodies up over the back of the horse, face down with limbs dangling.

I cast a nervous glance at Maygen, who also had mortal blood.

She smiled reassuringly before saying, "I'll keep my distance."

It wasn't bothering me because apparently, I am not a mortal, my mind whispered.

Kilian had claimed I was a forbidden creature, and the Shade, too, claimed I was not mortal, so perhaps it was the truth... but if I am not human, then what am I?

Chapter Eight

Hidden Desires

Reaching Silenus Forest was a due blessing upon us, as the Ashen Lands had nearly claimed our lives more times than I cared to admit. Between the dehydration, borderline starvation, and the run-in with the pack of Chimeras, we were lucky to be alive.

Aklys had managed to catch small fish in the river runoff, which made for a quick dinner to replenish some of what we had lost during our journey. Before resting, I had traded my bloody and torn clothing for the only other garment I had: the green dress I'd worn in the settlement.

I had been staring into the fire for a long while, studying the differently colored hues throughout the flames. I was comparing them to my gift, its evolving raw power, how unpredictable and dangerous it was... and red.

Closing my eyes, I listened to the sounds around me. I heard the rise and fall of exhausted chests, taking in deep breaths as they slept. They were my companions through the misery.

We hadn't had the energy to erect tents, so Maygen was curled up underneath Thibault's coat that he had graciously offered her. The Fae man slumbered next to her with Aloise cradled in his embrace. They fit together like two misshapen puzzle pieces, ones that present the illusion that they wouldn't fit until you place them together. Then, you realize this is where they're meant to be.

A sadness washed over me as cool as fresh spring water. I loved Thibault, and his decision to be with Aloise deeply wounded me, but

I forgave him. I forgave him for taking advantage of our situation when he found me in the settlement; I'd wanted that passion and comfort even more than he had. I truly believed that we had needed that moment and that it served as a kind of closure for us.

I forgave him for moving on from me, as I'd been gone for such a long time; for so many years, he had waited for a love he could never claim. I forgave him for loving another because seeing them loving each other was starting to feel okay.

Aloise was beautiful, and she was good. I was grateful my curse had done something decent in saving her life.

On the other side of the fire, Aklys was the most silent of the group. His breaths were nearly unnoticeable. His body completely still like he had become a statue in his unconscious state, so as to not alert anything nearby to his presence.

My gaze lingered on him for a few moments. The ruse of my disdain for the vampire continuously faltered. I clung to his betrayal in the keep, when he sat idly by as Kilian assaulted me. I understood his motives, but I could not bring myself to let it go.

Despite him rescuing me several times since, despite the fatal attraction fighting to take root between us, he had already shown me that I couldn't trust him entirely. Trust was something crucial to me, something that had continuously eluded me throughout this life. I couldn't allow myself to want someone that couldn't give me that security.

I wouldn't let it happen after Thibault had wounded me, nor would I let it happen after Asuras destroyed me.

Perhaps if he'd told me beforehand what would have to happen if I was caught, if he'd given me a strategy or a plan to fall back on, I might not feel this way. Maybe I would've endured that painful experience with more resilience. Had I known, I wouldn't have felt the despair I had in those moments where he watched me be carried away by those brutes; I would've known he was coming to save me.

What happened, happened. There was no changing it now. It was a stain that I would see every time I examined the tapestry we weaved as our paths entwined.

His lips parted slightly as he fell further into sleep; tips of fangs glinted in the warm glow of firelight. He was deadly, born of a curse, just like I was. We were alike.

The urge to move my body toward his, to curl up next to him, gnawed and gnashed at me like a monster's jaws. I didn't move, though. He would surely part ways with us as soon as we reached the cities, and I would not have to struggle with these desperate, intrusive thoughts anymore.

A rustling sound sent my body whirling, immediately descending into a low crouch. A hiss emanated from the bushes. A little hiss, sounding pathetic and nervous.

My eyes squinted, trying to make out shapes amongst the shadows. Two tiny eyes caught the reflection of the flames behind me, shining in the darkness. A small cat hid in the branches of a bush, just a kitten. I relaxed my body and rubbed my fingers together in an attempt to beckon it forward, only to be met with another weak hiss.

"Come on out," I whispered. "It's safe, and I won't hurt you."

Many moments of silence passed as I waited for the tiny beast to reveal itself. Sighing heavily, I lowered myself to lay on my side in the grass. My eyes began to flutter, for sleep was calling to me even as I fought against it, but I was not ready to be alone in the darkness.

Muffled rumbling sounds crept up to where I rested, and my head snapped up to see the kitten happily munching leftover fish we'd caught from the stream, purring. The smile that burst onto my face felt like it might split my skin.

What an unusual sensation it was, experiencing a small joy such as this, as I existed in mostly agony and despair.

I extended a larger piece toward the furry little beast. Warily, it stalked closer, snatching the food from my outstretched hand. I wondered if the starving creature had ever experienced kindness at the hands of anyone or anything in this cruel world.

The state of its body was not convincing that it'd been well taken care of. Tiny ribs were visible beneath the dusty gray fur, and its tiny tail had a kink at the end; it must've broken at some point. It was so small, no more than a few months old and had already endured such pain. Without a second thought, I gathered up what was left of the fish and offered it to the cat.

"You are kind," a far-off voice whispered.

Startled, I leapt to a standing, defensive position. The tiny creature at my feet seemed none the wiser to my sudden alertness and continued purring as it feasted.

"Who is there?" I demanded quietly, trying not to wake anyone.

I could handle any threats on my own. I could protect them as they got their much-needed rest. My mind wondered if it might be the Shade, but this seemed different somehow.

"You are kind after all you have suffered. You are kind despite the predisposition of your blood," It sighed.

The voice sounded vaguely familiar, almost comforting, as if I'd known it before. I felt compelled to seek it out, and my feet began moving toward it before my brain could will sense into me to stop.

Ducking low hanging branches, my bare feet were tickled by long grasses as I sought out the source of the mysterious words. The forest seemed to have its own glow, illuminating the plant life subtly, almost mimicking the moonlight above.

The moon was nearly full now, granting me enough light to navigate through the trees. I trekked closely by the Erotas River so I'd be able to find my way back to the small encampment where I'd left my companions. The water swirled to the tune of its own melody, soft yet strong, with the sparkling current whirling and twisting shades of deep blues.

Fireflies dotted the shadowed depths of vegetation, the closest things to what I imagined stars would look like if they still decorated the night sky. I felt entranced, like I was in a dream. The ethereal nature that surrounded me sang songs of night as nocturnal animals flitted about, calling out into the darkness.

A different sound snagged my attention away from the beauty unfolding before me. Did my ears deceive me or was someone humming a tune? The notes were silky and magical, a woman's voice swirled around my being, filling me with a gentle melody. My body swayed slightly, and my skin tingled, kissed by magic.

I slowly sank down to the earth, sprawling my body in the grass, letting the soft forest floor caress my skin — succumbing to the mysterious lullaby.

"Celessa," the voice whispered.

I did not wish to move from nature's embrace, so I only listened.

"Find Isonei, Celessa, she will bring you home," It sang.

Isonei? I knew that name.

I had touched her once, and she was magical.

Intoxicated by the forces of the forest, I found myself dipping my hands into the river. The cold water lapped at my skin, almost teasing me, begging me to dive in. My head spun as I drank from cupped hands; the liquid was almost sweet, soothing my throat and melting inside my body.

Giggling to myself, I stripped away my clothes, discarding them into the grasses beneath my feet. I dipped into the icy current, and it swirled around my body, holding me in its dancing waves. A low moan left my lips as I slipped beneath the water.

Moonlight filtered through the rippling surface, and it played upon my pale skin as I floated weightlessly in the magical depths, my hair gliding about my body. I moved as fluidly as a shadow, hidden inside an enchanted world all my own.

"Celessa?" I heard someone above the water. It was different this time, not the whisper that had lured me here.

I broke the surface, filling my lungs with warm, pine scented air. Truly inebriated now by whatever forces were at work around me, I searched for whoever had spoken my name.

A male figure stood on the river bank with a hand outstretched to guide me from the water. My skin was humming, and I watched him curiously. His skin seemed to hold the moonlight; his features obscured by brightness. He was a mystery.

My instincts willed me to go to him, so I waded back toward the shallows of the river. Playful laughter erupted from me as I slipped my hand into his own, allowing him to pull me from the magic.

He glowed peculiarly, a blur. I lifted my hand to his mouth, running a finger along his lips, and the velvety texture was pleasing to the touch. The blood beneath my skin was racing through my veins, warming me despite my body being naked and damp.

Pressing into the man, I moved toward his lips, desperate to capture the smoothness with a kiss. To my disappointment, he pulled away.

"Did you drink from this river?" he asked.

"Yes, of course, it tastes like sugar."

I giggled, advancing again.

His hands grasped my arms gently, restraining me from capturing the kiss I so desperately desired from the beautiful stranger.

"You're intoxicated! This is the lover's river. It's imbued with magics of desire," the voice scolded.

"You appeared before me, so that must mean you are my desire," I purred seductively.

The body before me went rigid, as if my words had struck a chord deep within. The hold on my arms loosened, and I pressed forward again. My bare body brushed against the fabric of his clothes, and the sensation of the friction was euphoric. I wrapped my outstretched arms around his neck, pulling him in.

"Lay with me," I whispered, forcing him toward the ground.

"Wait," he argued, reluctantly landing on top of me in a bed of grass.

"Kiss me!" I begged, guiding his face toward my own with my hands.

He didn't budge, gazing down at me, this being of starlight. I weaved my fingers into glowing locks of hair, tugging him closer. He sighed a small sound of defeat.

Smiling at my victory, I finally claimed him with my lips. The pleasurable sensation exploding throughout my body was almost too much to bear, and I parted his mouth with my tongue, searching and silently begging for more. At long last, he returned my desire, groaning and pressing heavily into my body.

We exchanged passionate kisses and caresses before a new powerful urge began to take hold. I wanted this strange man made of magic.

Tugging at his shirt, the fabric was forced over his head. He sighed again. Why was he not returning my affection? My bare breasts were pressed against his warm skin as I successfully undressed him. He was still hovering above me, so I lifted my leg and hooked his waistband with my foot, forcing down his breeches.

"You need to stop. This isn't right, and you don't know what you're doing. It's the magic."

His words sounded forced and almost pained. He was still trying to stop me, but it was obvious he wanted this. I wanted this.

Our naked bodies were entwined, sensitive parts pressing together, creating a maddening friction. I raised my hips against him so that he could feel the heat, feel the slickness of my body. He gasped and followed the sharp breath with a groan. The sounds sent shockwaves to my nerve endings. I ground against him again, every muscle in my pelvis tense and throbbing.

"Enough!" He breathed, forcing me flat against the ground with a strong hand.

"If we're going to do this, you need to be of sound mind."

"Don't you want me?" I questioned breathlessly, still lost in the throes of passion. The intoxication made my head spin, unable to make sense of the face above.

The man rumbled a low growl.

"I want you so badly it *hurts*," he confessed.

I caught him in another heated kiss, trapping him in my embrace.

"Then take me," I whispered.

He shuddered, firmly pressed between my thighs, alerting me to the truth in his statement.

Annoyingly, he pulled free once again.

"It's not the right time. I don't want you to regret this," he resolved.

I whimpered pitifully, realizing he would not satisfy the maddening desire that had my body writhing uncontrollably beneath him.

"Please."

I begged but he shook his head, and the glow that concealed him began to ripple and break apart. The forest that spun around us slowed, returning to its former stillness, trees calming from the dancing they had done in my mind.

"Not yet, milady."

I pulled my mysterious, would-be lover into yet another kiss, desperately tangling my tongue with his own.

Milady?

Awareness was returning, and the horror of my actions began to settle down upon my consciousness, making my blood run cold.

Oh, Gods. What have I done?

The man lifted away from my embrace, and as I looked into his eyes, his features began to make sense. I was staring at Aklys. My jaw dropped open, and I froze entirely, with every moment we had just shared flashing in my suddenly sober mind. I screamed internally, now fully conscious.

"I-I, um, Aklys, I..." I stuttered, unable to form a coherent sentence.

I released him from my hold, pulling my hands away to fist them in the grass. My face burned with embarrassment.

He remained where he had been hovering above me, elbows resting on either side of my shoulders, his lower body still pressed against mine. I throbbed from the unanswered summons of my body, with my sex still slick from arousal.

"I-I'm so s-sorry," I trembled.

"I thought I'd told you not to drink from this river?"

"There was a voice," I explained, "and I followed it here, I don't know what happened."

He watched me for a long moment, scanning my features, stroking my damp hair with his fingers.

"How do you feel now?" he whispered.

I felt embarrassed and confused. Sound of mind, and wishing I hadn't wandered off, I cannot believe I had foolishly succumbed to the magic. I felt warm from the heat of his body, still savoring the contact between us.

"This wasn't my intention," I confessed.

Aklys smiled at me.

"The magic in this river is meant to reveal and play upon desire. It's the magic between the lovers Silenus and Druantia, the nymphs for which the neighboring forests are named," he ran a thumb along my cheek as he spoke, "They would meet along the river that joined their homes, and they would make love in the water."

My cheeks grew ever warmer, a bright display of my shame.

"I knew you liked me," Aklys teased.

Confusion wrapped around my thoughts as I said, "Then why didn't you... you know..."

Unexpectedly, Aklys dropped a tiny, tender kiss to my forehead.

"The magic was influencing you. If you decide you want my affection, then I'll be here. I wasn't going to take advantage of what you aren't truly ready to explore, especially after all you've been through."

He lingered still, his bare body draped over my own like a warm blanket.

We breathed in unison for a long time without speaking, exchanging longing looks, with neither of us daring to move for fear of interrupting these forbidden moments.

"Before we go back to reality, where I resume my indifference..." I trailed off.

"Yes?" He pressed.

"Would you just indulge me a bit more?" I whispered.

Aklys' eyes widened in surprise, brows furrowing as he tried to uncover the meaning behind my words.

"I don't want them to know about this," my words referred to the companions we'd abandoned at the campsite.

Aklys must've woken to realize I'd disappeared and come looking for me.

"Just..." I shifted under his weight and slowly lifted my arms to caress his sides with my fingers.

He shuddered against the delicate touch.

"Kiss me a bit more? I want to pretend for a little while longer that this is okay. I want to pretend that there isn't any animosity and that perhaps we'd decided of our own will to sneak off into the woods."

My breathing grew heavier.

Not needing any further convincing, his lips met mine. The action was less hurried this time and more searching, more memorizing. Absorbing every sensation, like he was learning every small movement.

I wasn't ready to admit how I was beginning to feel about Aklys, as I was struggling to remain firm that I didn't want this, that I didn't want him. I was shattering as easily as glass, though, and he was the mallet that broke my resolve.

I arched to accommodate the arm he was sliding under my back to hold me closer. His other hand cradled the side of my face gently as if we were lovers locked in a truly tender embrace. I curled my arms up around his neck again, my fingers gliding through the locks of his dark hair.

Slowly, painfully, the former urgency was returning — this time it was a feeling entirely my own. The magic was gone from the atmosphere. Between our embrace, I could feel that his body matched the desperation of my own in the heated exchange.

"Aklys."

He tightened against me as I breathed out his name. His eyes searched mine looking for answers, for permission, for direction on where to venture next. For the first time since we'd become entangled, he took in the sight of my nude figure. A pained whimper left his lips as he gazed at me beneath him.

The hand that had been trapped under me freed itself, and he touched my neck, trailing down to caress my collarbone, drifting even further to explore the soft flesh of my breast. The grumble that left him as he explored my body made my core tighten, drunk on his touch. The fingers traced lower, gliding along my abdomen and dancing along my hip bone.

Aklys returned his gaze to mine, expression tightening as he wrestled with reason and restraint, losing the battle against his animalistic inclinations. Our mouths met and he flicked a hot tongue against my bottom lip before poking it gently with his fangs. The sensation startled me, and I jolted against him.

"Damn it," he grumbled.

His hand ventured lower, making contact with the moisture from my body reacting to the lust that had consumed me. My hold on his hair tightened, alerting him to what I craved. He breathed a sigh of relief, as if he had been unsure that he could stop himself at the point we had reached. His fingers slid gently across the tight bundle of nerves hidden between my thighs and I whimpered. My reaction ignited something within him, and he growled, his eyes darkening.

Aklys' gaze didn't leave mine, watching my expressions contentedly as he stroked my most sensitive area. Hushed moans escaped me, each sound signaling him to increase the intensity of his touch. Gently, a finger slid inside the warm opening. My muscles tensed and released around the intrusion, willing it deeper inside. After a few moments he skillfully added another long finger, stretching me a bit further. Another moan crawled up my throat as I processed the sensation, and his grip on the back of my neck tightened slightly.

He thrusted the fingers in and out of my body, occasionally fully withdrawing them to press against the nerves just above my entrance. Watching me closely, his lips parted as he guided me toward release. My hips were lifting with his touch, meeting his movements.

"That's it. Keep going," he sighed.

His voice fueled the raging fire within me, my climax nearing as I desperately bucked against his fingers. Aklys' grip tightened in my hair, and the slightly painful tug against my scalp added a heated surge to the boiling pleasure.

"I want to feel you come on my fingers, my beautiful lady. Look me in the eyes, I want to watch you shatter."

My whimpers prompted a wide, fanged smile from the vampire.

The throbbing intensified as he pumped in and out, and I was losing control.

"Oh Gods!" I erupted onto his hand, his fingers deep inside me, still urgently flexing in his effort to undo me. I held his gaze, watching his jaw clench as I completely broke apart beneath him.

Losing control, Aklys lashed out and bit me. His fangs pierced the soft tissue of my breast, sharp pain made me thrash in an effort to escape. Without warning, my orgasm intensified, the pain washing away as my body exploded with pleasure. I cried out, clawing at the vampire as he licked the blood running across my chest.

"You look so beautiful when you finish, when you're at my mercy," he groaned.

The release began to ebb away, my body relaxing and my mind spinning from the adrenaline coursing through my veins. Aklys withdrew from the tender flesh, and I watched closely as he slid the wet fingers into his mouth, tasting me on his tongue. I was intrigued by the act, my cheeks heated, taking in the image of him savoring the flavor of my climax. He hummed happily, bringing his face close to mine.

He whispered, "I'll find myself craving you for the rest of my life."

I had anticipated more, but found only disappointment as he rose from the ground, picking up his discarded clothing to dress himself.

"We should get back."

He handed me the dress I had abandoned by the riverbank earlier, extending a hand to help me to my feet. The illusion had fallen, and our time together came to an end despite my desire to experience him fully.

My legs wobbled as I was pulled upright, knees nearly buckling beneath my weight, still recovering from the intensity of the orgasm. Aklys caught me in his arms, holding me tightly in his embrace. As I looked up into his eyes, I was met with a sad expression.

I was confused. He had wanted this from me, I knew that much.

"What's wrong?"

"It's time to go back to reality. This was just a dream."

Aklys forced a smile.

He was right, and I felt something akin to the sorrow he displayed. Back to reality.

"Milady?"

My body was being jostled, and my eyes flew open, startled. I frantically sat upright and found myself staring at the Erotas River.

"Milady," the voice repeated.

Aklys knelt next to me only inches away, concern furrowing his brow.

"I, uh, I... um." I looked around, confused.

What had just happened?

"Why did you wander off?" he asked.

"I already told you? That voice..." I trailed off.

Confusion laced his features, and it was apparent that he had no idea what I was talking about. It actually had been a dream, and my stolen moments with Aklys hadn't been real.

I turned to look at him fully. He was clothed, hair tousled as if he'd just woken from a deep sleep. My dress clung to my body, damp and cold like I'd fallen in the river.

The throbbing between my legs muddled my thoughts. What had happened to me during those dreams? It seemed as though my body had truly responded to the illusions.

My face heated, realizing entirely that I had dreamed about *Aklys*. I had wanted it to be real; I'd relished in it, savored him. Our eyes met, and I wondered if he could sense the arousal I felt. A strange substance was present on my fingers.

Oh, no. I'd touched myself in my sleep... to a dream.

"Did you drink from the river? I told you not to do that because-" He started.

"It's magic. It reveals hidden desires," I finished for him, not breaking eye contact.

He watched me thoughtfully.

"Discover anything interesting?" He teased, inhaling loudly as he smelled the air, inching closer.

"Nothing entirely surprising," I whispered back.

I remained still, not flinching away from him.

"You know, something is amiss here..."

He breathed slowly, deeply.

"I don't know what you're talking about!"

My skin burned even hotter.

Aklys lifted a hand, tracing his fingers up my arm, to my shoulder. He gently brushed away the hair covering the delicate skin of my neck and lowered his face to the exposed flesh. I fought the urge to move closer to him, my body throbbed in response to his touch. His lips caressed my shoulder teasingly.

"I knew you liked me," he purred against my skin.

Losing control, I thrust myself toward him, toppling us both to the ground. Aklys laid out flat beneath me, and I straddled him between my thighs.

He looked pleasantly surprised by the sudden assault. I gazed at him for a few moments, allowing the longing in me to show through the usual facade, and I leaned down to place my mouth by his ear.

"I do like you, Aklys. I long for your touch, the thought of you exploring my body, the sharp pain that brings me pleasure from your bite," I whispered, "how I imagine it feels to have you inside of me."

Aklys went completely rigid. I felt strong hands ascending up the length of my thighs, pausing when they reached my hips, gripping me tightly against him.

"I know you can smell the arousal," I taunted him. "Could you smell my release when you found me sleeping? I was dreaming of you and all the things I want you to do to me."

I nipped at his ear, and his fingers tightened further, digging into my skin. I squeezed his body between my legs, grinding the dampness of my throbbing sex against him.

I barely recognized the person I was right now, this woman who was willing to take what she wanted. She was someone who was being honest with herself.

"Do you want me, Aklys?" I moaned into his ear.

"Yes," he breathed, shuddering.

I hummed, enjoying this power I held over him. It was on my terms, not coerced by the chaotic forces of nature. I lifted my face to meet his stare, then lowered myself back down. I met his lips with my own, granting him one gentle kiss.

Then, I stood abruptly and began walking away. The vampire laughed, but the sound wasn't quite right, as it was born of exasperation; maybe even frustration. A hushed noise like wind whispered behind me, and my body was suddenly forced against a tree. Aklys pressed in behind me, grinding against my rear. His hands were placed firmly on my hips, his mouth against my neck.

"How unladylike of you."

A hot tongue tickled the sensitive flesh.

We had begun playing a dangerous game.

I pushed back, unleashing a deep groan from the vampire. I leaned my head into him, further exposing the pulsing arteries that I knew he wanted to violate, to taste. He kissed the tender area with more ferocity than before, losing the hold he'd had on his self-control, gasping against my fragile skin.

I needed to keep the upper hand.

"Let me go," I demanded.

Reluctantly, he obeyed.

As he removed his hold, I turned to face him. Slowly, I raised my hands to the thin straps of my dress and began pulling them away from my shoulders. The fabric slipped across my chest, rolling below my breasts and catching on my waist. Aklys' eyes widened as I exposed myself to him. All I could think about was the bite he'd delivered to me in my dreams, I wanted to feel that sensation again. My hands captured his face, guiding him down to the swells of flesh.

"Here, I want you to bite me here," I whimpered.

Aklys dropped to the ground, pulling me down into his lap, he knelt and held me as I straddled him again. One arm wrapped around my waist pulling me close, the other snaked its way up my spine, until his hand was grasping the back of my neck.

"Bite me," I begged.

"I can't, not like this," he ground out, trembling, "I've never wanted something so badly, I might lose control."

"Do you want me?" I asked breathlessly.

"More than anything," he confessed.

"You can have me right now, have me in this moment," I offered.

He groaned as he pressed his lips to my breast, rolling his tongue roughly over the peak.

"If I take you... If I take you fully, you're mine. You'll always be *mine*."

He growled, something primal stirring to life within him.

"Just a taste, Aklys," I cautioned. "We can indulge, but just once."

He stilled, searching eyes meeting mine, the heat fading. The vampire looked almost sad; sad that I wouldn't submit to him, that I wouldn't hand myself over so easily.

He wanted me to be *his*. I did not want to belong to anyone other than myself, though I did want to experience him, just a little; despite it being selfish.

Faster than I was prepared for, his fangs pierced my skin. He began drawing blood from the wound on my chest, and I squeaked out a shocked cry. His grip tightened, and I was completely at his mercy, locked in an iron hold. The pain from the puncture along with the sensation of the vampire pulling the blood from my body sent a flood of heat to settle between my thighs.

I thrashed and bucked, desperately grinding my pelvis against him. Frantic thrusting overtook me, and the coil deep within me began to tighten.

"Please," I cried out.

Aklys raised his head to meet my distressed gaze. He pushed forward, laying me against the ground, animalistic hunger etched in his features. He crept down toward the lower half of my body. I lifted my pelvis in response to his advance, grabbing at the hem of my dress and hiking it up to leave myself completely exposed, save for the bunched fabric around my waist. A pitiful whimper left his lips as he lowered his head to meet the slick area.

The vampire slowly, torturously touched his tongue to the sensitive parts, dragging along every pulsing nerve. I moaned, reaching down to wrap my fingers in the messy locks of dark hair. He began a vicious assault, savoring me, skillfully ebbing waves of pleasure throughout my body. I had never imagined being touched in such a way.

"Say my name," he growled.

"Aklys," I whimpered.

"Louder."

"Oh, fuck, Aklys!" I shouted, legs shaking as my control faltered.

Pleased with my obedience, he returned to feasting upon the forbidden flesh. Every flick of his tongue brought me closer to the edge. The winding coil unraveled, erupting wildly, and I cried out into the night. Euphoria took over my sense of reason as I climaxed on the vampire's tongue. I grabbed at him, wanting him above me, inside of me. Aklys climbed on top of my body; his eyes were dark, and a deadly aura surrounded him.

"I want to fuck you, milady."

The growl that came forth had risen from the very depths of the vampire, raising an unusual feeling in me of fear mixed with arousal. I pulled him closer.

"I don't think you understand what that means," he said, "Once I have you, you're mine, and I'll kill anyone who tries to take you from me."

He propelled himself away, backing up from where I was still spread before him. I could see his instincts trying to send him toward me again, but whatever rational thoughts he clung to held the vampire at bay.

As much as I feared being marked by this man, the thought of him ravaging me was entirely too alluring. He watched me, face pinched painfully. Spreading further, I slid my hand down between my legs, running my fingers along the swollen flesh and slipping them inside of my body. I held his gaze as I dampened my fingers with my own essence.

I extended the hand coated in moisture toward the vampire, beckoning him to return. He groaned pitifully, falling to his knees. Slowly, he crawled closer, taking my fingers into his mouth. His tongue swirled around them gingerly, not missing a single drop.

"I can't," he huffed breathlessly, the shaking that rocked him becoming nearly violent.

It was his turn to beg. I raised my hips up from the forest floor, teasing him, before lowering myself back down and spreading my legs apart as far as I could manage. My hands grabbed at my breasts, pinching the tender peaks between my fingers as I splayed out before him.

"Please," I whispered.

He submitted to my will, bringing his body above my own.

Roughly, he forced down the pants that had been concealing him, the glistening tip of his length pressed against my body's entrance. Aklys brought his mouth to mine, invading the warm space with his tongue, moaning into me. Slowly, only the tip nudged inside, stretching me to accommodate him. He was panting, fighting against his urges.

"I mean it, I'll never let another man touch you. You'll be mine."

I couldn't answer him, as I wasn't sure exactly what I wanted, and he knew it.

Aklys pulled back, and I whimpered in protest until he graced my sensitive area with the presence of his tongue once again, this time adding long, skilled fingers to the assault. He pressed inside, the movements quick and vicious. The vampire unleashed his frustration of not claiming me fully upon my body. The release came quicker this time with the new stimulation, and I was unable to contain the explosive orgasm, rocking against his fingers and tongue.

I fell apart on that forest floor, simply crumbling into the waves of euphoria. The vampire's face appeared, nose to nose with my own. He kissed me passionately, unexpectedly. I melted into him.

"Someday, I'll have you."

"I wasn't stopping you," I breathed.

The look on his face was solemn as he considered my words.

"Yes, you were."

Chapter Nine

The Past, Present, & Future Of Pain

Lying next to Maygen, I found myself unable to sleep. I had shared very intense moments with Aklys, having been lured into the forest by a magical presence, and acted in a way I hadn't known I could. I was not someone who had been permitted to indulge lust, growing up a noble lady; only once before in my life had I ever experienced a man to such a degree, and that was *recently*.

On one hand, I couldn't stop thinking about the fact that the vampire wanted to claim me fully and wanted to make me his. I didn't know what to do with that information, considering how I felt about being at the mercy of another person.

On the other hand, I craved him. I wanted more. I wanted to feel him, taste him, and experience him.

My mind wandered back to the voice in the trees, how it had told me to find Isonei. I distinctly remembered the meadow Nymph, daughter of the Goddess Melissae; I had clung to the memory of her during my torment. A child's dream of meeting an elusive magical being was fulfilled.

Either the magic could invade my memories or there were things at work that I did not understand. Isonei had found me as a young girl, appearing out of nowhere as I sat alone by a brook.

I was an easily amused child, a girl who loved fairy tales and magical things. I'd wanted nothing more than for a magical creature to become my friend. When I laid eyes upon Isonei, I had immediately reached out for the woman.

She had beckoned me to her, whispering that she could not stay, but that we would meet again. The Nymph gifted me a glowing blue flower, asking that I steep it as tea and drink it, that it was magical.

I'd listened to her, but I hadn't felt any different after. I remembered being disappointed. I wondered now for what purpose the flower had truly been; what magic had she placed within me? What had she been doing there? Had she known what I was?

I had so many questions.

Wishing the sun would rise sooner, I squeezed my eyes shut, but to no avail. Restlessness drove me from the tent and out into the world.

The early morning air was crisp, fresh, and had a slight chill to it that hinted the season would change soon. Summer would give way to autumn.

A set of arms encircled my body, pulling me into an embrace from behind. My heart fluttered as Aklys squeezed me gently, nuzzling his face into my hair.

"Can't sleep, milady?" he breathed.

He couldn't be doing this, for I wasn't his and he wasn't mine. We shouldn't be embracing, whispering to each other, nor stealing quiet moments to linger undisturbed in simple affections.

I didn't want this.

Yes, you do, my inner voice whispered the truth I struggled against.

My throat squeezed shut as I contemplated moving away from him. My heart told me to return the gesture, to be sweet to the vampire. My mind was in disagreement, telling me not to trust the man, to draw the line at sexual exploration.

I could give him my body, but not my soul. I could not give my heart. I wasn't even sure if I had one left after all I'd endured. If I did, then it didn't truly belong to me anyways, not anymore.

Wriggling free of the hug, I turned to face Aklys, but as our eyes met, I lost my words.

He was breathtaking, the intimidating type of beauty that told you at first glance he was dangerous; that heartbreak was imminent. He was a deadly vampire, yet he did not scare me.

I'd seen what he could do, murdering men and challenging monsters, but I never felt afraid of him. I was not afraid even when he'd caught me in Thibault's house, nor when he touched me for the first time. I'd never felt true fear at his hand, as if somehow I knew he would not hurt me.

I hadn't been allowing myself to look at him throughout our journey, to take in every angle of his face, every shadow and color. His dark hair appeared black until the sun danced on the disheveled locks, unlocking glistening shades of brown hidden within the darkness. His hazel eyes were entrancing, ever changing, the colors seemed to move of their own accord. At times they were more green, but occasionally they appeared gold. Magical.

"Are you just going to stare at me all day?" Aklys grinned.

"Sorry," I mumbled, lowering my eyes.

His fingers crept up my cheeks, coaxing my gaze to look upon him again.

"I don't want you to stop. I like that you see me."

The vampire lowered to meet my lips, kissing me gently. My heart melted at the tender display, but my sense finally broke me from the stupor I'd been swimming in. Painfully, I removed myself from the affection, backing away from him.

Aklys frowned and dropped his hands to his sides.

"I can't," I whispered. "I don't want you to think that I can give you what you desire. I can't. I can share my body with you; I can't share anything else."

Wordlessly, the man straightened.

"It doesn't have to be that way," he grumbled. "I can be patient. As I said before, I'll keep trying my luck here. I know what I want."

Before I could speak, he began turning away, leaving my objections unheard. Irritation flared, and I walked after him as he disappeared into the tree line. I wasn't finished. He couldn't just tell me he would keep wanting me when I did not want him to do so.

"Aklys!" I shouted.

The vampire did not turn around. I picked up my pace, breaking into a run. Despite my effort, he disappeared. I could never pursue the speed he possessed.

"Damn it, that's not fair!" My voice carried through the trees. "You don't get to ignore my wishes and then run off before I've had a chance to even respond!"

Fingers snaked into my hair, turning my head. The vampire had made a circle and appeared behind me with little effort. Aklys backed us into a tree, pressing firmly against my body to pin me.

"Say what you want then, milady. I'm listening," he taunted.

Stunned, I did not speak.

"Do you want me?" He whispered, lowering his head.

I held my breath.

"Do you want it to be a secret? Are you afraid of what your friends will think? Or are you afraid to want me the way I want you?"

The vampire pressed his lips to mine, heating my core while simultaneously sending chills dancing along my skin.

"If you only want what my body can do for you, then take it, it's yours," he insisted.

Returning the affectionate kisses, I allowed myself a few more moments.

I'm so selfish.

"Let me pretend that you're mine, if only for a few stolen moments. Let me touch you, let me taste you. I've never wanted something so badly. I've never known a woman like you."

Aklys groaned against my lips.

"You cannot have me the way that you want me. I belong to myself."

"I want to belong to you, too."

His tongue pushed between my teeth, deepening the passion. I moaned into him. Unable to stop myself, I gave in and wrapped my arms around his neck as he lifted my legs to hook around his waist, pushing us against the tree with more urgency.

This wasn't what I had planned. My intention was to force him to swear off of his attempts to court me and to put an end to this fatal attraction, but it was useless. I could not resist him.

"I'll have you someday," he swore.

"Why would you want that? Why me? You could save yourself a lot of misery by pursuing someone else. Anyone else," I insisted.

Aklys didn't respond as he looked into my eyes, searching for something. Perhaps he was hoping to see through a lie or find hidden emotions that might give him hope I would change my mind. He would be disappointed.

"Whoa!" A voice sounded a short distance away.

We'd been discovered.

I was painfully aware of how this looked, our intimate entanglement. I groaned internally.

It was Maygen.

Aklys didn't budge as my expression froze with surprise and embarrassment. I wriggled against his hold to alert him that I wanted to be released, but he made no move to let me go.

"Put me down," I commanded.

"Am I interrupting something?" Maygen asked.

"No!" I snapped.

"Yes!" Aklys spoke over me without breaking his stare.

The woman shifted uncomfortably for a moment, tapping her hands against her legs.

"Aloise is ill," she pressed with a sense of worry in her tone, "very ill."

I glared at the vampire. A low growl sounded in the man's chest as he released me.

"We aren't finished," he muttered.

"Yes, we are. I meant what I said."

"Your actions said something entirely different."

A frustrated sound left my chest as I began stalking away from where he'd ensnared me against my better judgment. Further complications brought on by foolish lust was not an option. If I kept telling myself I did not want him, perhaps I would begin to believe it.

Why couldn't he be a normal man? Why couldn't he only be interested in the physical aspect of things and willing to let me go?

I didn't know if it was normal for vampires to act this way toward romantic interests. I hardly knew anything about his kind, outside of what I'd learned as a child. Those stories had taught me they were bloodthirsty and without mercy. I'd been led to believe vampires hunted and killed mortals for entertainment, that they laid waste to villages and held no regard for life.

None of those things were true of Aklys. He'd wanted to save the people of the settlement, and he treated me tenderly, only tasting my blood with my permission.

There were too many things that demanded my attention currently to be worrying about this. Getting safely to Euros with Maygen, ensuring Thibault and Aloise's safety, was the priority.

His affection was inconvenient.

When I arrived back at the encampment, Thibault's face was twisted with alarm as he held Aloise's weak body. She had emptied the contents of her stomach on the ground and was shaking uncontrollably. The woman sobbed as she clutched her lover's arms.

"What the hell happened?" I demanded.

"I don't know! She woke up like this, but she seemed fine last night!" Thibault whined.

"I'll forage for mint to help her stomach," Maygen offered. "Thibault you should fetch her some water, but boil it first so it's pure."

"Could she have picked up some sort of illness in the desert, or is it from dehydration?" I asked.

Maygen only shrugged as she turned to return to the forest.

"I'll come with you," I called after her.

I had wandered in a different direction than Maygen as we foraged herbs for the ailing woman. My knowledge of plants wasn't vast, but mint had a distinct smell. I walked along the river, staring at the swirling magic.

If it hadn't been for this water, my 'feelings' for Aklys would've remained dormant. I cursed myself for being foolish and placing another treacherous obstacle in my own way. Fate was mocking me.

Crunching leaves caught my attention; one of my companions was likely approaching. In no mood for idle conversation, nor any further debate with Aklys, I turned. Irritation pricked at my skin and my tongue readied itself to berate whoever sought to interrupt me.

Freezing in my tracks, I beheld a strange woman.

Her brown hair was so long that it touched the forest floor, running down the length of a pure white dress decorated with green ribbons. The woman's eyes were angled and her nose was incredibly thin, with skin as pale as the moon.

My breath was stolen as she stepped closer.

"Is this another illusion? Did I drink the water again?"

Confusion muddled my mind.

"Forbidden daughter," she addressed me, her voice was ethereal.

"Excuse me?" I asked, offended.

"What will we do with you?" she asked.

I didn't understand what the stranger meant.

"Who is 'we'? Who are *you*?"

"Have you killed?" The mysterious woman whispered.

"Yes." *Why did I admit that to a stranger?*

"Why?" Her eyes narrowed.

"The first time was an accident," I couldn't stop myself from answering her, as if my words were being forced from me.

"Tell me what happened."

She was face to face with me now, her eyes glowed with what could only be described as divinity.

"I have power, and it's dangerous. The first time it appeared, I killed a man without meaning to, but he had been hurting the boy I loved."

"Tell me more."

"I killed a Wyndiga. It was attacking my friend, Maygen. I killed a Chimera. It was trying to kill Aklys and Thibault. I also killed a man, an evil man."

"What evil man?" she asked.

"Kilian. He was an abuser, a tyrant. I had no choice, but I liked it, the way it felt to take his life and put an end to his cruelty." I continued as tears pricked at my eyes, "I killed his Mage, a girl. He corrupted her with dark magic. I tried not to, but it wouldn't stop. My power killed her even after the dark magic had gone."

The tears dampened my cheeks.

The woman touched my face with her fingertips, and a sense of calm washed over me, staving off my tears.

"Who are you?" I whispered, trembling.

"I am Melissae."

My blood ran cold.

I stood before a Goddess, a true deity. The Goddess of the Seasons, she was known to bless expectant mothers and to also have an affinity for the truth.

Body folding, I dropped to the ground to kneel before her.

"We expected the worst when we learned of you, but my daughter assured us you were good," she hummed thoughtfully, gazing down at me as I lingered at her feet.

"Your daughter?"

Gods and Goddesses were known to have many children.

"The meadow Nymph, Isonei. I sent her to you many years ago, and she had been tasked with bringing you to us, yet she returned home empty handed," the Goddess declared.

I lifted my head to look into her eyes; they shimmered with fascination and curiosity.

"She gave you a gift that day. That little flower suppressed your powers. She gave you her protection, child."

"Are you here to kill me?" I asked.

Melissae watched me thoughtfully for a few moments before speaking.

"I will not kill," she said finally. "My daughter shall come for you once more."

"Why?"

"You were created for a purpose. You must decide if you will fulfill it."

I did not understand. It was said the Gods were cryptic, but this was just frustrating.

"What am I?"

"It would appear that you are an Amalgam," she answered.

A divine child of mixed blood: one born of the merging of divinity with mortality. A forbidden creation. A dangerous creature.

"That's impossible."

My head shook away her words, refusing to accept the truth.

I leaned forward, placing my palms against the ground. My breathing was strained, ragged, and painful. Emotion surged beneath the surface of my skin. My power was crying out at its truth. I was not a true mortal.

That meant everything I had known about myself was a lie.

"My parents?" My voice had begun to crack.

"Your mother was of the last line of mortals brought into creation."

"My father?" I could barely force a whisper.

"A God."

My head hung low, and I let my dismay flow freely. I stared at the ground as my mind pieced together memories. Some things began to make sense. My mother's nearly unnoticeable aversion, something that only I could see. My appearance that slightly differed from my sisters. My power.

My parents had loved each other deeply, so I could not imagine my mother ever betraying my father.

"My mother would never..." I trailed off.

"Your mother was the victim of an unspeakable crime," Melissae snapped.

My heart broke, burdened with the weight of my existence. I was the product of an assault against my mother.

She was a kind, gentle soul, full of love and compassion. What sort of divine being could commit such an atrocity?

"Which God?" I asked, eyes still lingering on the grass below my palms.

Silence.

"Who is my true father?" I demanded, lifting my gaze.

The Goddess was gone.

Three days had already passed since we'd left our encampment by the river. Aloise rode our single remaining horse for the entirety of the trek through Silenus Forest, stopping frequently due to the sickness that plagued her.

Irritation bubbled inside my chest. While I had forgiven her, I was having a difficult time truly accepting her. Being comfortable in her presence was still out of reach. Any minor inconvenience began to feel personal, with every delay sending me further into a rage spiral. I knew my anger was misdirected, but I couldn't stop myself.

"If she continues to be ill, I'm going off on my own. The sound of her vomiting is sending me over the edge," I grumbled to Maygen.

"It's not her fault. It could've happened to any of us, right?" She shrugged.

Doubtful. She was the weakest and most susceptible of us, the only true mortal.

I huffed in exasperation and slowed my pace, falling behind the small group.

As Aklys passed by, he made a visible effort to avoid eye contact with me. We hadn't spoken since Maygen caught us in an incredibly foolish entanglement in the forest. An unfinished argument lingered between us, unspoken words filling the air with tension. I didn't know how much more of this I could bear.

Each day I look into the eyes of the man I wanted to love, I look into the eyes of the woman he chose over me, and I look into the eyes of a vampire with whom I didn't want to have feelings for. The emotional turmoil was enough to drive any sane person mad.

"How much longer to Briobar?" I called out to no one in particular.

"We should reach the outskirts by dusk. We'll camp at the forest's edge and move into town in the morning; we all need rest," Thibault responded.

The last time Thibault and I had seen each other before he was sent away, was in my family's estate on the outskirts of the city we'd once called home. The Umbraeon family home was located at the northernmost point of the city, near the coast.

I wondered what had become of it after my family's demise. Had it been left untouched to wither away and meet its end as my loved ones had? Has a new family taken our place? The thought of strangers living in my home made me uncomfortable. I didn't want to picture the long halls filled with voices that didn't belong to my sisters.

There would be no lady that could light up those dreary rooms the way my mother always had without even trying. There would be no lord that commanded the respect that my father had, which he'd spent his entire life earning through kindness and compassion for his citizens.

I hated myself for existing.

Had my mother been spared a horrific trauma, I never would've been brought into this world. My siblings would've lived long, full lives. My parents would have seen the ages together, growing gray and frail, loving the grandchildren that should have been, knowing the family line lay secure in the offspring of their daughters.

Necilia would've been an amazing mother, she had frequently mothered my sisters and I. Brushing our hair, reading us tales and tucking us into bed. I suppose that was what the eldest sister was expected to do. My heart ached; I missed her.

I needed to know my true paternity. I wanted to know which God committed such an atrocity, harming my mother and creating a forbidden bastard child. A child with terrible power, cursed with an existence plagued by endless suffering.

I would find him; and I would end him. Killing a deity was unheard of, and it may even be impossible, but I would spend the rest of my life trying. No God capable of rape and violence deserved to have any power over the realm and its people.

As I mulled through my thoughts, I wondered about the lore surrounding my affliction. Surely, I had more siblings. What if my true father had more Amalgam children? Was it possible I was not the only one? Perhaps I had more brothers and sisters that the Gods put an end to, to spare the world of the terrible powers that emerge when an offspring like myself is created.

All of the Gods and Goddesses brought forth children to fill the land with life, to spin the wheels of Fate. The mortal lines, humans, were created by several unions of Gods and Goddesses. It is said that they believed lives were meant to be short and fragile in order to be valued, to find the will to accomplish greatness with what little time they had. Those with an expiration date are motivated to accomplish more, apparently.

The Goddess of Mortal life and Birth, Nysa, and the God of Order, Hollin, created the first line of mortals. They were the first children to enter the realm. Nysa took a second union with the God of Wisdom, Arendiel, creating a line blessed with pure and beautiful magic, the first Mages. They were meant to be healers for their fellow men. The rest of the pantheon soon followed suit, bringing mortal and magical bloodlines into the world. It is said these peoples lived peacefully under the governing of their deities in the earliest years of the realm's creation.

Before long, the immortal lines were birthed, meant to be superior to mankind in every way. The Nymphs, the Elves, the Fae, and finally the Spectrals were beings blessed with gifts of beauty, strength, and long-lasting life. They were referred to as immortal, for they would live on through the ages if their lives were not taken from them.

A division between the immortal and mortal lines still exists today; the beings tend to keep their bloodlines separate from the 'inferior' mortals. Children of mixed blood were cast out, mistreated, and their parents were often punished or executed. Few circumstances allowed the merging of bloodlines, usually as a power play to gain a family name and inherit assets between courts; the mortal blood eventually bred away until there was hardly a trace, retaining only its inheritance.

It was different when a God or Goddess procreated with a mortal. When the deities combined magics during their unions, there was balance, with equal power offering control over the outcome. The intention of these couplings was to give life to a new lineage, but those that came from them would always be lesser.

When a divine being paired with a mortal or 'immortal', there was no balance. The deity's magic would amplify and mutate, as if it were made stronger by a host body rather than harmonizing with it.

Very few legends exist about Amalgam children. What I had learned was that the children from a mortal father and a divine mother were less chaotic. Being that the deity's body was the one to grow the new life, the magic had a higher chance of being contained, muted, less of a threat. For a mortal mother and a divine father, the woman was nothing more than a submissive vessel for power to evolve unchecked.

The deities agreed that these children were too much of a risk, ending relations between themselves and the peoples of the mortal realm.

I wonder if things were meant to be this way, so incredibly complicated. Was this what the original powers had anticipated? Had they known what would become of the existence they designed?

The Gods and Goddesses of creation were not the first beings; they had 'parents' for lack of a better term. Before these primordial beings were at odds with one another, and before good or evil truly existed, they combined many magics to craft each one of our deities for specific purposes.

"Lost in thought?" A low voice disrupted my internal delve into history.

"Yes," I hissed at the vampire.

Aklys was finally speaking to me. It had been days since he'd spoken a word, I thought bitterly.

"Dare I ask?" He arched an eyebrow inquisitively.

"I was thinking about our history, the realm's history. The Gods."

"Why?" The vampire scoffed.

My jaw clenched, "Because I want to know who my father is."

Aklys went rigid. The sudden disturbance that painted his features made my stomach twist; questions began to rise up my throat.

"The Goddess Melissae appeared before me in the forest the day we departed camp. She confirmed that I am an Amalgam as Kilian had said, but she didn't tell me which God hurt my mother. I need to know."

Aklys swallowed, the effort too forced to go unnoticed.

"Lord Altan Umbraeon was your father."

I narrowed my eyes at the man.

"No."

He knew something; I could feel it in my bones. I turned to stalk away, but a strong hand gripped my arm.

"Lord Altan raised you, and he loved you. He was your father."

Pulling from his grasp, "Yes, but I bear the blood of a *God*. I will find out which, one way or another," I snarled.

"And do what?"

He was challenging me.

"I'll ask him why he did it. What was the point? What is my intended purpose?"

"Don't ask questions that you don't want the answer to."

The vampire's gaze was unfaltering, sometimes I wondered if he remembered to blink.

"And then I'll kill him," I concluded.

"How are you going to kill a God? Just leave it alone. Live, instead. This will destroy you if you let it."

"It already has."

Disgust soured my mouth.

Aklys stared down at me for a long while. I expected him to argue further, to sway my mind away from my resolution.

"I understand," he said softly.

Scrunching my face, I tried to appear angry and disinterested in conversing with the man.

All I could think about, though, was my mother. Her pain and anguish, being cursed with a constant reminder of what had happened to her. She had been cursed with me. I was far enough gone that I had murdered a man in front of her, and she watched me descend into becoming an abomination. I was the reason she died, the reason she lost everything.

"You don't," I argued, swallowing down the sob that threatened to free itself.

I was tired of being unable to control my emotions. I was tired of being vulnerable in front of this infuriating man. Aklys reached out a hand to caress my face, but I pushed it away.

"I don't want your comfort. I don't need it," I growled.

Furrowing his brows, "Fine," he ground out.

The vampire stalked off, leaving me to stand alone.

Chapter Ten

To Hurt & Heal

In the distance, faint light from the setting sun cast shadows over the city of Briobar. From the tree line it looked nearly the same as it had over a hundred years ago. It looked like home.

Rows of small town homes lined the brick streets, windows aglow with firelight. People still milled about the outskirts, finishing their daily tasks in the crop fields that stretched from the buildings to the forest. Obscuring the fading rays of sunshine were dark storm clouds, steadily rolling in over increasingly unsettled sea water, with angry waves lapping at the pebbled northern shore. As darkness progressed, tiny drops of rain pattered against the foliage above.

"We should make for an inn – Aloise shouldn't continue to be exposed to the elements in her state."

Maygen had grown increasingly concerned for the frail woman, as Aloise's condition had yet to improve since she had fallen ill after we'd escaped the Ashen Land's clutches.

Thibault agreed quietly. He didn't sleep, he hardly ate, and he gave every ounce of energy he had to make sure Aloise did not succumb to whatever was plaguing her.

I'd be lying if I said I wasn't concerned, for I wasn't without compassion. However, every minor inconvenience only manifested as resentment inside of me. I was desperate to take time to work through my emotions, but I craved closure.

So close, yet still out of reach, lies a major piece of my life that I could access once more. I could access a place I loved. If I could see it once more, perhaps I would find a sliver of peace.

"We can't risk being signaled out; it'll take a while to scour the area to confirm it's free of Sentinel patrols," Aklys argued.

"The only one who is in danger is me. I can remain here until we are able to rendezvous in the morning. You should seek comfort and shelter for the evening. We will be able to locate a healer for Aloise come daytime," I made the suggestion half-heartedly.

Being alone for a short while could be beneficial to my mental health, giving me time to mull through my thoughts and create a clearer picture of my situation. Despite my ability to defend myself with my power, I doubted my companions would allow it.

There was no risk of vampires in Briobar. The major cities in Teskaria were entirely averse to the species, so any lingering vampires were generally found in Euros and Adristan, and even that was extremely rare... save for Aklys.

Come to think of it, I still didn't understand why *he* was in Teskaria in the first place.

"Celessa, as long as you remain hooded, then it should be fine, right?" Maygen inquired.

Aloise reached a weak hand toward me.

"We aren't going anywhere without you," the woman whispered, fervently hushed by Thibault who insisted she save her strength.

My heart squeezed at the sentiment, and despite all we'd endured I wondered if she might actually care for me, even if it was just a matter of human decency.

The thought of being trapped in a stuffy inn room for an entire night made my skin crawl, though the prospect of a comfortable bed had my muscles screaming for relief. Night after night on hard ground doesn't do well for one's back.

One would think my body would be accustomed to such mistreatment after lying on a stone table for damn near one hundred and fifty years.

"Perhaps we could send Thibault and Aklys first? Only men are allowed to procure lodging, and we have to be accompanied at all times. Thibault can take Aloise, and Aklys can take you and I?" Maygen suggested, eyes pleading as she looked at me.

Groaning, "Fine." I relented.

Thibault's brows furrowed with concern as he said, "After I have Aloise situated, I can assess the area before coming for the rest of you. We should check the area for information on persons of interest and any nobility. Anyone worth anything will be looking for you, Celessa. We should take every precaution."

Despite the risks, I planned to see my home. The more people left behind with me meant more people to argue with about my decisions.

"Take Maygen with you. If you run into trouble, or if it's not safe in there for me, the three of you should at least sleep comfortably for one night." I glanced at Aklys as I said, "Teskarians aren't exactly fond of vampires, anyway."

Aklys approached Thibault as he mounted our horse behind Aloise, reaching out a large, clenched hand towards the man.

"Money for the rooms," he said, dropping several coins into Thibault's open palm.

"Where did you get this?" Thibault asked the vampire.

"I'm always prepared."

Aklys shrugged, sauntering away. Probably to find somewhere to lurk.

"Go with them," I insisted to Maygen.

"We'll be back shortly, I promise."

She squeezed me tightly before trotting after the horse.

It hit me, watching her walk away, that she had quickly fallen into a place in my heart that had been reserved for my sisters. The reality that she was the only family I had weighed heavily on my mind. The urge to visit my home grew ever stronger.

Perhaps I could convince Aklys to escort me while we awaited word from our companions? I didn't see it as an issue as long as I kept to the shadows. If he refused me, I would go alone.

"I have a request," I started.

"So, you only want to speak to me if you require something?" Aklys scoffed.

"Can we resume whatever *this*," I used my hands to gesture between the two of us, "is at a later time, because this is important."

Rolling his eyes, the vampire pushed away from the tree he'd been leaning against and began to approach me. It was strange, but sometimes I swore his eyes glowed in the darkness, as if they held their own light. It was like they had their own magic.

"What is it you desire, milady?"

Clenching my jaw at how he addressed me, I resigned to stifle my argument toward the mocking title, for now.

"I need you to take me to see my family's home," I stated resolutely.

Aklys' eyes widened slightly, and a dark brow arched at my request.

"No."

"No?"

The vampire stood in silence.

"Why the hell not?" I challenged. "If you do not take me, I will go myself."

"Your home does not stand abandoned, milady. It took no time at all before the courts installed a new lord to take the Umbraeon family's place."

A striking blow hit my heart. I didn't know what I had expected, really. The possibility of a new family living at the estate had been something I considered, but knowing for certain that there were people in my home hurt me more than I had anticipated.

Children would've been raised in the courtyard where I'd played with my sisters. A new lady would've renovated all of my mother's past designs, and a new lord would've taken up residence in my father's office. It felt wrong.

"I don't care. I just want to see it," I whispered.

"Once you see it, you won't be able to fight the urge to get closer. Have you forgotten that we're on the run? Or that you're a wanted person?"

The vampire shook his head, silently scolding me as if I were a child.

"Please," was all I uttered.

"What?" Aklys seemed shocked that I even knew the word.

"Please," I pressed, taking a step toward the man.

He did not pull away as I closed the distance between our bodies, reaching my hands out to entwine my fingers with his own. Raising my chin, I looked into his eyes, summoning my most pitiful expression.

"I need this closure," I insisted, "to feel less... broken."

"Listen," he murmured, "they are a family of Mages. It could compromise your safety."

I did not blink, holding the vampire's gaze, squeezing his hands tighter.

He sighed with exasperation.

"Unbelievable. You're using affection to coerce me," he growled as I brushed my chest against him.

"That's awfully manipulative for a lady."

"I am no lady."

"You're my lady," Aklys said as he pulled a plump bottom lip beneath his fangs.

In a swift movement, the vampire pulled me into his arms, cradling me as I hadn't allowed him to do since we stood atop Grim's Peak. Casually, I slid my arms around his neck, nestling myself close to his chest.

"You torture me," he breathed.

"I truly do not understand where your interest lies," I groaned, rolling my eyes at the vampire.

"With you," Aklys smiled. "All of you."

We disappeared as silently as a whisper, moving like an untoward breeze through the forest, nothing but a shadow.

The estate was quiet and dark, nothing like it had been when my large family occupied it. The hired help and visitors had always milled about. Friends of my sisters often visited and would linger for lengthy periods of time, spending night after night in our home. They would take evening walks in their gowns, skipping about the courtyard and gossiping as young ladies often did. My mother frequently invited her own siblings to visit with us.

I wondered if her family had endured, or if my father's distant relatives had been affected by my existence. Did the generations of their families continue on, or were they delivered a similar Fate to my parents and sisters?

It didn't matter.

"Who lives here now?" I asked Aklys quietly.

"The Undergrove family."

I knew of the Undergroves. This family had been in a position of power even when I had lived here in my 'first life', but they didn't have the best reputation. Dispatched to our city by the noble families of Osceau to influence my father in court, a Lord Undergrove had been meant to serve as my father's advisor; though, he was an unwanted one.

I shouldn't be surprised, as the Umbraeon family had been one of the very few noble families left that were not imbued with magic or of an immortal bloodline. There was no one left here to speak for the common folk or to prioritize the needs of the most vulnerable.

My father had been so loved and supported in his position because he never let his people down, and he'd always cared for the lowliest. Under my father's governance, Briobar had been the most prosperous city in Teskaria for mortals, with our poverty rate well below that of the other cities.

Sadness simmered behind my eyes as I considered how those who needed the most help were most likely those left to fend for themselves; without a compassionate leader to rely on.

"I'm willing to bet they weren't too torn up over my family's demise," I grimaced.

Aklys squeezed my shoulder gently.

"Let's get a bit closer – I want to see the courtyard."

"I told you we had to stay away," the vampire argued.

Shrugging away from his touch, I pressed forward, running quietly through the grass to the shrub shielded fences that encircled a large portion of the property. I couldn't stop myself, because I *needed* to see it, my home.

Shouldering through the bush branches, my body pressed against the cool iron bars that guarded the yard. Peaceful relief washed over me as I beheld the familiar sight. It looked the same. How was that possible?

Entranced by the scenery, I did not notice a person lingering nearby until well after I'd been spotted. My heart raced as a man walked toward me. He was young and well kept, likely a member of the household. If I panicked it would raise suspicion, so I remained still.

"Can I help you?" he asked, his voice thick with a northern lilt.

Fumbling, "I just w-wanted to see the y-yard," I managed to spit out.

The man cocked an eyebrow at me.

"We don't typically allow commoners in."

"Yes, sir, of course. My mistake."

I moved to turn away, to escape, but a hand reached through the bars to snag my dress.

"The gate is open," was all he said before turning to walk the length of the fence.

This man meant for me to follow him to the entrance.

Where was Aklys?

"Come, you may see the courtyard, since you are alone. It is renowned in Briobar for its simple yet entrancing beauty."

The man beckoned me with an outstretched arm as I found myself in front of open barred doors.

Hesitantly, I placed my hand on his own.

This is a mistake, I thought to myself. I needed closure, so just for a moment I would step foot here again. The longing for my home clouded my judgment.

"Seeing you closer now, it would appear that you may not be a commoner? A fine woman such as yourself must come from a noble family, I assume?"

"No, my lord."

"That is surprising, as such beauty has become so exclusive to nobility in recent years."

I swallowed roughly; immortal families were known for their more 'pleasing' features, generally considered more attractive than mortals. Even mortals with magic were held in higher regard than those without. Most Mages were noble, as there were not many were left; at least, that was what I'd known before I slept for all those years.

"Tell me, how did you reach the property undetected?" the man asked. "We have patrolmen stationed nearby at night."

"I must be very quiet."

"Indeed," he chuckled, "or the vampire who brought you here is."

The blood drained from my face, and my pulse began racing. I pulled my hand away from the man and turned to run, but only found myself face to face with another stranger.

I'm such a damned fool.

"Are you who I think you are?" the first man inquired.

"If I am, then you should be afraid," I growled, my power welling beneath my skin, threatening to break free.

A faint glow had appeared at my fingertips, the red essence making itself known.

"Incredible!" the man exclaimed, falling to his knees.

Surprise overtook my senses, as I reeled from his reaction to the visible threat. The man behind me moved to kneel as well, and I felt more confused than alarmed.

"Are you daft?" I blurted out.

The fawning fools chuckled.

"You have nothing to fear from us, Lady Celessa. I recognized you right away. Though, I must say, I'm surprised you are so trusting, given your circumstances."

"Who are you?"

"Niall Undergrove, son of the Lord of Briobar, who happens to be away on a diplomatic matter. The matter is concerning you, by the way." He smiled. "This here is my friend and hired hand, Tomas, who happens to know your vampire."

Spinning, I searched for any sight of Aklys.

"Come, my lady. The vampire is retrieving your other friends from the inn. You're lucky my lord father is away, as he still suffers from an inexplicable loyalty to the courts. I'm not interested in such debauchery."

Niall extended his hand to me again. I cursed internally for being my usual naive self, and I cursed Aklys for leaving me without telling me I would be safe, *again*.

I didn't think these two had the manpower to subdue the vampire, let alone get information from him. The only way they'd know about my companions and where they were would be, was if he'd told them, or they had been spying on us.

Surely Aklys would have noticed, had that been the case. He must trust them enough to leave me in their presence, but should I? Should I even trust the man who lusted after me?

I walked silently through the courtyard with my newfound escorts, who carried on chatting as if I wasn't there, swaying me in different directions to admire the various gardens. It felt surreal.

At one point in my life, my father had invited young noblemen to our home to court me just like this, taking my hand and whisking me along the pathways. Before, when I was a lady, I was not allowed on the grounds after nightfall. I'd worn large, expensive dresses that were nearly suffocating, toted along like I was an exotic animal; a prize to be won.

Now, I wore a plain dress as simple in fabric as a proper shift.

These men were friendly for no reason, with no attempts to woo or flatter me. They simply minded each other while I observed the place that had once been my home. After a short trek, I was guided to a bench that hadn't been here before, a new installment. It was new to me, at least.

"Your friends should be arriving soon," Niall smiled as he spoke.

I only stared at the man. He shared an uncomfortable glance with Tomas.

"My lady, you haven't spoken; are you alright?" Tomas asked.

Turning my head, I looked away from the men and toward the ground. I said nothing.

"We'll fetch you when your rooms are ready. Out of respect for my family, only guest rooms will be available, I'm afraid. Your stay will have to be as brief as possible."

Niall touched my shoulder gently before disappearing with his companion.

In silence, I remained still and waited.

How much time had passed meant nothing to me as I watched the sky grow ever darker. Sitting in my yard that wasn't my yard, outside of my home that was no longer my home, caused anger to heat my core, the rage seething within every fiber of my being.

My descendants should be here. I should've lived a long life here. I should've married and raised children alongside my sisters. I should've been a true Umbraeon daughter.

Clenching my jaw in an effort of restraint made no difference to my power as it bubbled out of my skin. Tensing my muscles did not stop it from bellowing out around me in its thick fog-like appearance, blanketing the ground and creeping through the grass. Holding my breath did not halt its advance as it sought to destroy something, anything.

As I stood to observe the mist's reach, I feared I was truly beginning to lose control.

It did not hurt me much anymore when my power made its presence known, and it seems my half-mortal body had become more accepting of the curse. I was evolving with it. Each time I unleashed the mist, I felt more in tune with it, more connected to it.

Bring it back, my mind pleaded.

Let it go, a dark voice chimed from somewhere else inside of me — a voice I did not know by name, but one I've heard before.

Did I truly have control? Did I *want* control? If I wanted, I could raze this entire estate to the ground. I could put my home to rest with my family, the only people who belonged here. It did not belong to these intruders, these strangers.

It was mine.

"Celessa?" A voice broke through the haze of my rage.

Turning, I made eye contact with Thibault.

"Your eyes are glowing this time."

His concerned expression washed me with awareness, pulling me from the stupor.

My curse withdrew, sliding back into the gashes of my arms that I hadn't felt open, and I watched them close behind the blood mist as it returned to my body. There was no discomfort when the wounds closed themselves.

Fingers flexing, I observed the bending joints and contracting muscles, my hands lifted to touch my eyes.

"Glowing?" I whispered.

"Red, like your power."

Humming thoughtfully, I returned my gaze to the man.

"I don't think I'm in control anymore. I couldn't stop it from coming out, every thought I had was malicious, vengeful, and hateful."

"You are none of those things, Celessa."

I sat back down on the small bench, bowing my head. Thibault settled next to me, placing his hand lightly on my back.

"I think I'm becoming those things."

Carefully, Thibault rubbed my back in an effort to reassure me, to comfort me.

"I was whipped here," Thibault murmured.

I had forgotten that this was the very last spot that I'd seen him as everything went to hell. It was the first time my gift reared its ugly head.

Looking toward the ground, I noticed the grass wasn't quite as thick in the spot below the bench, like it refused to thrive here. We were sitting atop where the whipping post had been. Disgust rippled through me at the realization, and I leapt from the seat.

Thibault remained still, a smile gently tugging at the corner of his mouth.

"Why do you look amused?" I demanded.

"It's been so many years, yet you stand before me, untouched by time. It's hard to believe that we made it back here after my exile and your imprisonment."

"I should've lived here, died here."

"Yes," he agreed, nodding slowly.

We lingered in silence for a moment. There were many memories of this place. There had been love here, young and naive, pure and innocent.

"Despite your objections, I feel as though I should keep apologizing for my behavior," Thibault started. "I have great love for you, Celessa. You deserve a better man."

"You're still a good man, Thibault. You can't be faulted for making a mistake – you're just a person. I told you I've forgiven you."

"Before you bless me with your kind words, please let me finish."

Arching a brow, I waited.

"Aklys isn't the better man to whom I'm referring."

I groaned, "It isn't like that."

"Isn't it? You may forget, but I have the senses of the Fae, and I could smell him on you. Don't do this to yourself; don't let him have you. I know he's been decent with you, but he's a *vampire*, Celessa."

Thibault stood then, gripping my shoulders tightly.

"Stop it!" I demanded. "Save your concern for Aloise."

Judging by his expression, it still wounded him that I would reject his every advance regarding my well-being.

"You can't have it both ways, Thibault! You don't get to choose another woman and then try to stop me from being with other men!"

"No, not other men, just him! Celessa, have you even realized that he is a full vampire? Not half, not a descendant, just a vampire. The only full vampires are the cursed siblings, the First. Any others are watered down descendants with mixed blood. That means he's a child of the Gods, and it means he was one of the war lords that bathed the kingdoms in blood."

That wasn't true, Aklys had told me his family was the victim of a mimic curse. Yet, I found myself wondering if that was the truth. Perhaps his true intentions were to seduce me just to use me as a weapon.

If the vampires were able to wield my ever-growing power against the other races, they'd be unstoppable. The names of the First had been systematically erased from history to conceal their identities. Only the immortal beings who still existed from their reign knew who they truly were, as well as the Gods that withdrew their rule from our realm generations ago.

What if he was lying to me?

"As someone who cares deeply for you, I implore you, be with *anyone* else," Thibault pleaded.

"I appreciate the concern, but I'm not a child," I grumbled. "However, I already told him he couldn't have me, and I meant it. You have nothing to worry about."

Thibault sighed with relief.

"Isn't he your friend?" I asked.

"More or less."

"If he is worthy of your friendship and your trust, then why is it different where I'm concerned?" I challenged.

"Celessa, I've seen him use and throw away women he had seduced as if they were nothing. Is that what you need to hear? I know I hurt you, but at least let me spare you from him hurting you, as well."

"Oh," I breathed heavily.

Thibault sighed.

"May we sit together for a while?" he asked.

Forcing a smile, I whispered, "Sure," and returned to our seats on the bench.

Making conversation with the man who once held my heart, but had become my friend, was something I hadn't known I needed. Familiar chatter that lacked the former animosity granted me something precious, a hint of closure.

The thickness of night had fully enveloped the grounds, and it was late. Thibault had left me to return to Aloise; alone, I soaked in the late summer air. Soon, the seasons would change and traveling would become more difficult, so we needed to make it to Euros before then. Rising, I ventured inside the keep.

I loved these grounds, this building, and every memory the estate held. I'll allow myself one more day to enjoy it. After tonight, I would let it go.

Entering the front door felt like a dream for a moment until I realized the entire interior had been changed. Our family portraits no longer hung in the foyer, and the walls were redecorated with paintings of landscapes and strangers.

Niall appeared from the sitting room to the left, with Tomas and Aklys following behind.

"My lady, may I escort you to your room?" the young lord offered.

Nodding, I quietly took his arm and let him guide me to the guest rooms on the upper level of the home, painfully aware of Aklys' eyes on my back. The stairs seemed never ending.

"You'll have to forgive the simplicity, as my father lowered the taxes when the blight started, so our funding for the estate isn't what it once was. We sold many items."

I hadn't realized how empty many of the rooms were.

"Blight?" I inquired.

"This area of Teskaria has lost a large portion of its crops due to the unpredictable weather. The curse that was placed on Evelia has spread. Now, we rely mostly on imports from the larger cities and the few farms that struggle nearby."

"My lord, I assure you I am accustomed to much more unfavorable conditions. This is luxurious," I reassured the man.

We arrived at the furthest bedroom, and Niall opened the locked wooden door. Another change in the home, for none of the rooms had locks when my family had resided here.

"Does the lady wish to be alone?" he asked.

"What?"

"I ask on behalf of the vampire, Aklys. He did not want to intrude."

"I want to be alone."

Niall nodded and gestured for me to enter the room.

"He'll be just across the hall if you change your mind, my lady."

"Thank you," I whispered back.

He smiled warmly, "It is my pleasure."

I locked the door behind him.

Chapter Eleven

Loved & Lost

Asuras smiled at me.

I had started fancying him in no time at all. Though he was older than I, he was handsome, charming, and without a wife.

He whispered to me tales of faraway lands. He told me the secrets of Evelia, how perfect it had been, and how its lone city was so beautiful it was fit for the Gods. He spoke to me of the rebel country, Greilor, which was a wasteland teeming with vampires and outlaws. The Mage spoke to me of the wondrous beauty of the large cities in Euros: the capital, Licourt, and the sister cities, Pagon and Periveil. He spun tales of the regal Elvish families of Adristan and their beautiful southern coast.

He promised me the world.

Then, he gave me a prison.

"Give me your power."

The Mage's hot breath left moisture against the skin of my neck.

"No!"

I screamed, darkness trailing after me as I fled, its cool embrace paralyzing my limbs. My body crumbled to the ground, succumbing to the black haze, my cries were suffocated. I was left to float in nothingness. My Fate had befallen me once more, and I was trapped. Helpless. Hopeless.

My body thrashed, my mind screamed, and my power roiled.

I'll use my curse to free myself.

I will stretch it so far and wide that it will kill everything in its path until it finds the Mage. I would not suffer another hundred years. I would not suffer for one more day.

His face was all I could see, painted with a twisted smile. He was mocking me.

He will die.

I will kill him. I will kill every acolyte that aids him, and anyone who gets in my way. I will become a monster to save myself.

My wicked grin stretched wide as I summoned my cursed magic, my strength. Willing it forward, I will touch the edges of this world. I will destroy it all.

Screams erupted around me as my essence advanced, the sounds of fear. A poisonous thought entered my mind, *I was so powerful.*

The only obstacle that stood in my way of true power; the only beings I needed to fear, were the ones I could not conquer.

Vampires.

The world was erupting, and everything was shaking.

No, I was shaking.

I was being shaken.

"Stop, damn it, let go!" I screamed.

Two strong hands released my body, leaving me to collapse limply on the bed. My head was pounding at the violent thrashing that my once relaxed, sleeping self had endured. Pain burned in my neck. My eyes opened fully to spinning surroundings.

Something was wrong with it, the space I was in. It was blackened, with ash-like material fluttering through the air.

Aklys hovered over me, pinning me to the spot under his weight, his face was twisted with an unreadable emotion. What had I done?

"What happened?" I demanded, searching around more frantically.

It was like any trace of life had been sucked from the room, leaving no color, no kindness, just desiccation. Ruin.

"What did I do?"

"You were screaming in your sleep. Maygen was already on her way to check on you. She couldn't get the door open because you locked it, so she kicked it in and your power went after her. Luckily, I was close by, and it receded. The closer I got to you, the more it withdrew. I didn't know what was wrong, and you wouldn't wake up. I've been trying to wake you for over an hour."

Aklys touched my face gently with his fingertips.

"Is Maygen okay?" Tears welled, I was fearful and ashamed, knowing I could've ended her life.

She would never look at me the same again, and how could she? Knowing I'd nearly killed her, knowing that I have no control, why would she want to be anywhere near me?

"She's okay. Come here."

The vampire hauled me into his embrace, holding my shuddering body close. I couldn't fight him, nor was I sure I wanted to.

"Tell me what happened. Was it a nightmare?" he asked.

I nodded.

"What was it?"

"Asuras," I whispered. "He'd taken me, and I refused to suffer through that hell again. I can't. I'd rather die," I inhaled, then exhaled, "or kill anyone who tries to stop me from being free."

"I will never let him hurt you again," Aklys growled, startling me.

Looking up at the man who held me, something stirred. It was as though every feeling I'd been repressing was coming to the surface at that moment, fueled by his declaration. He wanted to keep me safe from what I feared, and I think that was what I truly needed most. To feel safe.

This hopeless romantic nonsense would be the fucking death of me.

What I didn't need was to feel safe and cared for by a vampire I barely knew. He was a man who could take advantage of me at any moment, who could betray me again, and who could easily be lying to me about who he was.

Aklys was the only person I had been exposed to since waking that had no reason to fear me. He was immune to my powers, and I was no match for him physically. In that regard, I had every reason to fear him. Except, I didn't.

Maybe I was just lacking that sense in my brain that alerted me of bad people and ill intentions. It wasn't too presumptuous, considering all I have endured from blindly trusting others. I couldn't stop myself from acting before I truly considered things. I don't have control over my inclinations or my power. A volatile creation, a danger to everyone around me, that's what I was.

I had been silent for a long time. Aklys lifted us from what remained of the bed and carried me across the hall to his designated room. The vampire didn't give me a chance to protest as he laid me down and wrapped my body in blankets, then started heading for the door.

"Where are you going?" I asked.

"To find somewhere to sleep," he said quietly before shutting the door.

I'd demanded he respect my feelings and give me space, so why was I distraught at his compliance? I was already missing his former banter, his playfulness, and his affection.

This was for the best, I reminded myself.

It will be better for everyone if I cut ties and disappear. This was all a mess.

I'm a mess.

Sleep evaded me. Pacing did my mind no favors, but I couldn't rest after what had happened. How was I meant to relax knowing I could murder everyone around me in my sleep?

The sun had not yet risen, with the outside world covered in a dark gray haze. I could leave. I could go alone. It was the safest option for my companions.

Slowly, I pushed open the heavy door and peered into the hallway. I needed to move quickly to collect provisions before I departed, and it would be easy because I knew every inch of this house. I'd find clothes in the family rooms, and I'd gather food and supplies from the kitchen. Before anyone awoke, I would be gone.

Satchel in hand and a large pack on my back, I hurried to the estate stables where our mare had been left to rest. Bright sunlight creeping over the horizon was slowly illuminating the waking world, and I was running out of time. The graceful brown horse was contained within a far-off stall, happily munching on the food that had been provided for it.

"I'm sorry to disturb you, but it's time to go," I whispered to the gentle beast, stroking her mane.

"May I ask where you're headed?" A voice sounded from behind.

Startled, I whirled to meet the too-friendly grin of Niall.

"I didn't expect anyone to be awake at this hour," I grumbled.

"Well, we couldn't rest soundly after the minor disturbance in the house." He winked.

We?

Tomas strolled leisurely into the barn, iron shackles in hand. Panic crushed my body like an avalanche, freezing my feet to the ground. Why did he have shackles?

Niall noticed my frightened expression and laughed deeply.

"Don't be alarmed, my lady!" He grinned as he said, "I mean to help you!"

"By imprisoning me?" I challenged.

"Oh, no, you misunderstand!" the man insisted.

Tomas had laid the shackles atop an anvil and with a smith's hammer he beat the chain between them. Bits of iron links crumbled away from the bracelets.

"You forget, Lady Celessa, I am a noble Mage!" Niall boasted. "I assume you mean to leave due to your unexpected outburst? You worry for the safety of your friends?"

I nodded slowly, still wary of the men.

"I mean to imbue these cuffs to help repress the affliction that plagues you. Normally, Mages use repression magic to help contain immortal or magic wielding prisoners, as it is easily imbued in iron such as this. My thought was that if we remove the binding, you may wear them like jewelry.

"Unfortunately, I did not have time to enlist a blacksmith to fashion something more appealing for you. When I heard rummaging in the kitchen, I surmised you were gathering supplies, so I retrieved Tomas and followed after you."

"Why should I trust you?"

"Yes, you have no true reason to believe I want to help you. I only shared my home with you, assured the safety of your friends, and fed you all."

"My lady, may I?" Tomas' voice turned my attention away from Niall.

The young man held out the cuffs to me, open and ready to be placed upon my wrists. This may be a viable solution to my problem, yet I found myself hesitating.

"How long does it last? This magic?" I asked Niall.

"As long as you like, my lady. Forgive me though, I am still unsure of the key's whereabouts. It's been quite some time since we have needed to shackle anyone," he teased.

The man was so friendly and light-hearted. Nauseatingly so, like he was forcing it. I wasn't sure if it was my paranoia influencing that thought, or was he truly trying too hard to earn my trust? Either way, the cuffs were no longer linked, so I wasn't going to be restrained.

Perhaps it was worth the risk, to spare others from this curse. My options were this or run away. Did I really want to leave them? The people who had put their lives on the line for me, the ones I cared for?

"Fine."

Reluctantly, I bared my wrists to Tomas, who clasped the cold iron around them.

"Wonderful!" Niall beamed.

"What now?"

The Mage took the bracelets into his hands and the metal began to glow as if they were placed in a furnace, turning bright orange. Watching in awe, I didn't notice they were warming like they were being heated as well, until my skin began to burn.

"Damn it!" I yelped, ripping my arms away.

"All done!" Niall clapped his hands together dramatically. "Test out my skills, my lady!"

"Don't you think maybe you should... I don't know, go somewhere else?" I suggested. "Like, further away from me?"

"I am fully confident in my abilities."

Scrunching my face at the man, I pushed the cursed power against my skin, bracing myself to attempt to pull it back from the people who lingered close by. I closed my eyes, willing it forward. It felt like I was being scalded beneath my flesh, my power thrashed internally, chafing against my bones and expanding painfully. My eyes opened to see the blood mist never left my body.

"It's... stuck."

"Excellent! A new beginning for you, sweet lady!" Niall embraced me tightly, stealing my breath. "Let us go tell your friends!"

Niall had sent Tomas to rouse my companions before further explaining his magic. As we walked along, the lord went on to tell me about his father's imminent return and the safest routes through Druantia Forest. He suggested we procure passage into Euros in Dawn's End rather than risking our presence in Ofror, a much larger and more dangerous city.

I half-listened, tuning out his voice to observe the cuffs that adorned my pale skin, gently pushing my power against them, testing their resistance.

Thibault sparred with Aklys in the courtyard, and it was the friendliest I'd ever seen the pair of men. It was the first time I'd witnessed Aklys wielding a sword, or any weapon for that matter. Their duel was a blur of black and copper hair, as if the fire of the sun battled the shadows of night. The men smiled, carefree, if only for a moment.

It was clear that the only animosity they possessed regarding each other had everything to do with me. I felt guilty. I wondered how they had been before I showed up, but I'd never asked. I knew they were familiar, that they were friendly with each other, but I didn't think about it any further.

Aloise and Maygen sat side by side on the bench where Thibault and I had talked the evening before. My heart warmed at the sight of them, they had become close while Aloise battled her illness. Maygen often busied herself helping Thibault care for the woman. She looked better today, some color had returned to her skin, the deep tones of her complexion no longer appeared hollow.

Honestly, I could watch them all like this forever. Joyful, playful, at ease. This was the leisure they deserved, not a life of misery on the run. Perhaps I should've left after all. Even with my curse suppressed, they would never be safe with me.

Aklys noticed me first as I approached with Niall and Tomas close behind. His gaze fixated on me, and his face fell into a mask of cool rage. Thibault hadn't caught on yet and swung his sword at the vampire, who caught the blade in his hand without so much as flinching. Maygen leapt to her feet at the sight of Aklys' blood dripping to the ground, holding the weapon in his grasp, still as a statue.

"Your hand! Why did you do that? Are you insane?" She shouted, shoving the vampire.

"What did you do to her?" Aklys snarled at Niall.

My companions all turned to look at me then, quickly noting the bulky iron cuffs clamped around my wrists. Embarrassed, I tucked my hands behind my back. This was meant to be a good thing, so why did they all look so appalled?

In a flash of supernatural speed, Aklys stood directly in front of me.

"Show me," he demanded.

I presented the shackles to him as if I were simply showing off jewelry.

"What the fuck is this?" He growled, grabbing Niall by the collar of his shirt.

Tomas reacted immediately, drawing the sword strapped to his side and baring it at the vampire.

"I wouldn't." Thibault threatened; he had moved to where we were standing, sizing up Tomas with the blade he'd been dueling with.

"Friends, please, nothing was done against Lady Celessa's will."

Niall grinned, raising his hands in submission.

"Aklys," I whispered, touching his arm gently.

He released the young lord and returned his focus to my wrists.

"Niall suppressed my powers," I spoke softly, unsure of how he might react. "I did it so that they wouldn't have to be afraid." Looking toward Maygen and Aloise, my heartbeat quickened as I continued, "So I don't have to be afraid."

Maygen's eyes met mine. She frowned.

Confusion rippled through me. I'd done this for her.

"I simply imbued the iron cuffs with a repression magic to keep the essence at bay!" the lord confirmed.

"Give me the key," Aklys demanded.

Niall *tsked* at the vampire, "I'm afraid I'll need to have one made." He shrugged nonchalantly.

"You allowed a Mage to place magic shackles on you without even having a key to undo this? Are you out of your mind?" Aklys' tone was condescending.

"Apparently," I grumbled, stepping away.

"Don't worry, we will take great care of her. Please, continue to enjoy the rest of your time here," the lord insisted.

Niall patted the vampire's shoulder as he passed him, following my steps.

"Celessa?" Maygen called, stopping me in my tracks.

I turned to face her, and my cheeks flushed with embarrassment.

"I'm not afraid of you, please take these off."

As she pleaded, she reached for the heating restraints. She flinched away after making contact, feeling the scalding metal reacting to my restricted magic.

"I am afraid. I am afraid *for* you, for Aloise, and for Thibault. This is the best option for now. I don't know of any other way to protect you from me."

I touched her face lightly and forced a smile before I continued on my way toward the edge of the property.

I needed to be alone.

Niall let me be after I ignored him for some time. It took a while, as that man cares to talk much more than I care to listen. His friendliness still made me uncomfortable and getting used to the idea of not having my gift to call upon blanketed my mind with wariness.

Have I made a mistake?

The only thing I'd said to Niall was that I needed a key. He promised to return with one if I would remain on the grounds and wait for him. Taking my time, I circled the estate property. I would have a good look at it all before we departed.

One last look at my home.

Closure, I reminded myself. Closing this chapter, and releasing this weight, would make my life easier. It was time to move forward.

I hoped I would no longer yearn for the evergreen trees, the salted northern air, or the stone pathways. There was hope that I would remember it with fondness one day when I found a new home.

Perhaps Lysenna's Keep would be all that Maygen had promised? It could be a safe haven, somewhere I could live out my days, somewhere that would bring me comfort and happiness.

Peace.

Laughable, that's what that was. I would never be able to live peacefully as long as Asuras roamed this world. There would be no rest as long as Teskarian Sentinels hunted me. There would be no contentment as long as I had to wonder about the identity of my bastard father.

I would never be able to repress my lust for vengeance, with the murderous intent solely reserved for the two men who had ruined my life. One gave me a cursed existence, and the other exacerbated it. There would be no happiness until they were gone from this world.

That was a thought that truly satisfied me. I would need my power for that. I only meant to keep it suppressed until Maygen was safely returned to Lysenna; I hoped they would accept Aloise and Thibault as well.

As for Aklys, I didn't expect the vampire would remain with us that long. He would return home, wherever that was, eventually. One of the first things he told me was that he did what he pleased when it suited him. This situation, being on the run, was hardly a suitable existence.

Reaching the largest tree on the property, an ancient oak, I let my mind quiet of its rage for a few moments. Lowering myself to the dirt, I pushed my fingers into the soil, digging between its deep delving roots.

This was a hiding spot, where I'd buried something at my mother's request.

"This is our secret, my Celessa. When you're all grown up, when you are ready to uncover all there is to know about the beauty that is you, you may have this. Until then, you must hide it, songbird. Hide it well."

Mother stroked my cheek gently and placed the small wooden box in my hands. I always listened to mother, for I only wanted her to be happy. I knew the best hiding spot, our favorite tree.

"I won't let you down, mother!"

"I know," she smiled warily.

My fingertips grazed something foreign - not a tree root, but a flat surface. A smile stretched my lips; it was still here. I found it.

Kneeling in a more comfortable position, I prepared myself to open the long-awaited mystery. It had endured over a hundred years, waiting for me. Prying the small latch open, I lifted the lid of the box.

Confusion and disappointment fell upon me, as I had expected something with a bit more grandeur, I suppose. Inside, my mother had left a ring and a piece of parchment.

The ring band was silver and decorated with a single gem: a white sapphire that shone like the coldest light in existence had been trapped inside. It was as pale as the moon, but with a vibrancy unlike anything I'd ever seen.

The parchment read, *Protect the key.*

Incredible! Thank you, mother, as if I hadn't dealt with enough cryptic nonsense recently. Discouraged, I slipped the contents of the box into the pocket of my tight-fitted pants.

The sound of crunching footsteps had me rising to my feet. Turning, I was surprised to see Tomas was approaching me when I had been expecting Niall. Summoning a smile, I attempted to stifle my mood and greet him politely.

"Tomas," I addressed him.

I was concerned with his paling expression, the life draining from his dark skin.

"What's wrong?"

"Niall sent Aklys into the city for supplies, and they came sooner than I thought they would."

He panted, making it clear that he had rushed to find me.

A hollow pit of despair yawned open inside my gut as I said, "Who?"

"The Sentinels. They're here for you, and you need to run."

Panic set in.

"Where are my friends?" I demanded.

"There is no time!" the man insisted. "Niall set you up. He rendered your powers useless for his gain, not to *help* you. They'll be expecting to take you into custody without struggle now, they have no reason to fear you! With Aklys indisposed, you're a sitting duck. I'm so sorry; I did not know he intended this; I would have warned you sooner if I had."

"Tomas, I pay you far too well to have you betray me."

The words came from Niall, who appeared from seemingly nowhere.

Some Mages were able to transport themselves short distances very quickly with apparition magic, but I hadn't expected the lord to be skilled with several magics. Usually, Mages focused on one specialty dictated by their noble family or by the courts. Allowing Mages to utilize many magics was considered too dangerous.

Tomas rounded, shielding me. The man drew his sword to his adversary and braced himself.

"Lady Celessa, let's not make this any more difficult than it needs to be."

Niall's smile was cold now, cruel and twisted.

He was exposing his true self, and my instincts had been right. The friendliness had been a facade.

I made yet another mistake.

"I'll go with you," I smiled.

"What?" Tomas shouted in dismay.

"Typically the pretty ones aren't so smart, truly I am impressed," the Mage teased.

"As soon as you give me the key you promised," I continued, reaching out my hand.

Niall threw back his head, releasing boisterous laughter.

"She's funny, as well!" He mused.

"I see," I said as I painted my face with a thoughtful expression, "you are afraid you're no match for me, so placing me at a disadvantage is the easiest route for you."

"Spare me, my dear. I have no pride left for you to play on. I'm simply following orders. I have no interest in going against that abhorrent power you possess. So, if you don't mind, they are waiting for you."

Tomas advanced toward the lord, lashing out with his blade.

"Celessa, please, run!" The man called out, "Your friends are just outside the main gate! Aklys is strong enough to remove your cuffs! Find him!"

Niall moved quickly with his magic, dodging each strike Tomas aimed for him. I was helpless in aiding the man, I knew there was nothing I could do.

An unearthly essence began to radiate from his body: black magic. Niall was corrupted. How had he hidden it from us? My thoughts flashed to Kilian's Mage, streaked with black, no humanity left within her. Niall's face transformed before me as his darkness enveloped

Tomas, a familiar black ink dripped from his parted lips. My protector's body contorted, a scream tearing from his chest.

I ran.

"Maygen!" I called, fully aware that I would attract the attention of everyone looking for me, but I didn't care.

I needed to know where she was, and I needed to know that she was safe. More than Thibault, more than Aloise, Maygen was my priority. She was the woman who risked herself to save me, the one who gave me back my life, she was my family. I had to find her.

Rounding the side of the building, my head swiveled frantically, searching for someone.

Anyone.

Pain shattered my focus, with bright white overtaking my vision. The ground welled up beneath me, my body jolting as it connected with the earth. Crying out, my limbs scrambled to find some bearing, desperately trying to regain composure.

"I'm a bit disappointed," a man's voice chimed through the thunder in my skull. "This is all the fight you have? You are so easily manipulated and have no strength without your curse, what a pity."

The voice belonged to Niall, the fragments of his face piecing together as I craned my head to look up at the man.

The metal cuffs on my wrists glowed brightly, searing my skin as if I'd lain my hands in a roaring fire. Thin fingers reached out to grab at my clothes, and Niall lifted me from the ground by the collar of my tunic, dangling my body in the air.

My mind raced to the altercation with the Wyndiga, a different sort of a monster than the one that held me now.

With little thought, I lashed out with a clenched fist and struck the man in the throat. He reeled, releasing me, and stumbled backwards. Niall sputtered and choked, gripping his neck. I aimed a kick at him, harder than I'd ever struck anything in my life, connecting with his groin. The pained scream was ear splitting.

Turning away from my assailant, I began running once more. The roaring in my head grew, and the metallic taste in my mouth was overbearing. Blood leaked from between my lips because he'd struck me in the face.

I was so tired of being hit in the fucking face.

Clanging of metal caught my attention, mixed with the horrified screams of a woman.

No.

Following the sound, I willed my body across the stone pathways. I begged for the cuffs to fall away from my wrists. My intention had been to protect my friends from myself, but I hadn't considered that I might need it to protect them from everyone else.

At last, I spotted Thibault locked in combat with a Sentinel. The enemy wore black and silver, heavily laden with protective armor, adorned with a crest of crossed swords and a spiked black crown.

Two men had restrained my other companions. Maygen was not one to be subdued easily, and the man who held her in his clutches must've realized as much, as she hung limply from his arms. He'd rendered her unconscious, blood smeared across her face. Meanwhile, Aloise was screaming, thrashing weakly against the grip of another Sentinel, who only grinned and sneered at her futile effort.

Thibault was losing the fight against the soldier.

"Thibault!" I screamed.

Every person in the courtyard turned to face the sound of my desperate cry. There were too many adversaries for us to face. We were outnumbered. Aside from the two men holding Aloise and Maygen, the man that battled Thibault, there were two more Sentinels nearby. At the sight of me, they began advancing.

Panic gripped me.

I was useless.

"Please!" I cried. "I'll turn myself over if you let them go, I beg you!" I said to no one in particular.

"Done," one of the men said.

The bastards restraining Maygen and Aloise threw their bodies roughly to the ground, while the man facing Thibault lashed out with his sword again. Thibault had been distracted with my submission and hadn't seen the blow that was aimed for his midsection. The sword slashed him in the abdomen, wrenching a pained howl from the man and a terrified scream from Aloise.

"No!" I screamed louder as I watched the man ready his weapon to deliver a fatal blow. Thibault faltered, falling to his knees.

Memories raced through my mind at the speed of light. Memories of a fiery haired boy taking my hand for the very first time, secrets shared and moments stolen, it was not enough time to build a life together. Fate separated first loves and Fate brought them together again, despite the relentless assault of time. Lust became heartbreak, and resentment became understanding. We were a man and a woman tested and tried, with a unique bond, who had finally settled into friendship.

If I did nothing, Thibault was going to die.

Screams were indiscernible now, with my entire being going numb, and I couldn't differentiate the sounds.

I couldn't fully register the two soldiers in front of me falling to the ground as the man behind them ripped their heads from their shoulders.

There was no awareness as my body moved toward the scene of my friend facing death. The world around me was muffled, but the ringing in my ears was loud. As my skin burned beneath my shackles, I willed myself free.

Power that swelled beneath the surface began cracking my skin, like the sun's rays breaking free of a blackened stormy sky. My bones felt like they were splintering; I felt my muscles shredding apart viciously.

This meager magic was never stronger than mine. It was never strong enough to hold me. With every ounce of strength I possessed, I pushed. The iron cuffs melted away, burning into the ground. My power absorbed essence, and this was simply a barrier that I needed to break.

I exploded.

A vision of angry blood red smoke like a plume from the eruption of a volcano enveloped the world around me. My friends stayed in my mind, and I decided my power would not touch them, for I was in control now. I had to be.

This dangerous extension of myself ended the lives around us, and the Sentinels screamed as I ripped them apart and disintegrated them into nothing. I relished it.

Save them, I begged myself internally. I begged whoever may be listening. I begged my gift that almost seemed to have a mind of its own.

I pulled back the deadly essence, praying I hadn't harmed those I care about. For a few moments, there was nothing but darkness, my body and my mind reeling from the shock of my outburst.

Flesh against flesh, the sensation of hands moving across my skin brought awareness back into my body. My vision was greeted by the face of Aklys, who wore a grave expression.

I had collapsed, frozen against the ground.

"Don't look," Aklys choked out, his eyes glazed with tears that threatened to fall at any moment.

Look at what? I wondered.

No, I must have hurt them. Maygen, Thibault, Aloise.

"No!" I choked, pulling my face from his hold.

The entire world fell apart around me as I surveyed the scene. The Sentinels lay dead, now piles of gore and nothing less than what they deserved. Maygen still lay unconscious on the ground, but she was safe, unscathed. Aloise wailed with the sound of heartbreak, earth shattering and gut-wrenching.

Thibault knelt on the ground, his head hanging limply and body crumpled into itself... so incredibly still, with the Sentinel's sword plunged deep into his chest.

Dead.

Chapter Twelve

Thoughts Of A Villain

F ood was repulsive, and sleep had become elusive. I existed purely in misery.

Three days had already passed since Thibault was murdered in front of every person left in this world that cared for him. Three long days had passed since the realization fully set in that his death was my fault.

It crushed me entirely.

Had my powers not been suppressed, or had I figured out how to break the barrier just a few moments sooner, he might be alive right now. If it weren't for my stupidity, he would be breathing, and we would be leaving this damned city: a place I never wanted to see again.

It's been three days since numbness washed over me so fully that I truly no longer cared if I lived or died. Right now, the only thing I could focus on was satisfying my hunger for vengeance.

Thibault was all that I'd had left from my first life; he was the only living and breathing reminder of who I once was. He was my friend. More than that, I loved him.

Now, I had no pieces, no shreds left of Lady Celessa Umbraeon for which the person I was becoming could cling.

Who would I become without the woman I was supposed to be?

"I want him dead."

Aklys furrowed his brows at my words. He had settled into a constant state of looking upon me with concern or pity since the devastating loss.

I didn't cry when Thibault died. I couldn't. I didn't deserve to mourn him when I'd had the power to change his Fate.

Incompetent. Pathetic. Weak.

The voice in my head grew ever louder. It mocked and tormented me. It was the same voice that encouraged me to be a monster, and it was right: I should've been.

I should be.

The magic beneath my skin cried out at my internal debate, for it wanted to be used. Perhaps if I truly embraced it, and no longer considered it a curse but rather an advantage, I could overcome every obstacle placed in my way. Every enemy and every threat, I had the power to destroy it all.

"I haven't extracted a sufficient amount of information from him," Aklys murmured.

Rage flared, expanding in my lungs and quickening my heartbeat.

"What fucking information, Aklys? What could he possibly have to offer you? You should've let me kill him days ago!" I shouted.

The vampire flinched. This man had grown accustomed to my vast array of moods. He'd seen me intrigued, desperate, hurt, amused, irritated, and even deep within the throes of passion.

My rage, though, was something new to him.

I've never had a lid on my emotions, not really. I could hide them for a short time if I wanted, to distract myself and pretend I felt otherwise. Everything has changed now, and pretending does nothing but cause me more suffering and more grief. Pretending doesn't erase Thibault's death.

"He may know something about Asuras; where he is, or how many people are looking for you. I just want to keep you safe."

Aklys' hand twitched, as he'd been refraining from touching me, but I could see how much he struggled.

"It makes no difference. Asuras will never stop, and the Sentinels will never stop as long as I remain in Teskaria. I will *never* be safe," I scoffed. "You know that to be true, we all do. There is not a single place in the Three Kingdoms where I will be out of his reach. Someone will *always* be looking for me."

The vampire went silent, and not even his breathing was loud enough to hear as he simply watched me.

"What?" I demanded.

"There's nowhere that I can take you where you will be safe – you're right."

Whatever self-control he'd been exercising dissipated as he pulled me into his arms.

"But I can kill every single person in this world who seeks to harm you."

I choked on the weight of his sentiment, if just for a moment.

"No," I growled.

His shoulders dropped slightly at my rejection.

"*I* will kill them."

With my harsh statement, I pulled away from his embrace and turned to leave the room. My footsteps were heavy, echoing through the empty halls of the keep as I made my way down the levels. There was only one holding cell in this keep. There was only one prisoner in that cell.

His name is Niall Undergrove.

I would be his executioner.

"Beautiful, powerful Celessa: so smart, so bold, so dangerous."

Niall chuckled from his place on the floor.

"The fabled cursed lady has come for me at long last."

He sounded mad, but that did not surprise me. Dark magic eats away at one's mind, erasing their humanity. Had Thibault lived, perhaps I would've found myself merciful enough to remove this affliction for him.

Silently, I watched him through the imbued iron bars. Cells such as this existed in most keeps of old, meant to hold all manner of magic or affliction, inescapable with any use of power.

"How are your friends, lady? All my friends are dead."

The Mage crooned, rotating his head to meet my cool stare as he said, "Are they sad? Do they mourn?"

He smiled, and the black inky substance that ran through his veins had coated his teeth, evidence of the extent of corruption.

"Do you mourn, my lady?"

Niall began to stand, but faltered, with his knees buckling and stumbling into the damp stone wall.

"Why corrupt yourself with black magic?"

It was a reasonable inquiry on my part, as so few survived corruption. Those that did survive became powerful beyond measure; there were only three in the recorded history of the kingdoms. Asuras was one of them.

Niall coughed, sending sickly fluid splattering against the floor.

"Even if I didn't desire to claim your death as my own, you'll be dead soon anyway. What could you possibly have stood to gain from this?" I asked.

The man snarled at me, appearing offended that I was asking exactly the right questions. They were questions with answers that plagued him. No Mage that was sound of mind made the decision to attempt corruption unless they were forced. Memories of Neina played in my mind, who had been forced by Kilian.

"Sometimes we are faced with no other choice: death or redemption. Though, it appears redemption carries a steep cost," he wheezed.

"You made the wrong choice. Now, instead of just you dying, your whole family will die." I grinned, meanwhile, Niall's face twisted into a picture of agony and despair.

Good.

"I'm responsible for the death of the Fae-man, not my family."

"How many are there? I know of your father. Does your mother live? Any siblings?"

He fell into silence.

"So many portraits in these halls, I'll have to discern who still lives with the records your father surely keeps tucked away in his office."

I hummed thoughtfully, tapping a finger against my cheek.

Niall squirmed under my gaze.

"Good news, though, you'll die last!" I smiled cheerfully at the Mage, clasping my hands together as I said, "We can commiserate over how it feels to see a sword plunged through the chest of someone you love. My sincerest thanks for your hospitality and generosity, my lord."

My feet carried me away from the cell, listening contentedly to the desperate wailing that began to fade away as my body drifted up the stairs. I could hear pleas for the lives of his family, bargains for information in exchange for their safety. I was not interested in making deals.

I was only interested in revenge.

I'd requested help cleaning up the mess near the gate, the piles of what remained of Sentinel trash still littered the courtyard. I'd decided to remove the evidence of what had transpired here. I wanted the noble family to arrive unsuspecting.

Aloise wasn't willing to leave her room, not that I expected anything else. She probably blamed me as much as I blamed myself for Thibault's murder. Maygen tended to the woman and respectfully declined aiding me.

I may be imagining things, but it seemed as though the aura around her had shifted, and my friend really had begun to look at me differently, exactly as I feared she would.

Aklys had wordlessly helped to remove the debris, not sparing me a single glance. It was good that he was inching closer toward indifference. The less he cared, the more I'd be able to focus on the tasks at hand.

Vampires should be ruthless, cunning, and driven by murderous intent or bloodlust. How was Aklys so different from every story I'd been told? Every legend, all the history seemed to be wrong. If he wasn't so compassionate, I could rely on him to help me. How could he be so quick to decapitate soldiers, but disagree with my plan to execute Niall?

Right now, I craved a monster.

Tell him what you want, that strange sentience insisted, intruding on my thoughts.

I wondered if the voice was the consciousness of my curse, or if it was something else entirely. There had been too many instances where the blood mist had entirely disregarded my will, acting out on its own. Was it possible that it was something else?

Truly, I was a product of chaos, as there was no other explanation for my abilities. Was this voice that of the divinity that flowed through my veins? Was it a link to the bastard that created me? Or was the voice just my own? Perhaps it was the truth of who I really was, who I would become.

You know how to get what you want, the voice's claws scraped enticingly over my fragile mind.

"Aklys?"

I rapped my knuckles against the wooden door concealing the vampire's new accommodations, the room he'd chosen after I destroyed mine.

I'd waited until night had blanketed the world, and Aloise's sobs paired with the comfort of Maygen's voice had faded away into silence.

Aklys had been missing the entire duration of the evening. No one joined me in the dining hall, not that any of us were able to eat anyway.

Silence invites madness, and loneliness embraces it with open arms. My thoughts were left to fester unchecked, with no voice of reason to sway my mind, rotting away all sense and reason.

Pressing my ear to the door, I listened. Faint rustling within the room was all that could be heard, muffled by the barrier. Lifting the handle, I found it unlocked and forced my way inside, quickly latching it behind me.

The sight before me was startling only because it was unexpected. Aklys was covered in blood, eyes dark and fangs bared. The vampire charged me, pinning my body against the door.

I was so small and insignificant compared to this beast of a man.

"What is wrong with you?" I gasped beneath the crushing force.

Awareness crept into his features.

"I fed," he said as he swallowed roughly.

I wonder how long it's been since he last drank blood, for I didn't know how often he needed it. I did know that there had been no indication of him sating his thirst since he had last bitten me in the forest, and that was over a week ago.

"On who?"

"The fucking horse," he growled.

What kind of vampire feeds on a horse?

"How often do you need blood?"

"More often than I get it."

Aklys pushed away from me, stalking toward the bed.

The horse blood had smeared all over my tunic, and the smell was nauseating. How could any creature stomach something like this? I followed behind the vampire, sitting carefully while he continued to pace around the room. Long fingers weaved between locks of dark hair, and he pulled against his head in frustration.

I watched him quietly.

"I didn't kill it, if that's what you're wondering."

"Actually, I'm wondering why you decided on horse blood for a meal?"

"Better alternative than the locals, whom I would absolutely kill without intending to," he groaned.

He was suffering.

"Do you lose control when you don't feed often?" I asked.

"I lose control when I can't have what I want."

Aklys was facing me now, fists clenched at his sides.

I knew what he wanted.

Me.

"Feed on me, then?" I shrugged as nonchalantly as I could manage, "Though, I have terms."

You know how to get what you want, the voice purred.

Aklys only grumbled in response.

"You can have my blood, Aklys," I whispered, standing, "but I need a vampire. If I'm feeding one, I need it to act like one."

Slowly, I slipped my tunic over my head, allowing the blood-stained garment to fall to the floor. My skin tightened as cool air caressed my exposed chest.

"The Undergroves will die. Anyone who gets in my way will die."

Approaching the vampire, I slipped my fingers around his hand, guiding it to the small of my back.

"Asuras will die."

Pressing my body against his filled me with warmth, and this time I welcomed the distraction from the rage and pain I fought against, the pain I didn't want to feel.

"You won't stop me."

The vampire's breathing was strained as my hands slid up the length of his torso, across his chest and around his neck. Coaxing him down with a gentle pull, his mouth met the tender flesh of my neck, heat now coursing through my body as furiously as wildfire spreads during a drought.

"Promise me that I'll have a vampire," I insisted, squeezing him gently.

Aklys went rigid, a low growl rumbling inside his chest.

"I could never refuse you, milady," he sighed.

The sharp fangs pierced my delicate skin, eliciting a sound somewhere between a cry and a moan. My fingertips pressed into his shoulders as I held him, savoring each pull of blood that he drained from my body. Was it supposed to feel good?

Aklys' arms encircled me, and I squirmed against him, desperate to feel more of his flesh against my own.

A fine line existed between pleasure and pain. In an existence riddled with agony, I deserved a few moments of relief. Release would keep me sane.

I needed something to save me from the torment that will come with Thibault's burial. Come morning, he would be laid to rest, and I would become absolute on my path of destruction.

Aklys pulled away suddenly, dropping my limp body against the mattress of the bed.

I stared up at him, taking in the sight of my blood painting his lips.

"Done with me already?"

"Never," he gasped.

Smiling, "I'm waiting," I teased.

To my dismay, he frowned.

"While I wish you wanted me for all the reasons I want you, I'm not going to stop you. I'll be the monster you desire, but I can't just be a convenient distraction from your pain. I'll feed on you when you allow it, but I can sense what else you want, and I don't think you're of sound enough mind to make that decision right now."

The last thing he expected and the last thing that I'd meant to do was laugh, but I couldn't stop the outburst. I laughed at him, at myself.

Rising from the bed, my jaw clenched to the point of pain; irritation apparent on my face.

"Goodnight, Aklys."

Niall had beaten himself bloody in a last-ditch effort to take his own life during the night. It was a pathetic attempt, considering he still breathed. He'd managed to break off a large chunk of stone from the cell wall and had used it to bludgeon his face and neck until consciousness was lost, but he lived.

I smirked over his limp body, listening to his raspy breathing.

You do not get to escape this, your death belongs to me, I have claimed it.

The rusted metal pail that dangled from my hand was filled with ice cold water. I could offer him hydration, assure that he would be fully aware as he met his death. He deserved to be tormented.

Releasing the bucket, the tin canister bounced against him, water poured over the filthy body at my feet. Niall writhed and gasped at the shock of the impact; his eyes too swollen to see me as he swiveled around to confront his assailant.

The blackened veins seemed even darker today, the poison within him making a final assault upon its host. It reminded me of a parasite, feeding until there was nothing left but a lifeless shell. It was an effective way to ensure someone's death, though it would be much more satisfying to watch my power consume him entirely as he begs for his life. That was what I wanted, and I couldn't wait much longer.

"Which one are you?" he croaked angrily.

My fingers toyed with the locks of his hair. He'd moved into a kneeling position, swaying weakly as he tried to remain upright.

"I'm tempted to have Aklys heal you with his blood, so that I can enjoy spectating another form of torment before I kill you. It would be more entertaining if you were fully healed and aware; you might last longer during your final moments."

"My lady, you honor me with your presence," the man spat, strands of black fluid hung from his lips. "I wonder how you would fair against black magic?"

Would that be his final stand? Did he plan to use corrupted magic against me when we removed him from the holding cell? What a joke!

Laughter erupted from my chest.

"I can do so many things, Niall. It keeps evolving, this curse, growing stronger and unveiling new potency each time I summon it. I have faced your affliction before, and unfortunately for you, I absorb black magic."

My fingers tightened in Niall's hair as I said, "I neutralize it."

Pulling against the filthy locks, I wrenched his head back so that his face was angled toward the ceiling.

"Your power compared to mine..." Grabbing his face with my free hand, I sunk my fingertips into the swollen bruises around his face and whispered, "...is fucking *nothing.*"

Niall screamed and flailed against my hold.

I did not relent.

Something had awakened within me, uncovered by the most recent of my traumas. I'd learned many manners of torture during my sleep, faced down terrible atrocities, and suffered greatly because of it. I listened to the voice in my head that was birthed by violence.

I had begun allowing my curse to consume me, to change me. The more I embraced it, the stronger I felt. So much so, my physical endurance had begun to transform, growing. We were evolving together.

I held the injured lord firmly in my grasp with little effort. Before I'd endured hell, I would never have possessed the strength or tenacity to do anything like this, even if he was in a compromised state.

"What are you doing?" A small voice from outside the cell stole my attention.

Aloise? Why was she here? She shouldn't be anywhere near this wretch.

"Having a conversation with Lord Undergrove," I responded.

Forcefully, I sent the man tumbling to the ground and turned to step out of the bloody cell.

The frail, sickly woman gazed at the battered body for a few moments before facing me fully. Her deep brown eyes were lifeless, and anyone could see that she had given up. She was making no attempt to hide it. The thin skin below her dark orbs was inflamed, nearly bruised from the violent sobbing that she couldn't fight these past few days. Her already compromised state had deteriorated further. She refused food or drink, and she barely slept. When she did manage to rest, it did not take long before the petrified screams of her nightmares burst through unconsciousness to pierce the air of reality, pulling her from slumber.

I hated to imagine she likely dreamt of Thibault's murder. Reliving it over and over again.

She wasn't much smaller than I was, but she felt so incredibly tenuous compared to me now. Aloise reached out a delicate hand, and I flinched.

"Celessa..." she started, "You don't have to do this."

Her fingers rested gently against my arm.

"He's the reason Thibault is dead; he brought them here."

Aloise closed her eyes tightly, battling against tears. I wished I hadn't said those words so carelessly to her. We both loved Thibault deeply, but she had been his, and he had been hers. They had something special, and it was ripped away from her, right before her eyes. She watched the man she chose to love die.

"I-I'm sorry, I didn't m-mean..."

My resolve was faltering, sorrow reaching its snaking tentacles through cracks in the anger.

She shook her head, silently requesting I stop.

"He is responsible, yes, but what good will this do? We can't bring him back, even if you kill this man or the others for which you have plans,"

How did she know about that?

"It will only bring you greater suffering. You are powerful, but I don't believe that your power makes you a monster."

Those words struck my heart like a blade, and I couldn't find it in me to argue with her.

"How fucking precious," Niall laughed, shattering my stupor and reigniting my burning rage. "And stupid. She is evil, a *monster*; every Amalgam born is nothing less."

Aloise squeezed my arm tighter in an attempt to redirect my attention from Niall's comments.

"How do you know what I am?"

The lord sighed deeply, "They all know, now. They're all going to try to earn his favor by handing over your head."

I'd allowed Aloise to coax me out of the lowest level, to pull me away from Niall. A new irritation had been burned into my mind in those moments below, and only one person had known about my plan to murder the Undergroves: Aklys. That meant he'd told Aloise and probably Maygen as well.

My lip curled up in anger, and I meant to confront the vampire the moment I saw him.

Maygen's presence stopped me in my tracks.

"Don't try to talk me out of it," I snapped.

"I won't let you. We don't know if his family had anything to do with this. I agree that Niall should die, but you are not going to just slaughter anyone you want to make yourself feel better! The woman I rescued was a beacon of hope, not a damn tyrant! You're supposed to make this world better, erase evil, not become it."

The woman whom I'd grown to care so deeply for put her hands on my body, and she pushed me. I stumbled, taken by surprise.

"If you go through with this, I will never forgive you," she snapped, bringing us face to face.

Maygen squared up against me with her breath trapped in her lungs, waiting for me to say something.

"If I become what they think I am, then they'll have a real reason to fear me. You'd be safer that way."

She wailed in frustration, raising her arms to push me again. I let her.

"Do not pretend you are doing this for anyone but yourself," she hissed. "I meant what I said. I won't forgive you!"

Watching her walk away, I braced myself to react emotionally.

I felt nothing.

"Milady."

The deep, sultry voice of the vampire echoed from somewhere in the keep, from somewhere behind me.

I hadn't heard him creep up on the confrontation, a quarrel ignited by his ineptitude where keeping his mouth shut was concerned.

"Why did you tell them?" I asked without turning.

"I thought they may change your mind," Aklys mumbled.

"We made a deal," I reminded him. "Vampires aren't supposed to care for the feelings of others. I said I wanted a true vampire, and I meant it."

"As you wish," he growled, heavy steps retreating.

Inhale, exhale. A conflict was rising in me. Do I prioritize their safety or their feelings?

What consequences will follow the path I choose?

We weren't ready to bury Thibault, but if we waited any longer, then his body would be compromised past the point of preservation; becoming foul and rotten.

Aklys had managed to bring in two healers from the city: one to quell Aloise's sickness and the other for our fallen friend, to suppress the bodily changes that take place after death. We needed more time, but it had run out. The vampire spent the earliest hours of the morning digging a final resting place at the border of the estate property, and had carried our friend from the keep to be returned to the earth.

The Undergrove family still had not shown themselves. It had been six days since we'd arrived in Briobar, and Niall had led us to believe his lord father would return the day following our arrival.

Where were they?

Many grotesque fantasies had formed in my mind as I waited to deliver my wrath upon them. I wanted them to see the body of the man they'd condemned to death. I had planned to force them to look upon his lifeless face, skin so incredibly pale and hollow.

He was slightly discolored now, looking less and less like the man who had defended us. The man who risked everything for us, who paid for our safety with his life.

The last of my first life would be laid to rest with him today. What was left of who I was would join him in the ground. Here, in the place where we had once thrived, he would be buried.

An invisible hand squeezed my heart, watching helplessly as Aklys lowered Thibault into the freshly dug grave.

"Thank you for your sacrifice, Thibault," Aklys whispered as he released him, the weight of his body softly thudding against the dirt. "I pray you see the stars, my friend."

Aloise sobbed softly as Maygen held her. I could feel her eyes on me, and I could sense her waiting for me to break, to allow myself to feel the true weight of his loss. She hoped for my humanity to bring me back to who she needed me to be.

All I could think about was Niall's life slipping away as payment for what he'd done. A life for a life would balance the order of things. Thibault could rest knowing I'd avenged him.

Traditionally in Teskaria, the family members of the deceased would take a handful of earth to be spread across the body during the burial and whisper their wishes for their loved one's afterlife upon it. We had been born here, raised here. Even though this country and those who dwelled within had turned their backs to us, this was our home. I was able to bury him where we grew up.

Taking a fistful of soil, I approached the grave.

I faltered, tripping over my own feet as my vision blurred. For a moment, it seemed as though he was looking back up at me with evergreen eyes. A fleeting illusion conjured by a traumatized mind.

"I wish for you to find peace. I wish for you to rest knowing you will not be forgotten. I wish for you to always guide us." My voice cracked as I said, "Until we meet again."

The dirt slid between my fingers, dusting the still body.

My mind wandered elsewhere as Aloise and Maygen whispered their goodbyes. There was nothing that plagued me in this moment. There was no anger, no sadness. I didn't daydream of my revenge, nor did I wonder about what comes next. I simply lingered there for a while, existing.

Numb.

Looking down at Niall on the cell floor, a far-off feeling of pity stirred at the sight of the broken man. How were these sensitive emotions shouldering their way through the flood of rage and resentment? I allowed those feelings to consume me, there shouldn't be room for anything else.

Despite my hatred, I was finding it difficult to become the monster I desired to be. Deep down, I don't think I truly *wanted* to be evil, vicious, or malicious. Try as I may, I couldn't convince myself that I could be someone worthy of fear.

I had allowed memories to seep in: good ones, precious ones. Memories that made me ponder who I wanted to be, versus who I had been expected to be. Memories of who I was and the question of who I could become, gave me the potential to live a decent life, if I was willing to try.

The facade needed to remain strong for now. At the very least, if I could appear as a villain, then it would keep my friends safe. If people were afraid of me, then I could protect them.

I did hate Niall, and he deserved to die.

So, I would start by killing him.

"Aklys informed me that your family's cavalcade has entered the city. They should be here soon," I grinned.

With a rag, I wiped away the blood that had crusted around his eyes. The swelling was still severe, but movement behind the barely opened slits revealed that he could see me.

Mustering a vicious grin, I knelt before the restrained man.

"I'm feeling generous."

"Don't leave me waiting on bated breath, Lady Celessa. What do you have to offer?" the man ground out.

"Would you prefer your death be presented to your family first? Or would you rather watch them die?"

Niall thrashed wildly against his bindings. "Evil bitch," he hissed.

Scoffing, I said, "You seem to forget how demure I was before you tried to collect a bounty on my head and summoned the Sentinels, who murdered the man I love."

"The Fae-man was your desire? Tell me why I assumed it was the vampire? How sad for you! I, too, know how it feels to be a victim of unrequited love."

The action was pure reflex, and I hadn't even a thought to stop myself as I struck the man in the face, the sound of the slap reverberated through the space. Niall groaned, as he spat blood mixed with the corrupted black fluid from his mouth and onto the floor.

"You know nothing, so keep your poisonous mouth shut," I commanded.

"Have you wondered why the vampire acts so timidly towards you? It's so terribly out of character for his kind. That bloodlust does a number on one's humanity, you see. I wonder what he wants from you?"

"Shut up."

"It makes sense, I suppose. He's immune to you. How incredible it would be to possess a weapon that you need never fear." Niall hummed thoughtfully.

"I'm not sure what you hope to accomplish with this nonsense, but you will be disappointed."

The reality was that I had already considered this. It troubled me often. He must've sensed my discomfort, chuckling quietly.

"Perhaps another offer of information may prolong my lifespan?" Niall suggested, "I'm dead anyways, my lady." He wiped inky strands from his lips with cuffed hands before continuing, "At least you could gain something more than petty revenge, if you're smart."

Squeezing my eyes shut, I turned my face away.

Kill him, the voice coaxed - but something told me I needed to hear what he had to say, even if it wasn't the truth.

"Fine," I whispered, lowering myself to the ground a short distance away from Niall. "Speak."

The lord smiled, and I noticed amidst the blackness painting the inside of his mouth that several teeth had broken. They hadn't looked like that before I hit him. A shiver ran down my spine at the realization.

"Do you wish to learn more about yourself," he paused, body shifting against the chains, "or those in your company?"

Based on the tone of voice, I knew which he'd prefer to divulge.

"Tell me about vampires."

Chapter Thirteen

What Could Be Worse

Aloise's body shook as she heaved the contents of her stomach into the large bowl on the ground. I held her tightly, cursing the useless healers that had done nothing to cure what ailed her.

They'd been too afraid to even look at her much, forced to come to her aid by a vampire. Caring for the sickly woman had been enough of a distraction from the impending execution that I was able to mull through some of the information that Niall had given me — most of said information was useless in itself, but that was what he wanted.

He wanted to tell me things that would make my mind wander helplessly, imagining every worst-case scenario and drawing my own unfortunate conclusions.

Loose strands of hair fell toward her face, my clumsy fingers nearly jabbed her in the eye as I fumbled trying to clear them away.

"Maygen is much better at this than you are," she wheezed.

I couldn't help but smirk.

"This is my first time playing caregiver, as I usually find myself in a position where I'm the one who needs to be tended to."

Aloise scoffed weakly, "One more thing we have in common, I suppose."

Trembling, she attempted to lift her body into an upright position. I lent her my strength as she continued trying, with me now bearing her weight. It was strange holding her like this, supporting her.

It wasn't more than a few weeks ago that I'd hated her for Thibault's decisions. The last time I'd really touched her was in

Kilian's cell in that dim dungeon, when I unwittingly sucked the black magic out of her body and saved her life.

"Aklys told us you spent a significant amount of time with the lord."

She sighed, reclining onto the tufted bench where we sat.

"Yes, until he interrupted us half way through what felt like a nonsensical history lesson."

"What did he say to you?"

Her deep brown eyes were still hollow, the only emotion residing within them was a deep and impenetrable sadness. It was the kind of anguish that touched every fiber of your being and settled into the marrow of your bones, flowing through your veins as if it were the very blood your heart worked so hard to circulate. It consumes you.

"He tried to feed me vampire lore and tales about the Gods."

I shrugged, unwilling to divulge everything until I'd had time to decipher fact from falsehood.

"Is he trying to turn you against Aklys?" Her voice grew more concerned as she said, "I think he's a good man, Celessa, especially for a vampire. I may be biased because he's the only vampire I've ever met, but as far as men go, I have met plenty of those."

The internal groan my mind unleashed was so loud, I feared she may actually hear my thoughts.

"I think that despite every other ill intention thus far, he was trying to make me more aware of who I kept in my company."

I paused for a moment, carefully choosing my next words.

"I'm too trusting; with a slight show of goodwill, I blindly follow along. I just did it with him, so he knows it to be true firsthand. I did it with Aklys in Kilian's keep, and he betrayed me."

Deep breath.

"I did it with Thibault, thinking he would still want to be with me. I did it with Asuras, thinking he actually wanted to show me the world and make me happy."

My jaw clenched.

She remained still for several heartbeats, the silence quickly becoming deafening. I squirmed, awaiting her response.

"Honestly, I understand," she said at last. "We are at the mercy of men, hoping that they'll have our best interest at heart if we lend them our trust."

Aloise was right. We were unusually vulnerable to the whims of men: both of us, it seemed.

"Perhaps women are easier?" I suggested lightheartedly.

The chuckle that left her made my chest warm. Despite all she had endured – being tortured, nearly dying, leaving her home for good, her sickness, the death of her lover... she found it in herself to laugh.

If she could find a way, then I think I could too.

"I think we may be just as difficult," she said and offered a smile.

The screams of a man doomed to die rang through the halls, the sounds scared and desperate. He begged and raged.

My fingers itched in anticipation. My power slid across my bones, dancing beneath my flesh, as if in answer to his cries. It wanted to end him as much as I did.

The newfound attunement to my curse gave me a sense of comfort and control. Perhaps Niall had done me a favor, because my gift and I could coexist now that I had decided to embrace it. We were becoming one.

Patience was wearing thin as I paced around the property, eagerly awaiting the appearance of Niall's family. Aklys had spotted them in the city, but they had yet to arrive at the estate.

Worry that they were aware of our presence weighed heavily in the air. If they knew about us, or even suspected, it would make for a more dangerous situation. Surely Aklys wouldn't let us remain here if that was the case.

I may not trust him fully but, at the very least, he wouldn't put *himself* at risk like that. Moreover, I believe he genuinely cares for us and wouldn't knowingly allow us to face another threat. We wouldn't be in danger again so soon.

Growing tired of the suspense, I'd requested that the vampire bring our prisoner to the grounds. The bench I'd rested on when we first arrived here was gone. I destroyed it in a fit of rage, leaving the bare ground beneath exposed to the world once more. We then installed a post similar to the one my father had ordered Thibault whipped upon.

It was a fitting place for Niall to die, I thought to myself, *overlapping a horrific memory with one of justice and revenge.*

"No audience?" Niall hissed, struggling against Aklys' hold as the vampire secured his bindings to the post.

"Shouldn't be long now. Hopefully, they don't miss the show. They are the main event, after all. You already had your time in the spotlight, didn't you? What a shame that you blew it!" I teased him, flipping my hair with my hand in a dramatic fashion.

"After all you've learned, you're still keeping the blood sucker around?" The lord gritted his broken teeth in a pitiful looking sneer, "Vampires will be your demise, Lady Celessa, they're the only ones you can't kill."

My eyes flashed to Aklys, who appeared entirely unbothered and frankly bored with the situation. That was new. I'd seen him feign disinterest many times, always knowing it wasn't genuine. Now though, he truly looked as though he had wished this to end many times over.

At the very least, I had resolved to ask him about his heritage, his family, and his curse the moment we had time alone to speak freely.

I couldn't be involved with the war lords of the early kingdoms; I'd dealt with my fair share of tyrants already and expected there were more to come. I didn't want to subject myself to any additional distress.

Niall had teased me with speak of the rogue territory, Greilor. The land was rumored to be barren and teeming with those cast out of the Three Kingdoms, where the vampires and all of their loyal subjects had been exiled after the war.

If Aklys was one of those vampires, how was he in the kingdoms now?

The mountain range along the coast of the country, in lore, was teeming with monsters and unpassable once you'd entered the country. Once you were in, you never left. It was essentially a geographical prison.

Maybe now he seemed indifferent because he was trying to maintain the illusion? The lie? What if there was truth to Niall's claims and Aklys had been seducing me into becoming a weapon to retake the kingdoms? My brain cried out in fear, but my heart refused to accept the accusations.

"Milady?" Aklys touched my arm gently and without realizing, I flinched away from him.

The beaten lord grinned viciously. "The seeds have been sown, *skamelar*."

Aklys stiffened at the insult. I'd only read the slur in books and never heard it spoken out loud. A derogatory term from the old dialects, the profanity was used against beings of mixed blood and against vampires. It meant parasite, abomination, scum. The vampire glanced at me, and I gestured with my hands to the man before us, a silent offer.

He backhanded Niall in the mouth, the violent maneuver happened almost too quickly to register.

It stirred something in me, something wicked. Seeing him become aggressive with the traitorous pig was almost... arousing. Heat flooded my cheeks; to have such thoughts in this moment was absolutely despicable and embarrassing.

Aklys turned to look at me, eyes darkening as he breathed in the air that now felt as if it was shifting with tension. I knew that he was aware of my momentary lapse in reason, and he could sense my body's reaction to him.

Avoiding his cool stare, I stepped toward Niall's kneeling figure.

"Lord Undergrove, it's time you met your demise." I bowed dramatically as I introduced, "My curse."

The color drained from his face as a sinful smile revealed my bared teeth. Blood red magic trickled down my fingers, kissing my skin like the fog that lingers against the ground on a damp, dreary morning.

Gentle and loving against my body, my curse was only kind for me. Everyone else was a perceived enemy. Niall was an enemy.

It throbbed as it crept across the ground, inching closer to the subdued man.

Panic twisted his features. "No, I'll do anything. Slit my throat, or break my neck!"

"I can't personally attest to how it feels to have the very essence of your being shredded apart, to be disintegrated into nothing other than the bare foundations of the body, but I imagine it is excruciating."

I hummed happily as I willed my power to move slowly and torturously, taunting him. "It usually ends so quickly. Shall we see what happens when I take my time?"

Niall's swollen eyes widened further than I thought possible. This kind of fear was exclusive to that of meek prey finding itself in the clutches of a vicious predator.

Satisfaction heated my core. The memory of dismembering Kilian surfaced, as it had been my first true act of intentional wrath. I could still hear his screams.

A wispy tendril brushed against Niall's leg, and I concentrated the energy there and began pushing it slowly into his flesh. The man wailed, and my eyes fluttered shut in response to the sound.

I could see it clearly in my mind, I could feel it even, the sensation of assaulting his body. An extension of myself was crawling beneath his skin, ripping muscle and tendons as it worked its way around the bones of the squirming man. Subconsciously speaking to my curse, the command to break him was met with reverberations of what felt like pleasure.

My power loved being used, for it desired to destroy. It wanted me to feel the same euphoria. Together, we splintered his femur.

A gut-wrenching scream opened my eyes.

The red mist had pooled out onto the ground. Crimson waves were lapping against my feet and billowing like smoke, blackening the ground and encircling the lord. Amusingly enough, it reminded me of a cat ready to pounce on a mouse as it swirled and crashed around him.

Niall's face was purplish in color, wet with sweat and tears.

"Before you die, give me what you possess."

The request left my own lips, but it felt like it had come from someone else, someone who knew something I didn't. I didn't know why I craved this tainted power.

Draining the black magic out of his body, the familiar burning sensation traveled up my arms and ignited inside my ribs. It was painful, but the last time I did this, it felt like it changed and strengthened my magic.

I needed strength now, so I would take his. The darkened veins receded from his arms and neck, and the color returned to his skin, brightening his eyes. Two things pleased me about removing the affliction: I gained power from absorbing the dark gifts, and he regained his humanity.

With his mind intact, he was becoming fully aware of everything he had endured and inflicted. He would feel it all: every emotion, every regret, and every ounce of pain.

"Forgive me," he begged.

"I would. If only it were possible to trade your life for the one that was lost."

It was time for Lord Undergrove to meet his end. My power advanced, enveloping his quaking figure.

Suddenly there was nothing: no sound, no visuals.

For some reason, I had returned to the darkness.

A light assaulted my vision, one that wasn't quite right, and the world around me seemed almost unreal.

My fingers threaded between blades of grass. I was lying on the ground. Faint shouting disturbed the ringing in my ears.

The reality of what was happening shocked me into awareness. I'd been attacked. Twisting, my body stacked itself upright to face my newest adversary.

This never fucking ended.

The face that stared back at me shocked me so thoroughly, I found myself unable to move. A man towered over my small frame. Tall and pale, with shoulder length hair as black as the night and blue eyes as pale as a moonlit ocean tide.

Blinking, the illusion was disrupted. The stranger had appeared for a moment as my greatest fear, Asuras, but this was not the dark Mage.

Whoever this was, I'd never met before, but he smiled at me.

The smile was adorned with fangs.

A vampire.

"What the fuck?" I shouted.

My eyes searched frantically for Aklys, but what I saw instead was an older man hauling away the half-ruined body of Niall Undergrove. The lord still breathed, for I hadn't had a chance to carry out my vengeance. Anger bulged my eyes as I scrambled to advance toward them.

The strange vampire closed the distance between us, grabbing my throat with one of his hands and tangling my hair in between the fingers of the other.

"Now, now. Needn't worry about such petty nonsense, little lady," the man purred.

Willing my power forward was pointless, and I was met with nothing. There was no mist, no answer from my curse. I was alone.

I choked against the hold on my neck.

"We have a message for you."

The vampire twirled my body, pulling my back against his chest and pressing his lips to my ear.

"From who?" I whimpered.

Wicked laughter erupted, "From your daddy."

My heart stopped.

"Who is he?"

He clicked his tongue, "Unfortunately, I'm nearly due to take my leave. These pathetic mortals, at the very least, completed their task in keeping you here, so that we might look upon your precious face. He didn't want us to intervene, but I just couldn't resist, we've been waiting for you for so long."

Squeezing me tighter and forced the air from my lungs, I began to fall limp in his arms, gasping. He continued, "He wants you to come to him of your own free will, when it's time. I know you'll make the right decision, won't you?"

The vampire turned us to face a different direction so that I could helplessly watch as the carriage fled from the estate. Niall had been loaded into and safely stolen away in that carriage.

Aklys was engaged in a brawl with another man, a man that exhibited the same strength and speed of the person in which I'd become so familiar. His adversary rivaled him flawlessly, his equal: another vampire.

No one in the Three Kingdoms encountered this many vampires in an entire lifetime, never mind one day.

"My dear brother seems to be at odds with your friend there," he whispered in my ear. "Let's wrap this up before one of them ends up dead, what do you say?" A throaty chuckle sounded as he lowered his head.

Fangs sank into my neck, and I screamed.

Aklys' head snapped at the sound, and he'd begun to make a mad dash toward me, only to be thwarted in his attempts by his adversary. His body crumpled to the ground, for the man behind him struck his head with such force it would've ended the life of any mortal in an instant, the sound of the impact echoed through the air.

Smiling, the other vampire sauntered over lazily. Long, bloodied fingers caressed my cheek.

"Outstanding," the second vampire snickered, producing a small vial from his pocket which he pressed against the wound in my neck. He was collecting my blood.

"He'll be so pleased," the first man sighed as he pressed his fingers into my chest. "Here's your message, *my lady*."

Searing pain scalded the flesh beneath the hand of the assailant, and it felt like he was burning me, reducing my skin to ashes. I couldn't even scream as the pain ripped through my chest and then ceased without warning.

"Until we meet again," he whispered the promise as my body fell heavily to the ground.

Damp warmth spread gently across my skin, and a soft cloth wiped away the mess that adorned repeatedly battered limbs. Muffled voices faded in and out, and light touches attempted to rouse my consciousness. Soreness radiated through the muscles and bones that made up the frame of my body.

I was familiar with this kind of abuse, this pain. It wouldn't stop, no matter how hard I fought, how long I held on; would I ever escape this?

"Celessa?" A female voice rumbled through the wall of dissociation that gripped my mind.

The call of my name rolled like an ocean wave crashing against the shoreline, loud yet disrupted, as if I were being called to from outside a prison of glass. Every part of me had given in to defeat. With my attempts at revenge stripped away and retribution lost, failure crept into my bloodstream like a deadly poison that strips away one's will to live.

"Celessa?"

Clearer now, I shattered the barrier, and I was finally breaking the surface of the imagined water. The lighting of the room was dim, and two faces hovered nearby wearing expressions of worry.

"I'm still alive?" I wheezed.

Maygen touched my face, eyes watering as she sighed.

"That's unfortunate," I grumbled, hissing at the pain that jolted through my limbs, forcing myself upright.

We were back inside the keep, in the too formal sitting room with obnoxious and uncomfortable furniture. No wonder my back felt like I'd been sleeping on stone, even the forest floor was more comfortable.

"How long was I out?" I asked the pair.

"Several hours," Aloise spoke softly, her voice laced with concern, but also something different. It sounded like fear.

"Where is Aklys?"

"After he recovered, he went to search for the other vampires. He didn't speak to us much, only told us to watch over you until he returned."

The frail woman shifted her position, inching closer to where I sat.

She continued, "Aklys scared me when I first met him because of what he was and all the stories I'd been told of vampires. Then getting to know him, he wasn't so horrible like those monsters of old. Those men today..." She trailed off.

I placed my hand on Aloise's, squeezing it gently in an attempt to comfort her. Comforting people wasn't my strong suit.

"Aklys is different, and his curse is different."

I had been at the mercy of true monsters, yet I lived. I wasn't sure I wanted to know why.

Slow footsteps sounded near the entryway, heavy and exhausted. I turned to meet Aklys' shadowed eyes, blackened by rage and defeat.

"I failed you all," he growled as he approached, kneeling before me, "I stayed with you to keep you safe, and I keep failing."

I couldn't move, couldn't speak. Aklys extended a hand toward me, brushing his fingers along the curve of my collarbone, near the bite mark.

"I couldn't stop them from hurting you," his voice was barely above a whisper.

I knew he cared for me, but I was not his responsibility. None of this was his fault, and knowing he felt like it was squeezed my heart painfully. I wished that he would stop caring, that he would save himself from the turmoil and anguish that followed every step I took.

"It could've been worse, right?" My voice was shaky, unconvincing.

He furrowed his brows before looking at Aloise and Maygen, the women lowered their eyes and remained silent. The tension was heavy in the room, something was going unspoken, something important they did not wish to tell me.

"What?" I insisted, unable to bear the weight of the untold.

"You've been marked," Maygen said.

I didn't understand. I'd been marked for misery at birth, marked for death by my mortal blood, marked by the Gods for being an Amalgam child. What else could there possibly be?

Aloise handed me a small hand mirror.

Looking into the reflection, my blood chilled.

"What is this?" I exclaimed, my gut squirming at the unsightly marking.

The imprint of a snake curled around my neck, draping along my collarbone, its head resting on my sternum. The pain I'd felt, the burning; somehow, that vampire had delivered a brand upon me. A tattoo of a serpent had been painted on my once clear skin.

The worst part was not even the violation that I felt from being marked against my will, rather it was not knowing what the symbol meant.

"It's a curse," Maygen's voice cracked as if she were fighting back tears.

"It's not a curse," Aklys snapped, "but it does make things a bit more complicated."

"As if that's even possible! Are you kidding me?" My hands fisted the vampire's shirt, commanding his attention, "*What is this?*"

"A God's mark."

"And that means what, exactly?"

"It means that whichever God has bestowed the mark can always find you; it's an outdated way to lay claim to a being of the mortal realm. Now, if another God or Goddess comes calling upon you, then they have to answer to the one who has branded you. It's like a gross perversion of tug of war: in the early ages, deities would seek champions with exceptional gifts or skill and stake their claim for power."

Aklys' eyes resembled a new moon's night, no light to be found, utter darkness.

"This mark belongs to my father, doesn't it?"

Aklys nodded slightly, "I would imagine."

"The coward couldn't come do it himself? He sends vampires to do his dirty work? How is that even possible?"

Covering my face with my hands, I folded my body, stifling sobs that were born of anger and frustration. Nothing made sense. Why would vampires do any God's bidding? Why wouldn't my bastard father reveal himself to me?

"We should leave," I decided, rising to escape the overbearing presence of my concerned companions.

Tumbling out of the front door, I sprinted a few paces from the keep's entryway before collapsing into the grass. I needed to leave this place, and I wanted this life to be no more than a memory. Ultimately, I wanted to be free of chaos.

My fingernails scratched at my skin, clawing desperately at the mark on my neck. The deity responsible for my creation had earned my hatred a thousand times over. I wanted him to pay for every second I drew breath in this hellish existence in which he cursed me with.

The painful burning of my flesh finally became enough to stop my emotional efforts at unburdening myself. Blood coated my fingertips. Rage flared to life inside of me as I beheld the shining crimson. Self-control left me as I battered my fists against the ground.

"There's no point; it's a mark of divine magic, and it will heal," a voice whispered. "Your wounds are already closing."

Large hands wrapped around my wrists. I pulled them away in an attempt to free myself, to no avail. Deep red fog enveloped my body, my power bursting forth angrily. It was a cyclone of vicious energy, swirling violently and glowing in the darkness of night, changing the world around me...the world around us.

Aklys knelt with me, holding my hands within his own, silhouetted by crimson.

He was a beautiful sight amongst my chaos, a beacon of light in my storm.

I couldn't stand it.

༺❀༻

Every instinct was pushing me away from the city of my birth. I couldn't remain here any longer after all that had happened. We would travel through Druantia Forest, named for the other lover of nymph lore, Silenus' desire.

Maygen's direction would take us through the forest to the mouth of the river at Limnade Lake, where we would cross into the open lands toward Dawn's End. From there, we would procure passage into Euros.

If we'd had a ship in the settlement, we could've been spared from so much. We wouldn't have encountered the Chimeras or endured the misfortune of being betrayed by Niall. Thibault wouldn't have died at the hands of a Sentinel. Vampires wouldn't have come looking for me in Briobar. If we'd had a ship, we could've crossed the bay to Dawn's End in just a short time, or better yet, gone straight to Euros. We could've been at Lysenna's Keep by now.

Fate wanted me to suffer, and in turn everyone around me suffered. I should be alone.

"Can't we just go around?" I yelled over the thunderous roaring.

Two grueling days had passed since we left the city. We were sleep deprived due to our quickened efforts through the forest, in hopes of shortening our time in Teskaria. We only stopped to relieve ourselves, never to rest. The sooner we left this country, the better.

However, I had never traveled near the lake or river in my first life, and no one told me that it emptied into the Erotas River by waterfall. I could barely hear myself think over the sound of violently tumbling water.

"It would take another day or two to go around, I don't think we can afford that kind of time. We were in Briobar far too long," Maygen called as she paced along the water's edge. She and Aklys had been searching for the shallowest point to cross.

"I can't swim on no sleep. I'm so exhausted I can barely move," Aloise whined from the ground.

Sitting beside the sickly woman, I beckoned for her to lean against me so that she might rest, and she happily accepted the offer and placed her head in my lap. I sighed.

We were all battered, and we needed to camp for the night. There was no bridge to be found, and unless we built a raft, wading the waters was our only option to cross. We would surely drown from exhaustion.

Aklys hadn't spoken a word since before departing Briobar. He didn't make eye contact with any of us, traveling far ahead or far behind the entire way to the lake. I wanted to know what thoughts plagued him.

This is better, I reminded myself. This distance, being uninvolved, was better. It was in our best interest. Yet, I couldn't help but yearn for the sound of his voice and the feel of his touch.

Aklys let us rest as he erected the pair of tents we'd brought along, securing the reins of our horse to a nearby tree. Maygen built a fire and helped boil stew before settling in for the night. I couldn't stop myself from hoping that he would join me in the tent, despite knowing it was foolish.

Night had fallen, but the vampire hadn't entered the shelter. Restlessness got the best of me, and I rose to investigate his whereabouts. Pushing away the flaps of fabric that concealed the inside, I peered into the darkness to see the shadow of a man sitting beside a low burning fire, silent and unmoving.

I settled myself next to him on the ground, glancing into my peripheral vision at his solemn expression. The orange firelight shadowed and danced along the angles of his face. I'd never seen him appear so mysterious and brooding, so sad and angry all at once, but in the calmest way possible.

"It reminded me of who I really am," he whispered finally, gathering my full attention.

I turned to face him as he stared into the flames.

"The true nature of a vampire?" I asked.

He frowned deeply, "No, the nature of a *monster*. No matter what you are, consciousness and free will grants choice. Vampires are capable of decency, but choose to be beasts. Yes, we suffer from bloodlust, but moderation and a willing source makes it easier to control."

"You don't commit such atrocities; you are decent."

A lone tear escaped his eye, sliding down his pale cheek as he spoke, "You don't know me. You don't know the things I've done, who I am. You've only seen what I wanted you to see, the man I wish I was." He inhaled deeply, stretching his shoulders before he continued, "You make me want to be better because that's what you deserve, but do not be fooled: you asked me to become a monster without understanding that I already am one."

Words escaped me, for I couldn't imagine the man whom I had become so unexpectedly attached to, hurting innocents or raining destruction upon the land. It didn't seem possible.

"Tell me."

"What?" Confused, he squinted his eyes, fighting against the evidence of his sorrow.

"Tell me what you've done so that I understand," I insisted, "It won't change anything, Aklys. I've killed people, I've brutalized and tortured, and I am not innocent of monstruous acts."

"Every person you have ever harmed was in self-defense or retribution. The lives taken at your hand would not have hesitated to turn the tables on you."

He snaked long fingers through dark locks of hair, obviously in turmoil.

"You have never killed just to feel life leave a body, just to revel in the sensation of a person falling limp as you drain them of everything they've ever been. You haven't torn apart families because you craved the despair of innocent people losing their loved ones. You haven't tortured simply because you wanted to feel more powerful."

Aklys buried his face in his hands. "I have done unspeakable things. I will always be a monster, and my affliction makes it too easy."

I watched him in silence for a few moments.

"How many?"

"*How many?*" His tone grew more exasperated.

"How many lives have you taken?"

The vampire scoffed, "Too fucking many."

"Men?"

"Countless."

"Women?"

"Far more than I care to admit."

"Children?"

"No," he snapped. "I'm an abomination, but I've never harmed a child, not intentionally."

"Then you're less of a monster than many in this realm, Aklys."

Wide eyes stared back at me, filled with surprise that I was handling his confession so well, that I was so accepting and understanding. He reached toward me, brushing his thumbs against my cheeks. Heated flooded beneath my skin as I gazed into the shadowy hazel eyes.

"I was meant to be a monster to you, too."

"What is that supposed to mean?"

Aklys bit his lip roughly, throat bobbing as he tried to swallow his words.

Understanding struck my skull like a hammer. I pulled away from his grasp and stood, pacing back from the vampire.

"Please, milady, don't." His arms remained outstretched, beckoning me back to him.

"Don't lie to me," My voice was shaking as I said, "Did my father send you?"

"No! I swear!" He stood, moving toward me.

I backed away further, "Then what did you mean?"

Aklys hesitated, jaw clenching.

"When the Mage took you, it was believed that you'd died after some time. Many sought him out to uncover information about you because certain people were aware of your power. You've been viewed as an asset ever since its emergence, considered the ultimate weapon; persons of power and influence want you. I was meant to find you."

The vampire shifted uncomfortably as he continued, "Then I met you in the settlement, and couldn't believe it was possible someone so frail could be so powerful. You were a fighter, and that intrigued me. I'd planned to just grab you and take you to finish off Tobian before being on our way, but you fought me. A sickly mortal girl stabbed a vampire and put up a hell of a fight despite the disadvantage. Seeing everything you did in the keep... I've been in awe of you since. My respect for you grows with every passing day. Every part of me wants to protect you."

This was surreal, for I had been right the entire time. I couldn't trust him. He was just like the others, only interested in the prize that was my power. Denial and understanding waged war inside my mind, equally powerful with the potential to drive me mad.

"Please, I'm sorry!" Aklys moved closer still.

"I trusted you," I whispered, wrapping my arms around myself. I felt violated.

"You can trust me! You can still trust me!" He pleaded desperately.

"Can I?" I snapped. "You're the same as the others, sent to procure the all-powerful weapon, the *object*! Thibault was right about you, and I should have listened to him."

"No, I-"

"You're a deceiver, a typical vampire. I guess you were being honest about that! I'm such a fool, and it proves to be true again and again."

Aklys grabbed my arms, forcefully closing the distance between us.

"I care about you. I know what I was sent to do, but my conscience didn't allow it. I waited to see who you were and found that you deserve so much more than what you've been given. I want to make sure you have that. I want to take you to your new home, and I'll tell everyone I've ever met that the girl with the Gods' power doesn't exist. I will spend the rest of my days keeping you as safe as I can."

Tears escaped my eyes. Not tears of sadness, but tears of anger, of betrayal.

"I trusted you, but you..." His hold on me loosened as I spoke, and I stepped away. "I wanted... I thought..." I couldn't finish my thoughts and turned away.

My feet carried me toward the tree line, desperate to escape the weight of the only confession he delivered tonight that had the power to change my mind about him.

"Please!" He begged, repeating the word as I retreated into the forest. The moment I reached cover within the trees, I broke into a run, fleeing from my heartache.

He touched me, more than physically, and he was lodged deeply within my brain. The air I breathed was thick with his scent, and my thoughts were poisoned with his presence. I let him feel me, taste me, and I exposed every part of myself to him.

Aklys appeared in front of me, hands outstretched to halt my escape. I was no match for his vampiric speed, despite my muddled divinity.

"Get away from me!" I screamed, throwing my arms out in front of me.

Tendrils of power lashed out like whips, colliding with the man's body and propelling him backwards into a tree trunk. Shock stilled me, for my curse had never touched him before, and in the past, it wouldn't. Couldn't.

Aklys appeared equally surprised, realizing what I'd just done, what it meant.

He forced a smile.

"Now you're a liability to the monsters who want you, there's no enemy you cannot conquer. Please, just let me try to keep you safe," he begged.

Without warning, something exploded from the ground. Tendrils different than my own appeared, but my power had already retreated beneath my skin. Whatever was happening was not under my control. The coils extended toward the vampire, wrapping around his arms and legs, pulling his body to the ground.

They were tree roots.

A woman's figure emerged from the depths of the wilderness, arms thrashing wildly, the roots mimicking her movements. She was using magic, manipulating nature to subdue Aklys.

I'd frozen in my panic, unsure of what to do. I only stared at the green skin and glowing eyes that approached me: a Nymph. The breath stole from my lungs as I watched her bind the vampire.

Aklys fought back against the assault, but her magic was strong, quickly replacing every root he managed to break through.

"Let's get this over with quickly, monster." Her voice was light like a breeze, but as powerful as the magic she wielded.

"Don't hurt him!" Sense had returned to me, and I leapt toward the woman.

"You cried out from fear just a moment ago! Have you lost your mind? This is a vampire!" She scolded me, and her ethereal appearance enthralled me still.

"I'm just upset with him, but he hasn't hurt me!" I glanced at the imprisoned man. "Physically."

Aklys groaned.

"Your neck," the Nymph gasped. "You've been marked."

Her attention returned to the vampire.

"Did you deliver this unto her, you beast?" She shouted.

"No! No, he didn't! He protects me! Let him go, I beg you!" I cried, surprising myself at how desperate I felt to save the man who had spurned me yet again.

The woman glared at me for a few moments before releasing Aklys. Breathing out a sigh of relief and dropping to my knees. I pulled at the roots that clutched his limbs, attempting to free him. He watched me struggle, lying completely still, entranced.

"What's wrong with him?"

"I've paralyzed him for a moment. He's strong, so it won't last long. We must leave immediately!" The Nymph grabbed my wrist, pulling me away.

"What the fuck are you talking about? Let go!" I hissed at the woman.

"Have you no memory of me, Celessa?" Her expression was genuinely puzzled.

My stomach dipped, treasured memories taking shape in my mind, "Isonei?"

She appeared confused that I hadn't expected her.

"The Goddess Melissae said you'd come for me," I whispered.

"So I have, now let us leave this place," she insisted.

"To go where? What do you want with me?" I argued, fighting against her grip.

"I will take you to Evelia."

Evelia was lost ages ago, destroyed by the Gods, so she couldn't mean to take me to a wasteland? Dumbfounded, I only gaped in disbelief.

I wouldn't abandon Maygen and Aloise, so I responded, "I can't leave them."

"Who?"

"My friends."

"What are they?" She asked, glancing nervously at Aklys.

"Aloise is mortal, Maygen is *mostly* mortal."

Isonei was becoming disgruntled. "I can only take one. There is but one ship secured for passage, and the lone spot belongs to you. You have no time for farewells."

"I said I can't leave them; did you misunderstand?"

The nymph bared her teeth at me in frustration.

"Evelia is lost!" Aklys' had finally broken through the hold of her magic.

"To creatures such as yourself, yes, it is lost," she snapped.

"Then why would you try to take me there? My power is deadly, I could kill you right now!"

"The deities want you, and it is time for you to join them."

I'm meant to join the Gods?

Chapter Fourteen

Fateful Inclinations

Evelia was hidden, not destroyed. Powerful magic concealed it, so it appeared as a ruin to those who were unwelcome. It was impassable without the blessing of the Gods who resided there. The people of the mortal realm were led to believe in its destruction in order to protect those within.

Isonei claims to keep the Gods safe from vampires. I didn't ask why Gods needed protection from a creature without divine power. I assumed the answer would be vague, as were her answers to most of my questions. I received the barest of information as she attempted to sway me into accompanying her return to the lost country.

Maygen and Aloise were shocked to find the mystical woman at our camp when they awoke. I hadn't bothered to disturb them before dawn, since they needed their rest. It proved troublesome explaining to them what had happened without revealing too much about Aklys and I's conversation. Explaining to them that Isonei intended to spirit me away to the land of the Gods was even more difficult.

Maygen had objected with such ferocity I feared she would burst at the seams with rage; I'd never seen her so angry, though I understood the outburst. This strange creature wanted to steal away her family, her friend, someone she'd fought and nearly died for.

Wary of the intruder, and quieter than usual, Aloise had hastily retreated to hide in her tent for the majority of the argument between Maygen and Isonei. I was surprised because I'd seen her face down monstrous people like Aklys and... myself. She hadn't shied away from us, but our most recent encounters with strange people acting under a guise of good intentions *had* left us in ruins.

"There is no discussion to be had. She is coming to Euros. She belongs with me; I am her family!" Maygen gestured to herself angrily while facing down the Nymph.

"She is not safe there. Do you think you are able to provide protection better than the Gods? Foolish girl," Isonei hissed.

The two were giving me a migraine, and I wanted to scream.

I looked toward Aklys, wondering if he felt mortal pain as simple and annoying as a headache. The vampire had been banished several meters away, with Isonei's distrust and dislike of him resulting in the erecting of a magical barrier between us. It was almost like looking through warped glass, with the image of him slightly obscured.

We could hear each other, see each other, but he could not approach.

Good. I was pissed off.

He'd been out to collect a bounty, and while things didn't play out that way, I had no idea when that task actually changed for him. Was it before or after I'd let him taste my blood? Was it before or after I'd let him taste my body? What if I hadn't shared intimacy with him? Would I have been handed over for coin by now? I shouldn't care if he experiences headaches. I hope he does. I wish I could give him one myself.

"Celessa, would you just scare her off with your power or something?" Maygen cried out in aggravation.

Rolling my eyes, I heaved an exasperated sigh. "Isonei, I told you I won't leave them. I meant it. The lure of lands untold and powerful deities isn't enough to rip me away from the people I care most about. They're all I have."

Aloise had appeared from her tent then, carefully walking toward me.

Isonei gasped and then groaned in frustration.

"You're telling me you won't leave because of them?" The nymph gestured to Aloise with an outstretched hand.

"Yes, I'm staying with my friends," I confirmed.

"Friendship is fickle, you simply care for new life."

Isonei crossed her arms over her chest.

"As much as I enjoy deciphering riddles, could you just be straightforward? I'm already in physical and emotional pain from your incessant bickering."

I rubbed my temples.

"You aren't aware?" She scoffed.

Arching a brow, I waited for her to elaborate.

"This mortal is with child."

The nymph glared at Aloise, unblinking as a breeze loosened strands of sweetgrass hair, twirling around her delicate features.

I was going to be sick.

Aklys had risen and pressed himself against the nearly invisible barrier. "If that was true, I would've known; I can smell it."

Whipping my head around, I stared at him dumbfoundedly.

His cheeks flushed a bright shade of red, embarrassment and shame.

"Vampires suffer from bloodlust. Pregnancy enriches the blood. It's like leaving an open bottle of aged wine within reach of an alcoholic," he admitted.

"She's been in survival mode, monster, so her body protected itself from the likes of *you*. That goes without considering your attention and inclination has been directed *elsewhere*," Isonei hissed.

"The sickness," Maygen whispered, "It's a baby?"

She went to her knees at Aloise's feet.

"That's not possible," Aloise breathed. "How would you know something like this? I've been in your presence for a handful of moments."

"Nymphs were healers and midwives for the first mortals. We bestowed gifts upon children, delivered babes, and cared for mothers. Mortals have a glow about them when they are with child, apparent only to those designed to care for them."

Isonei approached Aloise, touching her arm gently with her pale green fingers.

A gentle golden hue illuminated her skin, the truth revealed. Aloise was pregnant with Thibault's child.

It was a miracle.

No, it was more like a death sentence, for she was always in danger. How could I protect her like this?

"Take her," I demanded.

The three women all turned their attention to me, puzzled.

"Take her to Evelia, you must give her my place."

"Are you mad? If I go against the wishes of my divine mother-" She argued as Maygen clutched her arm, "Release me!"

"Please. You said you cared for pregnant women and babies. Take her."

Maygen's entire demeanor had changed toward the woman. Anger and distrust were replaced with desperation.

"You do not understand what is at stake..." Isonei trailed off.

"Is your life in danger if you displease them?" I asked.

"Of course not, my mother is a Goddess."

"Will you be punished?"

"Reprimanded, perhaps."

"I beg you, take Aloise to Evelia," I pleaded.

"Do I have no say in the matter of my life?" Aloise piped up.

"No!" Maygen shouted, though I could not speak.

I, too, had been the victim of being robbed of choice many times over.

"Yes," I whispered. "You have a choice to go, and you have a choice to carry this child if that is what you want. I won't take your free will from you."

Aloise's hands cradled her flat belly, for there was no tell-tale of a babe within her womb, but we knew Isonei's magic was true.

"I want this child. I want Thibault's child," said Aloise.

Tears welled in my eyes.

If Evelia was truly safe enough to hold me, there would be no safer refuge for them. I'd had no intention of going with the nymph in the first place. She'd promised me passage, though, so I would give it to Aloise. No one in this realm deserved it more than her unborn child.

"Thibault's child is not safe here, and it isn't safe with me. I can't protect you, Aloise."

Understanding passed between us. I refocused my attention on Isonei.

"I will not go with you either way, so please give her the safety she deserves."

"Why are you so desperate to protect a child that bears no blood of your own?"

The nymph eyed me suspiciously.

Swallowing roughly, "I loved the father. He died because I couldn't protect him," I forced out, twin tears tumbling down my cheeks.

Aloise clutched my hand as she said, "You blame yourself?"

I only nodded, unable to find words.

"He was relieved when you suppressed your powers. It gave him hope that perhaps you'd be able to live without fear of hurting us, and it pained him to see you become so withdrawn."

She sighed and continued, "Thibault was never going to stop loving you, Celessa, even if he chose me. I was dealing with it because you protected me, because you saved me. You forgave us. I owe you my life, and I've grown to care for you. Speaking for us both, you are not to blame, and no one holds you accountable. He died for all of us, to keep us safe, and we all saw how hard you tried to save him."

Her voice shook, thick with sorrow.

"I cannot just take your place... you owe me nothing." Aloise frowned.

Dismayed, I gripped her hand.

"I am indebted to Thibault for his sacrifice, and that has extended to this child and to you. I will find a way to take you there myself, if she will not."

My eyes darted back to the Nymph; her face frozen in awe.

"Your heart has not changed," Isonei whispered. "As a girl you were blossoming with love and generosity, and I left you to your life. Taking you away from all you held dear seemed wrong, and it seems it may be wrong again, but what you are asking is not within my power."

"I am not asking. I am begging."

Green eyes flicked between Aloise and myself.

"Fine," Isonei agreed, turning away.

A deep sigh of relief escaped my lungs.

They would be safe.

Isonei still refused to allow Aklys near our small group, insisting now that it was more for the safety of Aloise than the rest of us. We had rested one more day at the lake before deciding to move forward; Isonei promised to ease our crossing of the falls.

"How do you propose we cross, Nymph?" The vampire shouted from the stump he perched on a distance away.

"*We* will have passage. You may swim if you insist on following, monster," Isonei sneered.

The woman stood at the water's edge, barefoot and garbed only in a fitted garment that mimicked the texture of tree bark. It hugged her thighs like shorts, crawling up her hips and midsection, covering her chest and stopping below her armpits and collarbone. I'd never seen any clothing like it: it was almost like a second skin, like it was part of her.

The gently lapping lake water nipped at her toes as she angled her head toward the sky, extending the wingspan of her arms far from her body. Roots crept forth from the nearby forest, snaking along the ground at the Nymph's command. The tendrils twisted and braided together tightly, interweaving as more approached her. They began forming a structure thick enough to comfortably walk upon and reached out to extend over the water.

Isonei was manipulating nature to build us a bridge. It was breathtaking to behold.

When she finished, the root-woven bridge stretched out over the crest of the wide waterfall that roared below, its particles misting the air. Water droplets dampened the crossing, darkening its color. It contrasted the deep blue-green of the lake beautifully.

I was baffled that such beauty could exist in a forsaken place such as this. A land with cities built upon bones and teeming with bloodthirsty monsters, man and beast alike, could still be awe-inspiring.

I took a moment to breathe this in.

The three women of our small group went before me, at my insistence. I'd wanted to see if Aklys would attempt to cross, or if he would swim like Isonei had commanded. To my surprise, he made no attempt to even touch the bridge, diving into the depths and effortlessly cutting through the water. Amused, I watched him swim nearby, taking notice of his eyes catching my own every few moments. I kept reminding myself that I was angry with him, but I could not look away from the man. He stopped when he was parallel to my position, treading the water and facing me fully.

"I know you're angry with me right now," he shouted over the deafening roar, his damp hair clinging to his forehead and face, like the tentacles of an angry octopus stuck to his head.

"Angry is an understatement," I returned. "I'm only trying to enjoy this petty punishment you've been given while it lasts."

The vampire smiled, fangs bared, and the thought of the pricks against my skin warmed the lowest depths of my body. Furiously suppressing the lustful thoughts, my mind cursed my body and my heart for continuing to long for the man.

"At the expense of my pride, I would endure countless petty punishments for you, milady, if only in hopes that you may one day forgive me."

Rolling my eyes, I turned to continue across the bridge.

"Don't linger too long, wouldn't want you to drown," I grumbled.

"Be still my heart, she cares for me," the man called out.

"I'll drown you myself. You aren't as amusing or as charming as you think you are."

I lifted my hand to offer him a vulgar gesture, to which a deep and boisterous laugh carried over the rushing current. I couldn't fight the slight smirk that escaped my self control, twitching my lips.

No, I don't think I truly wanted to hold on to resentment, anger, and despair. I don't think I wanted to be a villain or a monster, or at least not a real one, despite all of my suffering. Perhaps, I would simply appear as one to those who desired my monstrous power, or perhaps I would give them what they deserved and rid the world of them myself.

I would only allow those who deserved it to feel the depth of my love, a secret hidden away from the rest of the realm.

Once Isonei whisked Aloise and the unborn child away to Evelia, far away from this hellscape, I would have more room to take greater risks. Aklys was a vampire, so surely he knew where many nefarious figures resided, ones that I could dispatch on my own or with him by my side. I would see Maygen to safety in Euros, and I'd accompany her all the way to Lysenna's keep.

If Fate allowed it and Aklys remained, I would ask him to help me better this world.

Flickering brightness alighting in response to loud roaring startled me.

Grass kissed my bare ankles, flattening beneath soft feet. Angry wind bellowed across an open meadow, looking out over a dark and angry sea. Waves reached for the blackening sky like desperate drowning hands, foam hissing as they collided against the surface of the ocean, returning home.

It was lightning that jolted across the expanse above, answered by booming thunder. A storm brewed, sweeping over earth and water alike. Chaos called land and sky together as one, joining in a dangerous waltz and leaving any who lingered at the mercy of their might.

Only when rain began to fall did I realize that my body was bare against the elements, no protective layer of clothing against my skin. The droplets of water caressed me lovingly, and I didn't mind being exposed to the storm.

I was alone, after all, at least physically. Why didn't I *feel* alone?

My body swiveled, allowing me to observe my surroundings. Behind me, at the end of the meadow, were towering mountains. They were so monstrous, the clouds in the sky swirled around their peaks, obscuring the entirety of their great height. My eyes returned to the sea, growing ever angrier, waves creeping further up the dark sand that separated saltwater from grass. The rain grew heavier, battering my tender skin, dampening my hair so that it clung to my shoulders and chest.

Violence incarnate struck the ground before me, one of nature's most powerful forces. I'd seen lightning strikes before, and they spelled disaster and death to any unfortunate souls or structures that encountered their wrath. I remained still, unaffected by the assault, and it lingered there.

A beam of light danced before me. I wanted to touch it, and I reached out, hoping to graze my fingertips against the magnificent display of power.

When I made contact, the thunder grew louder, angrier. The sea mimicked the call, increasing its speed and ferocity with how it berated the shoreline. Dancing light spasmed as if it were wounded, and before my eyes it darkened, becoming something evil and twisted. It shrunk down into a roiling mass, floating in the air, inches from my face.

What had it become? Something that was once a pure product of nature's emotion had become another thing entirely. A high-pitched ringing sounded, interrupting the thunder and piercing my skull.

Like the waves, the darkened mass of lightning ebbed and crashed into my body. I absorbed it into myself, despite the pain it inflicted. Stabbing, burning, stinging, itching, aching: every discomfort all at once invaded my being.

Rain grew heavier still, the very earth beneath my feet groaned in protest. Through the walls of falling water, I watched the sea turn dark like ink, like the infection of black magic. Droplets of water changed from crystal clear and cool, to a thick crimson that coated my skin, sticky and warm. The sea was corrupted, and the sky rained blood.

Fire raged within my chest, the tattooed brand upon my neck sprung to life, the form of a giant viper. It towered over me, larger than any basilisk, a true monster.

The snake hissed, "Child of death and decay, lady of blood and bone."

The creature's mouth did not open, but rather it spoke to me with its eyes, in a voice that was deep and rich with magic untold.

"It is time you took your rightful place; you are the unbreakable sword of the mightiest force known to existence."

The voice echoed inside my skull, filling my thoughts with its intended purpose and infecting me with its poison.

"I will not!" I protested, anger burning my heart as I faced down the beast.

The snake began writhing at my proclamation, with mortal emotion filling the black orbs that were its eyes, brimming with disbelief and rage.

"You have been given life, and unimaginable power by my deliverance! You dare refuse me?"

"I don't even know who you are!" I called out against all of the deafening noise.

All at once, the ocean stilled. No waves lapped against the land. Storm clouds above blanketed in a smooth and unwavering formation, with no thunder to be heard. The rain ceased, leaving fallen blood to cake against the earth, filling my nose with a foul metallic scent.

"I am the only being worthy of ruling the realms, with you by my side."

"You're a bastard and a coward."

I pooled saliva in my mouth and spat at the serpent.

The creature hissed angrily, coiling into striking position.

I would welcome my death rather than join a tyrant. I bared my flesh to the foul creature in acceptance of my end.

Deep laughter rumbled as heavily as the thunder had.

"You shall suffer greatly."

In a shuddering movement, the viper collapsed into itself, changing form. A man appeared in place of the large beast. He was tall, but I couldn't decipher much else, for his features were obscured by darkness.

The man reached for me, taking my head between his strong hands, and he squeezed.

I screamed as he crushed my skull in his palms, thrashing wildly and blinded by the pain of being broken apart. The cracking and crunching of bone erupted in my eardrums, which followed suit, exploding to leave me in excruciating silence.

After a few moments, life left my body. My consciousness, my essence, and all that I was now hovered above the gruesome scene. Despair twisted my consciousness as I witnessed my own broken, dead body lying on the blood-rain soaked ground, limp at the feet of a murderous creature.

I realized he must be my father. My own father had killed me.

The apparent God cocked his head, revealing a vicious smile and a body streaked with blackened veins. His mouth was all that I could see of his face.

As the hand reached toward me again, I attempted to flee, but the divine being effortlessly captured whatever form I existed as now: the very essence of my soul.

"You will suffer misery untold," he whispered, "until you decide to join me. Only with my grace will you find relief from life's cruelty."

In a swift, violent motion, I was thrust back into my ruined body.

Gasping, my body jolted upright. I rolled over, vomiting onto the ground next to my makeshift bed. Shooting pain lingered in my skull, and my stomach answered with twisting nausea.

I sobbed as the images of the nightmare replayed over and over in my mind. My cries woke Maygen, who now shared a tent with me rather than Aloise, leaving the pregnant woman with Isonei.

Her delicate hands smoothed the fabric of my tunic, and despite knowing it was my friend, I jumped away from the physical contact.

The sensation of the man's hands on me was still fresh, and I trembled as a result.

"What happened?" She whispered.

I was grateful my power hadn't made an appearance like it had during my last nightmare; I was so wary of Maygen sharing my space because it felt like she was being put in harm's way. Her presence and comfort were most welcome, but it did not satisfy what I needed.

"Aklys," I coughed, avoiding her gaze.

"You had a nightmare about him?" She asked, confused.

"No," I choked out, swallowing roughly.

Understanding settled over her, and she inhaled deeply.

"I will keep a close eye on the Nymph. He's just outside her barrier, and you can push through."

"How?"

"Your gift - absorb the magic?" Maygen suggested.

"What if I hurt Isonei?"

Concern began to replace my irrational craving for comfort.

"You won't. Step lightly. Hurry," she urged me quietly.

We both peered out of the tent to observe the area around us; Isonei and Aloise's tent was close to our own. Maygen waved me forward.

Stepping out, I was careful to make as little noise as possible. I made eye contact with the woman once more before she gave me a knowing smile and a small nod. The silent understanding offered me much needed relief.

My feet carried my body soundlessly over the flat ground. There was very little cover in the open land north of Key's Keep, and only a few stray oaks stood dotted across the terrain. We'd traveled for nearly two days to get here.

Isonei's shield against the vampire hadn't faltered even once. She mostly ignored his presence unless she was cursing him or insisting he leave. I never spoke on the matter and silently hoped he would continue to linger nearby, regardless of how much I pretended I didn't want him to do so.

It was uncontrollable, my yearning, the emotions I struggled against. All I could think about in this moment was Aklys holding my body with his own, with my face against his chest listening to the sound of his heartbeat.

Finding the wall of Isonei's barrier was the easy part, but absorbing her magic just enough to escape scared me. What if I took away too much? What if it affected her? Was I making a mistake? Perhaps it would be safest for us all if I simply returned to my tent.

My hands rested against the warped glass-like wall, and I pressed my head against it, allowing tears to fall in hopes that it would release some of the distress I felt.

"Milady?" That sweet, sultry voice drew my gaze.

Aklys stood just a pace away from the barrier, watching me. Tears fell heavier, for the floodgates I'd put up around my emotions were breaking, unleashing every single repressed feeling; they were quickly escalating beyond my control.

I looked at him with cloudy eyes, face hot with sorrow, still reeling from the trauma my subconscious had endured.

The vampire placed his hands on the barrier, lining them up to where mine rested against the magic. Only the damned wall was standing between us. At least, physically — emotionally, there was entirely too much to unpack. For now, I simply wished to touch him.

"Breathe, I'm right here for you," Aklys murmured, pressing his forehead against the magic.

This was almost enough. The barrier hindered the movements of physical beings, so neither of us could cross. The elements could cross over, though; the crisp night air carried a breeze, sending me the gift of his scent. I breathed him in, clinging to the small comfort, for it was the only one within my reach.

"I'm here," he promised.

I closed my eyes, imagining I could feel his warmth seeping into my skin. I imagined his strong arms encircling my body, holding me close and offering the affection that I refused many times before, but so desperately craved in this moment.

Right now, I didn't dare to think about his intended purpose where I was concerned, how he had betrayed my trust more than once, or how I didn't know who he truly was or what he really wanted. Just this once, I would give control to my heart rather than my head.

Long fingers threaded in between my own, closing over my hand. Soft lips pressed against my forehead, and my shaking body fell into the embrace of the vampire.

Aklys squeezed me tightly. How? My power hadn't appeared, and I didn't feel any magic enter my body. Glancing nervously about our surroundings, I caught sight of the pale green Nymph.

Isonei watched us closely with narrowed eyes.

"If you harm her, you will face my wrath, monster." She stated coolly.

Aklys nodded his thanks to the woman, who immediately turned away to return to the encampment.

The vampire lowered our bodies to the ground. He sat with legs outstretched and pulled me into his lap, wrapping my thighs around his waist and curling his arms around my body.

I tucked myself into his chest, nuzzling the loose shirt, and he rested his chin atop my head. We lingered in the quiet, just breathing, exchanging heat and heartbeats.

Drowsiness settled deeply into my bones, despite my fear of returning to the nightmares. Every so often, my limbs would twitch in protest to my faltering consciousness. Each time, Aklys would tighten his embrace, reassuring me that I was safe.

"I'm here," he promised again, "I have you."

During the day following my nightmare, it felt like the blood was singing in my veins. Every particle that made up my being vibrated and hummed in answer to the summons I'd received from the bastard God.

My power yearned to go to him, to fulfill its purpose. My head cursed him and all that he was, all that he had caused.

He was a malicious deity, eager to control and abuse me for my curse. I couldn't allow that to happen. A small voice echoed within, warning of chaos and carnage if I did not submit.

The fear of this deity could not sway me from my place alongside my friends. There was much at stake, and ensuring the safety of the three women in my company was the only thing that mattered right now. In just a few days, Isonei and Aloise would be safely stowed away in passage to Evelia, where they could live in peace and comfort. They could be without fear of what evil lies within the Three Kingdoms.

Key's Keep was an unusual sight. The small stone fortress loomed before a network of bridges that branched across small sandbars throughout the water south of the structure, connecting to smaller buildings. What was the point of such a set-up? Not that it mattered, as we were only passing by.

I couldn't help but feel a pull to the strange place. I felt a desire to explore. It stood abandoned. Aklys had told us the last family to inhabit this place had renounced their nobility and fled decades ago, claiming it was cursed.

Perhaps it was my own curse that wished to witness such claims, like calling to like. It craved more, more essence to absorb and more magic to devour. With each act of wrath, it grew stronger, especially when the intake of magic occurred.

We couldn't afford such a delay for my foolish curiosity, as Dawn's End was just two days away. It was so close I could nearly feel the relief of departing this country washing over me. I was ready to be rid of Teskaria, hoping to never return. Not much longer would I breathe in the familiar air, nor feel the grass of my homeland beneath my feet. I would leave every painful memory behind.

Aklys' warm breath melted into my hair as he pulled me into an embrace from behind, his chest rising and falling against my shoulders. Allowing him to hold me felt right and wrong all at once. The very open display of affection in front of our companions made me uncomfortable, but after the events last night, they knew I needed him. I knew I needed him.

Fight it as I may, the truth only continues to break down my barriers with each passing day and night that I yearn for his presence. I had to believe people were capable of change, over time or on a whim. I had to believe that Aklys' intentions for me had changed for my best interest. It had to be true, because if people couldn't change at their heart's command, then there was no hope for me at all.

The vampire hummed, the sound reverberating through my skull, creeping down my spine and sending chills throughout my body.

He tightened his hold, inhaling my scent and sighing contentedly. This was strange, these feelings, the reality of them.

I had never been permitted to receive the affections of a man as an unmarried lady of nobility. The only one who had ever given me true intimacy before Aklys was Thibault.

Only innocent gestures occurred during my first life, filled with stolen kisses and secret hand holding, until attempting the ultimate disgrace, discovered and punished. There were the few moments of meaningless passion I wished I could forget, for that had muddled so much between us.

Affection from Aklys was different. His touch lingered on my skin long after the physical contact ended.

"What troubles you?" he asked.

"I was only thinking about the keep."

It was half true; I was thinking about the strange fortress, among other things.

"Shall we go and see it?"

"We don't have time," I reminded him.

"I am very fast. I'll have us there and back to the party in no time at all."

Strong arms squeezed me tighter.

"They won't be safe without us."

Aklys chuckled, "I think Maygen and the Nymph would be very offended to hear you say such a thing, so you should speak softly, milady."

I smirked, enjoying the playfulness. I really did want to see the keep, if only for a few minutes, just to settle my curiosity.

"Let me test the waters," I whispered, wiggling free of his arms.

A brief conversation about Aklys and I visiting the old keep left Isonei irritated, but Aloise and Maygen were encouraging, insisting we should go. Maygen winked inconspicuously, as if we were escaping to engage in physical intimacy, and my cheeks heated at the unspoken suggestion. Isonei informed me that she would be erecting the barrier once more in our absence and that she was uninterested in waiting for an extended period of time.

I promised her we would be quick.

"We're off on an adventure!" Aklys smiled.

He was radiant, like the moon in all of its mysterious beauty, shrouded by darkness, but alluring and magical. I readily wrapped my arms around his neck as he swept me up.

Vampires were incredibly strong, more so than many other beings in the mortal realm, and it was intimidating. He felt the shift in my posture as I tensed against him, looking down at me with an arched brow.

"I'm not sure if I've mentioned it before, but you're beautiful," he whispered.

The urge to deny the sentiment rested on my tongue. I hadn't truly looked at my own appearance in much longer than one normally would. I'd been too afraid of myself since my rescue and after everything I'd done. The one time I'd seen my reflection was to look upon the brand that tarnished my skin. If I looked in a mirror, I feared I would see nothing more than a shell of my former self.

Upon some observation of my body, it was easy to tell I'd been moving about enough to build some muscle and eating enough to gain and maintain weight. I was grateful for my body's slow return to normalcy. I had no desire to remain in an emaciated state, a constant physical reminder of the abuse I'd endured. The reduced visibility of my collarbone, ribs, and pelvis were a welcome sight.

I wasn't as radiant as I'd once been, but I was getting better. Before Asuras had imprisoned me I'd had curves, a generous natural figure, and I glowed. I missed the girl I once was; I mourned her.

Aklys' speed would never fail to amaze me, for what would have taken at least an hour to reach at a normal pace appeared before us in a matter of minutes.

"Is it tiring, moving like that?" I asked, genuinely curious.

He smirked as he said, "It takes time to adapt, like anything the body can accomplish. Imagine it like running for a mortal, but enhanced. While I move much faster, it only lasts for bursts. Vampires get tired, out of breath, and weak in the knees."

My attention was quickly stolen by the interesting display ahead, as the structures were damaged. From a distance everything had appeared intact, but seeing it up close, it resembled the ruins of a place tarnished by war. Uneasiness settled in the pit of my stomach.

Looking at Aklys, his expression mimicked my own.

"I think we should go back," he mumbled, voice low.

Howling echoed from the building that towered above us. The sound was not that of an animal, but of something deadlier. This excursion wasn't supposed to end up this way; I had only wanted to ease my restlessness, experience something new, and enjoy myself. Now, we faced down an unexpected danger once more, a danger neither of us had anticipated.

Several Wyndigas crept forth from the mouth of the keep. The creatures snarled, frothing at the mouth, claws outstretched in anticipation of prey just within their reach.

Aklys growled, and the sound was primal, summoned from the darkest depths of his being. It was a warning from one cursed creature to another.

The Wyndigas hesitated, crouching as they observed us with hollow black eyes.

"They won't hesitate much longer - it's time for you to go," the vampire commanded.

Disbelief sparked, pulling me from my shocked stupor.

I glanced between the man and the beasts. Someone or something had put them here, for Wyndigas were only known to dwell in Tamaa Forest. Maygen had told me as much when we were ambushed during the escape from Sanctuary.

Whomever moved them here had to be powerful enough to manipulate or subdue the creatures. They were here for a reason. They were here for me.

My gift gnawed at my flesh, restless, plagued by an insatiable hunger.

I could only assume one being was responsible for this offering of violence.

Removing myself from Aklys' arms and stepping to the ground, my curse sparked to life, erupting from my hands and lashing out like whips. The skin on my arms split apart violently, the crimson mist tinged with blood of my own. Cocking my head towards Aklys, a voice left me that didn't seem quite my own.

"It's time for *you* to go."

The vampire hesitated, and I prayed he remembered what had happened in the forest, where my power touched him. He was in danger now, too. He held my gaze for a moment before retreating.

My essence had made contact with the first of the beasts, wringing the life from its gnarled body. Euphoria ignited my cells, pleasure replacing where pain had once dwelled. I no longer feared the mist, and it no longer hurt me.

Four beasts dared to make a stand against me, unknowingly ending their lives simply by acting on their twisted instincts. I paced forward, allowing my power to roam freely, destroying the once mortal beings one by one.

The screeches and howls fueled my desire to wreak havoc. Little time passed as I reduced the Wyndigas to nothing, taking their power, and their darkness for myself. My toes curled at the onslaught of magic entering my body.

A loud voice blared angrily inside my head.

"Beware, daughter of despair. With each corruption you consume, you shall falter, akin to the monsters you slaughter. You will fulfill your purpose."

Pain seared where the tattoo was decorated onto my flesh, and my neck tightened. It wasn't possible, but it felt like the marking of the snake was alive as it had been in my nightmare, and now it was strangling me. My body crumpled to the ground, writhing against the invisible hold, trying and failing to gasp for air as my limbs flailed desperately. Clawing at my throat with my fingertips, I begged silently to be released.

"Answer the call," the voice demanded.

Squeezing my eyes shut, I summoned all of my strength to reply to the invading presence.

"Fuck you," I choked.

"Which path will you travel?"

I'd encountered such a presence before, this being that simply exists. The sentience that was neither good nor evil, it just was.

"We have met before."

"*Yes,*" it answered.

"Are you Fate?" I asked.

"*Many beings call me many things, I accept them all, for I am.*"

"Do I still get to choose?"

"*You will always get to choose.*"

Calmly floating, the energy comforted me, cradling me in its infinite embrace.

"*The walls will fall, magic laid bare, all will be at your mercy.*"

"I don't understand."

"*Heed this warning: war is waiting.*"

"War? Who is fighting the war?" I asked.

Plummeting, I knew I was being returned to my body, to my realm.

My body was still being cradled, in the physical sense now. The scent that surrounded me was a mixture of woodsmoke and the salty bay breeze. It was so comforting, inviting, mouthwatering.

I squinted against the sunlight, as the features of Aklys' face came into focus. He was carrying me. His eyes met mine, wide with concern. I tried to muster a smile but my body felt battered, too exhausted to move.

"You won't be doing that again."

Aklys spoke sternly, the dominant tone of voice took me by surprise.

"Excuse me?" I mumbled, summoning all of my strength just to speak.

"You leveled the damn buildings. Key's Keep is gone."

Uncomfortable silence settled between us.

Our lone horse trotted slowly ahead of us with Isonei and Aloise perched atop. Maygen walked next to them and had been craning to see if I was fully conscious after hearing Aklys speak. She let out a dramatic sigh of relief.

"You're making a hobby of fainting, Celessa. Maybe you should eat more," she teased.

"As if that is the issue," Isonei snapped. "Her power is out of control, she has no guidance, and still she refuses to join the divine beings in Evelia."

"We were ambushed, Isonei. What would you have me do when lives are at stake?" I challenged.

"Train your physical abilities to defend yourself or flee, Celessa. Each time you use your gift, it grows stronger, and each time you absorb cursed magic it grows darker!" The Nymph shouted in frustration.

I stretched to free myself of Aklys' hold only to be met with a stern expression, and I rolled my eyes at the vampire.

"What do you mean it grows darker? I haven't had any side effects from my power absorbing anything," I argued.

Isonei turned to meet my gaze, and her clear eyes that shifted from green to blue were penetrating, full of magic. "You truly believe there are no consequences to consuming the most wicked forces that exist?"

Her words struck a chord in me, because this was not something I had considered.

It made sense. When my power consumes dark essences, it feels stronger, reinforced. I was feeding it what it craved.

"Each time you absorb corruption, your own will grow, spreading like a disease. It will not harm you, nor will it kill you, but it will turn you into the very thing you've been fighting against." The words carried a burdensome weight, heavy with truth.

"We're only one more day from the port."

She changed the subject quickly, her own words affecting her more than she had meant to reveal.

"Which direction?" Maygen asked.

"Due west."

"The only ports in this area are attached to Dawn's End," Aklys spoke, challenging the Nymph's directions.

Isonei hissed in frustration as she responded, "It is hidden, monster. Only allies of Evelia have access to it, as it is concealed by magic. I shall erase the information from your mind myself before we depart."

The vampire's chuckle was the mockery of a challenge. It seemed he had no intention of giving up his mind to her, earning him a threatening glare from the green woman.

"How much longer until we make camp?" I asked.

"Once we reach the forest north of Dawn's End, we'll have enough cover to make camp. At daybreak, we will escort Aloise and Isonei to the port and make for the city to procure passage into Euros."

Aklys brushed his lips against my forehead in an attempt to comfort me.

"I can walk, you know?" I teased.

"I know," he replied, pulling me tighter against his chest.

The vampire never broke a sweat, despite carrying me for what felt like hours, despite my objections. Occasionally he would take notice of my staring and offer me a wink or a smirk.

With each affectionate, playful gesture, my body grew more aware of the tension between us.

The way his broad chest flexed beneath his clothing made me feel the need to press my thighs together. I watched his long fingers and large, strong hands collect firewood for the campfire he built. Thick arms stretched and tightened as he moved about and lifted our provisions, readying our encampment for the night.

Aklys was easily the most attractive man I'd ever met. Vampires, Fae, and Elves were exceedingly beautiful when compared to mortals. Their divine parents had intended they be better than humans in every way: stronger, faster, fairer.

He was beautiful and has lived a long life. I found myself wondering about how many women have lusted after him the way I was presently. I was curious about how many had experienced this man that my mind, body, and soul craved.

My cheeks warmed with jealousy, followed by embarrassment at my irrationality. I was surprised at my own audacious emotions. What a trivial thing to find myself hung up on, considering all that was transpiring in the realm and all that was at stake for those in my company.

I should be diligent in worrying about procuring the safety of the women in my company, not fantasizing about Aklys and finding myself bitter about hypothetical women past.

All that mattered right now was making it safely to the port, and getting Isonei and Aloise onto the ship to Evelia.

Sighing deeply, I relented to my body's will, moving toward the tent to rest for the night. The thought of getting restful sleep after today's events was most welcome.

My thoughts dominated my senses only until I felt strong arms wrapped around my waist.

"Do you remember what I told you in the forest?" Aklys whispered against my ear.

His hushed tone sent chills across my skin and heat flooding to my core.

"I wonder if you might indulge me?" he asked.

Turning to face him, my eyes settled on his full lips, on the tips of fangs that peeked out from between them.

He was so tall that I needed to rise up on my toes to press my mouth against his own. The warmth was intoxicating, with his breath sweet yet metallic. The kiss was deep, passionate. It was everything I wanted and needed.

My vampire consumed me in his passion and I submitted to him entirely, blissfully content in our embrace.

Chapter Fifteen

Famous Last Words

A klys had insisted we take a walk through the night consumed forest, dark and alluring, with a mischievous grin playing on his lips.

I hadn't felt hesitant in the slightest, we were starting anew, the truth laid bare. My feelings had been hurt but his honesty settled within me comfortably. No longer would I harbor feelings of resentment for mistakes that were made.

Rather, I would allow myself to become comfortable with how I felt for the vampire. I deserved more than an escape through physical intimacy. I deserved what I'd searched for in all the wrong places: to be loved, chosen, cherished and protected.

Hopefulness had blossomed within me that this man could be the one to fulfill my desires. My hand was tucked tightly within his own, fingers woven and palms pressed firmly together. Sweat slicked our skin within the grip as he tugged me along happily.

We had made camp in the thick woodland north of Dawn's End, patiently waiting to see Aloise and Isonei to the hidden port in the morning. Though I had planned to rest, spiriting away with this man was enticing, leaving no trace of fatigue, which was whisked away by his touch and enthusiasm.

Anticipation set my nerves ablaze, a tingling sensation rippling throughout my body as I let Aklys lead me through the trees.

"Where are you taking me?" I whispered.

Aklys hushed me gently, "You'll see. Every forest in Teskaria harbors secrets, hidden magic, reserved for those who dare explore their depths."

"How do you know where to find these supposed treasures?"

Offering me a solemn smile, he responded, "I was born in the northern region, I spent my entire mortal life here."

Stunned, my jaw dropped slightly.

"Which city do you hail from?"

"My family came before the cities. Teskaria was the last of the land to be settled, the final addition to the Three Kingdoms, but I was born where the city of Ofror now stands."

Aklys was Teskarian, as well.

A fleeting fantasy took root in my mind. If he'd been a noble mortal, he would've been an ideal suitor for me in the eyes of my father. A small smile crept forth as I imagined meeting him for the first time. If Fate had played out differently, if we'd only been human...

"Where is the rest of your family? Do they live?" I asked.

He had mentioned his family only once, when he told me about their curse and their sleep. An uncomfortable silence settled between us, and his steps slowed slightly. Some of the former excitement and lightheartedness stripped away.

Suddenly, I wished I hadn't asked.

"They live, but they are far from here. It's been fifty years since I last saw them, with the last summons I received being one year ago, in the form of a letter."

He stopped altogether, turning to face me.

"It does not matter, let's enjoy our evening, milady."

My heart thundered in my chest as our bodies pressed together, lips meeting in a passionate union. A coiling sensation had settled low in my body, waiting, and longing.

Aklys kissed me in a way he hadn't before, for it was the deep, yet delicate kiss a lover placed upon their intended, a show of devotion. The emotion that transferred from one to another held promises of more.

"Come, we are almost there."

Chills shook my frame, as I hadn't expected to be released from such an embrace so suddenly.

He led me through the darkness once more, and our steps had increased to a pace so hasteful we'd nearly begun sprinting.

A giggle escaped my lips at the sight of the vampire skipping along with the carelessness of a child.

His head whipped around at the sound.

"Tell me what I can do to hear that again."

I only smiled at him. It felt strange to genuinely smile. There were so many reasons not to — reasons that I let prevent me from feeling anything akin to joy. Horror after horror plagued my existence.

There were so few things to find happiness in, but he was one of them, so I would grin at this man who made me feel things that were good.

Aklys pulled me into his arms, lifting my feet from the ground, and he twirled us around. Another giggle erupted from my chest, and I found I had lowered my walls. Tonight, I would feel carefree. I would be happy.

"I am so in awe of you, milady. For all you have suffered, you have the most beautiful smile."

The vampire squeezed me tighter. Sharp fangs glinted in the moonlight that streamed from between tree branches, decorating the forest floor and allowing just enough illumination for me to drink in his beautiful features.

I brushed his cheek with my hand.

"I didn't want to feel this way, but I can't help myself," I admitted.

Aklys sighed, pressing his forehead to mine.

"You make me feel alive again," he said.

He began walking again, still holding me in his arms.

"I left my sleep over two hundred years ago, and I have been walking this realm, a ghost of the man I once was. Being around you has awoken the desire to live within me."

Hazel eyes glowed, shimmering with deep magic, forever mixing shades of light brown and deep green.

"I had not intended this either, if I am to be truthful with you, milady. I have always had self-control when it comes to women, to infatuation."

A tiny kiss pecked my lips.

"Celessa Umbraeon,"

Aklys never used my name, it was strange to hear his voice speak it out loud.

"You are the one person in all the realms that could bring me to my knees, if you wished it. You are so powerful, and yet you needn't use any magic to shatter every wall I've ever put up. You hadn't even intended it."

He lowered me to my feet, moving his hands to caress either side of my face.

"This may not have been my original intention, but it is everything to me now. I need you to know that."

The man extended his hand to gesture away from where we stood, beckoning my attention to the place we'd been searching for.

A shocked gasp caught in my throat, and I found myself wonderstruck.

In the thickest part of the small forest, hidden deep within moss laden and twisted trees, lies a pond. The waters were blue, but not a naturally occurring shade, rather light in tone and glowing vibrantly.

Surrounding the pond and decorating the small clearing within tangled barriers were beds of pillow-like moss; tiny purple flowers dotted the ground following little, swirling paths around the spongy mounds. Leafy vines hung from the branches above, swaying gently like ribbons in the breeze.

Floating in the air, which was perfumed with the floral essence of the flowers, were strange orbs of light. Similar to fireflies but larger and different in color, they blinked to and from existence in slow flashes of magic.

"What is this place?" I asked breathlessly.

"Pixie Glen," Aklys chuckled.

What a childish name for such a magical place, I thought. How had I never heard of such a wondrous occurrence before? How did this unnatural sight, that existed so close to a bustling port city, remain hidden and untouched by man?

"Pixies are creatures of myth meant for children."

"They're technically Sprites, and they exist, but they cannot thrive where corruption lies. A small handful of places like this one still remain in the kingdoms, secret sanctuaries for the tiny creatures. My youngest sister discovered this one when we still lived in the country, so we let her name it. My siblings and I were avid explorers."

The vampire sighed at the memory.

"Will you tell me more about them?" I asked.

"Someday," he promised.

The rustling of fabric drew away my gaze to see the man dropping his clothing to the ground, leaving himself stark naked. I gaped at the masculine form that appeared to be carved by the Gods themselves. His fingers toyed with the garments covering my skin.

"Join me?" Aklys requested.

Nodding my acceptance, the vampire beamed with satisfaction and eagerly removed my clothes. We stood facing each other, bare and glowing, basked in pure magic. Aklys was a light in the darkness, physically and figuratively, silhouetted by mystical shades of dusk sky blue and emerald green. He was as mysterious as the beauty around us.

Taking my hand gently, he led me to the illuminated water. The vampire slid in so effortlessly, making no show of how the temperature affected him, leaving me nervous to discover for myself if it was agreeable. Dipping my toes, I withdrew immediately.

"It's cold!" I yelped.

"It's much better once you're in, I promise."

He smiled, reaching toward me.

Backing away, I shook my head.

"I'm not freezing for your amusement."

The vampire leapt from the water, wrapping my naked body in his cool, wet arms.

"Don't! Don't you dare!" I bit out, struggling against him.

Aklys did not listen, propelling our bodies forward into the pond, my senses immediately overwhelmed with biting frigidness. Before I could berate him, warmth crept over me, the water heating pleasantly around my skin. I couldn't help but relax, still in the arms of the admittedly infuriating man.

"I told you!" He teased.

Playfully, I stuck out my tongue. Aklys leaned in and captured it between his lips, locking us in a deeply passionate exchange. Strong hands wrapped around my bare thighs beneath the water, lifting them to hook around his waist before settling on my rear, holding me tight against him.

"If you only knew what you do to me, milady," he whispered against my damp, swollen lips, squeezing my flesh teasingly. "I've never felt desire burn as fiercely as this, what have we done?"

Water sloshed around us as he moved, wading toward the bank. The space between the moss beds and the pond water was not sand or mud as one would expect; instead, it was composed of countless tiny, shining pebbles.

They glimmered like gemstones, slick with the luminescent splashes we delivered upon them when Aklys laid my body onto the shifting surface. Hovering just above, the vampire planted kisses onto my lips, trailing across my jawline, down to my neck.

A hot tongue caressed the delicate flesh of my throat. A low growl rumbled through his body and reverberated into my own as his mouth pressed against throbbing arteries.

Without hesitation, I pushed myself into him further, silently inviting him to taste what he desired. My blood warmed at the thought, skin tightening with anticipation. I never imagined myself in a position such as this. Not only was I completely exposed in the middle of the forest, I was stealing intimate moments with a man while unmarried... again.

Moreover, I never pictured myself readily offering my blood to a vampire, much less enjoying it. My fingertips pushed roughly into his flesh the moment fangs pierced my skin, the sensation rattling me to my core.

Wrapping my legs around his waist from beneath, I forced him down, closer. My pelvis ground against his, the evidence of his arousal pressing firmly against my own.

Aklys released me from the bite, blood glossy on his teeth, and a single warm drop fell to my lip. He moved to wipe it away, but I pushed out my tongue, licking the metallic tasting liquid away.

"Fuck," he grumbled, pushing our lips together with urgency.

He rocked gently against me, one hand wrapped firmly in the locks of my hair, the other tracing the curves of my body.

I whimpered, and the vampire went completely rigid.

"You sound as delicious as you taste, milady."

Aklys began trailing kisses further down, across my collarbone, between my breasts.

"Your breathing and your heartbeat are rushed — do I truly excite you this much?" He teased.

I nodded a breathless response.

"Tell me," he demanded.

"Yes," I answered. "You excite me. I can hardly stand it," I whined.

Sharp teeth teased the sensitive flesh of my breast, pricking the skin but not puncturing, the act sent me writhing. I was desperate for more.

"Please," I begged, my fingers threaded in his locks of dark hair.

"Please, what?" He asked.

"Bite me again, please!" I urged him closer, pulling his head down.

"How could I ever refuse you?" Aklys growled, piercing my flesh and relieving the tension that coiled my muscles, my body falling limp as I relished the euphoria.

Moans escaped me as he drew blood, each pull of my veins pushing me closer to the edge. It was unbearable; the ecstasy of his bite sent me spiraling, and my body throbbed with release as I cried out the vampire's name.

He hadn't even touched me in the way I thought was necessary to achieve an orgasm. My face flushed with embarrassment at the realization.

"What a magnificent creature you are, so perfect."

His praise set my skin on fire.

"You have kept me suffering for weeks, my beautiful lady. I have longed for the feel of you against my skin, the taste of you on my tongue. You have plagued my every thought, my dreams."

I watched him lick my blood from his lips as he drank in the sight of me, bloodied and panting beneath him.

Aklys brought his fingers to his mouth, pushing two inside and dragging them back out slowly, slick with blood and saliva. Reaching down, he stroked my most sensitive parts, teasing me. My pelvis kicked up in answer, legs shaking with each gratifying touch. He pressed harder against the throbbing nerves, and I cried out at the pressure.

"Don't worry, I'll take care of you."

His breath was hot against my chest, the heat traveled across my skin, reaching every part of me. Soft lips made their way across my abdomen, delivering consistent affection as he explored. My body shuddered with each brush of his skin against my own, growing more aggressive, more unbridled.

"I want to taste you again."

Aklys' eyes met mine. Nearly all traces of hazel were gone from his irises, replaced with the shadows of hunger and desire. I was startled by the change in his demeanor.

"I'm yours," I breathed, opening myself to him fully.

He froze, "You don't mean that the way I wish, do you?"

I remembered what he'd said before, when I'd hoped he would ravage me, that if I allowed him to take my body, he would claim me entirely.

"Aklys..." I trailed off, holding his gaze and watching his expression change. I swallowed down the words I couldn't say, the confession that threatened to spoil these moments.

Sharp pain invaded my senses, as his fangs sunk into the soft flesh of my inner thigh. I released a shocked scream, moving to escape the unexpected assault.

Aklys pushed my hips back to the ground, holding me still. When he pulled his head back, a new kind of urge had taken over, changing his expression to one of a ravenous and insatiable hunger. My back slid across the pebbles, as he pulled my body down to his face, raising my hips and pushing his head further between my legs. Blood was trickling from the wound he'd just inflicted, painting his cheek red.

The thick, hot tongue I craved began thoroughly assaulting me, the way it had in Silenus Forest. Another climax had already crept to the brink of eruption, every sensual and painful moment we'd shared bringing it closer.

"I can't take it!" I moaned, my pelvis ground against his parted lips.

"Come for me, milady."

He moaned, sparing only a moment to speak before returning his attention to my body. Two fingers pushed into my entrance, pumping gently inside, beckoning my release forth. The winding coil sprung free, and my body went taut as waves of ecstasy overtook my senses. I cried out into the night as Aklys continued guiding my orgasm, groaning contentedly as I finished on his fingers and tongue. As the euphoria subsided, he lifted himself above me, his expression twisted with painful want.

"Please," he begged, "I'm desperate for your touch."

I offered my hand to him, which he guided down to his hard length.

"Just for a moment..." Aklys whispered.

The vampire moaned as I wrapped my fingers around the girthy extension.

He folded his hand over mine, guiding me in stroking him roughly, the slick tip of his manhood rubbing along my throbbing sex.

"I want to come with you," I whispered, and my muscles were tightening again, feeling him press against my nerve endings.

Aklys groaned, his control faltering as I pumped him against myself. His essence was hot on my skin, the quivering of his body such an incredible sight I couldn't contain myself, coming again as I felt him cover me in release. The vampire collapsed, trembling, his lips pressed to my neck.

"Someday I'll have you," he swore, lifting us to return to the water.

The coolness that came before the comforting warmth did little to awaken my senses, my body thoroughly spent and overcome with drowsiness.

Aklys stroked my skin lazily, wetting my hair and wiping away the pebbles that clung to my shoulders, occasionally brushing a gentle kiss against my forehead and cheeks.

Someday he'll have me, I thought.

Morning had arrived. I must have fallen asleep in the glen, as there was no memory of returning to camp when I awoke cradled in Aklys' arms.

His back was propped against a tree, holding me upright, nestled in the opening of his legs which were crossed at the ankles.

I smiled at the sight of him completely relaxed, head tilted back and eyes closed. His dark lashes were full and long, and I took a few moments to admire the construction of his face. A strong jawline, thick brows that arched only slightly, full lips, and a straight nose crafted his handsome features. All were framed by the unruly dark hair that always looked slightly windswept no matter the conditions.

Eyelids popped open, and he peered at me suspiciously.

"Like what you see, milady?"

I thought back to the keep when he'd asked me this question the first time and smirked.

"I do," I confirmed.

Aklys smiled.

"I'm always right," a sleepy voice chimed in.

Maygen had emerged from her tent and sauntered about happily, a wide grin spread over her face. She was looking at the two of us, thrilled with her declaration.

I had brushed her off before when she'd inquired about my thoughts on the vampire, denying any interest. She had given me the time and space I needed to sort it out for myself, even waiting to proclaim her victory as I recovered from my night terrors and the events of Key's Keep.

A disgusted sound left the woman who followed, Isonei, who kept no secrets when it came to how she felt about Aklys and his kind.

I frowned slightly, not about her feelings toward him, but at the realization that she was due to depart. I would likely never see her again after today, and though she wasn't always agreeable, she held a piece of my heart. She had protected me at a young age, confident that I would not become the monster my father had intended.

What pained me more was knowing I would never see Aloise again, a woman whom I'd grown to care for, who had become my friend. I would never meet her child, Thibault's child. Reassurance in the knowledge of their safety was all that contained my reluctance to part with them.

The vampire lifted us from our position on the ground, leaving me to stand on my own.

I sought out Aloise, who had yet to emerge from the tent.

"She is sick again," Isonei stopped me before I could enter the shelter. "Let her rest a while longer. Walk with me," she insisted.

We began making our way from the encampment, stopping only when we were out of range for our companions to eavesdrop on the looming conversation. Isonei did not allow Aklys and Maygen to be far from her sight, though, making sure we had just enough privacy without intrusions.

An uneasy feeling had settled in my gut, watching her worried expression.

"The suspense is killing me," I offered playfully.

Isonei shot me a glare, and I noticed her eyes were blue today, clear and bright.

"You are not funny," she hissed. "Serious matters are at hand."

Clearing her throat, she continued, "When we reach the port, your monster must stay away."

"Why? He is no threat, and we are better protected if he is nearby," I argued.

She rose a pale green hand to silence me.

"We will be received by my divine mother."

"Melissae," I clarified.

The Nymph nodded as she spoke, "She will not be alone; the Goddess of Beauty will accompany her."

Surprise pushed the air from my lungs.

"Calaeya?"

A mother of mortals, a consort of the God of Chaos. My skin prickled at the thought.

"They expect to receive you, not your friend. I have no interest in being labeled a failure *again*, so if you would be so kind as to state your position to the Goddesses, it would be appreciated."

"You pulled me away to ask me to cover your ass so mommy doesn't scold you?"

"Celessa, you are most disagreeable."

She wrinkled her nose dramatically, feigning disgust.

"Forgive me," I winked. "I will speak with them and I will ask Aklys to stay behind. It won't be an issue to receive Aloise in my stead, right?"

Isonei sighed, "Many years ago it was the mission of the Nymphs to procure the most vulnerable peoples of the realm and escort them back to Evelia. There have been internal wars raging within the Three Kingdoms for as long as they have existed, corruption is rampant and the innocents suffer. We were once a safe haven."

"What changed?"

"Infiltrators. People who secured passage with the intention of bringing down our barriers. While I am aware that Aloise is innocent and in need of aid, the deities may be skeptical."

Her bare feet shuffled in the grass.

"There's something else — what aren't you telling me?" I asked.

The magic laden irises gleamed, "Calaeya did not want you in Evelia, she will be most relieved to hear your decision. She fears you."

"Why would a deity need to fear me?"

She stepped close to me, pressing her lips to my ear, as if she were worried someone would overhear.

"It is because your divine power is capable of challenging their own," the Nymph whispered. "Deities cannot be killed by the mortal or immortal beings of the realm, they pose no threat to them because of the difference in their magic and their blood, as well as the control they possess over it. Amalgams retain their divine blood, they mimic deities, and *that's* the true reason they are considered dangerous."

My heart fluttered and then stilled. What Isonei had just revealed changed everything for me. It gave me a renewed hope for my vengeance and an answer to my most daunting question: Could I kill a God?

I now knew it was possible. The only image my mind could conjure was the viper.

"You do not know what you have done for me, Isonei. Thank you."

Her brows furrowed, and fear laced her features.

"When I uncover my father's identity, he'll be dealt with. I'll be free of him, and the realms will be free of him."

The woman relaxed slightly.

"Do you know who he is?"

Her hands flew to her face, clasped tightly over her mouth.

"Are you okay?" I shouted.

The act had been involuntary, for *something* was stopping her from speaking.

"I'm sorry, I'm sorry! Don't tell me!" I panicked.

Able to release herself, her arms hung at her sides, she faced me with a solemn expression.

"Any who interfere in such a way may face his wrath, we cannot risk it."

The voice that came forth from her in that moment did not belong to the woman, it was a response left within her by magic, an answer brought forth by my request.

"I'm sorry."

I touched the soft skin of her shoulder with my fingertips, and, to my surprise, she pulled me into an embrace.

"No, Celessa. I am sorry. Forgive me, for I can no longer aid you, we have already risked and lost so much," she whispered.

"It was my intention to see you to safety. I should have taken you all those years ago but it just seemed so wrong to pluck a flower from where it thrived. We never foresaw the dark Mage intervening in your Fate. What he did changed everything."

I didn't ask her anymore questions for fear of a magically induced reaction, I only attempted to dissect the words she spoke, my mind coming up blank.

I would find no more answers here.

Dusk was beginning to change the blue of the sky to hues of violet and rose, pastel clouds painted the horizon looking west over Galazio Strait.

I had sailed these waters but once, with my father and my older sisters: Necilia and Arecelle. We had gone to Licourt, capital city of the Three Kingdoms, at the request of the High Court. We'd been introduced to the Achreios family, powerful Fae that presided over the kingdoms, the ruling nobles.

High Lord Cohen Achreios had summoned my father to introduce his eldest daughters, with the intention of arranging matches for us. I had only just come of a suitable age, and my father had been reluctant to expose his daughters to all the manners of debauchery that took place within the capital courts.

Micah Achreios had sent a formal proposal to my father only a fortnight after our visit, requesting betrothal to me. My father had been disgusted and outraged that the Fae man had sought after the youngest of his girls.

As Cohen's eldest son, Micah, too, was an immortal being. While he appeared to be a man in his early twenties, he had been nearly one hundred and fifty years old at that time. Fae families rarely sought unions with mortals, and it was unheard of for the ruling family to extend such an offer.

Lord Altan had wanted to refuse, but the decision was left to me, as I had reached adulthood. I had been so deeply in love with Thibault that I'd never even considered the offer, hopeful that my father would relent and allow me to marry him instead.

I would like to see the city again someday. It was magnificent, surrounded by clear waters and an enchanting forest, the buildings stretched out over the majority of the island it sat upon. The inner-city structures were crafted from white stone, bright and beautiful, they seemed so large until you stood before the castle.

Castle Licourt shamed every building that existed in the realm, for it towered over everything, casting a shadow so far, it shaded large sections of the city as the sun crept across the sky. One day, I would return and create new memories, when I lived a simpler life and could exist safely within these lands.

Isonei had insisted the port was not to be revealed under the exposure of daylight, so we waited patiently for sunset. Aklys' arms encircled me from behind, and together we stared out over the open water, watching the fading rays change the colors of the world. I turned to face him, the glow of day giving way to night shone brightly upon his skin, painting him gold.

"You'll have to wait for me somewhere."

I sighed, pressing my cheek to his chest and wrapping my arms around his waist.

Aklys rested his chin atop my head, his body bowing to reach. He was much taller than I was, at least twenty centimeters, which was admittedly impressive because I was of average height for an adult woman.

"I know, the Nymph already threatened me." He snickered, squeezing me gently as he continued, "I wonder if Calaeya would remember me if she looked upon my face."

Intrigued, I craned my head to look into his eyes.

"Have you met her?"

"I have," he smiled as he said, "I have crossed paths with many of the deities in my life, though it has been many years."

"Which ones?"

Excitement pressed me closer, eager to learn which divine beings the vampire knew. The deities were shrouded in mystery, meant to be far out of reach from those within the kingdoms.

"Perhaps when we have more time, I can tell you the stories of how I came to meet each of them?"

A gentle kiss brushed my forehead.

"Nightfall is nearly upon us, we should prepare ourselves, milady."

Disappointed, I nodded.

I could wait, for I knew we had plenty of time.

Isonei appeared from the cover of the brush, returning with a small bundle of herbs for Aloise as we waited for the full coverage of night to offer safety. Aloise had been fighting with the strain of her changing body throughout the day, sicker than usual and unable to travel without some sort of remedy to quell her symptoms. The Nymph had informed us that the gestation of mixed bloodlines tends to take a greater toll on the mother as the pregnancy progresses, especially when the mother is mortal.

Admiration of the woman had grown within me exponentially, for carrying on and clinging to life after Thibault died. I wished I could see her through to welcome their child into the world.

When the sickness had first appeared in Aloise, we'd feared the worst, unaware she was experiencing the symptoms of pregnancy.

Learning that it was due to pregnancy, the only thing that mattered was ensuring her safety.

The safety of Thibault's only child.

He never had the chance to know he was becoming a father. Despite the reassurances of my companions, I couldn't help but continue to blame myself for his death.

I found myself wishing often that Maygen and I had made it through the pass without being attacked, without having to journey to the settlement where we'd been put through hell. After all, it was the place where Thibault had found me and our paths became entwined with Aloise, with Aklys. If I had never been there, Thibault would be alive to share the joy of their union with the woman he loved, with the woman he had chosen.

My only hope was that Aloise and her child would be safe in Evelia, as Isonei had promised. They would have the opportunity to thrive and to be happy.

The herbs the Nymph offered were meant to subdue the harsh symptoms she endured. If they worked to their full potential, she would be free of the violent vomiting and her energy would be restored. Her body would be without pain, enabling her to make the journey toward their salvation.

"You weren't gone long," I mused.

"There is not much time to spare. It won't be long now; my mother will reveal our vessel, and we will have to take our leave quickly. It is best to bid farewell now."

Isonei's eyes flitted to Aklys, which struck me as odd, for she rarely looked to him unless she was planning to berate him or deliver an insult. I wondered if it was because he hadn't left us yet, when she had expressly requested he make himself scarce.

"Monster," she said, facing him with a stern expression. "A word," she requested, gesturing him away.

For Isonei to even entertain a conversation with Aklys, to want to speak with him privately, was puzzling. I hoped after their departure he would share their hushed words with me, and I prayed it was something that wouldn't be detrimental to our efforts to procure their safety or to continue our journey into Euros.

As if my subconscious had called out to her, Maygen appeared at my side.

"Do you think it's serious?" She mumbled.

My shoulders sagged as if being weighed down by the secrecy.

"We know better than to hope for anything else."

Maygen huffed her agreement, joining me in my silence for a few moments.

"Soon there will only be three of us. We have managed to gain three, lose one, gain another, and now we wait to lose two more. Fate mocks us."

"Perhaps Fate is showing us that we will never be secure in our position and that we always stand to lose something," I returned.

"How morose." Maygen sighed. "You're probably right. This is all we know. Loss and turmoil." She smiled tightly before stepping away to gather her things.

The three of us who remained had agreed to travel through the night into Dawn's End, with the plan being to secure passage in the morning to leave Teskaria at long last.

Aloise had consumed her herbs, quickly regaining more control over her body, and rose from her place by our smothered fire to stand by my side. Her abdomen was appearing more distended than usual, revealing the life growing within.

A warmth settled over me, and I was happy that she had this piece of Thibault to cherish forever. He would live on through his child.

"Is everything okay?" she inquired quietly.

"Isonei is acting out of sorts, and she is speaking with Aklys."

Aloise's eyes widened with shock, and I chuckled my understanding in response.

"I'm just as surprised. She seems concerned, and she didn't speak to me much upon returning."

The frail woman frowned slightly, and the sight stirred strange emotions within me. So much animosity had existed between us at first: we'd been jealous of each other and at odds due to our love of Thibault, not to mention his love for each of us.

When he'd made the decision to be with Aloise, I had hated them both. Throughout the trials we've faced, I found it in myself to forgive them. When I gave myself time to understand it, and to understand him, I couldn't bring myself to truly hate him for moving on. I'd wanted him to be happy, and Aloise made him happy.

Repressing my feelings for Thibault had also given Aklys the space to worm his way into my heart. His crude banter became charming, the teasing nickname he used for me was no longer annoying, and his advances toward me became more irresistible. The night in Silenus Forest exposed feelings I hadn't expected to ever have for the vampire, and I had since struggled to prevent them from blossoming into something more.

I felt the sadness returning, knowing that these would be our last moments as companions. The woman had become my friend, and I truly cared for her. I deeply cherished the small bundle she held in her womb, a precious gift I would never have the opportunity to know, but would gladly lay down my life to preserve.

"I wish you would come with us," Aloise spoke finally.

Her words deepened the sorrow I felt at the prospect of their looming departure.

Forcing a smile, I reached out a hand.

"If I don't stay, I'll never see this life through the way I need to, and there is still so much left for me to uncover. I was never meant to hide in Evelia," I whispered.

She took my hand, and I allowed her to lean on me, supporting her weak frame as we waited for Isonei and Aklys to return. The last of the light in the daytime sky filtered away like our remaining moments together.

The vampire's mood prior to speaking with Isonei had been relaxed, happy even. Now he stood rigid, his expression pale and unsettled. Concern took over my mind, wondering what Isonei could've possibly told him to make his demeanor shift so drastically. I continued eyeing the man until my presence dawned on him, and he returned my gaze. The corner of his lips lifted in a pathetic attempt at a smirk, but the act did nothing to alleviate my worry.

"We must leave the moment my mother summons us, and you must depart this place. Secure your passage to Euros, for Teskaria will never offer you safety," the nymph commanded, taking long looks at Maygen and myself.

Aklys had made himself scarce a distance away, concealed within the tree line. Four women stood side by side on the shoreline, waiting for something to appear.

An unexplainable urge overtook me, and I turned to look upon the faces of my friends. I pulled Aloise into an embrace, tightening around her more than I had expected. She happily returned the gesture, summoning moisture to my eyes. I tried to blink away the tears before anyone noticed.

Upon releasing her, she grasped my hand, placing it upon her swollen belly.

I melted; the tears that had threatened to spill before flowed freely now.

"Celessa, always remember that you are the reason we are still here. Your *gift*," she took my hands into her own, "it saved my life, this baby's life."

Realizing she had most definitely been pregnant when I had found her in that cell beneath the keep, when my power wrung the black magic from her body, nauseated me. If I hadn't been able to save her, although it had been unintentional, they would all be gone right now.

Thibault was lost forever, but because of his love for Aloise, a new life would grace this world.

"Thank you," she whispered.

"Perhaps we will see each other again someday?" I suggested half-heartedly, knowing in my core that it was merely a foolish fantasy.

Isonei embraced me as well. The disgruntled nymph was precious to me, and it pained me to let her go. I truly hoped I would be reunited with them eventually.

"Lady Celessa, at long last."

A thick, captivating voice sounded from behind me, stealing my attention from the women with whom I'd been sharing affections.

The divine being who stood before me was decorated in gold adornments, a white cloak draped over her deep, rich skin. The contrast was stark, bright ivory against glowing ebony. Eyes equal in depth stared into my very soul, so dark they threatened to consume me within the most tranquil night. She was the most exquisite woman I'd ever laid eyes upon.

Calaeya, the Goddess of Beauty.

Chapter Sixteen

The Hardest Goodbyes

"Do you believe yourself to be so powerful that you need not kneel in the presence of divinity?" Calaeya snapped, shattering my awe.

"Forgive me, Goddess."

Bowing my head, I dropped to my knees, embarrassed to have insulted the deity.

"Unnecessary formalities," a familiar voice hissed. "She is one of us, divine blood runs through her veins, unbridled and ever changing; as is her purpose. You should mind your manners, *myn lykyng*."

Raising my gaze, I was met by the glowing being that was the Goddess of the Seasons, Melissae. She lifted me gently by my chin, guiding my body upward to stand before her.

"We meet again," her lips pressed firmly together, disappointment apparent on her face. "I understand you will not join us in Evelia. This is a mistake, Celessa."

Before I could give my thoughts a voice, Calaeya scoffed.

"A mistake for whom? She will serve her purpose, and we will be safe from the wrath of the one who sired her."

Her voice was thick and rich, and I dared to imagine her performing a beautiful opera like the talented vocalists I had adored in my childhood.

"The vampires circle her like birds of prey, and we grow more endangered with every moment spent lingering in her presence!"

I felt disappointed that the deity looked upon me with such disgust, whereas I found myself mesmerized by her. I was ashamed of the power I possessed, ashamed of the truth of my birth, ashamed of who and what I was.

Melissae cupped Calaeya's face in her hands, pressing their foreheads together lovingly.

"She did not choose this," she reminded her.

The Goddess of Beauty offered me one final glance, the magic in her eyes glimmering. A ship rocked against the small dock of the secret port, and Calaeya moved to make for it, to disappear from these lands once again.

Her steps stilled for a moment, and she turned slightly. "Turn away from the north, for war awaits those who dare draw near."

Without another word, she took her place on board.

"My Goddess Melissae, I humbly request to give my position among you to another."

My head turned to Aloise, who stood nervously cradling her belly, flanked by Isonei and Maygen.

"You wish to protect the unborn, a noble gesture. I will grant you this kindness, Lady Celessa, if you will consider braving the journey to Evelia in nearing days. There are many who wish to meet you."

Her pinched expression radiated more warmth than before as her gaze passed between myself and my companions, gentle eyes fell lovingly upon one face in particular.

"It is time to return home, my child."

Melissae reached out for her Nymph daughter.

Isonei led Aloise forward to bow before the deity. Melissae gently touched the swelling evidence of the life within.

"A healthy girl." She smiled.

Aloise beamed, and my heart warmed. *Thibault has a daughter.*

The women bid their farewells to Maygen and myself, and parting ways was bittersweet. Fighting the urge to follow them, I prayed they would find their way safely.

Melissae lingered for a moment more, her energy shifting and her aura darkening.

"I fear you are not prepared for what lies ahead." Her voice had deepened, the tone nearly threatening. "The threat follows you. Beware of those who bathe in blood, heralds of chaos and war. Your heart's desire will be your undoing."

In a blinding flash of white light and vibrant blue flower petals, they were gone.

Somehow, we knew that Isonei and Aloise had gone to Evelia, and we knew they were escorted by Goddesses. Memories of where we had been, and how they had departed, were gone.

Vaguely, I recalled releasing our horse, but couldn't remember why. We had returned to the forest, taking a path meant to lead us to the city. Maygen and I had been enchanted, sauntering along until Aklys reached us, his presence returning us to awareness.

He had trouble recalling the exact location of where we'd said our farewells to our companions as well. I'd remembered Isonei threatening to remove the information from our minds, it seemed she had made good on her promise.

Few words were exchanged as we all processed the departure of our friends, walking through the long night in an effort to reach the port city. The gray of dawn offered hazy light and just before us, down the long slope of a rounded hill, sat the bustling settlement of Dawn's End. Ships docked around the jutting ports, and the town had just begun to come to life, with the earliest risers beginning their work at the water's edge.

Soon, we would make for Euros, leaving Teskaria behind at long last.

"This has been exhausting," Maygen spoke loudly, examining the sun's rays that filtered through the leaves of large trees that surrounded us, "I think a short nap is warranted before we book passage. Enjoy your alone time." She snickered at the implication.

Maygen had wrapped a blanket from her pack around herself and was snoring on the ground in a matter of moments.

Aklys was staring blankly, his face as pale as it had been after his conversation with Isonei. The vampire stood before me, swallowing hard as I gazed up at him. A hand lifted toward my face, and I leaned into the affectionate gesture. The connection I felt growing between us both excited and frightened me. As much as I wanted to embrace it, whispering reservations ignited my smothered fears and gave them new life.

Slowly, I stepped into him, gently brushing my body against his. Hazel eyes searched the area, scanning for any hidden threats, before he scooped me up into his arms and darted a distance away from our dozing companion. My breath stole from my lungs, my arms clinging to him as he carried me off.

Aklys set me down gently near a small stream, hands lingering on my body, as he waited to assess my intentions.

"Milady."

Desperately fighting the smile that threatened to expose itself, I looked toward the ground, biting my lip. Long fingers tugged at my chin, beckoning me to return my gaze to his face. I needed his comfort, and I craved his intimacy. My heart was burdened with the sorrow of losing our friends, despite it being for the best. A few stolen moments with this man would grant me a reprieve, and it would allow happiness to mask my sorrow, if only for a little while.

"May I?" He whispered, slowly lowering parted lips to brush against my own, closing the distance between us.

My breath caught in my throat as the awareness of his desire made its presence known, pressing against my abdomen. Our bodies and minds seemed to be in sync where lust was concerned.

"Do you want me?" He breathed, pushing against me until all I could think about was the erection that taunted me beneath the fabric of our clothes.

"Yes. I want you," I reassured him.

He groaned and captured me in a passionate kiss, forcing his tongue into my mouth. I melted into him. Strong hands slid down my back, firmly grasping my rear and forcing every inch of my body into contact with his own. I was certain that the only way to be any closer to him was by having him inside of me, and the thought made my legs quiver.

The heat between us dampened our clothes, sweat already clinging to our bodies. Aklys pulled away to remove his shirt, and I watched every fluid movement, taking notice of every muscle that rippled underneath his smooth skin.

The vampire lowered himself to a kneeling position, looking up at me hungrily from the ground. His hands snaked their way underneath my too-long tunic, and fingers hooked the waistband of my pants, tugging them down and discarding them after my feet had been pulled-through. Before I had a moment to protest, he lifted my legs up to rest on his shoulders, parting me before him.

I gasped, trying to steady myself.

"Lift your arms, and grab that branch. Don't let go." He commanded, and I breathlessly nodded my submission.

A satisfied rumble vibrated from his chest as I secured my grip onto the thick branch above, holding my weight just enough for him to comfortably wedge himself between my thighs. Aklys teasingly planted kisses along my legs, slowly creeping toward my most sensitive area.

I whimpered and wriggled in anticipation of what was to come. Waiting for him to finish his playful teasing had me utterly in pieces, entirely at his mercy, and throbbing with desire. He was fully aware of my struggling as he breathed hot air onto the aching body parts.

"I love how eager you are, and the way your body responds to me."

His hot tongue ran along the tender flesh of my inner thigh; he *wanted* me to squirm.

"Do you think about my tongue on you every time you look at me?"

I whimpered helplessly in response.

Two sharp fangs pricked at the sensitive flesh below, and I failed to stifle the moan that tumbled from my lips.

"Tell me how much you like it, and I'll think about tasting your blood, milady."

He grinned tauntingly.

"I want to feel your fangs on my skin — I *crave* you."

I was struggling to speak, mind spinning.

His grip on me tightened, and I braced myself for the quick pain that comes with the bite. My body shuddered when he pierced my flesh, leaving my core clenching at the sensation of his long tongue lapping up streams of blood that trickled down my thigh.

"Mmm, my second favorite flavor."

Aklys licked the crimson from his lips.

"But my first..."

His head inched closer.

At last, he made an intrusion into my body's entrance, stretching the delicate space, and savoring the taste of me. His tongue trailed upwards to swirl around the most sensitive part of my center. My pelvis bucked forward, and a low moan carried out from deep within my chest as he began to satisfy the desperate, throbbing urge.

I had no control over the quivering that jolted my legs against his shoulders. With my grasp on the branch above faltering, I was desperate to reach down to touch the vampire, trying to steady myself in the process. Releasing slightly, I moved a hand to touch his soft locks of hair.

"Hands above you," he snarled in quick response.

I returned my grip to the tree, holding as tightly as I could manage.

Aklys assaulted the tender area thoroughly, paying special attention to the nerve endings that caused my body to shake and twist with pleasure. I cried out into the forest, begging for release. He savored me as though I was the sweetest honey to ever touch his tongue, and plunged into me deeply, desperate to taste as much of me as possible. The moans of pleasure that he breathed into my body brought me closer and closer to shattering.

"Don't hold back, milady, I want every drop of you."

He groaned, the only pause he took from pleasuring me was to seduce me further with his words. He was relentless.

"Come on my tongue. I want to feel you - show me how much you enjoy this."

I couldn't take anymore, the internal coil snapped, and my eruption sent me screaming in an explosive release.

Aklys moaned into me as I orgasmed for him. He didn't stop feasting, his tongue carrying my body through the waves of euphoria. I whimpered as my grip finally faltered, giving out and losing hold on the support above.

The vampire didn't budge despite the sudden drop of my weight, and I twisted my fingers into his dark hair, clenching tightly as I collected myself.

Aklys lowered me onto his lap when I began to still, the release subsiding. He circled his arms around my quivering body, holding me tightly to his chest as I attempted to catch my breath, and I relaxed into him. I let him hold me for a long time before lifting my head to look into his eyes; intrusive thoughts already plaguing my mind.

"Are you suffering?" I blurted out.

He arched a questioning brow at me.

"Your pleasure is more than enough to keep me satisfied," Aklys chuckled.

I moved to kiss him, and satisfaction glossed over his eyes while he absorbed my affection wholeheartedly. The moment was sweet, and I greedily savored every second.

Then suddenly, his body went rigid, and he lifted us to stand.

Puzzled, I looked around, seeing nothing that should raise alarm.

"What's wrong?"

"Get dressed," he demanded, hastily tugging on his shirt and collecting my discarded clothing, which he helped me back into.

Aklys lifted my body into his arms again and began running in a new direction, away from where Maygen slept and away from our tree by the stream. He sprinted for only a few moments until we had reached an open field, and then stopped abruptly, dropping me to my feet.

"Aklys, what's going on?"

"Stand behind me, and don't say anything," he commanded.

The darkness in his eyes startled me.

"Pull your shirt up, and cover your marking with your hair. They're here."

He mussed my long locks, arranging the brown hair around my neck to conceal the snake tattoo that was branded on my skin. Who was here? I hadn't seen anyone for a long while, scanning the forest that surrounded us.

"When you turn back, start heading back north - stay straight on, and you'll make it back to Maygen. You go to her, and don't look back," Aklys whispered.

A group of four armored men appeared from the forest's edge, hastily approaching and leaving me no time to question the vampire.

The insignia upon the metal breastplates was not one with which I was familiar, for these were not soldiers of Teskaria or Euros.

They stopped only a short distance away from us, and upon further examination, I surmised they were not from Adristan either. These men were vampires.

Aklys angled himself in front of me, squaring his shoulders, and prepared himself to receive the caravan of strangers.

"We've been looking for you, Aklys," spoke a blonde-haired man.

"I've heard," Aklys replied, his voice low and laced with suppressed rage.

"It's time to go home, as you have some very unhappy people waiting to receive you. I believe you have some explaining to do."

The man's eyes flicked in my direction, wearing a suspicious frown as he inspected me. I cowered under the intensity of his gaze.

"Let's not waste any time then, Euric," Aklys agreed, moving to commune with the men.

My eyes bulged as I realized he was attempting to leave with them. I lashed out, grabbing his arm. He looked back at me with an expression that was cold and unusual, as if he had put on a mask.

"What the fuck is going on?" I hissed.

"I'm leaving," Aklys said flatly.

Leaving? His declaration felt like a slap in the face. *Why would he leave with these people?*

I didn't loosen my hold, my eyes fixed on his, silently demanding answers. We had just reached a place of mutual understanding, trust, and emotion. I had finally allowed myself to feel everything I'd been repressing, and I had lowered my defenses.

His face twisted, eyes darting between the caravan and my trembling figure before him. A deep sigh pushed through his pursed lips, and he looked toward the ground to avert my questioning gaze.

I was confused and hurt. *Had he planned to leave all this time?*

He'd made this journey by my side. He chose to continue on despite every trial, every bleak moment of despair, and every danger.

We'd shared life-altering experiences together. He'd waited for me to reciprocate his affections. Aklys had held me in his arms, been patient with me, and earned back my trust. He had made me feel safe and protected, confessed his emotions for me, and showed me hidden pieces of himself. Now that he finally had me, he would abandon me?

Was every moment worth nothing? Had it not been enough? Had I not been enough? A unique kind of sadness overwhelmed me, weighing me down and reaching the very depths of my soul.

It felt like my heart was breaking.

I loosened my hold and skimmed my palm down his arm, wanting to hold his hand in my own, desperate for him to return my touch.

Aklys withdrew, avoiding my advance, further deepening the internal wound.

I couldn't understand why this was happening. I had held hope he would give me just a bit longer to work out the kinks in my life, in my feelings, and in the very fibers of who I was. Couldn't he just give me a little more time?

Was I not worth it?

My insecurities took hold, and my darkest thoughts made sense. Who would want someone so beyond damaged as I was? Who would be willing to wait for someone to give them what they wanted?

Aklys was making his disdain abundantly clear in these passing moments, eyeing me with a stare that was devoid of emotion, blank and cold.

The welling in my chest was reaching the surface, tears threatened to spill from my eyes as I took in the disdain of his demeanor.

"Not here," he growled, grabbing my arm and pulling me away.

"Time is of the essence," one of the vampires spoke up. He was an armored man with dusty brown hair, wearing a fanged sneer upon his face.

Aklys turned to face him, emanating an aura of power and authority I'd never experienced from him before. It was like he'd transformed into an entirely different person, a stranger, not the man that held my heart in his palms.

"I will have a few moments to rectify this situation," he gestured toward me with his free hand, "and then we will go. You will wait."

The man glowered; his face painted with disgust as he glared at me.

I followed Aklys away, out of view of the vampires. The shaking had surpassed a point of control, my body trembling as though I'd been dropped in a bath of ice water.

Safely out of earshot, Aklys swiveled my body behind a tree to conceal us. His eyes were dark, not empty as they had been, but still masked, hiding the truth. He was hiding himself.

Tenderly, he ran his fingers down the length of my arms, his breathing becoming ragged. An imaginary, clawed hand was gripping my throat as the silence between us grew increasingly painful. Waiting on bated breath, I watched him, hoping he would tell me it was a ruse.

Just tell me we are going to run away.

We could run away from this summons, away from the people awaiting him, away from everything.

"I'm sorry," he whispered.

I lost the battle then. Disbelief overwhelmed me, and tears overflowed onto my cheeks, leaving behind warm, wet evidence of my pain.

His face twisted, contorting into something miserable.

"I don't understand," I whimpered. "You're really going to go? Why? Aklys, please…"

I didn't entirely understand what it was I was pleading for. I think I longed for him to stay with me because I needed him, and I wanted him for so much more than just our physical intimacy. That had been something I could only admit to myself; it was something I hadn't told him because I was afraid.

I had been afraid to feel something like this, afraid to connect with someone in a way that only leads to heartbreak. I was afraid to love him, and I'd let that fear hold me back in the time we'd been together, continuously tested by Fate. I had pushed him away again and again, wounding him.

Now, I was paying for it.

Aklys looked uncomfortable as he searched for his words, the right ones.

"I'm not ready to let you go!" I proclaimed.

He hushed me fervently, gesturing to his ears, as he didn't want anyone to hear us.

"I don't have a choice," he whispered.

"There is always a choice, Aklys! You chose to find me that day in the settlement, and you chose to stay by my side all this time. You chose to share things with me, to share *yourself* with me, and to change your mind about what you'd been meant to do. You're just going to leave it all behind? You're going to leave me behind?"

My words spilled forth without restraint, my despair getting the best of me.

Perhaps if I had been better, he wouldn't go.

"I-I'm sorry, I know that... That I wasn't giving you what you need t-to want to stay with m-me... I wasn't ready, but I am now, please!" I stuttered as sobs began to shake my body.

This wasn't happening; it couldn't be.

Time and time again, I am forced to lose those I love.

Aklys took my face in his hands, searching my eyes. He shook his head, the mask he wore nearly shattering.

I found myself against his chest, pulled into an embrace.

"Please," I begged, "Please don't leave me."

Aklys' own body began to tremble as he held on.

"I must go, milady."

He sighed into my hair, pressing soft lips to my scalp, seeming unwilling to release me from his hold.

My sobs became more violent and more desperate. I was ready to admit to myself that I felt love. I loved him with every cursed part of my being. Even though I felt disgraceful for feeling so much for a man I'd sworn I didn't want, and even after telling myself I'd never love again after the betrayals I'd endured - I love him.

The words reached my tongue, but fell flat, unwilling to be released into existence. If I don't tell him, he won't stay. I have to tell him…

I couldn't.

"Look at me," he commanded, returning his strong hands to my face, aligning our gazes. "There are many things that you don't know about me."

Aklys bit his lip, dragging the sharp fangs against the delicate skin.

"I have obligations, obligations that are now calling me back to a place where you cannot follow. I don't want to leave you, please know that, but I won't endanger your life for my own selfish desires."

"I don't understand, we're always in danger. Where could you possibly go that we couldn't be together? This doesn't make any sense!" I argued.

It had to be an excuse, and he was trying to make the blow upon my heart less painful. He had to know it wasn't working, that I was suffering.

Aklys remained quiet for just a few seconds, but those seconds felt like hours, torturous and unending. His resolve had melted, and a single tear fell to his cheek.

"Greilor," he said flatly, reluctantly.

Greilor?

Greilor was a country of ruin and outcasts, a hellscape that harbored the worst manners of people. It housed the vampire lords that had survived the Blood War and what was left of their armies.

As a child, my parents taught us the history of the Three Kingdoms. All we knew of the far-off kingdom was that the lands were forbidden, desolate, and corrupt. No one who ever journeyed there returned.

Why would he be summoned to Greilor? How was that possible? I had so many questions.

The only conclusion I could draw was that he lied.

"If they find out who you are, I don't know if I can protect you. I can't risk it." Aklys was referring to my power and that I was the only Amalgam in the realm, a forbidden and coveted creature.

A weapon.

He lifted his head toward the direction in which we'd strayed from, hearing the men beginning to grow louder. The party that awaited him was growing restless and irate.

"We will see each other again." Aklys swore, touching his forehead to my own.

I held onto him with every ounce of strength in my body, silently begging for him to stay.

"Please, I need you. I..."

Just tell him, my heart screamed. *Tell him that you love him, give him what you know he needs to keep him by your side. Tell him the truth.*

I still couldn't tell him.

He caressed my cheeks, wiping away the wet warmth with his thumbs, and pressed a tender kiss between my brows.

My fingers twisted into his clothing, my grip on him tightening fiercely. I wouldn't let him go.

Aklys angled my face to capture my lips with his own. He kissed me deeply, passionately, the kind of kiss that only two lovers share. It was desperate, and it was sad. He was kissing me goodbye.

When he finally began to pull away, I cried out pitifully. This was unbearable.

"It won't be so bad if you close your eyes, milady," he whispered.

I shook my head, silently refusing.

"You have to let me go now. Close your eyes. Please."

More tears glistened on his perfect face, the face of a man who had unknowingly worked his way into every fiber of my being, who had become a part of who I had become and all I hoped to be.

Reluctantly, my eyes squeezed shut, fighting against the instinct to keep holding on. His touch slowly lifted from my skin, our contact ending. An emptiness grew around me, drowning me in misery.

Another small kiss pressed against my lips, light and sweet.

"Don't open your eyes, my beautiful lady. Everything will be okay."

I shuddered, breathing in his scent one last time.

"We will be together again," Aklys promised quietly.

Footsteps began to carry away, indicating his departure. I screamed internally, struggling against every urge to open my eyes and to follow him. The steps paused, lingering a moment more. I listened intently, praying he would change his mind.

"*I love you.*"

The whisper echoed through my skull, repeating over and over. Every day we had spent together, every word spoken between us, and every stolen moment we shared replayed in my mind. Had I only imagined the words? Had my mind granted me the illusion of what I so desperately sought after? Was it a blessing to be loved or was it another curse left to damn me into oblivion?

I collapsed to the ground, unable to control the chaotic storm raging inside my chest. My eyes popped open, but Aklys wasn't there. Whirling, I searched for any sight of him. He was gone.

I needed him to come back; I had to tell him that I loved him too. This wasn't right. Forcing myself back onto my feet, I pushed forward, running in the direction we had come and the direction he must have departed.

They were gone. No sign that the vampires had ever been here was visible. Not a soul was in sight, nor was there a footprint to be found.

No. *No.*

An excruciating pain exploded in my gut, and my power began pulsating and bursting forth from my skin in waves. It twisted and writhed, as if its own sentience shared my agony. An unearthly scream tore from my throat, echoing through the trees and across the land.

I screamed and screamed.

My power was lashing out all around me, wringing the life from the ground below. It ripped gashes in my skin, violent and painful, but I pushed it on; I clung to the pain because I could feel nothing else. I didn't want to feel anything else. I was erupting like a volcano, another deadly force that had no place in this world.

Waves of cursed power burst forth, and the earth cracked and shook beneath the force of it. All I could see was red. Dark, angry, red swirled all around me, leaving every part of my body crying out in rage and despair.

I lost control again.

My fingers dug into the blackened soil, feeling the ashen remains of what my essence destroyed slip through my fingers.

Aklys left me, betrayed me again. I had let another man wound me, shatter my heart.

I hated myself.

After what felt like an eternity, the misting tendrils made their way back to my body, ebbing softly like ocean waves lapping at the shore after a storm. I barely registered its return as I curled up helplessly on the ruined ground. The land around me was left in chaos, the life stripped from everything within a few meters distance of my crumpled form.

Bringing my knees to my chest, I held onto my quaking body tightly, and I wept.

Chapter Seventeen

Going Through The Motions

My body laid still for hours, shocked. I made no effort to leave the place I ruined.

We could have left Teskaria today, the three of us, together.

I was so exhausted with being hurt, with losing people. Battered and heartbroken, I simply lingered in the ash and the decay. I felt consumed by it.

Maygen was frantic by the time she found me, dusk casting rays of orange light over the burned ground, the scene mimicking the destruction of a wildfire.

I hadn't spoken, but a few words, to my friend after Aklys' disappearance. She asked once what had happened, but I couldn't find it in myself to answer her. I was on the verge of shutting down, drowning in a pool of despair and overwhelmed by the turbulent floodwaters that his presence had helped keep at bay.

He left so easily, and I still couldn't make sense of it. The biggest part of me hoped it was a ruse, and that he would return under the cover of night having eluded those who had come to claim him.

A small, smoldering ember rooted in my chest, and it screamed out that it never wanted to see him again, he who left after all that had transpired.

"We'll need to book passage across the strait. It's in our best interest to avoid the cities, but if I can't find a ferryman to take us up the river, we'll just make ourselves scarce in Periveil."

Maygen sighed, leaning against a tree, gazing down the hillside over the bustling port city of Dawn's End.

Periveil was a major city across the river from Licourt, which was the capital city of Euros and the center of the Three Kingdoms. Licourt was where interkingdom matters were handled, as the capital was the meeting point of the high lords. It was at least three times the size of any other city in the countries, and it contained a damned cesspool of corrupt nobility and evil people belonging to every race. Periveil was not much better, although significantly smaller in size.

The bustling of people and town life loosened my emotion's grip. I cleared my thoughts to focus on my surroundings and the mission of fleeing this country. Distant memories took hold for a moment of when I had traveled here during my first life. I had been young, just a girl, chasing after my older sister along the water's edge.

Most of the time, I was able to repress thoughts of the past because I was too afraid to confront it. Aklys had been a welcome distraction amidst the chaos of our journey, smothering my pain and trauma with his affection. Now, I could not stop myself from wondering about my family's murders. It would be impossible to move on without facing it, no matter how miserable it would make me.

I wouldn't allow myself to hope it had been quick and painless. Cruelty knew no limits, especially when it came to unfortunate innocents, that much I knew for certain after all I'd endured and seen firsthand. An entire family suffered for Fate birthing a girl who possessed an unexpected and unfortunate power.

Life was unfair.

"Celessa?"

Maygen's voice cleaved through the misery like a white-hot blade. She was the one person I had left, and she was the only one I should've been with from the start.

We would have been spared so much if we had been able to escape Sanctuary some other way. Due to the string of misfortunate events, names were branded on my consciousness now: by love, sorrow, pain, and death.

There would have been no run in with Thibault and Aloise, nor would there have been torture in Kilian's keep, and I wouldn't have Neina's blood on my hands. Niall never would have had the chance to turn on us; therefore, Tomas would not have met his death defending me.

Isonei may have been spared the trouble of her mission to procure me, and we wouldn't have needed to part ways. Maybe if she had found me sooner, I would have agreed to go to Evelia with her.

I never would have met Aklys.

Though, come to think of it, how did Maygen get to Sanctuary in the first place?

"How are we going to get out of here?" I asked, committing the earlier question to my memory for a later time.

With the vampire gone, there was no man to escort us. As long as we remained in Teskaria, we were at greater risk due to the backwards laws regarding women.

I wondered how or why such restrictions had fallen into place. Only noble women needed escorts in the time before my imprisonment, as was custom. Were the laws put into effect when I'd been taken, in the event that I escaped? Did Asuras have that much sway over the courts? How much influence did he have in Teskaria? How far did his reach extend through the Three Kingdoms?

"I'll find an escort."

Maygen spoke confidently enough that I believed in her wholeheartedly. Perhaps she knew some of the locals?

"What should I do?"

I didn't want to be useless. More than that, I didn't want to be alone.

Her eyebrows pulled together, pinching her face as she debated internally.

"Are you familiar with the area?"

"No, not really."

I didn't want to lie and wind up making things more difficult for her, simply because I felt vulnerable, when realistically I would be fine on my own. I could defend myself against all manners of monsters and men.

Truth is, the fear of abandonment had soaked into every fiber of my being, saturating me with the despair of being forgotten and left behind. Since I've awoken, every person in my company has become lost to me in one way or another, except Maygen. I was terrified to lose her too.

She summoned a weak smile, seemingly aware of my silent struggle. In an act of comfort and reassurance, Maygen pulled me into an embrace. The tight and affectionate hug left me speechless. It was everything I needed at that moment, but now tears threatened to break free, and I'd had quite enough crying recently.

"You don't have to worry," she promised, "I won't be gone long, and I have a plan. You'll be safe here, and it'll be easier for me to sneak around unaccompanied."

I shifted uncomfortably, realizing I would be an inconvenience.

Maygen released me, turning away to take her leave.

"Swear to me," I demanded, voice shaking.

Her eyes were soft as she said, "I swear to you, Celessa, I will *never* leave you."

This very day, I had witnessed the sunrise with the man I had hoped to love. The day prior, he had held me as the sun disappeared over the horizon. I watched the sunset now, alone.

Hours felt like an eternity as I awaited Maygen's return, anxious as the prospect of night affected me more intensely than I'd expected. So long I had suffered in darkness, but found it didn't frighten me as much with my companions around, especially with Aklys' attentiveness and comfort. That reassurance was gone now, and I was terrified.

Several citizens of Dawn's End had passed by the tree line where I lingered, concealed from sight. Each time someone passed, I shrunk further into the trees. I felt like a creature of the night, lurking in the shadows; a monster lying in wait, poised to pounce on an unexpecting victim.

Preoccupied with peering through the branches, I'd been oblivious to the sound of someone walking up behind me, until a strong hand squeezed my shoulder.

My entire body bristled, whirling to meet the intruder. Thoughts raged like a hurricane, with each wave lasting only a second as my brain rattled off questions. Is it Maygen? Has Aklys come back? Has Asuras found me? Is it a Sentinel? Is it a random stranger curious as to why a lone girl was hiding in the forest?

Eyes as dark as night stared back at me, not the kind of dark that was threatening, but that kind that was warm and welcoming. They were the deepest shade of brown. The strange man was broad-chested and built like a warrior, toned against the harshness of the world. His skin was a deep shade of umber, and his black hair was cropped close to his head, dark stubble traced a strong jawline.

Through the slight part of his lips, I saw the glinting hint of... fangs.

Another *fucking vampire*.

Listening to my instincts and heeding Isonei's warning about my power, I fled into the thick of the woods, running as fast as my feet could carry me. If I was going to fight him, I would need my curse, though I shouldn't use it - I had to find another way.

Physically, I was no match for a man of his size, without considering the vampirism. Unleashing my curse was never safe, so I couldn't use it in close proximity to the town. I didn't want any innocents caught in the crossfire.

Too late, the vampire was before me, as I was no match for his speed.

He put his hands up, palms facing me in an attempt to halt my escape.

"Listen, I jus-" He started, but I lashed out to strike him.

"Wait, damn it!"

I swung, aiming closed fists at his face, again and again. The man dodged every attempt, swaying from side to side, remaining clear of my frantic assault. He grabbed my fist as I threw a right hook, and I pulled back with such force it should have dislocated my wrist. Instead, I found myself free of the vampire, who appeared just as shocked as I was.

I didn't waste a second, rearing back to swing at him again, this time punching him square in the nose. Blood sprayed my hand and painted his lips red.

"Why!" He cried out, grabbing his face in an effort to stop the bleeding.

"What the hell is wrong with you?" the man demanded.

Without answering, my muscles tensed, lifting my leg to deliver a pushing kick to the man's midsection. His body propelled backwards, landing heavily on the ground. Never before had I possessed such strength - What was happening to me?

The man groaned, rolling in the dirt, now clenching two injured body parts. I wouldn't have another opportunity to flee, so I took it, trying once more to escape.

I am so fucking sick of vampires.

Bursting through a heavily draped thicket, laden with vines, I collided with another body. Bright lights exploded in my vision as I fell to the forest floor, the air knocked from my lungs. Scrambling, I fought to regain my bearing and came face to face with a very stunned Maygen.

"Are you trying to kill me?" She yelped, hand against her chest as she asked, "What are you running from?"

"A vampire!" I wheezed. "We need to go, right now, before he heals!"

"Heals? What did you do to him?" Her tone was heavy with worry.

Confused, I shook my head, "What? Did you not hear me? Vampire!"

Tugging the woman's hand, I pulled us both up from the ground, desperate to escape.

To my dismay, my companion shook me off, sprinting in the direction from which I'd come.

I trailed after her, begging, "Maygen, stop!"

She was much faster than I was, her body accustomed to the world, to life. Despite my newfound strength; my own body still lagged behind, catching up slowly, one day at a time.

My power roared to life beneath my skin at the sight of my friend in the arms of the strange man, breaking free and spilling onto the ground. His startled expression at the unveiling of my abilities only fueled my rage, and in his fright, he gripped her tighter.

"Let her go," I demanded, blood-red mist thrashing angrily against the earth.

"Enough, Celessa!" Maygen shouted, freeing herself from the embrace and stomping toward me.

The man's eyes trailed her as she approached, alert and anxious.

Fog stilled against the grass, swirling around my feet like a puddle of rainwater, recoiling at Maygen's advance for fear of harming her.

"Put it away."

It listened, retreating into my body to find dormancy once more. It cowered like a beaten dog under Maygen's assertive stare.

"I don't understand," I whispered. "He snuck up on me in the trees; he's a vampire."

Her eyes softened, and she sighed, "I'm sorry, he's faster than I am. I told him not to spring up on you like that."

She ran a hand through her dirty blonde locks, ruffling the wavy mess.

My eyes flicked to the vampire, who met my gaze and smirked.

"Celessa," Maygen demanded my attention. "This is Cian."

She reached out for the man, who took her hand in his own as he approached.

"He is my..." she started.

"Intended husband," he finished for her.

Her pale cheeks blazed red at the confession.

Dumbfounded, I simply stared at the pair with a slackened jaw.

Maygen was engaged? Maygen was engaged to a *vampire*?

She had told me once that she didn't consider men to be essential, yet she'd also told me vampires were the most fun. I hadn't given it a second thought at the time, nor had I considered what kind of person she might be outside of the perilous journey we were suffering through.

She was descended from nobility, but vampires held no social status in the Three Kingdoms; no noble house would permit a lady to marry a vampire. Would they?

"She looks faint," the man mumbled.

"You never told me..." I managed, ashamed that I was unaware of something so important about the woman I considered my closest friend. She was my only friend, really.

"Yes, well, you have had so much going on," she chuckled nervously. "I hadn't planned to force you into a *normal* friendship role until we at least made it back to Autumnmoor in one piece. I was saving all of those little things for a less overwhelming time. I wanted you to be safe and comfortable first."

I truly did not deserve this woman.

"I'm sorry for punching your fiancé in the face."

Embarrassed, I rubbed the back of my neck.

"Don't forget that impressive kick to the chest!" He laughed, light-hearted and forgiving, "I'm pretty certain you broke my ribs, so good thing my blood is half-cursed monster."

Maygen elbowed him in the side. A *half*-vampire, a child of one of the First.

"What? It has its perks."

He smiled, planting a kiss to the top of my friend's head.

Sea sickness was a bitch.

I certainly had not been so sensitive to the rocking of a ship in my first life; the nausea kept my head over the railing of the boat during most of the day. Boarding the vessel and departing Teskaria had, at long last, been uneventful. People didn't notice me amongst the crowds, but they noticed Cian.

The vampire had kept Maygen and myself on each arm through the city and to the docks, so no one spared a glance at the women he escorted. They certainly cowered away from the powerful aura he emitted.

Dawn's End was the one place in the country where you *might* see a vampire, due to it being the busiest port in the Three Kingdoms, right in the middle of it all.

A moment's peace in the waking hours couldn't be found while we remained on the water. It was a transportation vessel, so the noise of people chatting and flitting about rarely ceased. Only one man had dared approach me during the trip, whom Cian nearly sent off shitting himself.

I found him to be a very amusing man, and his self-deprecating humor made me feel comfortable with not only being in the presence of another vampire, but with myself. He often made jokes about curses, vampirism, the Gods, and Fate being a 'damned dirty whore' as Maygen highlighted the events of our journey for him.

According to the updates given by the quartermaster, we'd arrive in Periveil by evening. We had boarded at night, sailed straight through, and would arrive at the end of this grueling day. The shores of Euros were within our reach - we made it.

I prayed to the Gods that our journey to Lysenna's keep would be the exact opposite of our time in Teskaria, that it would pass by both quickly and safely.

Maygen rubbed my back affectionately as I heaved into the current below.

"Not much longer," she promised.

"Unless Haleth sinks us because she won't stop vomiting all through his waters," Cian snickered.

My cheeks burned, I was frustrated enough that I couldn't stop myself from being sick, but to think the God of the Seas might be aware of it made my guts twist further. I imagined a watery hand reaching up and dragging me deep into the murky depths, never to be seen again. I vomited again; my stomach thoroughly emptied of all its contents. My midsection felt like it'd been filled with daggers.

"Just another hour or so and we'll be docked at the shoreline of the city. If you can't handle a ferry ride further up, then we can go by foot."

"Will it take longer to walk?" I ground out.

"A day or two longer, depending on how tired we get. There are more opportunities for danger."

Cian picked at his fingernails nonchalantly.

I groaned in response, I just wanted this to be over and to be safe. If that meant enduring more time on the water, so be it.

The very solid, very *still* ground beneath my feet was a blessing I silently thanked Fate for a thousand times over.

For being a sister city, Periveil was more grandiose than I'd expected. The tall, inner-city buildings mimicked the white, marble structures of Licourt. The difference, though, was that the menacing castle towering over it all was black, boasting massive towers topped with crimson spires. Even from the shoreline on the outskirts, it loomed in likeness to a large black wolf, watching you with red eyes and teeth, waiting to swallow you whole. It was like stepping into an entirely different world.

The people of Euros had more freedom than those who dwelled in Teskaria; they didn't cower at the sight of a stranger or avoid each other in hushed passing.

Midday gave way to evening as we arrived, with the daylight hours coming to their ritual close, and shadows cast from buildings along cobbled streets. Cian flitted about the docks, conversing with person after person in search of a ferryman to take us upriver to Autumnport. Maygen followed behind him closely, happily clinging to his hand as he bartered.

It was like watching a completely different person; she was still the brave, strong, humorous woman I'd come to know, but someone else too. She was also a beautiful, happy woman, who was deeply in love. There was no need for escorts in Euros, as we'd left that obstacle behind in Teskaria, so I wandered a small distance away while still discreetly keeping the couple in sight.

I stared into the commotion around me absentmindedly, perched on a rock by the water; listening to sailors shouting about cargo to merchants who waited to purchase imported goods, the little cart vendors who made an array of different foods to sell to the passersby who came and went from the vessels.

My stomach grumbled angrily as I inhaled the different scents of street food. I hadn't eaten since before boarding the ship in Dawn's

End, and my body had rid itself of any shred of that meal throughout the trip to Periveil.

"Might I treat you to some food? The crepes from Honey's Creperie are exquisite. Crepes actually originated in Periveil - did you know that?" A songlike voice chimed from behind.

My head lifted to locate the source, meeting the watery eyes of a tall, lithe woman. She wore a cloak to cover her head and shoulders, and a few wisps of long white hair escaped the hood. I couldn't tell what manner of person she was, as her ears were covered; she smiled with closed lips that were painted rose red, which pushed her blush dusted cheeks up toward the ocean blue orbs.

Please don't be another vampire, I begged no one in particular.

"I'm sorry if I startled you, but I could hear your stomach growling and your friends there seem none the wiser," she chuckled as she spoke.

"Not startled, just wary of the kindness of strangers these days."

I forced a tight-lipped smile in return.

The woman giggled again, "I understand."

She moved to sit next to me despite the implied dismissal of her presence, and I eyed her suspiciously.

A hand extended toward me in formal greeting, "My name is Ophelia."

I shifted uncomfortably, not entirely sure how many people knew of me and what I could do; I was unaware of how far Asuras' reach extended and who might be swayed by his influence.

"That's okay," she said, as I shook her hand without giving my own name in return. "I know who you are," she whispered.

Bristling, I moved to slide away from the stranger, but she caught my hand again.

"You don't have to be afraid of me, I swear. Very few here know of your identity or the forces that seek you."

"How do you know who I am?" I demanded.

Ophelia slid the fabric of her hood slightly, revealing a pointed ear; she was Fae.

"I'm a Lady of the Myrkvior family, twin sister of Lord Maxim, heir of Periveil."

As a person of nobility, she would know, as of course the courts would be aware; the matters of one kingdom are the business of Licourt, making it known within the neighboring lands.

"If you're looking to collect a bounty, I wouldn't."

I allowed my power to filter out slightly, glowing along my fingers.

Ophelia released a hushed squeal, not of terror but of excitement, grabbing my hands to look at them closer.

"That is incredible!" She exclaimed.

"What?" My eyebrows pulled together in confusion.

"Lady Celessa, you have nothing to fear from us. Asuras has no sway in Euros, for he is most unwelcome in the lands overseen by Periveil and Pagon's courts."

"Ophelia."

A deeper voice summoned the attention of the Fae woman. A man with hair as white as snow approached.

"Is she ready?" He asked, inspecting me with glowing blue eyes.

"Ready for what?" I hissed, ripping my hand from Ophelia and glaring at the pair.

The man was unenthused, furrowing his brows and twisting his lips at my abhorrence. He folded his arms over his chest, casting an irritated glare toward the woman who still fawned over me, watching me with wide eyes and an even wider grin.

"We mean to escort you, at least to Autumnport. I have a private barge, so you won't have to beg a ferryman to travel at night, and there won't be a mess of civilians invading all the space," Ophelia chirped happily before returning her attention to the man. "Lady Celessa, I'd like to introduce you to Lord Maxim Myrkvior, my brother," she beamed while facilitating the introduction. "He's still unmarried, in case you were wondering."

"I wasn't," I snapped.

Maxim raised a dark brow at me, and I wondered how the twins' eyebrows so starkly contrasted their pale hair.

"This offer is only extended to you on behalf of my sister, as I'm not terribly interested in immersing myself in the affairs of an Amalgam. You can accept it, indulge her curiosity, and find yourself in Autumnport before morning; or you can find lodging and figure out passage tomorrow, as no other barge will take you after dark," the Fae lord grumbled, turning to stalk his way down the graveled river shore.

Ophelia beamed a hopeful smile at me as she said, "He's impertinent, so don't pay him any mind. Please, seek counsel with your friends, and if you decide to accept my aid..."

She opened my hand, dropping coins into my palm before continuing, "We'll be at the furthest dock waiting, until night has fallen."

I looked toward the filtering sky, slowly giving way to darkness.

"Don't forget to try the crepes," said the strange woman.

With that, she trotted away, her steps light and bouncy.

What the hell?

"The Myrkvior twins offered us a ride?" Cian mused.

"Is that surprising?" I countered with a mouthful of cream cheese crepe.

I didn't know these people, but it seemed the vampire did.

"Not for Ophelia, she's... different," Maygen sighed.

"How did they know we were here?"

I wasn't taking any chances, not after all Maygen and I have been through.

"Maxim has been waiting for us since we left, as he saw us out and gave Maygen the information she needed to extract you from

Sanctuary. If they had ill intent, it would've become apparent some time ago, I'm sure. The Vargens have been friendly with the Myrkvior family for generations." Cian clarified and began walking in the direction I'd informed him they'd be waiting, to my dismay.

"I don't like it," I argued, swallowing my questions.

How had they known anything about Sanctuary, and why had they bothered helping free an Amalgam? Maxim had *just* claimed he wanted nothing to do with it.

"You don't have to like it. I'm ready to go home; it's been months. I'm not waiting any longer than necessary!" The vampire threw back without turning to entertain any further argument.

I scowled at the dark-haired man, following along in his shadow. Maygen fell back to link our arms.

"Who are the Vargens?"

Maygen beamed and pointed an index finger at herself as she answered proudly, "Me! My family is the nobility of Autumnmoor."

I was blindsided again.

As we walked, my friend told me of the family that awaited us. Her godmother was also her aunt by marriage: Lady Lysenna Vargen, maiden name Belemont; she was a Mage. Maygen has two cousins, sons of Lysenna - one older and one younger than she.

She told me how her family had taken in Cian as a boy, as well as his brother. The younger cousin was betrothed to a woman who had also found the hospitality of the noble house as a child. It seemed Lysenna had a habit of taking in the misfortunate, so perhaps I would be truly welcomed as Maygen had claimed.

Ophelia clapped her hands excitedly as we sauntered down the dock, hopping from a finely decorated barge to greet us. It looked like an event boat, similar to one I'd seen before when departing Licourt with my family; it had been the after-party for a wedding, containing all manners of people roaring with laughter and stumbling after consuming intoxicating, rich wines. Necilia had turned up her nose, calling it improper and debauchery.

I had been entranced, for I craved that bliss, that excitement.

Along the polished railings were wrapped vines dotted with white flowers, decorating each post. Overhead were strings of lights, swinging to and from the corners of the vessel. Wisteria hung from the lighted strands, swaying carelessly in the wind. Draped benches sat in the middle of the deck, surrounding a hole in the floor. Upon inspection, it appeared to be a pit meant for fires, safely contained within the opening. It was admittedly incredible.

"Sit," a low voice demanded. "Cian tells me you have a weak stomach."

I glowered at Maxim, with his outstretched hand gesturing toward the cushioned seating. Though it was comfortable, I kept my discontented scowl etched into my features.

Ophelia leaned against the railing as she chatted with Maygen, who lingered comfortably in the warm embrace of her lover. Cian held her from behind and rested his chin atop her head.

A fire roared to life in the pit, with the flames turning from blue to orange and casting bright light over the length of the barge. The ship lurched, pushing out into the waters to begin its journey up river. My stomach immediately recoiled, the heavy food inside quickly threatening to reappear.

Maxim plopped a pouch into my lap as he strode past.

"It'll stop the nausea," he grumbled, "I don't want you vomiting on my boat."

Inside I found what appeared to be a large sugar cube, with tiny leaves that speckled the white dust. I looked to Maygen, holding up the mysterious gift and raising an eyebrow. She nodded at me reassuringly, so I ate the unexpectedly bitter treat. The turning in my stomach subsided in a handful of moments, and the relief was euphoric.

"Thank you."

"How old are you?" Maxim asked.

Taken aback, "Old," I snapped.

The man rolled his eyes.

"Why?"

"You don't meet an Amalgam every day, and you were imprisoned before I was born."

I scooted further down the bench as the Fae man plopped down next to me, stretching his arms over the back rest.

"I thought you didn't want anything to do with an Amalgam, so why do you care?" I hissed, "How old are *you*?"

"Thirty-five," he answered quickly.

"I was twenty when I was taken, and then I slept for one hundred and forty-two years. My body hasn't aged, but that still makes me one hundred sixty-two, I suppose."

My frown deepened as I realized my birthday must be soon, with autumn making an approach. I decided I wouldn't tell anyone, as it wasn't something I wished to celebrate; the passing of my life didn't feel like something that was worth noting.

Ophelia fluttered by, handing us large goblets of wine and dancing about whimsically.

"A toast!" The white-haired woman announced, twirling with drink in hand. "To the admirable endurance of Lady Celessa, and to the safe return of our friends. May your lives be long and the days be kind to you all."

Everyone happily cheered to her toast, drinking deeply, as I eyed the cup suspiciously.

"This may come as a surprise, but not everyone you meet has ill intentions."

Maxim gestured to my cup with his own.

"The last person who claimed to have good intentions for me ended up causing the death of a man I love," I retorted.

He scoffed, "A man? Are there more than one?"

I paused for a moment, "Not anymore."

Pouring the sweet red down my throat, my skin warmed as it settled pleasantly in my stomach.

"If this is poisoned, I'm going to be really pissed."

"It won't poison you, lady, but it is Faerie wine!" Ophelia giggled. "In no time at all you'll be loosened up and enjoying yourself. Shall I summon our bard for some tunes?"

How long has it been since I last heard music, since I last sang a song?

"That sounds lovely," Maygen answered for me, already refilling her drink.

I couldn't help but laugh at the woman. I wasn't sure what kind of drunk she was, but if our likeness held true in this arena, then it would make for an eventful evening.

Two hours upstream and Ophelia's promise of intoxication held true, for I'd found myself thoroughly inebriated, swaying about the deck. The bard's music was enchanting.

Maygen and I had engaged in dance, locking fingers and spinning each other in circles. The Fae woman joined us for a time before laying her head on a cushioned bench and snoozing with a contented smile plastered on her face. Maxim draped his sister in a plush blanket before settling at her feet to watch the smoldering fire. Cian had taken Maygen into his arms, and she appeared to be so much smaller against his chest; he plopped down with his intoxicated lover to nap. To be so effortlessly happy, so relaxed, what a dream.

I watched the dark water swirl around the side of the barge as we sailed when the musician, after prolonged silence, began strumming a familiar tune. My heart clenched at the depressing melody as I imagined the faces of those I'd loved and lost: my parents, my sisters, Thibault.

They were gone from this world forever, far from my reach. Father had called me his songbird, but I could not remember when I'd last let music sway my voice. A lone tear slid down my cheek, and I allowed myself to sing a few solemn verses.

"In the stillness of the night
The stars fall from the sky
Our end has found us now
This is the final goodbye
Don't dare ask the Gods why
As I take your hand in mine
For there's a song that only we know
It's the song of sinking low
It tears us apart
You always seem to have to go
I will find you in the next life
We won't leave this realm alone."

There was no point in wiping away the free-flowing tears, for each one that dried was quickly replaced. I felt so down, despite the drink, despite being surrounded by bright and happy people. I sobbed more freely when the bard picked up his instrument and headed back to wherever he'd come from. There was so much I hadn't allowed myself to feel. All I had wanted was to find closure in every place that needed it, every place that needed to be healed. One wound after another has found its way to me, with mark after mark being branded on my skin and my soul; my pain seemed endless.

"Celessa," a familiar voice whispered.

I spun, searching, desperation overriding my already compromised senses.

"Milady," he sighed.

Aklys.

He was somewhere, somewhere close. I looked to my friends, all still peacefully resting near the fire, blissfully unaware that Aklys had come back for me. I didn't want to wake them, so I wouldn't bother them now - I had to find him first.

"Celessa," he beckoned again.

Peering over the railing, I was shocked to see his face in the water below. He was reaching for me from the murky depths. Overjoyed, I reached back, frantically grabbing for his hands to pull him onboard. He was too far away, though. Shouldering off my cloak and kicking away my boots, I braced myself.

I had to get to him, had to be with him. I needed him.

So, I jumped.

Chapter Eighteen

Passageway

Cold, it was so very cold. The water was frigid enough that it sent my body into a state of shock, freezing my limbs. I couldn't move, couldn't breathe, and was wriggling weakly; I was lost inside the black abyss. My lungs ached as the oxygen ran out, leaving me on the verge of unconsciousness.

The plummet into the river had been an act of desperation, born of loneliness and heartache. My lover had returned, he'd come back for me, and I'd do anything to claim him. I wouldn't let him leave me again.

The alcohol in my system had taken over my better judgment, leaving only enough willpower to focus on the man I craved, not to preserve my life. I was a strong swimmer, growing up on the shores of Briobar, so I knew better than to dive unprepared into tumultuous waters, especially under the influence.

But it was too late.

Aklys was before me, watching me die, his watery figures obscured by the currents. My fingers flexed, desperate to touch him. His face twisted, changing into something otherworldly and horrifying. As his eyes blackened, the fangs in his mouth elongated, the rest of his teeth following suit. Clawed hands reached out for me, and I couldn't even whimper protest; I was numb and dying.

"Celessa," it groaned, bubbly and garbled.

I closed my eyes as my body was squeezed. I was tired, and I wanted nothing more than to take a breath. The darkness invaded my mind, giving way to slumber.

"Aklys," I mouthed, as water flooded my throat, drowning me.

Hot hair invaded my lungs, expanding my chest, pushing apart my ribs. It made me want to choke. Water sputtered from between my lips, and my eyes fluttered open. The world was blurry, and a figure loomed over me.

Aklys.

I reached out to touch his face, to caress him. He swatted my hand away.

"You're a fucking imbecile," he hissed.

Not Aklys.

His hair was white, his eyes blue: the polar opposite of the features of my vampire.

"Why did you jump? Do you have a death wish?"

I was uncomfortable, the ground underneath shifting and rough. It was the river's shore. We weren't on the boat. He lifted away from me, sitting down on the gravelly surface, clothes clinging to his skin; drenched.

Maxim had jumped in after me and pulled me from the river, but where was the barge?

"I saw something," I wheezed.

"You saw something and jumped off of the fucking boat into the river at *night*."

Rubbing my eyes, I sighed as I conceded, "Yes."

"What did you see?" He asked.

"A man I love."

I pulled my knees up to rest my forehead on them, circling my arms around my legs.

"No. You saw a Siraen, creatures of the night that lure weak minded sailors to their deaths by taking on enticing forms. It tried to drown you, and it almost succeeded!" Maxim spat, "This is why you don't travel the fucking waters at night; Ophelia is testing my sanity."

I heard him sigh, a sound caught somewhere between frustration and understanding.

I curled into myself, cold and broken. A malevolent force made me imagine him. Was I really so desperate I'd jump to my death for an illusion?

"It's easier not to care," Maxim mumbled.

Peeking an eye above the shield of my arm, I raised a brow at him, and shot back, "Maybe I'm not built that way. I can't just *not* care. I feel deeply, and I love and I suffer with every piece of myself. Feeling love is the one thing that has pulled me from despair and from the agony of losing so much."

Tears warmed my cheeks again.

"Everything has been taken from me. My family, my life, my friends: it's all gone. Maygen is all I have now, and the love I have for her is pushing me forward. In fact, it's seeing me through to the end of a journey riddled with chaos and despair. Every waking moment I've had has been by her grace, however difficult it's been."

Maxim sat silently for a moment, analyzing my words. He rose from the shore, extending a hand to help me from the ground. I allowed him to guide me up, struggling to regain composure; even after that ordeal, the Faerie wine still lingered, making my body sway and my mind swirl.

"Your feet are bare."

He looked as irritated with me as I felt with myself.

"Mhm," I grumbled back.

"Autumnport isn't far. As much as I don't want to, I can carry you there."

I thought about Aklys' arms, how safe he made me feel.

"Fortunately for you," I said, "I'd rather walk."

Every pebble felt like a knife. I stumbled and winced at each sharp pain as we walked, and the trek felt endless. How far was 'not far' for the Fae?

"Are you honestly that fucking stubborn?" Maxim growled.

"Are you honestly this much of a dick all the time?" I snapped.

To my surprise, he laughed. I couldn't tell if it was the product of being offended, if it was a response to his anger, or if I caught him off guard.

"Yes, usually," he responded. "That's a hell of a 'thank you' for saving your life."

"I didn't ask you to save me."

"Next time, I'll let you drown."

"Good!"

Maxim laughed again before allowing a long silence to pass between us.

"To be immortal is to exist in misery, over and over again," he says eventually.

He slowed his pace, walking beside me rather than ahead of me.

"Mortals have it easier, their lives are shorter, but because of that they *feel* more. They accept death from birth, expecting their own and dealing with the ones that happen around them. They know Dameniel waits for them, looming around every corner, hanging on every breath. Knowing nothing is certain, they love more fiercely, they hate but with more chances of respite, they hold on to every moment in earnest. You thought yourself mortal, so you don't have the predispositions we immortals suffer from.

"Hold on to that. Hold on to your mortality because it will help you recover, it will pull you from despair, and it will lift you from your pain. Little is known of Amalgams, and little is known of your imprisonment. Maybe Asuras slowed your aging to preserve you, and your body will age and die with its mortal blood. Maybe you stopped aging in mimicry to the deities and your divine blood will grant you immortality. Your entire existence is uncertain, but if you allow your misery to consume you, you may waste your best years wallowing."

Wrapping my arms around myself, I continued walking, unwilling to make eye contact with the man. I hadn't considered much about how my life would progress, nor had I thought about aging or if it would claim me. Many beings of mixed blood *did* age, where even if it halted, they died of it eventually; they simply had a bit more time than mortals.

Did I want to spend it all being miserable? How much time is acceptable to spend hurting and recovering? I felt like I was owed time for everything I'd been put through. I was allowed to feel anger, anguish, and hopelessness.

"What do you know of loss and the havoc it wreaks?" I grumbled. "Who are you to tell me that my time spent mourning is time wasted?"

The Fae man's eyes appeared to glow in the dark, and he emanated an aura of anger and power. He felt like a threat.

"You think I would speak from ignorance? Do you think I am unaware of the specific type of suffering you play upon for pity?"

"I don't want your fucking pity!" I hissed.

He grabbed my arm, forcing me to face him.

"You are not alone in suffering, and you have no right to act like it."

"Who are you to berate me for my sorrow? I have lost *everything*!"

"My mother was murdered in front of me, in front of my sister, pregnant with our sibling. I was *nine*. Murdered by her brother, my uncle, for not *obeying* him. It sent my father into madness. He became despondent before turning to substance abuse to numb his pain, which in turn resulted in the abuse of his children. Every time he looked at me, he saw the uncle to whom I bore resemblance."

Maxim ripped the collar of his shirt, exposing a scarred chest.

It was no easy task to scar an immortal being with rapid healing abilities.

"He hates me so much that I am forbidden to love, as he wants no grandchildren from me. He waits for Ophelia to produce a son, a new male to name as his heir. I found love but once, and he made her the subject of his *hunt*. He chased her down and slaughtered her, and he brought me back her fucking head, like a trophy. For what? Because of the structure of my face, something out of my control, I will suffer endlessly!"

I couldn't react, couldn't speak.

"Most of us do not get happy endings, Celessa. Accept what has passed, and *move on*. There is little else you can do."

"Why stay, then?" I blurted.

"What?"

"Why stay at court? Why continue to suffer?"

"If he were to grace me with his death, I would become High Lord of Periveil. If that happens unexpectedly, and I am not there, then Ophelia falls to the jurisdiction of the other noble families. The courts are cruel, and she'd be auctioned off like a brood mare to be left at the mercy of a husband she doesn't want, forced to bear some unworthy bastard's children. If I'm here, then she never has to worry because I will protect her."

Maxim began walking again, his shoulders stiff and his fists clenched.

"Do you feel responsible for her because of your mother's death?"

The word vomit was out of control.

"I *am* responsible for her because she is my sister. She is the only person whom I care about in this world. She can't protect herself, and she hasn't been right since our mother's death."

Despite torturous conditions, he endures for love, the very thing he condemned me for mourning. Perhaps he hoped to serve as a lesson to me, showing an example of what caring can put someone through: that love means pain, that hurting is inevitable... one cannot exist without the other.

We walked quietly for a long while, where the only sounds to be heard were my occasional gasps of pain from sharpness underfoot, followed by his disgruntled sighs and groans each time he heard me.
"What was her name?" I asked.
Startled, he turned slightly. "Who?"
"Your mother."
"Calendine."
"Your lover?"
"Jela."
"Will you tell me about them?"
He huffed at my request.
"It'll pass the time, and you seem like you could do with an emotional release."
After a brief silence, he relented, talking about the women he loved who had been taken from him so brutally. I could feel in every word how much he'd loved them, and I knew in my heart that he loved his twin even more fiercely. This was a man who was kind and noble, but twisted by cruelty at no fault of his own. Ophelia was the shred of hope and love that he clung to, that tethered him to the ground and spared him from madness.
I hope he never loses her.

Maygen was pissed. I'd expected her to be upset, of course, but not angry.
"Why? How could you?" She cried tears of rage, something else I hadn't anticipated.

Cian attempted to console and calm her, to no avail.

"I didn't mean to-" She cut me off.

"You don't get to give up like that! I know you've been through a lot, but you don't get to just fucking do that!" The woman screamed.

Realization snapped into place, "You think... that I tried to kill myself?"

She paused, watching me with wide, teary eyes.

"That's what we all thought," she confirmed.

My shoulders sagged.

"I didn't. I thought I saw him, and I was drunk, so I was just trying to get him on the boat." I lowered my gaze as I spoke, too ashamed to even look at her.

"It isn't her fault; the reason transportation vessels don't travel this river at night is because of the Siraens. They use their illusion magic to lure people to their deaths." Maxim spoke, placing a hand on my shoulder, an act meant to comfort me; but it made me shrink.

Maygen reached for me, pulling me roughly in an iron embrace.

"I'm sorry!" She cried. "Promise me you'll stop making me fear for your life," my friend begged.

"I promise."

Ophelia and Maxim offered us each a pack with a few provisions to last us the day as we made our way to Lysenna's keep. I pulled on my jacket and laced my boots tightly, eager to get moving; we were so close. Cian had signaled our departure, but as we said our goodbyes and turned to leave, a hand wrapped around my bicep. I turned to look at Maxim, his white hair dancing against his forehead with the rising wind, pale in the early morning light.

"What?" I demanded.

A shadow of sincerity passed over his eyes as he released his hold on me.

"Never stop singing."

With that, the Fae returned to their barge, and we started the very last leg of our journey.

We were almost home.

Passing through Autumnmoor had been easier than expected. Almost too easy. I had grown accustomed to the persistent difficulties Fate tested me with, loss after loss, one trial after another. At any given time, I expected to be hurt, whether it be physical or emotional.

No one deserved to live this way, and I hoped that reaching Lysenna would mark the end of these perilous chapters of my life. I craved peace, calm, and ease. I wanted to wake in the mornings without dreading what the day might bring, and I was tired of the relentless pain.

Maygen's dusty hair tumbled around her shoulders, wild and unruly, made even more so by the unseasonably strong winds that rolled across the wooded path. The trees sounded as if they were screaming, leaves beating together noisily, assaulted by the angry weather. I took a moment to close my eyes, breathing in the fading summer air; a few leaves had begun to change, threatening to give way to the next season.

I allowed myself to enjoy the array of the forest's colors, listening to the tunes of nature's songs. Birds sang merrily, unaware of the chaos that was the world. Flying above it all, looking down, and only viewing the beauty of the land must be a life of bliss.

Being a bird would be peaceful, I thought. If I were a bird, though, I'd likely be a bird of prey as I was hardly peaceful. With my curse, I'd be a monstrosity to behold; a vulture.

Flying was an intriguing thought, to have feathered wings and a light body. How easily you could flit from place to place. If I could fly, I would see the world. I would not just visit the Three Kingdoms, but everything. No one paid any mind to birds, so I would be undisturbed in my travels.

Perhaps I would go to Evelia, to visit Aloise with her swollen belly. I would see Isonei caring for her as she progressed through her pregnancy. The thought made me smile, knowing that they were safe and thriving.

My smile faltered as I thought of where I would travel next: Greilor.

Aklys' departure replayed in my mind often, and to make matters worse, his face plagued me constantly. I would never escape him. I would never escape any of my losses.

Maygen has been my companion throughout it all, and I was so very grateful for her, but the person I wanted by my side was Aklys.

I wanted the vampire who had betrayed me and then broke my heart as soon as I had let him into it. I should hate him, and I tried to each and every time he appeared in my thoughts. He chose to leave me, with a proclamation of love, no less. It was cruel.

Cian trailed closely behind Maygen and I, watching her. Smirking to myself, I fell back, allowing the two to walk side by side. Their happiness brought me some semblance of contentment, when I managed to swallow down my envy. I wanted what they had, but I hated the thought of finding it with anyone other than Aklys.

The two entwined their fingers, locking hands as they walked along. These moments should never be taken for granted, and I committed the image of their bliss to my memory.

I fell further behind, increasing the space between the pair and myself. I gave myself a healthy distance to wallow and be a miserable prick. I never wanted them to feel guilty for what they shared simply because I was in pain.

Angry wind continued its assault on us, becoming a nuisance to travel in, causing sticks and leaves to tumble across the ground frantically. The display almost felt like a warning. Convincing myself I was merely accustomed to danger, I pressed on.

We'd been making the trek from the port town for a few hours, passing Autumnmoor and nearly reaching our destination; the sun was lowering in the sky. My canteen was empty and the craving for hydration was reaching a point of irritation. I'd never been so damn thirsty in my entire life, like I still hadn't recovered from the salty water I'd nearly drowned in earlier.

"I need a drink," I declared.

Cian rolled his eyes and said, "We're nearly there, Celessa."

Maygen nudged him.

"A short break won't affect our progress." She smiled. "Let's take a quick rest then get back to it, and we'll still make it there before nightfall."

I strode off toward the sound of flowing water. Cian had told me earlier that there was a stream not far off the trail, and I wasn't waiting for further argument to keep us moving. Fallen twigs crunched under foot as I sought out the source of refreshment. A sense of urgency propelled me forward. When I spotted it, I threw my pack to the side and rushed forward, dipping my fingers into the cold current.

The last time I drank so carelessly from my hands like this had been at the Erotas River, deep within Silenus Forest. The magic of the liquid had enchanted me, and it was the first time I'd shared true intimacy with Aklys. I savored the memory of his touch as I sated my thirst. Gasping from the haste of my drinking, I stopped to catch my breath, gazing into the water.

Before my eyes, the swirling stream seemed to slow, nearly stilling. My reflection stared back at me as if I were looking into a mirror. Chestnut brown waves had fallen loose and were framing my angled jaw, drooping toward the water, nearly touching the glasslike surface. I couldn't remember the last time I'd truly looked at myself. Round hazel eyes gazed back at me, as I absorbed my almost-foreign features.

I was stereotypically attractive, the true picture of a northern Teskarian lady with full lips, arched brows, and a slightly upturned, thin nose. Yet, I couldn't help but feel disappointed as I stared at the woman in the water. Being pretty doesn't save you from being used, abused, tormented, hunted, or heartbroken. I lashed out, striking the water.

As the ripples pieced the surface back together, my reflection remained distorted, despite the water calming. Panic crept up my spine, causing the hairs on my body to stand at attention.

A woman stared back at me from the water, fully aware and her own being entirely. I leaned in, despite my better judgment, examining the image before me. She was me, but different; her eyes glowed red, with hair full and writhing, darkened to a shade that was nearly black. The snake tattoo on her neck twisted in the reflection, coming to life.

Her mouth parted, too far, jaw unhinging to release an unnatural scream. A scream that I could hear clearly in my mind as if she were real, the sound berating my eardrums. It pierced my skull, and I fell backwards onto the ground, gripping my head.

"Turn around!" The ethereal voice screamed.

I rolled onto my stomach, taking in my surroundings, frantically searching for signs of danger. I saw nothing.

"Turn around, turn around, turn around!" The shrieking ripped through my head worse than any migraine. I wailed from the pain, frantically kicking at the ground, squeezing my head — silently begging for it to stop.

"Turn around!"

"Fuck off!" I screamed back, thrashing wildly as if I could force the pain away through means of violence. My power cracked through my skin, swirling around my body, and reaching out in search of the source of the assault.

"Stop, don't get close!" Cian's voice broke through the agony.

I could see Maygen running toward me, my power was still splayed out, searching for the cause of my pain so it could destroy it.

"Don't! Don't! Stop!" I shouted at her, attempting to scurry further away, summoning my power back to me despite the pain I still suffered.

"Celessa!" She cried.

Suddenly, the pain was gone. Bright white overtook my vision, and my ears rang, drowning out every other sound. I melted into the earth, time halting around me.

"Celessa?" Maygen?
I hear you.
"Celessa!" She called again.
I'm here! I hear you! I yelled back.
Nothing; silence.
I saw nothing. I felt nothing.
"Turn around." That voice again.
Go to hell.
"Turn around!" It was demanding.
I did turn around! I saw nothing!
"TURN AROUND!"

I sat up straight, gasping. The world around me was returning to normalcy.

Focus.

I felt the ground under my hands, and I smelled the sweetness of the season riding the breeze, chilled by nightfall. Looking down, the earth below my body was charred, drained of life.

Maygen. Cian. Frantically, I scrambled from the ground, but the two were nowhere in sight. Panting, I grabbed my pack and slung it over my shoulder, breaking into a run toward the direction I had left them on the trail. They weren't waiting where we'd parted.

Turn around, the breeze whispered.

I turned around, searching, but seeing nothing. My attention turned toward the path we'd been following, the path that led to safety, to my new life. I sprinted, pushing as fast as my legs would carry me.

Reaching the brink of exhaustion, I nearly collapsed into the dirt. Night had made its descent upon the world, the setting around me bleak and shadowed. My companions were lost to me, and despair settled deep into my bones.

This couldn't be happening again. I couldn't bear it.

"Are you alright?" A new voice spoke behind me softly, a man trying not to startle me with his presence.

"No," I said flatly.

He approached slowly, obviously wary of me. It was strange for anyone to treat me as a threat, unless he knew who I was. I turned to look at him.

He was young, just reaching adulthood. His hair was as black as night and cropped close to his skull, the rich darkness of his skin resembled Cian's. He *really* looked like Cian.

"Who are you?" I demanded.

"Daevian."

"Do you know Cian?"

"He's my brother."

I nodded, willing myself to stand on wobbling, weak legs. Huffing in frustration, I stumbled as the muscles protested. The boy reached out toward me, as if he meant to catch me, but stopped himself and began backing away.

I choked on a dry laugh.

"Do I frighten you?" I asked.

"Yes."

"Where is Maygen?"

"At the keep."

I'd never been so grateful in my entire life - we had been granted a small mercy.

"They're resting," Daevian mumbled. "Cian sent me out after you. Maygen is all out of sorts and frantic. The keep isn't far."

I forced myself to walk with him, the only thought motivating me was seeing for myself that they were alive and well. A nervous bug was gnawing at the back of my mind as I thought about the psychic attack I'd experienced and the warning it carried.

It had kept telling me to turn around, but what had it wanted me to see?

Dim light flickered inside large windows that decorated a beautiful stone keep, and the torches illuminating the outside of the building gave it an enchanting glow. Light and shadow danced against the rock.

It wasn't nearly as large as I'd expected, as most keeps I'd visited resembled small castles, an attempt at making lords of lesser lands feel more important. This one looked like a home. It appeared to be loved and tended to, with gardens lining the bottoms of the walls, and vines of ivy creeping up and nestling into cracks in the rock.

A handful of people milled about outside, finishing up the day's work.

Another man took notice of us and immediately discarded his task to extend a greeting.

"Welcome to the Vargen estate." He grinned.

"I thought it was called Lysenna's Keep?"

My tone came off more irritable than I had intended, but the man continued smiling.

"Lysenna is my mother. My name is Erelim Vargen, and it's nice to finally meet you."

The hand he offered radiated the desire for friendship, but I only eyed it suspiciously. Retracting, he relaxed his grin, but carried on appearing amused.

"Right. Well, I'm Cel-"

"Celessa Umbraeon, daughter of Altan and Sybette Umbraeon, the last of the noble line, aside from Maygen I suppose."

The man looked awfully proud of himself for being well informed.

"Good job. I love being interrupted," I grimaced.

Erelim scoffed, then extended an arm toward me.

"Please allow me to escort you inside, my lady."

The formal term stung me like a wasp. Aklys' voice rang in my ears, *milady*.

"I won't acknowledge you if you call me that again."

"Understood." He shrugged. "May I?"

I looked over to Daevian, whose face was painted with indifference.

"Thank you for bringing me here."

I offered a tight-lipped smile, for it was all I could muster at the moment.

Daevian nodded, turning his attention to Erelim as he spoke, "I'm going to bed. Don't scare her off, or Cian will be pissed," he grumbled.

"With my charm and good looks? Nothing scary about me..."

"The fact that you think you're charming or good looking is scary in itself!" The young man tossed the joking insult back over his shoulder, as he made his way toward the entryway of the building.

"I imagine you're good friends?" I questioned.

"Practically family. Their parents were my parent's best friends."

He gazed lovingly where his friend had disappeared inside the home. As his eyes returned to me, I was fascinated by the color; a shocking shade of blue. They were deep, striking, and almost appeared to hide shades of violet within.

"Before all of them met their ends, save for my mother."

"My condolences for your losses. I know how hard it is to exist in a world without those you love," I offered. "My family is gone, too."

I took his arm, settling my hand in the curve of his elbow.

"I know, and I'm sorry. This way," he gestured toward the building, "Time to meet the family."

Erelim led me through a door around the side of the keep rather than using the main entryway, guiding us up a flight of stairs to a higher level.

"I thought you were about to parade me into a crowd of welcoming guests."

He chuckled. This man was entirely too good-natured and pleasant to be exposed to the likes of me, miserable and sarcastic.

"I assumed you may want to freshen up first, considering you're covered in dirt and leaves."

The door opened, revealing a large and comfortable room. I nearly fainted at the sight of the plush bed, clean clothes, and large tub already filled with steaming water.

"Does it suit you, Lady Celessa?"

"I am no lady." I withdrew my hand from his arm and whispered, "I won't be long."

Erelim led me down to a grand dining room, where the occupants of the house sat about feasting and laughing, enjoying one another's company. Feet shuffled against the floor, and I turned my head to see Maygen rushing in my direction. Relief swelled in my chest, nearly bringing me to tears. I extended my arms to embrace her.

"What did I tell you? Stop making me fear for your life! I didn't know what happened. You were screaming and cursing, your power... we had to run, it was trailing after us, and we ran."

I clasped her face between my hands, shaking my head, and I said, "I'm sorry. We made it, it's over."

She graced me with the biggest smile I'd ever seen. Maygen has always remained optimistic and mostly cheerful. Despite everything she's endured, despite every hardship, she has maintained steadfastness. She and I were like night and day. She was the morning, promising and full of light, and nothing could obscure the beauty of the rising sun that was Maygen. Meanwhile, I was midnight — cold, sad, and dark.

"Celessa, I'd like for you to meet the Lady Lysenna."

Maygen gestured to a woman well into middle age, who still retained the beauty of youth. Dark brown hair descended down her shoulder in a large braid, blue eyes shone brightly despite the dim light of the room. She was full-bodied and had one of the most comforting presences I'd ever felt.

"It's an honor to meet you, and I'm so grateful for the hospitality you have offered me."

I tipped toward the woman to offer formalities, but she stopped me with a delicate hand.

Intrigue glimmered in her eyes as she beheld me.

"Look at you," she breathed. "All you have endured, all the time that has passed, and here you are at long last. Beautiful, brimming with power and potential."

I felt like a con-artist. It seemed most people either saw me as a pretty face, a proper lady with an incredible gift, or a dark and dangerous weapon to flee from or fight against. I was none of those things, not really. I was a broken, beaten, sad, and scared girl. I was someone who was hiding beneath layers of self-protection disguised as sarcasm, carelessness, impulsivity, and lewd behavior. I was a mess.

The strange woman took my hands into her own, examining them.

"You are as lovely as the moon, yet capable of such destruction. How confusing that must be for you, trying to find where you belong between peace and beauty, chaos and ruin."

She hummed, caressing my skin.

My throat tightened at her words, with the emotion I was fighting against furiously threatening to rise to the surface and breach the walls of its containment.

"You are safe now, so there is no need to fret," the homely woman murmured, resting a warm hand against my cheek.

"Welcome home, Celessa."

Chapter Nineteen

Consequences In Lust

Months of silence.

Not in the sense that there was no sound in the world, my days were filled with bright smiles, laughter, and light. There was only an absence of chaos, but that void made me uneasy. No amount of calm could convince me that darker days would remain far out of reach.

Whispers of the unknown filled my thoughts, invading my mind day and night. The time had not yet come that I didn't constantly look over my shoulder, that I enjoyed sweet dreams rather than nightmares, that I didn't battle my innermost demons.

Each night I tried to drown the trauma, and the effects of it that battered me every waking moment. I was tired. I was tired of pretending I was okay, tired of holding in the essence that squeezed my heart and lungs, and tired of fighting the internal war between who I am and who I wished I was.

Someday, I will be free of it all; Maygen promised me. Someday, I would be happy, and I would find peace. I would rest. Not today, it seemed, as I breathed in the warming air of late spring, perfumed by blooming flowers and pollen on the breeze. It would not be today, even as my skin was set aglow by the evening sun.

I walked barefoot around the estate grounds, enjoying the feeling of grass against the soles of my feet, wedging between my toes. The towering stone walls had become a familiar sight, a welcome one, promising shelter and safety. I loved the property, with its beautiful yards and gardens encircled by vast forest.

It was everything I had hoped for in my first life. As a young girl, I'd dreamed of marrying a handsome lord with a beautiful keep that I would, one day, call my own. Now, there were suitors who vied for my attention and affection. I was even a guest in one's house.

However, I yearn for another, and this place does not feel like home.

Grateful would be an understatement of how I felt for the Vargen family. Maygen Vargen had been my companion, my best friend, and my savior from the darkness. She wanted nothing but happiness for me. I knew it wounded her that I continued to suffer after all she'd given, all she'd sacrificed. She was the reason I endured — perhaps I should tell her as much.

If I gave her reason to believe that I would achieve normalcy, escape depression and angst, she could relax a bit. She trailed after me most days, clinging to my arm. In the mornings, she would wake me and urge me from bed to take part in day-to-day activities. She brushes my hair and helps me choose dresses. In the evenings, she spends time in my room; relaxing, chatting, and drinking. She's been putting forth her best effort, and has never stopped trying. Yet, here I linger, still ensnared deep within the throes of self-pity.

Most of all, she was careful with me. She spoke as little as possible about vampires, even though her lover and his sibling shared the afflicted blood. Aklys' name hasn't been spoken aloud in some time. At first, she insisted I should be hopeful, that perhaps there would be a correspondence of some sort and that we would hear from him again.

I had wanted to believe he would contact me, that he would come back for me. Long days passed, turning into weeks, without a word nor trace of the man. He broke me. That vampire had let me give him my heart and then abandoned me with no explanation.

Yet I loved him still.

The dress I wore today was a sage green, pale in color to mimic the beauty of spring. How long has it been since I noticed color, or since I cared? How long has it been since I looked at my clothes, my body?

The winter that had passed was merely a blur of memories, none too significant. I had simply been existing, distracting myself by any means possible. My figure had filled out, returning to what it had once been: healthy. I had the curves of a woman, with rich food always readily available. Offering my aid in the household chores and groundwork had helped me maintain muscle. The defensive training Cian offered a few times each week helped tone everything out, despite my disinterest in participating. I did it for Maygen, so I might protect myself without endangering others with my power, without endangering her.

If only the mind could be mended as easily as the body.

Turning my head, I took notice of Cian and Maygen strolling nearby, arms linked. I took air into my lungs, feeling how they inflated and expanded my chest. It felt good to breathe. Walking towards them, I did something I had not done in a long while. I smiled.

Maygen's face beamed, a radiant grin answered my own, while Cian appeared startled.

"Have you done that before? I thought you'd just never learned how," he teased.

"Don't discourage her! You're an ass," Maygen snapped, jabbing an elbow to the man's ribs.

I had never seen a couple so playful. They argued often, but never without quick reconciliation, and no affection was ever lost. They spent much of their free time together, simply enjoying each other's company. They fought in training and embraced after each altercation, exchanging crude insults softened by loving reassurances.

I had something like that once, for however short a time, and it had ruined me. A love like this either meant the happiest end or the most bitter one. I would never say it out loud for fear of Fate overhearing, but I hoped they would make it to the end together. Maygen deserved good things.

She threw her arms around my neck in a tight embrace, smelling of cinnamon, cloves, and the comforts of a loving home.

I returned her affection, absorbing the warmth shared between two friends and between family.

Upon entering the keep, the usual scene unfolded before us. The hired help milled about finishing their tasks, setting the table with dishes on which we would receive supper. The room smelled of roasted chicken and herbs; my mouth watered.

Aithen Vargen sat nearby with his intended, Chessane Clearwater — slightly older than Aithen, nineteen to his eighteen, and a commoner. Lady Lysenna had informed me early on that Chessane was gifted with magic, a Mage. She suspected the girl was an illegitimate offspring of the Letum family of Pagon, but never said as much in idle chat. They had offered her sanctuary in the keep when she was a child, her mother passing from illness shortly after taking refuge with them.

Her skin was a radiant shade of deep sepia, glowing with subtle golden undertones. I admired her light brown locks of hair and the ringlets that framed her lightly freckled round face, shocking green eyes danced in the firelight. The young lord was absolutely smitten with her. Who wouldn't be? She was beautiful and kind, warm and welcoming.

Chessane waved from the couple's seat near the fireplace, offering a genuine smile while leaning into the embrace of her lover. Aithen looked at me with stifled contempt.

It was only he and Daevian who had been wary of my presence here. I never blamed them. I'd even agreed that they were putting themselves in danger by opening their home to me. Aithen had been vocal when Daevian had not, until Lysenna had endured enough of their outbursts.

According to Maygen, the lady of the keep had berated them with curses they'd never expected from the woman, and have held their tongues since. The exchanges between the young men and I had softened recently, but a cloud of animosity still lingered in the air.

We exited the room and began to ascend the stone stairwell to the next floor. Maygen insisted we dress properly for mealtimes, for the sake of her noble aunt.

The long evening gown I chose was a sleek material that pooled around my ankles, with a slit in the fabric trailing up to mid-thigh. I'd describe the color as that of a cloud slightly heavy with rain, but reflected as if mimicking the water of a clear pond. It hugged my curves lovingly, soft against my skin. Although the sleeves reached my wrists, the collar hung low to reveal the bare tops of my breasts, my snake tattoo on full display.

I allowed Maygen's friend Lelia, a member of the household help, to arrange my hair. She chose to twist it into a waterfall braid that hung over my shoulder, decorated with gem pins. For the first time in a long time, I felt beautiful.

"Lady Celessa, if it's not too bold of me, may I say you look enchanting." The woman chirped happily, "The lords will be in awe of your divine beauty."

Divine. The word soured my tongue. I wanted nothing to do with my dark divinity, but I smiled at her comment nonetheless.

Before she left the room, Maygen had whispered something to her friend, who nodded in understanding. She always noticed the very moment when something bothered me, taking great care to keep me comfortable.

I stood to rummage in the ornate wooden wardrobe that loomed in the corner, searching for something to calm my nerves. Revealing a bottle of spirits, I offered it to Maygen, who took a small swig before handing it back. The liquid burned my throat on its way down, warming me from the inside.

"You shouldn't drink so much," Maygen whispered.

"I'll stop when you do."

At that, my friend laughed. We'd fallen into an unfortunate cycle of unhealthy coping mechanisms, typically drinking. Occasionally, we would smoke tobacco laden with mentheae flowers, giving a head high and a calming effect over the body. It was rare we talked about what had forced us into such habits — the trauma we had endured side by side, as well as on our own. Maygen had slowed down in partaking in these indulgences, whereas I kept getting worse.

One more sip turned into several before we remembered we were expected at dinner.

Returning to the dining hall, it was rather obvious we were late, with all the food having been served and waiting on the plates. The members of the household sat in their respective places, with Lady Lysenna at the head of the table. On either side of the noble woman were her sons: Aithen on her left and Erelim to the right. Daevian sat next to Erelim, followed by Cian. Chessane sat at the side of her beau, and I was meant to be seated next to her, while Maygen would take her place beside her lover.

Every eye in the room had fixed on us.

Unexpected dinner guests had arrived, two familiar faces framed by white hair: the Myrkvior twins. Ophelia waved happily from her place at the end of the table, sat beside her brother, who watched me with furrowed brows.

I grinned at the pair, struggling to conceal my intoxication and apparently failing, as Maxim shook his head at me slightly, fighting back a smirk.

"My, my," Lysenna hummed, taking notice of our unsure steps.

Dipping my head to the woman, "I apologize for the delay, my lady."

"No need, my dear. You both look lovely." She grinned at me, her teeth were remarkably well kept, glistening white. "Doesn't she look vibrant?"

Erelim rubbed his jaw, taking me in fully. "Stunning," he acknowledged.

The rest of the table hummed their agreement, except for Maxim, who continued watching me contentedly. When most of the heads had turned, I cast a questioning glance because he hadn't taken his gaze away.

He winked at me quickly, nonchalantly, sending my thoughts whirling with shock. The Fae man was never personable or even remotely flirtatious during the frequent visits the twins made to the keep. Most of our exchanges consisted of bickering with an occasional threat, and Maxim reminding me often that he had saved my life and I had yet to do anything grand with it. He was generally a prick.

Dinner time crept along silently, with few words exchanged between present company. A heaviness hung above us like a storm cloud. Something was not quite right, and nervousness radiated from the bodies around me, stirring the dormant power beneath my skin. My fingers twitched as if attempting to flick away the quiet, and I prayed someone would engage in conversation to free us from this awkwardness.

"Have you given any thought to what you might do now that you seem to be recovering, Celessa?" Aithen spoke without looking away from his plate.

That was not at all what I'd had in mind.

I'd go south, I thought to myself, *to investigate the mystery of the rebel country, to find Aklys.*

"I have had quite enough of your boldness, Aithen," Lysenna snapped at her son. "She is a part of the house now, as Maygen is her last remaining blood. Respect my decision, or I'll see to it that you dine in your room from now on." She thought for a moment. "Chessane will continue to join us, for at least she is well-mannered. I did not raise you to be so crass."

My emotions must have been playing upon my face because Maygen stood from her seat and hurled a biscuit at her cousin, striking him in the face. It seemed our pre-dinner drinks had gotten the best of her sense.

"She was *actually* smiling today, and you had to go and ruin it! Look at her! Do you feel better now, you oafish cunt?" She shouted.

"Maygen, I implore you to rein in your curses at the dinner table, especially in the presence of guests."

A heavy sigh left Lysenna, as she leaned to whisper in Erelim's ear.

Ophelia giggled, excitedly watching the exchange with her hands folded beneath her chin. Maxim stared daggers at Aithen. The pair of cousins insulted each other back and forth for a few moments before Cian attempted to placate his fiancée.

Erelim stood from the table abruptly.

"Lady Celessa, would you care to join me for some air? I would like to get you away from my family's barbarism for a moment."

He smiled, politely gesturing with his hand to the door.

I rose from my chair and turned my back to the members of the house, exiting as quickly as possible, far ahead of Erelim. The eyes behind me burned into my back, both the stares of friends and less-than acquaintances.

My gown swirled around my legs, caressing my skin, which used to be a comforting sensation that now only made me more aware of how much I could feel: uncomfortable.

The young lord caught up to me moments after I escaped the keep into the darkening world. With a full moon, the grounds were more illuminated than usual, awash with pale light a distance away from where the warm hue of glimmering torches reached their end. I was slightly more relaxed in the open air.

"Celessa?" Erelim spoke from behind me.

My skin prickled at the sound of his voice, not in aversion but in anticipation, nervousness. He offered his arm to me, and I rested my hand on it, hanging loosely.

We walked in blissful silence for some time, wandering a short distance away from the estate grounds, along a forest path beneath tall trees decorated with blooming flowers. With every gentle breeze, blossom petals fluttered around in a magical scene, performing the dances of the season — early spring's waltz.

I had been in awe of my surroundings before the man that escorted me halted our advance, stealing away my attention.

"Are you alright?" His question was unexpected.

"Of course," I swallowed, stumbling slightly.

He looked at me with a raised brow, "Are you drunk?"

"No!" I snapped, reeling, "Not entirely."

Erelim snickered, guiding me along the trail surrounding the property.

"Shall I escort you back to your room?" The man offered.

"I think that would be appropriate."

I wouldn't sleep off the alcohol, but rather I would wait for the house to retire for the evening to fetch more, to be alone in my wallowing.

We rounded to return to the keep. My body was tensing at the fading inebriation, itching for more drink to bring back the comfortable numbness of my mind. Emerging from the trees, a white-haired man with arms folded over his chest came into view, waiting alone.

I could've sworn I heard an irritated sound leave Erelim, but upon examining his relaxed features, I wondered if I had only imagined it.

"A word?" Maxim was looking at me, paying no mind to the man at my side.

"Celessa is retiring for the evening."

Erelim's arm tightened against my hand.

"I'm sure she can find her way without you, when I'm done speaking with her," the Fae man grinned mockingly as he spoke.

They both looked to me for any indication of what I wanted, but all I could think about was finding a bottle of wine.

I shrugged, "I know the way, thank you my lord."

Erelim released me, sizing up a smug Maxim as he made his way inside.

"To what do I owe the pleasure?" I sighed, leaning against the stone wall.

"Is it a pleasure?"

"Not usually."

Maxim huffed, stepping away into the courtyard, beckoning me to follow. Rolling my eyes, I pushed away from the building and trailed after him.

"Are you going to tell me a secret?" I grumbled.

"No."

"Then why are you taking me further away from the wine cellar and my bed?"

He produced a small bottle from his pants pocket, tossing it to me. The clear liquid smelled spicy: spirits.

"Alright," I took a drink, draining half the contents of the glass container, "you have five minutes."

"What *are* you going to do?"

"Excuse me?" The tone of his voice was always off-putting and abrasive.

"Asshole Vargen asked you what you're going to do now, and you didn't answer him. He isn't the only one who is curious."

"Why do you care?" I snapped, the alcohol quickly refueling my courage and carelessness. "Not that it matters, but as long as I have Maygen, I'm not going anywhere. I won't leave her."

"Though it's something you've considered, otherwise that wouldn't have been the first thing you mentioned," he speculated. "Where is it that you want to go, Celessa?"

Greilor.

I wanted to go to Greilor. I wanted to know what had happened to Aklys, where he was, and I wanted answers. As a prospective High Lord, I would never tell Maxim that I desired to explore the forbidden, rebel country. It was a land rumored to be teeming with hell spawn, dangerous territory, and a death sentence. Greilor was where the enemies of the kingdoms resided. Soldiers had come from that mysterious place to claim the man I loved; soldiers serve, so who led them? What secrets lay beyond the mountainous barrier?

"Nowhere."

My eyes lowered, watching the shining fabric that shifted around my feet.

Maxim hunched over, bowing to search for my gaze.

"You're a terrible liar."

Annoyed, I turned away, making for the keep. The man appeared in front of me in an instant. I often forgot that the Fae rivaled vampires in speed and strength, as Maxim and Ophelia never cared to exercise their abilities in my presence.

"What?" I demanded, "What the fuck do you want?"

"I want your help."

Stunned, "With?" I asked.

Maxim lifted a hand, as if he was tempted to touch me. His fingers flexed before clenching into a fist that fell back to his side.

"Ophelia has convinced my father to step down as High Lord, as the court has deemed him unfit and overruled his decision to name my sister's potential future sons as his heirs. I am to take his place."

"That's-" I nearly gasped, considering how much his quality of life would improve. His father would be gone. He would be safe from him. "I'm happy for you, this is a good thing."

"I am expected to take a wife, and make some heirs of my own," he continued.

No, absolutely not.

"Maxim, don't," I started.

He frowned, "I know we don't have an ideal relationship; we're barely friends. You still desire your disappeared lover, and Erelim sniffs at your skirts like a damned dog."

I shook my head, covering my eyes with a hand.

"You're powerful, strong, and you would make an exceptional High Lady. Many would bow to you. I would commit my resources to helping you locate Asuras, to help you rid the realm of him."

He was trying to use my biggest fear, my greatest weakness, to sway me into accepting the most half-assed proposal I have ever heard in my life.

Though it was a tempting offer, I didn't want to be a High Lady, nor did I want that responsibility. We didn't have a good relationship, that much was true; I had no affection for this man. It had seemed that it was mutual, until now. Whether he simply desired a powerful match, or if he was the worst person in the world at showing interest in a woman, remained to be seen.

This was life for a person of nobility, particularly women, to be sought after and courted; a line of nobles vying to lay claim to you. I had experienced it in my first life, time and time again offered proposals. Since waking, the line of men had hardly shortened; Thibault, Aklys, Erelim, Maxim...

I was not a prize to be won or a piece of property. If I was to marry, it would be for love, and I doubted I would allow myself to feel that again for a long time.

Seven months wasn't long enough.

"I would court you if given the chance. I don't expect you to accept my proposal without at least an attempt at sincerity."

"Goodnight, Lord Maxim. I'll take your *proposition* into consideration."

Finishing the spirits, I tossed the bottle back to him and turned to take my leave, body buzzing with irritation.

Maygen's words rang in my head, '*Men aren't essential, but they can be useful.*'

If I was to be sought after for what I had to offer, then why not give men the same treatment?

∞

Sweat slicked our skin, our bodies sliding against each other with ease. I gasped, gripping the sheets with one hand and the hip of the man above me with the other.

He had me close, so close; he was thrusting in perfect rhythm while stimulating my nerve endings with skillful touches. His lips were pressed to my neck, holding me still with fingers wrapped in the tangles of my hair. I lifted my pelvis from the bed, wordlessly asking for more. The man obliged, plunging into me with more force and urgency.

My head spun, dizzy from my indulgences. The entire bottle of wine I'd swiped had found its way down my throat prior to seeking out another one of my vices. This was wrong, using intoxication to feel numb enough to sneak around in search of pleasure. He wanted more from me. I only wanted a distraction from my pain.

I often imagined Aklys was the one ravaging me, making me bend and break beneath him. I pictured dark hair and sharp fangs, eyes swirling with green and gold.

The illusion shattered as he moved to join our lips. I turned my head away - I never allowed him to kiss me. I didn't want to develop feelings for this man, as I only meant to use him; caring only about how selfish that made me when I was sober. Never considering how he felt, or how anyone felt for that matter, was easier.

Maygen had been less than thrilled when she discovered my indiscretions, yet she continuously found ways to conceal it from Lysenna. The lady of the estate hoped I would marry, unaware that I no longer had my virtue and that I'd been 'tarnished' before ever arriving in Euros. Not that it mattered, because the man she wanted me to marry was her son, Erelim - the very man who was deep inside my body at present.

"Celessa," Erelim gasped, "please, let me kiss you," he begged.

I placed a hand to his mouth gently, parting my lips for him to hear me moan.

"I'm close, don't stop," I requested breathlessly.

Unfortunately, it was becoming monotonous, this sneaking about. I wanted more excitement, more danger. I wanted to feel something.

It was hypocritical to yearn for a state of existing that I had fought so hard to escape. Yet here I was, bored with being safe, and bored with a man whom I knew had good intentions where I was concerned.

He picked up pace, grinding into my body and driving me to the edge with each push, never fumbling the finger stimulation he offered. Erelim was a selfless lover. He was always finding ways to ensure I enjoyed myself, always making the climax euphoric, and claiming one orgasm after another. He was good, very good, and I suspected he had taken lovers before me. Not that I cared, as it only enhanced my time with him due to his level of experience.

Grabbing my wrist, he pulled my fingers away from his mouth.

Was he really going to speak again?

He lowered his face, desperate to catch my lips.

"Erelim, no," I snapped.

I was the assertive one, telling him what he could and couldn't do, giving demands. To be honest, I wasn't sure why he entertained my consistent discourteousness. Erelim was very good looking, well-built with an infectious smile, and those enchanting purple and blue eyes. Chocolate locks of hair fell in waves over his forehead, handsomely kept and soft to the touch.

Surely based on his skillset in the bedroom, there should be women lining up to crawl beneath him. Autumnmoor was teeming with young, unmarried women.

Something felt different in the seconds I'd spent in my head, thinking about a great many things when I should be focused on the release I craved. The pace changed, becoming frustrated and desperate. Erelim took his hand away from our intimate union, grabbing both of my arms and pinning them above my head.

"What are you do-?" I started.

Flattening his body against mine, he changed the angle of how he entered me, making every thrust push my body to its limits. He was filling me up in a way that seemed like it should've been painful, but instead it drove me mad with ecstasy. Having effectively subdued me, Erelim forced his hot tongue between my teeth, kissing me deeply, passionately - all while bringing me to the edge.

I cried out into his mouth at the explosion of my climax, met with the hot throbbing sensation of his own release spilling inside of me. He didn't stop, pushing through each wave of our orgasms with his movements, never releasing us from the affectionate act.

We lingered like that for a moment after he stilled, just lying there in our forbidden union, with him still sheathed inside of my body. I said nothing when he pulled away from the kiss, searching my eyes for some sort of change. He kissed me again, tenderly; once, twice, he savored me. I returned it for his satisfaction, a silent thanks for what he'd done for my body.

Little did he know, I considered ending our affair with the kiss I'd repeatedly denied. Embraces like this lead to infatuation, which leads to everything I no longer wanted.

The return of affection had Erelim stirring, igniting something in the man. The once subsiding erection had begun filling me up again, stretching my tender flesh that had only just started recovering from the intimacy. He'd released his hold on me, moving a strong hand to grip the back of my neck and another to cup my rear, pulling me as close to him as possible.

Extra sensitivity from the previous release and the essence of this man made it come faster this time, more uncontrollably. He pumped roughly; Erelim usually tried to display restraint when we would engage in such activities. Now, he was unbridled, like a secret side to him had been unlocked.

"Just one more, give me one more," he begged against my lips, pushing harder.

"I don't think I can have another - it's too much!"

My legs were shaking against the sensual assault. Despite the overstimulation, I didn't want him to stop, as he was guiding me further into bliss.

"I never want to stop fucking you. You feel so good." He moaned. "You're so beautiful, so perfect."

Squeezing his hips between my thighs, I tried to slow him down to prolong the pleasure. He fought against the hold, forcing himself in again and again. It was too much, and I lashed out, digging my fingers into his shoulders and trying to hold on; but I couldn't contain it.

This time, I wasn't able to bite my tongue in an effort to be discreet, screaming my release out into the night. He captured my mouth with his, frantically trying to muffle the sound. Groaning, he met my orgasm again; this time he held himself so deeply inside of me that I felt every pump of his release.

A rattling sound broke us from the stupor, and Erelim leapt from the bed, draping a blanket over my naked body and wrapping a shirt around his waist.

His brother, Aithen, burst through the door. The young man looked alarmed, likely having heard my unexpectedly loud scream. His eyes flicked between his brother and myself in the bed, and he ran a hand through his hair, face turning red.

"You've really fucking done it this time," Aithen spat.

"Get out, you prick!" Erelim growled, advancing toward his sibling.

Lady Lysenna appeared in the doorway, stunned and holding her face with cupped hands.

Great.

Close behind were Maygen and Cian; my friend mouthed the words, "*I'm sorry*", while her vampire lover struggled to contain his laughter.

"What have you done?" Lysenna snapped at her son. "Taking advantage of her while she's vulnerable, what kind of man are you?"

Erelim was dumbfounded at his mother's harsh words. He and I knew full-well it hadn't been he who had started this, it was entirely my doing.

For several months after arriving at the keep, I'd found myself in a pattern of waiting until the household had gone silent, then swiping bottles to drink myself into oblivion. It helped me cope. I would drink and write long letters to the friends I missed, Isonei and Aloise.

I would drink more and write angry ones to the man who never came back for me, to Aklys.

I wrote them letters they would never read.

The young lord caught me once, offering to escort me back to bed. I hadn't allowed him to leave my room, already intoxicated as I was, and had insisted he drink with me. We hadn't indulged in each other that night, but rather we simply drank and talked, falling asleep on the floor.

However, the next night, full of liquid courage, I'd shown up outside his bedroom door wearing nothing but a long night robe. Erelim had let me inside, accepting the drink I offered him, fully expecting more innocent conversation. Then I undressed, Maygen's words about men being *useful* burned in my mind.

He'd attempted to talk sense to me, not on the premise that he was uninterested, but instead regarding what his mother would think. When I made it clear I didn't care, he was more than willing to take me up in the torrid affair — especially after learning about Maxim's proposal a few days prior, something I wanted to forget entirely.

The relationship was entirely at my behest, and he let me come to him when I wanted. Every boundary I'd set had been respected until tonight with that damned kiss.

"You've ruined her chances at finding a match of nobility with anyone else!" Lysenna continued, obviously referencing the Fae lord. "Clean yourself up, and come to the study immediately," she demanded of Erelim, casting a sorrowful look at my lightly-covered figure.

The brigade exited the room, leaving us in awkward silence.

I tossed the cover away and stood from the bed, knees wobbly. Stalking over to the naked man, I glared at him. He opened his mouth, but I lifted a hand to demand silence.

"Your little stunt with crossing my very clear boundary would have been the deal-breaker here," I gestured between the two of us, "but *now*, I imagine we're fucked."

He looked amused as he said, "Fucked? In the literal sense, we most definitely are, and can be again." Threading his fingers into my knotted locks, he pulled my head back gently, guiding me forward to press our bare bodies together.

"That's not what I meant."

Erelim sighed.

"My mother is likely going to want to discuss our future together, now."

My brows pulled together, irritation surging underneath my skin.

"Don't be angry with me! I wasn't the one screaming." He leaned down, landing another unwanted kiss as he said, "You exposed yourself."

"That was not my intention! I hadn't expected you to behave so, so..." I groaned in frustration.

"So amazingly? So incredibly? So wonderfully?" He teased.

I was the furthest thing from amused, as my lapse in judgment would surely be the undoing of the ease in which I'd been floating during my time here. My days were calm, and I was free to do as I wished; some time later my nights had become what I craved, relieving; riddled with sex and alcohol.

Perhaps I should've started sneaking into the town nearby to engage a lover with whom I didn't share a dwelling, one who wasn't a lord, and one who wasn't the son of the woman who had offered her home to me.

I wondered if I could have talked Maxim out of his proposal and offered him my body instead, no strings attached, because at least I didn't have to see him often. His impertinent demeanor would have made him a suitable candidate, he didn't seem like the type that would ask me to spend the night.

Erelim had asked me once if I had considered marrying, if I wanted to be with him; he'd made it known that was *his* intention. That was when my visits to his bed chambers lessened in their frequency. While he was a decent person whom I didn't mind spending time with, and certainly had no objections to screwing, I didn't want that kind of life.

I didn't want romance, marriage, or love... not anymore.

"Want to go again before someone wonders what's taking us so long?" He whispered, gliding a thumb across my bare breast.

My stupid body throbbed in answer to his suggestion. If I wasn't so riddled with lust and could control my craving for intimacy and attention, I wouldn't have found myself in this precarious situation.

Silently cursing myself, I wrapped my arms around his neck. I allowed Erelim to carry me to the bed again, rather surprised at his stamina and impressive ability to perform multiple times in one evening.

Now, he had to face his mother, and I would make the shameful walk back to my quarters.

Maygen had been waiting in my bedroom when I opened the door.

"I told you it was a bad idea, and I told you that you'd get caught eventually."

She sat cross legged on my bed, dressed in her night clothes.

"Yes, well, after a few months of it, I assumed luck was on my side."

Flopping down onto the bed, I grumbled, burying my face in the comforter. It had been just over two months of sneaking around that had played upon my arrogance, making me believe there would no be no consequences.

"What did you expect? To carry out the rest of your days screwing her son thinking she'd never notice?" Maygen nudged me with an elbow. "You know she's been hoping you'd show some interest in him, but I don't think this is what she had in mind."

"Please stop talking."

She giggled. "You probably woke all of Autumnmoor with that scream."

Sitting up, I grabbed a pillow and smacked her with it.

"It was an *accident*," I stressed.

"That's what you said every time I caught you leaving his room, too."

"I don't understand what the issue is," I sighed, pinching the bridge of my nose and squeezing my eyes shut.

"You're a lady, and you're supposed to be virtuous."

"You're a lady! You screw Cian all the time!"

"We're discreet… and engaged. Your point is invalid."

Maygen shoved my shoulder lovingly.

Engaged: she was to be married, though the couple didn't speak of it often. I eyed the delicate band on her ring finger, as she had only started wearing it after we'd arrived in Autumnmoor. It was almost copper, and the band curved slightly in a way that reminded me of a gentle wave. The gem that sat on it was deeply green, an emerald. It was a beautiful contrast of colors.

"When did Cian propose?" I attempted to steer the conversation in a different direction.

She smiled slightly, "We were in the north, though I can't really remember why. I think because Cian knows I love the snow, the brightness of it, the cold. I'd never seen the forbidden lands, or the frozen expanse, and it was beautiful. He even got down on his knees despite the icy ground; I'm surprised he didn't slip and fall."

She sighed a bit as she reclined, "I couldn't have asked for a more sincere proposal. At the very least, the men here are genuinely good. Lysenna made sure of that."

We laid on our backs, staring at the ceiling for a long while, just being comfortable in each other's company.

"I don't want you to think I don't find Erelim to be a good man, I do. I think he would treat me well, but I only wanted a distraction. I needed a release, a way to cope. I'm sure I would be interested in more with him if..." I trailed off.

"If you weren't still in love with Aklys?" She finished my sentence.

She turned her head to look me in the eyes. I returned her gaze, sad and uncertain.

The sound of his name being spoken out loud made me wince, as if it was physically painful, like I'd been stabbed in the chest.

"I've seen the letters with his name written in big, sloppy, angry handwriting." Maygen sighed, but noticed my eyes widening, "I didn't read them!"

"Yes, I'm still in love with him, but it's been ten months since he left. He isn't coming back. If I thought he was, I wouldn't be doing this. I held out hope, and it was crushed. What was I supposed to do? Wait for him forever in uncertainty?"

Rolling to the far side of the bed, I reached into the nightstand, opening the drawer to reveal an herbal concoction.

"At least you're taking precautions," Maygen chuckled at the contraceptive tincture.

"This was a mistake."

"Well, if you really don't believe he will come back, it might do you some good to move on. Marry Erelim, inherit the manor, oversee Autumnmoor. Have some scandalous, mixed lineage babies. Those were things that you wanted before, right?"

Yes, I had wanted all of those things once.

I'd wanted those things before that version of me was ruined.

Before that part of me died.

Chapter Twenty

What Lies In Wait

I spent the better part of the next two weeks avoiding Erelim, save for one drunken night when I'd stumbled into his bedroom, remembering what had happened and retreating promptly. Even more fervently, I avoided Lysenna.

The lady of the estate often trailed me with her eyes in the common rooms, and her gaze made me shrink like a grape in the sun. For all her generosity and care, I'd never been made to feel indebted to her. Knowing she hoped I would marry, and if she had her preference then it would be to her son, she never forced the suggestion on me. She never made demands of me. I feared her expectations would soon change, and I was not in the right state of mind for what that would entail.

Ophelia was set to arrive today, followed by her brother who traveled separately; Maxim was allegedly delayed. We expected she would be making the announcement of Maxim's appointment to become High Lord of Periveil. A few months had passed since he had informed me of what would unfold, when he made a fool of himself suggesting I become his High Lady, his wife. I had never attended the ceremony that grants a person of nobility more powerful standing in court and assumed we would be invited to the city to attend; I suppose I should feel excited to bear witness to such a thing, but I was not.

Scooting around the hanging garments, delving into the depths of my wardrobe, I uncovered a most unfavorable sight; my bottles were gone. My limbs ached due to the absence of alcohol, as my body had become dependent on the relief it provided. The vessels in my head had begun tightening, threatening to give birth to a migraine. Sitting on the floor, I grabbed my face with clammy hands and groaned.

Who would have taken them? Who knew of the hiding spot? Maygen did, but I didn't think she'd remove them without telling me. Sure, she wanted me to slow down, but she wouldn't just *take* them. Lelia also knew because she was oftentimes the one returning my clean clothing, arranging numerous gowns and cloaks on the hangers. The only other suspect was Erelim - after we'd finished our wine the night I had invited him in, I'd revealed my stash so we could continue drinking.

"Lady Celessa."

A familiar voice spoke with more of an authority than I had ever expected, having entered the room without attracting my awareness as I fretted over my misfortune.

Standing from the floor, despite the protest of my joints, "Lady Lysenna," I addressed the woman, bowing my head slightly. "I did not expect to see you this morning."

"I have noticed you have been taking great care to avoid seeing me at all since the *incident*," she said carefully.

An audible swallow struggled down my dry throat, "Yes, my lady, as I haven't found the words to apologize for my indiscretions."

"I have," Lysenna said as she gestured to the door.

"Walk with me."

Maygen paced the grass directly ahead of where I sat, hand covering her mouth to contain her frustration. I rested lazily on the ground, skirts sprawled around me, still reeling from the conversation that had taken place just a few hours prior. My friend was the furthest thing from pleased, and was also confirmed *not* to be the culprit behind my vanished vices.

We shared a bottle of sweet red wine, enjoying the warm summer sun. This area of Euros was considered northern, offering mild summers, often agreeable for spending time outdoors.

"I have no words!" She blurted finally; arms extended outwards in frustration.

Sighing, I sipped from my glass, appearing proper in the presence of company; normally I'd just squeeze the bottle by its neck to chug it the way men do with their ale in taverns. Ophelia had arrived with her ladies in waiting, absent of her most loyal bodyguard. The group of giddy females lingered nearby, fawning over their lady and giggling at men as they passed them by. There were six in total - four appeared to be mortal, while the other two were Fae.

"She can't! I'd go with you, and I know she doesn't want that," Maygen hissed, falling back to the ground to sit next to me.

"Lysenna is the lady of the estate, so I have to do as she bids," I sighed.

"You shouldn't be forced to do *anything* you don't want to do! She knows damn well how much you've been through, and her ultimatum is unfair!"

I grimaced, as the drink wasn't settling well today. Despite the reprieve it granted my body, my mind wasn't as accepting. I had nearly lost control this morning, something I had thought I was past.

I thought I'd overcome my curse, but Lysenna's importunity had sent me reeling, awash in a tidal wave of disbelief and resentment. Part of me knew she was being reasonable, that I owed her much and had no right to refuse her. Though, the other part told me I was above the demand, and that I had earned the right to live and do as I please.

Perhaps I was the one being irrational; ungrateful, even. A stranger had allowed her niece to endure many hardships to save me, and she opened her arms as well as her home, giving all she had to someone she did not know. She took those risks for the sake of a long-lost bloodline and a power they never tried to use.

Maybe I had been ignorant in assuming I would never have to resume my position as a lady, as my noble blood demanded. I was so blinded by my pain and preoccupied with drowning it that I never really spent time thinking about anything else.

"You have to decide today? Why?" Maygen demanded.

"Lord Maxim will be here this evening, that's why. The twins only mean to stay a day or two," I rubbed my throbbing temples as I uttered each word, pressing my fingers against them in an attempt to alleviate the stress.

"If you go to Periveil, then I will come with you, and so will Cian!"

Maygen looked to her intended, who leaned against a tree nearby, listening to our conversation.

"The last thing I want to do is pull either of you from your home and your family. It's not right, and I would be fine on my own if that was my decision."

"Or you could stay here and marry Erelim? We can all keep living our lives as we've been, and I mean, what's really going to change?" Cian scoffed.

Everything.

Everything would change the moment I accepted a proposal from Erelim *or* Maxim. It would change because I had no choice in the matter, because Lysenna made it clear that I was to settle on a suitor and procure myself a title before anyone uncovered my indecency. She made it clear that it would tarnish her reputation and likely Maygen's as well if word of my *obscene behavior* got out. That was the last thing I wanted. I knew how fast rumors spread, and how nasty the courts can get; it was bad enough already that she was harboring an Amalgam.

She'd argued that a match with Erelim would be ideal. Not only would I remain here, but any insinuations of our premarital relations would be nullified by our betrothal. She also suggested that Maxim would offer me the most security, by placing me in one of the highest positions of authority in the kingdoms. The people would have no choice but to respect me as a High Lady, regardless of my affliction and the taboo surrounding my very existence. I would be untouchable where Sentinels were concerned.

Ultimately, my decision would boil down to Maygen and if she truly meant to remain with me, to follow me. She had already given so much.

Cian had some semblance of a point: the only thing that would change the current dynamic is that I would be expected to share quarters with Erelim after being wed.

The conclusion was too simple, and I could feel that my brain was trying to lessen the blow.

I would become the Lady of Autumnmoor. He would be my *husband*, and I would be a wife to a man whom I admittedly enjoyed, but did not want to marry. He was a man who was pleasant and humorous, who was a skilled and generous lover, but he was not the man whom I desired.

Rising from the ground, I bid a sharp farewell to my companions, bracing myself for what lies ahead.

Ophelia stopped me on my way through, embracing me and twirling my hair around her fingers as she exclaimed, "My potential sister! Have you given any thought to Maxim's proposal?"

"I have."

Her smile was wary, as if she already knew my decision without the words being spoken.

"I know he would understand if you weren't inclined to accept his offer. While you are a beautiful, incredible woman, Maxim gave his proposal from a place of generosity; as your friend. He did not offer it as someone who intends to have a pretty bride by his side — but someone who longs for a partner with the means to change the world from a position of power."

Long, delicate fingers caressed my cheek, "You would make an unstoppable match, and I believe what he offers is in your best interest."

I stared into the eyes of the friendly woman, returning her smile.

"I value the friendship you both have offered me."

Hurriedly, I hugged Ophelia once more before making my way into the keep.

There were things I needed to consider before I finalized my decision.

One final letter I needed to write.

"Dear Aklys,

In the event you ever read the letters I have written, there are some things I wish to make clear.

You have imprinted yourself so heavily on my heart, mind, and soul; I have deemed it impossible to truly move on. I have now found myself in a position where I am left with no choice. In an effort to numb my pain, I have made questionable decisions at the behest of a less than desirable state of mind, and now I'm paying the price.

Today I will make the decision to marry. I will accept the proposal of a suitor and begin the next chapter of my life.

This comes after what has felt like an eternity of suffering in longing for you. You left me alone, left me confused and broken, hurt and angry. I have turned to all manner of coping mechanisms in an effort to dull my emotions. I can't imagine your reason for leaving and never fucking coming back, never sending word, ultimately disappearing from my life completely. You knew what I needed, and you gave it to me, then you ripped it away the moment I had finally let you in. You took away the trust we had built the moment I had truly given myself to you... when I had allowed myself to love you.

For Maygen's sake, I will triumph over the darkness that plagues me; I will rise above from all that has wounded my body and my mind, every painful and torturous experience. I will heal from the loss of my life, the loss of my family, and the loss of Thibault. I will beat back my nightmares, the fear of my power, and my aversion to the voice within. I will find peace in missing Aloise and Isonei, surprised at how much so, though I find reprieve in knowing they are safe and Thibault lives on through his child. I will overcome every obstacle. I will recover from you.

I wish I could say I was choosing peace, happiness, and health for myself. It turns out, Maygen is the only reason I haven't hunted you down and laid waste to those in this world who seek to harm me. She keeps the force that is in me at bay; for her sake, I have not pursued Asuras or the mystery of my divine father.

The ten, long months since you left have been more peaceful than I had cared to notice, but that changes now. I will be better for her, and eventually I will be better for myself. While this letter comes off as incredibly angry, fueled by rage and spite, it is quite the opposite.

I know I will never stop wanting you, and I refuse to believe that what we shared, in whatever short time spent together, wasn't real. I suffer because my feelings for you are true, and they run deep; my yearning for you is unending. It will not disappear overnight. It will take a lifetime to fade away and become little more than a shadow in the back of my mind: hidden, yet everlasting. I will hold on to the memory of you in a way that I haven't before, with resigned fondness.

Because I will always love you.

— With undying affection, your lady."

With that, I sealed the envelope and tucked it away.

Evening in the courtyard was the epitome of noble luxury; it was busier than usual, as the house was preparing to enjoy an outdoor summer feast, a final celebration in the warmth of the season before it gives way to autumn in the coming weeks.

The sky was an enchanting shade of indigo, with the final rays of blazing orange sunlight falling over the horizon, leaving distant trees to appear as nothing more than blackened silhouettes. Wooden poles had been erected to string lights about. The bulbs were powered by the Vargen family's magic, illuminating the space.

Long tables had been set end to end, with enough chairs to comfortably sit three large families. The hired help had been buzzing about, lining the ivory cloth draped surfaces with platters of food and table settings.

I watched it all with a grimace, retreating into the shadows.

My attire this evening was chosen out of spite. A future bride was expected to dress in light colors, such as pastels, ivory, or white; I wore black.

The dress skirts were tulle, and the dark material mixed with underlying shades of forest green, which gave way to a lace midsection. Crawling over my breasts were leafy strips of what appeared to be vines, extending past my collarbones from the bodice, and falling over my shoulders in loose strands. Golden cuffs squeezed my biceps.

A dainty golden collar decorated my neck, lying loosely atop the snake tattoo which was in full view, due to the depth of plunge in the front of the fabric. As much as I hated the mark and what it meant, I found my favorite styles were those that exposed it. I wanted everyone to see it and to never forget who I was or what I was.

Unruly curls spun around my head, untamed. Lelia had insisted after curling many small locks of hair that I allow her to pin the pieces, but I'd refused. Kohl painted my lids in a winged fashion, and I used a shade of red lip paint similar to Ophelia's to deepen the fullness of my smile. I wasn't sure where the dress had come from, as I'd never noticed it in my wardrobe before, not that I paid much attention. Although, I think something with such grandeur would have caught my eye sooner rather than later.

Despite my elegant appearance, I walked barefoot. Heels were never my friend, and I enjoyed the feeling of earth underfoot. They're also hard to run away in. The shadowed forest felt more like home than the noisy keep nearby, for it was quiet and mysterious... it felt like an embodiment of myself.

I wondered if Euros' forests held secret magic like Teskaria's, and I wondered if Sprites were able to live in this part of the world.

Frowning, I allowed small tendrils of my curse to escape, and glowing power danced along my fingers. The sensation was relieving, like pulling off boots after a long day spent walking uphill. It mimicked what I imagined holding fire would look like, only crimson. The red hue illuminated the dark path I walked along, allowing me to see a bit further ahead.

Something changed in it within seconds, barely enough time for me to notice. The blood mist reared up as if it sensed something, thrashing wildly around my wrists in warning.

A foul scent invaded my senses: something rotten, something dead. I searched for the source, the pungent odor becoming stronger with each step forward. In the middle of the trail was the dismembered body of a feline, with nappy gray fur and a broken tail.

My skin tightened, hair bristling. Surely, this was a coincidence, as it wasn't uncommon for ferals to end up with injuries to the tail, and gray fur wasn't some rarely seen anomaly — but I couldn't suppress the feeling of dread, that this was an omen of sorts, or a foreshadowing of what might come to pass. The last I'd seen of a cat such as this was on the outskirts of Silenus Forest before I'd been lured away by intoxicating, ancient magic.

As I turned to flee, my power wrapped around my arms like protective sleeves.

I was halted in my escape by a familiar face.

"You come across a single carcass and are too distracted to assess your surroundings? I could've been someone with malicious intent," the white-haired Fae grumbled.

"I didn't even know you were here," I scoffed, pushing past the obstacle.

"I see you found my gift!" He called out.

Confused and startled, I turned to face him before speaking, "Gift?"

"The dress, it suits you."

Maxim gestured to my attire.

Of course.

"Wouldn't have assumed you'd be one to give gifts."

"Call it bribery. I wanted to discuss my proposal."

I shrunk as he advanced toward me, and even more so as he offered his arm.

"There is nothing to discuss."

"Because you are uninterested in the position I've offered or because Erelim has been bedding you?"

The bluntness of his statement stunned me.

"How-"

"I'm not blind, and I can see how he looks at you. I see how you try to avoid it. It's a knowing gaze and a shameful aversion. I've taken my fair share of ladies to bed, Celessa."

"Yet your offer still stands?" I mused.

"It does."

That was not what I'd expected.

"Why?"

"You're unique, powerful, and you don't tolerate my bullshit. I hold you in high regard, and I respect your resilience. My proposal is meant to offer you something you need in return for something I need. You need acceptance and resources, and I need someone by my side who would secure my position.

I want you to accept, but would not hold it against you if you did not. Not everyone is willing to enter into marriage with an acquaintance, only to find themselves in an eternal platonic arrangement."

Ocean blue orbs stared down at me, blazing into my skin, scorching my face.

I considered his words for a few moments before responding, "What you're saying is, you want a partner in power rather than a wife?"

"More or less."

"You did say we'd be eternally platonic."

"I mean this in the most respectful way imaginable, Celessa; you would be too much for me romantically. We're both dominant beings, so we both want to be in control. That does not bode well." Maxim shrugged.

I laughed, "You don't want someone romantically that *rivals* you?"

"Did I not offer you everything else?"

"After all I've endured at the hands of men, I have no interest in suffering a loveless marriage for the rest of my life."

Withdrawing from his arm, I stormed away, praying he would not get in my way again.

Appearing in the open, I marched to the tables where people were being seated and where Erelim stood with Cian, smiling and chatting. Through his peripheral vision, the young lord caught sight of me, fumbling to conceal something in his pocket. I knew what he was hiding, and I knew what this celebratory setup was truly for.

Cian's face hollowed as I approached, and I realized my power was still dancing on my hands, while likely also making my eyes glow.

Swirling in black and red, I imagined I was the picture of beautiful chaos.

Erelim watched with a nervous expression as I summoned the curse back to its hiding place, deep within myself. Once loud voices had hushed, lowering to murmurs. I could feel Maxim at my back just a distance away, and my flesh heated under the excess of attention now focused on me.

"Ask," I requested.

The violet of his eyes swirled with magic at my request.

"This isn't the most ideal moment, and I'd envisioned something a bit more... romantic," Erelim whispered, his smile turning.

I could feel my power pulsing beneath my skin, angry at the world and at me, an extension of myself; it bore the truth of how I felt. Not wanting to be in this situation, though I recognized it was my own fault.

"Ask," I insisted with a more stern tone.

He swallowed, lowering on shaky knees, producing a box with trembling hands.

The entirety of the courtyard had fallen silent.

"Lady Celessa, I humbly request your hand in marriage."

His voice was so sure, whereas his expression was concerned, likely expecting refusal.

"I vow to love and cherish you for the rest of our days," the trembling lessened as he spoke, and I gazed down at him, unmoving. "I swear to uplift and honor you, to see you through the difficult times as surely as the pleasant. I will respect you as my equal in all things, as the Lady of Autumnmoor, and as my wife, if you would do me the honor of accepting my proposal."

Beautifully moved gasps of awe were elicited from the onlookers. Meanwhile, I felt cold.

Even as I looked down upon the face of a man who was sincere in his affections and treated me well, even as I took in the beauty of the ring he offered, I felt nothing... save for icy indifference.

He had presented me with a band of tiny, intricate golden leaves, with a cut and polished stone of deep blues and purples in the setting - mimicry of the Vargen's eye color. The ring was gorgeous, and anyone would be lucky to be in my position.

"I accept," I forced the words out.

This was something I had dreamed of in my first life, something I had craved so desperately even after waking — to be desired, to be loved.

Yet, I have found myself numb.

Erelim stood, beaming with a grin that could've shamed the stars if they still decorated the night sky, and he pulled me into an embrace. The attending party clapped: even Ophelia, who hoped I'd accept her brother, and even Maygen, who knew I still loved another.

This was a good thing; it would be a good thing. I just had to allow it.

Erelim slid the impressive ring onto my left ring finger, opposite the silver band with a white gem that sat on my right. He kissed me in front of everyone, in tender confirmation of our newfound arrangement, and I let him.

Once again, I have found myself burdened and unprepared.

Lysenna was overjoyed with my decision, praising her son and blessing me several times before dinner had ended. The Lady of the estate made it known that she was excited to resign her position to me upon my betrothal to Erelim, heir of Autumnmoor. It had become quickly apparent that she'd been planning the events to follow my acceptance for some time.

She announced to the present company that a ball would be held in celebration of our engagement on the autumnal equinox. The wedding would follow a fortnight later, in the thick of the season, as was tradition for the nobility of northern Euros.

In less than two months, I would be a wife. It didn't seem like long enough for an engagement. It made sense, though, as we had been living in the same household for nearly a year, and we'd been physically intimate for a few months; I knew it wasn't my place to object.

At dinner's end, Maxim announced his coronation ceremony to become High Lord of Periveil, inviting all who dwelled within the Vargen estate to attend. Every person leaving offered me congratulations, whether it was well-respected guests or the hired help.

Maxim had bid me farewell, and I wondered if this would end the frequent visits he made with his twin; Ophelia had kissed both of my cheeks before departing and wished me success in my endeavors, rather than the blessings of happiness I'd received from everyone else.

I wished I could feel the joy everyone around me exuded, as I wanted to be a part of it. It was for me - and about me - but it was not within me. Sadness weighed heavily on my heart, with my mind repeating the same thoughts again and again. What if I made the wrong choice? What if this discontent never fades? What if the man I desire returns to me one day?

It doesn't matter.

I'd allowed myself to fall into relations with Erelim, and despite my intentions being impure and without emotion, I couldn't imagine Aklys would ever want me again. I needed to do with my love for him as I'd done with the letter I wrote; tuck it away.

As the day of the ball crept closer, my unease only grew. I hadn't expected to be exposed to all manners of people, but when Lysenna offered me a review of the guest list, I realized she'd invited nobles from all the kingdoms... even Teskaria. The only relief I felt was due to the absence of the Undergrove name.

I wondered what had become of Niall, the man I'd meant to murder to achieve my vengeance — vengeance that I was denied by those bastard men, those vampires, who haven't appeared since.

I rubbed my neck, trailing my fingers along the snake tattoo that curled around my throat, to where it rested its head against my sternum.

So many questions still remain unanswered: Why was I branded? Who was the father that assaulted my subconscious? How did he have the power to send vampires in pursuit of me? For what reason did they need my blood? What was my purpose?

Maygen's voice invaded my wandering thoughts, as she spoke to her Lady aunt about the parchment in my hand, "Do you think it's appropriate to invite so many nobles, considering Celessa's *heritage*? It is deeply ingrained that Amalgams are dangerous creatures, beings who are to be destroyed at the behest of the Gods. Why extend the invitation to the nobles of Teskaria, who sent their Sentinel troops to track her down?"

"Has she not encountered Goddesses during her journey home? They did not destroy her; therefore, none should fear her," Lysenna countered.

Referring to the keep as my home made me cringe. Too soon would I become lady of the estate, overseer of Autumnmoor: Eurosi nobility.

"If we did not extend the offer to houses of each kingdom, it would be unbecoming, and it could create tension," she clarified.

"Tension was created when they actively dispatched special units to hunt her like she was some wild animal!" Maygen hissed.

I admired her ability to stand up to her blood, as I'd never possessed such tenacity when it came to expressing myself to my parents in my first life.

"My dear, I think you're being a *bit* dramatic," the woman sighed, sweeping long brown hair over her shoulder. Lysenna rarely wore her hair in any style, often leaving it to fall naturally in its great length.

"Have either of you chosen your evening gowns for the event?"

She eyed me subtly, and I knew she had reservations about my ability to select formal wear after my attire the night Erelim proposed.

"I'll have it taken care of, with the blessing of my lovely cousin and bride-to-be," a deep voice chimed from behind.

Turning my head slightly, I caught sight of Erelim approaching seconds before he slid a warm hand around my waist. My face burned. I was not accustomed to this manner of affection, and truthfully, I found it almost unsettling, to no fault of my fiancé. I enjoyed his company, I was very much physically attracted to him, and the decision to accept his proposal was *mostly* my own. I also made the decision to let go of my past, yet still struggled to actually do so.

What a fraud I am, such a hypocrite who is never true to their word.

A liar.

He deserved better than a preoccupied wife.

"The day I trust you with my evening wear, the stars will return to the sky in pure shock and disbelief, just to catch a glimpse of whatever monstrosity you attempt to dress me in!" My friend scoffed playfully, feigning disgust before smirking at her cousin.

"I trust you," I murmured.

Gentle fingers beckoned my chin upward, to look him into the depths of magical eyes.

"That makes me happier than you know." He smiled, leaning down to whisper in my ear, "I'll bring it to you myself, rather than stuffing it in your wardrobe without your knowledge like some wayward stalker."

I rolled my eyes, and Erelim winked in return. It was a jab at Maxim's gift. The Myrkvior twins were among those receiving invitations, and I wondered if they would come or if he felt too slighted to attend. Something in me wished he had never made a passionless proposal in the first place, and that we'd maintain our strange friendship.

Hypocritical of me, wishing Erelim *hadn't* proposed from a place of endearment.

"It has armor?" I asked, confused.

A gown of glittering deep blues and gold had been sprawled across the bed, and Erelim beamed with pride. The corset was golden plated metal, fashioned with scales to mimic that of a serpent, with a plunging bust to display my God's mark. It came with intricately designed cuffs and a delicate, golden crown of leaves to match the ring on my finger. The entire design appeared to be a play upon the beauty of war; though, I was probably the last person who required armor. It was beautiful.

"Not that you need it. I just want everyone to see you for who you are, the way I see you."

"How do you see me?" My voice was barely above a whisper.

"Bold, beautiful, and brave. Strong, resilient, and powerful. You are a warrior and a survivor."

He reached out slowly, catching a stray lock of chestnut brown hair to tuck it behind my ear, craning to gauge my reaction.

"Do you not like it?"

The hint of a frown tugged at the corners of his lips.

"I am mesmerized, truly! I just hadn't realized you thought so highly of me," I chuckled nervously.

"How could I not? After all you've been through, and all you have shared with me?" He returned.

Unfortunately, I had few memories of my drunken ramblings, and I was unsure of how much I'd divulged to the man during our late-night lewdness.

Apparently sensing my discomfort, Erelim withdrew.

"I'll send Lelia in to help you dress... our guests should be arriving soon."

He flexed his fingers at his sides as he spoke, fists clenching with hesitation.

"We attempted to send word to Evelia, to contact your friends that dwell there."

That was kind, generous; I missed Isonei and Aloise terribly.

"My mother also sent word through a forbidden channel, to contact those who dwell within Greilor," he continued.

My heart sank. They had connections to the rebel country? They sent word of what, my engagement? Why had no one spoken of this before? What if Aklys hears of it? Why would they even consider doing such a thing?

No, no, no.

There was nothing I could do but gape at the man.

"I was unaware until this morning, Celessa. I'm sorry. She claims that she needs all of the realm to know what is transpiring here. I'm unsure of her motives. I was blind-sided, and I do not wish for you to be as well."

Erelim's eyes lowered, ashamed. What did he have to be ashamed of when his mother had done something so serious behind his back?

What would happen if the vampires of Greilor showed up here, among the nobility of the Three Kingdoms? It would certainly spell disaster, as the tyrants were banished centuries ago, having bathed these lands in blood.

"Thank you for telling me," I forced out. "It makes no difference."

I tried my hardest to summon a convincing smile, even allowing Erelim to kiss me before he took his leave.

The passing hour of dressing and preparing to be seen by the courts swept by in a blur, with my head a torrential current of potential scenarios. I couldn't focus, nor could I fully comprehend what he'd confided in me. It felt surreal... and wrong.

Something was amiss, and I feared it would be a great undoing of the peace to which I so desperately clung.

Chapter Twenty-One

The Final Straw

Spinning, twirling — I was on the verge of vomiting. If I was passed off to one more stranger to be flung about the dancefloor, I was going to puke on their shoes.

The alcohol I'd consumed to make this evening bearable was reacting with agonizing protest to the amount of movement I was forced to partake in. My brain was bouncing inside of its bone cage, with my stomach twisting into the most intricate of knots. The squeezing of the metal corset only made matters worse. It was heavy, and I was exhausted.

Someone please end this.

A strong arm wrapped my waist, gracefully lifting my body and pulling me to the sidelines, as if in answer to my silent plea. I was spared from the beginning of another painful waltz, not by my intended husband, but by Maxim Myrkvior. He actually showed up.

"You look like you're going to faint," he grumbled, as disagreeable as ever.

"Dancing was never my *thing*," I panted, still reeling.

"It doesn't seem like any of this is your thing."

I looked around the room, taking in the excess of decorations and guests, the luxury of it all.

"It was once."

Maxim hummed thoughtfully before speaking, "If you had accepted my proposal, I wouldn't have put you on display for the amusement of these imbeciles. You could still change your mind and leave with me for Periveil right now. I'm sure no one would even notice amidst all of this merriment and nonsense."

"If that was meant to convince me, be assured you've done the opposite," I whispered.

Maxim chuckled, "You're a terrible liar."

Huffing a sound of discontent, I only gave the man an irritated glance. Although, I did find the offer to be mildly tempting.

A disgruntled expression appeared in my line of vision, one that wasn't too pleased at my present company being pressed so close.

I hadn't seen my fiancé in at least an hour, as he was whisked away by Lysenna after the opening dance. The performance was an excruciating experience - every person in the room watched as my soon-to-be husband tried to prevent me from stumbling and misstepping. My heart wasn't in this, and my nerves were thoroughly shot.

"Lord Maxim," Erelim offered a monotone greeting.

The white-haired Fae barely acknowledged his presence, still watching me for any sign of change concerning his offer.

"I see you have wasted no time in interrupting my fiancée's evening."

"Celessa was visibly uncomfortable, so I did her a kindness." Maxim shrugged. "Perhaps you would do well with some fresh air?"

"*I* will escort you."

Erelim pushed around Maxim, reaching for me, but his adversary stepped purposely in his way. They sized each other up, nose to nose.

My acquaintance had taken on the role of a shield, effectively blocking Erelim from taking my hand. The two began exchanging curses, but I couldn't focus on what was being said.

My nausea had reached its limit, boiling over. I was going to be sick, and flight-mode had taken hold.

Fleeing the building, I made my way into the brisk night to spare myself the humiliation of being sick in front of all the kingdoms' nobility.

"Fuck this!" I hissed, spitting at the grass, desperate to rid my mouth of the contents of my stomach.

The vomit reeked of alcohol, but I was only irritated by the inconvenience of losing some of what fueled my intoxication. Lysenna had instructed Chessane to keep a close eye on my consumption this evening; it was difficult to sneak drinks when she rarely found herself occupied.

I was smarter than them, though, so I would not be deterred.

Checking my surroundings to ensure I wasn't being watched, I disappeared into the forest, kicking off the heels I hadn't wanted to wear to run in my bare feet. Earlier in the day, I had stashed a bottle of spirits beneath a bush just a short distance away from the courtyard, hidden by the outskirts of the forest. There was no way in hell I'd go back to that party without refreshing my buzz.

I'm a miserable, miserable person. I should be enjoying myself. I should want to be sober. I should want to dance with my soon-to-be husband and friends.

My fingers made contact with glass after several minutes of rummaging in the dark, producing my vice. I sighed with relief, twisting off the lid to indulge.

Before I could bring the bottle to my lips, my fingers twitched, ears catching a subtle sound. I heard twigs snapping.

Footsteps were approaching.

Rising, I demanded, "Who is there?"

There was no response.

If it was anyone from the estate, or the friends from Periveil, then they would've answered immediately. My breathing quickened, heart racing. I let a trickle of power wrap around my wrists like flaming bracelets.

"Show yourself!"

A low hum vibrated from the chest of the intruder, bathed in shadow.

"Lady Celessa," a man answered.

This voice did not match any of the faces with whom I'd become familiar.

"Who are you?"

My power flared brighter, illuminating the space with a red glow, revealing the identity of the man.

He was a vampire.

But he was not the vampire who I hoped would come back for me; he was not the one I yearned for. This was one of the bastards who branded me. I could still feel the sensation of his fangs in my neck.

My resolve fluttered, breaking. I was afraid.

The man took a step.

"Don't come any closer, or I'll reduce you to *nothing*!" I spat.

"Is that how you treat a guest?" He grinned. "I even brought you a gift."

In his hand, he held a large pouch.

The fabric was wet, dripping. Droplets of fluid fell to the ground as he raised it for me to see: *pat, pat, pat.*

"I imagine you wanted *all* of your friends to attend. How unhappy you must be in their absence, especially without your would-be lover, *skamelar.*"

How did he know anything about them or their whereabouts?

I was trembling now, overcome with fear.

"How lonely you will be, little lady, how utterly and entirely *alone*!"

The man tossed the pouch to my feet.

I backed away, startled. Even my curse faltered, as we were both compromised by what lingered of my intoxication. To add insult to injury, it was never at full capacity in the presence of a vampire. As far as I knew, I could use it as a weapon against the cursed beings, physically touching them with it, but it didn't kill them and couldn't destroy them the way it did everything else.

"Don't be rude, Celessa, open your gift. I worked so hard to procure it for you."

I crouched carefully, taking the drawstrings between my fingers. The only light available in the thick of the trees was that which came from me, making what fell from the pouch even more horrific, awash in a red glow.

It was a head.

I didn't see the face before throwing myself back, falling to the ground and scrambling away from the gruesome sight.

The man was on me in an instant, reaching for the bloodied contents and pulling it into view. It was the head of a woman.

A familiar woman.

A Nymph.

Isonei.

It was dripping on me - the blood from her severed head dribbled onto my skin, creating little streams that ran down my chest. She was dead. He killed her. He murdered her and brought me his prize. The invitation sent to her had been a death sentence.

I couldn't move, couldn't breathe, strangled by horror and disbelief. The vampire dropped her head into my lap.

I wanted to scream, but I choked on it.

"It was too easy," he hissed, "I needn't say anything more than I was a friend of *Aklys*," the way he spoke the name was both mocking and disgusted. "Just a fellow vampire helping him safely escort Lady Celessa's guests. She should have known better, I think, considering you aren't marrying that pathetic waste."

Lowering himself, he brought us face to face, and I couldn't escape it because my body had frozen from shock.

"Did you really believe that the most wicked forces in the realm would offer idle threats? Did you not see the warning I left for you, the sweet little kitty? I've been watching you since you were '*saved*', Celessa, and now we're tired of waiting!" The man growled.

Screams replaced the once-joyous sounds that had filled the night air, ripping through the darkness.

I couldn't even blink, and instead I only stared at the grinning monster.

"I hope you enjoyed your evening, and I hope you kissed your loved ones goodbye."

As the sounds grew louder, my adversary licked Isonei's blood from his fingers.

"An appetizer. Time for the main course."

He was gone, so fast, too fast for me to catch him – if I could only move.

I stared into the glassy eyes of the bloody face that drenched my dress. This wasn't real. This was a nightmare.

Screams became more desperate, more shrill.

I was struggling to regain a direct train of thought to process what was happening. Tears were hot on my cheeks; my body shook violently as I moved the head to place it on the ground. The nearby cries were blood-curdling, for they were the screams of the dying.

I had to run, had to save people, had to save my *family*.

My feet were moving before I could comprehend that I was running, running back to the keep and towards the sounds of chaos and carnage.

There was fire, the scene before me a mess of flames and bodies.

How did this happen? Why is the keep on fire? I was only gone for maybe twenty minutes, but those twenty minutes were enough for everything to go to hell. Everything I feared had transpired.

I needed to find the members of the house, and most importantly, I needed to find Maygen. The guests were fleeing, some escaping down the road that leads to Autumnmoor and some stopped in their tracks by monsters that ripped them apart.

Monsters disguised as men.

A scream climbed up my throat, calling out the names of those I cherished. They had to be alive, I hoped they managed to escape.

"Maygen!" I screamed, the force of it straining my neck.

"Celessa," a calm voice spoke amidst the violence and the horror. "Come with me. I'll keep you safe."

Maxim.

"Please, have you seen her? Where is she?"

My power felt stuck, trapped beneath sheer terror.

"Let me take you away from here," he insisted, reaching out a hand.

"Why aren't you helping anyone else?"

I whirled, catching the gruesome sight of a vampire tearing into the throat of a girl that had been crying for help. The girl was Lelia, and she was being murdered by a vampire who took on the appearance of a familiar woman.

A woman... with white hair.

I turned back to Maxim, the blood draining from my face, seeing him as I hadn't before. There was blood on his hands, on his lips. His entire demeanor had changed, the features of his face shadowed, save for a slight glint between parted lips.

"B-but... you're Fae?" I stammered, stumbling away.

"I am," he confirmed, taking another step forward, hand still outstretched. "And I am something else."

I willed my power forward, but was met with nothing. There were too many vampires.

"My mother was a vampire, Lady Celessa," Maxim growled as he grabbed my wrist. "One of the first."

I fought against his hold, as strong as an iron trap.

"They call us Dark Fae, half-breed descendants of the original vampires. We can conceal our vampiric affliction if we choose. There is no need to fear me, Celessa - I mean to help you. Your acquaintances made their bed with the wrong allies long ago, so this was inevitable. You were merely the catalyst."

"You were my enemy the entire time! How could you?" I hissed, remembering that once he had felt like a threat when he was angry with me.

He felt dangerous because he always has been.

"You don't know who your enemies are!" Maxim shouted.

A familiar voice called out my name. It sounded desperate, pained, scared: Maygen. New strength erupted inside of me at her call, giving renewed life to my magic. I had used it to fight monsters before, and I would do it again.

Concentrating the power under my skin, I set it off in an explosion against the hold on my wrist, similar to what I had once done in battle against a Chimera; thought it lacked potency. Maxim was sent flying a great distance, ending with his body crashing to the ground. An angry cry crept closer, and I realized Ophelia was advancing toward me. I hesitated for a moment, as this woman had been my friend, but the bloodlust in her eyes held no semblance of the woman I thought I knew.

I lashed out with red tendrils, striking her from the ground, sending her colliding with the stone wall of the keep. Blood splattered against the surface, her body falling limp as I withdrew. I heard the scream again, the plea of my friend.

She was inside the keep.

I rushed through the entryway, despite the doors burning, flames lapping at the frame. A few bodies were strewn across the floor, one whole and the others in pieces. I felt sick, so sick.

I spotted Cian among the fire and smoke with a broken beam protruding from his midsection. This was not fatal to a vampire, but as long as it remained in his body he would not heal. Dropping to my knees to grab the foreign object, I was stopped as he pushed me away. Gasping, he pointed to a far wall... he pointed to a man.

The vampire who had given me Isonei's head now held a woman in his hands.

Maygen cried, thrashing against his grip on her hair and throat.

"Don't!" I shouted. "Let her go!"

"You were warned, were you not? He promised you untold suffering!" The man hissed, squeezing her tighter. "Watching you all this time, it would seem this little darling is what you hold most dear. I'd thought perhaps that person might be your intended husband, but you don't *really* love him, do you?"

His expression twisted into a fanged sneer as he continued, "The others had the right idea, to flee for their lives. What a shame that she wouldn't leave without you, forcing her lover to stay behind. Now, they'll both die because of *you*."

I moved toward them. I would save her, and I would kill this tyrant.

White-hot pain ripped through my shoulder, driving out toward my chest and bursting from my skin. I fell to my knees, overwhelmed with agony. Someone had driven a long dagger through my back, the tip of the blade protruding beneath my collarbone. I gasped, unable to move; it was excruciating.

Lifting my head, I searched for the identity of the assailant, to find a woman I'd never seen before - another fucking vampire. She grabbed my hair, wrenching my head forward to look at my friend. My power trickled out pitifully from my fingertips, subdued by the presence of so many afflicted enemies, my initial intoxication, and now my newfound injury.

"Watch!" She commanded.

"Please," I forced, feebly begging the man to spare the only person left in this world that I loved.

Maygen was my best friend, my only family.

"He needs his monster, and the creature he meant to create wasn't supposed to be whatever it is you've become," the man spat in disgust, "A weeping, drunken whore. You're pathetic! It's time you fulfilled your intended purpose, God spawn."

His fingers arched, his hand now resembling a predator's claws. The tips pushed into Maygen's neck, breaking the skin as easily as pushing a knife through butter. She wailed, screaming against the assault.

"Please! I'll do whatever you want! Just spare her!" I cried over my labored breathing, fighting against the pain.

My power snaked slowly along the floor, desperate to free her.

"It's nothing personal - you see, we have no choice. It's our lives or theirs, so there is no decision to be made..." the vampire trailed off.

His face flickered a solemn expression, almost too quickly to notice. It was gone as fast as it had come.

"Become the weapon you were meant to be, or this will never end."

"I will be whatever he wants! Let her go!"

My injury was twisting my ability to make sense of what was truly transpiring.

Wild eyes met mine, and Maygen's features twisted in pain, fear, and sadness. She opened her mouth, and blood trickled from her lips.

"I will *never* leave you, Celessa," she gasped, straining. "I love you."

The vampire pressed again, tearing his fingers through her flesh, ripping open her throat. Cian screamed from behind us; it was the scream of someone who had lost everything, the sound of a heart breaking. Maygen's blood sprayed the floor, and the light left her eyes as her limp body slumped to the ground.

This isn't real; it's just a nightmare. She's not dead. She is not gone...

Maygen is not fucking dead.

My heartbeat throbbed, drowning out everything around me, filling my ears with thunder. The woman behind me ripped the dagger from my body, freeing me of the blade.

That was a mistake.

I stood abruptly, turning to grab her by the throat, as whatever divinity resided in my blood gave me strength in my despair. I squeezed harder than I thought possible, so hard that my hand ruptured the fragile stalk that held her head to her shoulders. With my bare hands, I ripped her head from her body, bathing myself in crimson.

Her black hair was laced between my fingers as I refocused on the vampire that had murdered my savior from the darkness. She had been the one tethering me to the light, the only thing that kept me from the chaos that gnawed at me day and night.

My arm tensed, and I hurled the woman's head at the murderer; striking him in the chest. It hit him hard enough to make him stumble. He stared at the corpse at my feet with shock and dismay.

"You will die. You will all die!" I screamed, but the voice that left me did not seem like it was my own; it belonged to something that had no place in this world.

Reaching down, my fingers wrapped around the blade that had been lodged in my shoulder, and I wrenched it from the limp hand of the decapitated woman. I flung the weapon in the same manner I had the body part, and it found its place in the man's chest. Stalking toward him, I unleashed my power, letting it bellow around me like deadly fog.

"Is this the monster you wanted?" I growled, reaching for the stunned vampire, "Am I now everything he desires?"

I saw bright lights, followed by brief darkness. When my eyes stopped fluttering, I realized I was on the ground.

I am so fucking tired of getting hit in the head!

Who hit me? My gaze searched, seeing no one. Not even the vampire that I had wounded. He was gone.

No.

No!

I would not be robbed of retribution again!

My chest was tearing apart as fire collapsed the building, but my screams did little to reveal the extent of my pain, my rage, my despair. I couldn't breathe, as the smoke inhalation and grief were overwhelming, suffocating.

I crawled to Maygen's lifeless, maimed body. My fingers brushed against her already cold cheek. Pulling her against me, into my arms, I wept. I wailed. I cursed.

This life was not worth living without her, so I let the flames consume us, praying I wouldn't have to endure it any longer.

I'm awake. I'm still alive.

Sitting up from my resting place, I hoped it had all truly been a nightmare.

But it wasn't.

Before me was the crumbled keep, with broken stone walls, frame reduced to ash, still smoldering against the foundation. A gray haze lingered, with smoke and soot thickening the air. Dawn had not quite broken, and the sky was cloudy and bleak.

Everything was hurting.

My joints ached, my head throbbed, and my lungs burned. Every breath was painful, like I'd been scorched from the inside. The wound through my body still oozed, the blood struggling to clot.

I looked at my hands and at my ripped, bloodied dress.

Maygen was not in my clutches as she had been, and my last memory was holding her in my arms; she was gone.

I was alone.

Someone had pulled me from that fire, though so many bodies lay dead on the ruined ground. Lives were taken, but for what?

Nothing.

No greater purpose could ever excuse this: no rivalry, no motive.

A hand rested on my shoulder, and I jumped away from the contact, wincing at the state of my body.

"They're all gone," Cian whispered, eyes swollen, dusted in the remnants of what was once his home.

The other lives with whom I'd found myself entwined crossed my mind. What had happened to them? Did they survive and escape? Were they among the dead? Had they been reduced to nothing in the fire?

"Have you checked the bodies?" I croaked.

Cian shook his head, rising from my side to begin searching.

He had saved me, but there was no one else left.

We searched the corpses strewn about the courtyard. It was a daunting task, as we were both injured and suffering the aftermath of shock and heartbreak.

Ophelia's body was where I'd left it; though, upon some inspection, it wasn't blunt force that killed her; I think my power did. Her chest had been caved in and opened, leaving behind a heartless hole. Enemies hidden behind good intentions, all this time they'd been watching and assessing. They were half-vampire, half-Fae hell spawn; offspring of the first, the evil tyrants responsible for countless atrocities.

If their mother had truly been murdered by her brother, then that meant their uncle was an original vampire who may still live. That meant they were all related. They kill their siblings and bring carnage to the realm - ruining everything they touch, and leaving devastation in their wake.

Monsters.

There was no sign of Maxim. He must have recovered from my attack and fled, leaving his dead sister behind.

What would have become of all these people if I had accepted his proposal over Erelim's? What would have become of me?

Every decision I have ever made resulted in the deaths of the people I love.

I was a walking, breathing calamity.

What felt like hours passed before my lone companion summoned me.

"Celessa!" Cian called, holding the hand of a ruined body.

He cradled a horribly burned woman. It was a miracle she still breathed.

Lysenna.

Half of her face was unrecognizable, and her once long and beautiful hair had been scorched from her head. She was bloody and wheezing. How had she endured these injuries through the night, and how had she not succumbed?

Mage blood granted you many things, but it did not grant the rapid healing with which immortals were blessed.

"I had expected..." I was stunned that she could speak, though it was strained and barely above a whisper, "that there would be... chaos." Lysenna wheezed as she spoke, "I had not... that everything would be taken from us. They were supposed to protect us from them."

"I don't understand," Cian whispered, tears washing away the gray on his face to reveal his deeply rich skin.

Lysenna sighed. She was clinging to life, but barely.

"Now, everyone will know what has been lurking in the shadows, and what they have created," blood dribbled from her lips as she spoke.

She raised a shaky hand to gesture to where Ophelia's corpse was crumpled on the ground.

"Dark Fae?" I asked, receiving a slight nod in return. "You knew?"

"I suspected," her body was shuddering more violently with every word spoken. "I never would have let him take you, but the decision needed to be yours." She gasped, "I am so happy you chose my son."

My heart skipped, for I *had* chosen her son. I knew she had wanted it, knew she planned for it, but she never forced him on me; until she was left with no choice.

"Where are your sons, Lysenna? Where is Daevian?" Cian asked, trembling.

"Gone from this place."

Her eyelids fluttered.

"Lysenna!" I cried out, wishing I could save her, but knowing I could not. There was no dark magic at play in the wounds she suffered, so there was nothing here that my power could fix.

"I'm so sorry."

"No." She reached a weak hand toward me, grasping my own with what little strength she had left. "This is what we chose. We knew what it meant to bring you here."

I felt that she was referring to Maygen, that Maygen knew, perhaps Erelim as well.

They had done it anyway, and paid for it in blood.

The Lady of Autumnmoor died in the arms of a man whom she had given a home and a family. She had been close to a mother to Cian, and he sobbed violently at the loss. He didn't deserve this.

None of them deserved this.

We never found the bodies of our friends, and we prayed that they'd somehow escaped, but we were unsure of where they could have gone. We did uncover what remained of Maygen, an ashen corpse that was mostly charred bones. I walked to the spot where Isonei's head rested, sick to my stomach that she'd endured a death so horrific. Cian carried Lysenna to her final resting place.

We buried them with the sunrise and sobbed into the earth, cursing Gods and vampires.

We cursed Fate itself.

"We can't let them get away with this," I spoke through clenched teeth, never taking my eyes away from the women's graves. "Not a single one deserves to live."

There was a time when I had contemplated becoming a villain, when I had wanted to succumb to darkness, if only to keep those I loved safe. Perhaps if I had, they would all still be here. I had no one left to protect now, no one left to keep me complacent.

"I will follow you to the ends of the realm in pursuit of them," Cian swore. "We will lay waste to everything in our path."

The first target appeared in my mind.

Traitor. Deceiver.

"I doubt Maxim returned to Periveil, and he'll expect me to come looking for him. We have to go further than that," I decided.

"Where?" He asked.

We needed to go to the one place we weren't supposed to go.

"To where vampires dwell, where our enemy hides."

I looked Cian in the eyes, bloodshot and puffy.

"We will go to Greilor."

Chapter Twenty-Two

Chasing Retribution

As we'd expected, Maxim Myrkvior was nowhere to be found. There was no trace of the vampires that have effectively destroyed our lives.

Cian had demanded an audience with Viggo Myrkvior, father of the Dark Fae twins, and reinstated High Lord of Periveil. He wanted to discern what the man knew about his children, their afflicted relatives, or where Maxim may have gone. The white-haired man informed us that Calendine, their vampire mother, had been murdered at the behest of his treasonous children. Maxim had revealed to his uncle that Calendine was a defector to the 'enemy', a matter which Viggo declined to speak on.

Allegedly, the treatment his son received at his hand had been exaggerated by both twins in an effort to overrule Lord Viggo, to gain control of Periveil's courts. Maxim had gone as far as staging the slaughter of his lover, in an effort to garner sympathy, and scarring himself to feign abuse.

He had no knowledge of where his son might have gone and wasn't too devastated at the loss of his children. It was impossible to tell who may be the liar in this situation, and we left cursed with more questions than we'd arrived with.

We had nothing to go on other than a few names in the forbidden chain of connection to Greilor. Those whom Cian was aware of resided in Adristan, the southernmost Kingdom. We had to decide if we would attempt to cross the country border through Steepwater

Fortress or take the longer route through Harm's Pass toward the desert. The latter was too risky and would take longer than I had patience to spare.

Word had spread about what transpired in Autumnmoor. Several noble persons from Adristan died that night, and many of the bodies still lay unrecovered, as far as I knew. I could very well be blamed for the deaths, making passage to any destination even more dangerous. If people didn't fear me for being an Amalgam, they would fear me now, knowing that death follows wherever I travel.

Hooded cloaks were worn at all times to disguise our identities. Whispers passed in the areas we traveled through about vampires and Dark Fae. Some spoke of the Gods' will, saying the world would end or change and that war was coming. Many were vocal about their aversion to vampires and 'half-breeds', taking up the argument that they should be purged from society by any means necessary - in the name of the realm's preservation. Few made hushed conversation about the Amalgam, harbinger of ruin and despair.

It was crucial to remain hidden. Cian and I were in danger every step of our journey: both of us mixed beings and therefore perceived enemies of the kingdoms.

Our path after Steepwater Fortress would take us to Rosenshire. After passing across the open country, we would make for the coast of Crimson Bay and follow it to Ossarion, where Cian claims we should be able to find a smuggler to leave us on Greilor's shores. It should be easier now to locate nefarious persons, as we had become some ourselves.

It was tiring to travel like this again. I'd only been granted less than a year of peace since awakening — peace I would not have found if not for Maygen, and it was time I had taken for granted. I would return to my sleep for a thousand years if it meant she would still be alive.

Cian and I cried more often than we spoke, overwhelmed by devastation and rage. Nearly two weeks had passed since that fateful day, but it seemed like endless days of every waking moment feeling like hell. I had not been so affected by the loss of my first life as I was by losing Maygen.

My body was in physical shock, as well as emotional. I'd quit drinking and was suffering symptoms of withdrawal. It was necessary, for I didn't believe I deserved to be numb to this.

I needed to feel all of it.

We camped under the cover of trees near the fortress walls that guard Adristan, without fire and only thin blankets to keep us warm during the cooling night. The weather in the south was more agreeable, but winter was beginning its descent and had begun riding our backs. Due to my condition, we were forced to stop frequently to rest.

Cian dressed the wound to my shoulder that was left behind by the vampire woman - the *dead* woman; I smirked ever so slightly at the thought.

"Your healing is accelerated. It's not to the level of an immortal, but it's much faster than any human or mage that hasn't used healing magic. Has it ever been that way before?" He asked, securing the bandage that he'd wrapped around my shoulder.

"Only on my God's mark."

His fingers stilled a bit, waiting for me to elaborate.

"I tried to dig it out of my skin..." I paused, "with my fingernails."

Cian huffed, "Maybe the things you've been through are awakening a response from your power. Your divine blood might be taking hold over your mortal parts, or something."

"What about yours?"

I pictured the long beam protruding from his body, having impaled him through and through. It was a miracle, or lack thereof, that he'd had the strength to pull us both from the fire.

Rising to step around me lightly, he pulled up his shirt to expose a scarred midsection. The wood had left a mark, a big one; it was purplish in color, but the wound was sealed.

"I'm glad you're able to recover like a vampire, because if you were mortal, you'd be dead. I don't understand much about how mixing blood works in favor of the offspring," I said.

I sighed, rubbing my shoulder.

He explained, "It's easy to reproduce with a female of mortal blood, their anatomy is submissive so the curse bonds easily — that's why it's most common to find a half-vampire that is also half-mortal, rather than with another immortal lineage.

"Mortals are fertile often, whereas immortals are not. Otherwise, the world would be overrun with them due to their long lifespans. Lysenna told me when I had asked her about Daevian and I's parents," his eyes squinted as he spoke his brother's name. "I am physically closer to a vampire than to a mortal. Akin to them in most ways; I am just a little slower, a little weaker, and slightly more fragile. I can fall ill, and I can be scarred."

When he turned away, it was clear he was done with the conversation. This had been the most we'd spoken since the audience with Lord Myrkvior.

"How long will it take to reach Ossarion?"

The Elvish-built city was at the southernmost point of the kingdoms. It was also the closest piece of land to the mountainous barrier of Greilor's coast, a peninsula that was bordered by both the Glistening Sea and the Southern Gulf.

"Perhaps a week, if we face no unanticipated delays. We should seek out those with the names I remember from Lysenna... to find out what they know. If these people are connected to Greilor, they likely will have information about how to pass the barrier. Moreover, they may know what lies beyond, and who we might find there," Cian grumbled, rummaging in his pack.

"Where do we need to go?"

"The easiest target also happens to be the closest one, the Rosewick family: Elvish nobility that oversees Rosenshire. Namely, we need to see the head of their court, Harmyn Rosewick. As far as I know, there are five of them. Harmyn has a son and three daughters."

"Do we approach them respectfully, or do we use force?" I asked over a mouthful of the dried meat Cian had handed me.

Neither of us had an appetite, but not eating meant no energy, and that meant being even more vulnerable.

"Anyone in connection to the deaths of our family is an enemy. Fuck them," the vampire hissed.

I silently nodded my agreement, wrapping myself in my blanket in an attempt to lessen the shaking. The shivering was a product of nightfall's chill, but it was also from withdrawal. I knew no amount of warmth would stop it. Shortly after closing my eyes, I felt a slight shift in the weight on my body. Cian had covered me with his own blanket and his jacket.

"Thank you," I whispered.

"Another day or two and you should feel better," he mumbled, settling against a tree to sleep.

For once, luck had been on our side. We'd found a damaged stormwater drain, and a small, iron-gated entry beneath the towering walls. It had been a tight squeeze to fit through, mostly for Cian with his broad shoulders. I considered thanking Fate that the ground had been dry due to the lack of rain, but I forced away any inkling of gratitude.

Fate can get fucked.

Little passed through my mind during the nearly two-day trek to arrive deep within the alleyways of Rosenshire, under the cover of darkness; we listened for any talk of the noble family, or where to find them outside of their manor.

"A lady of the night?"

My lip curled up in disgust, and I turned to see if the comment was directed at me.

"What's your price, beautiful?" A half-drunk man smiled.

Use him, that small voice whispered.

I grinned something wicked and foul, instantly changing the man's demeanor from flirtatious to unsettled.

"Information," I purred, stalking toward him.

My power danced in my veins, showing along my fingers.

The man stumbled, and I pressed him against the wall with my advance, glaring down at his trembling figure.

"W-what information?" He stammered, gripping at his pants.

He'd pissed himself. I almost laughed.

"Where can I find a member of the Rosewick family outside of their estate?"

"The Black Rose!" He exclaimed. "I can take you!"

"Who will I find there?"

"Lord Kairin and Lady Bryalyn gamble there!"

"Show me," I demanded.

The drunkard escorted Cian and I to a shady entryway at the back of a stone building, where the stairs descended to a noisy, smoke-filled, underground bar. The patrons were all manners of drunk. Scantily clad, mortal women danced and sat on the laps of different men throughout the establishment. Large tables were set up in the corners for gamblers to place wagers on various card games.

Gambling was outlawed in the Three Kingdoms, save for the battle events held in Licourt annually, where everything was closely monitored and the people were heavily taxed for betting.

"Where can I find Lord Kairin or Lady Bryalyn?" I asked a woman serving drinks, who lazily gestured to the gambling setup in the furthest corner.

An Elvish man and woman with similar features sat side by side. Long, pointed ears parted the pale blonde hair that fell from their heads in waves, a stark contrast against their deep, golden skin. Kairin had half of the milky locks pulled back tightly, save for the strands that fell over his forehead and brows, the rest clinging to his neck. His sister's hair was unruly, a long and wild mess that draped over her shoulders and chest, falling against the table as she reached for cards. The pair were visibly intoxicated.

I'd arrived at the most opportune time, as their game had ended and the table cleared, save for the siblings. I pulled up a chair, sitting directly across from them.

"What's your game?" The Elvish man slurred, shuffling the deck.

Bryalyn paid me no mind, scooping up the coins they'd won on their previous bet.

"Murder and mayhem, it would seem," I replied, catching their attention.

The two watched with curiosity as I pulled away my hood, bringing my power to the surface for my eyes to glow in tell-tale of my identity.

She gasped, "The Amalgam."

"What luck, we've been hoping to make your acquaintance," Kairin grinned.

We entered a back room, a space obviously reserved for the higher-class members of the secret establishment. The door was guarded by a large Elvish man dressed in armor; the breastplate decorated with Adristan's crest of crossed arrows that were encircled by thorny vines.

I hadn't planned to have a private conversation. I wanted to rip them from the underground and demand they take me to their father. Perhaps less violence would prove favorable, although my murderous inclinations were making my eyelid twitch.

Kairin gestured toward lounge chairs, beckoning Cian and I to sit. My vampire companion hesitated, pulling a seat in front of his body. I sat in the chair while he loomed over my shoulders, staring at the pair of siblings.

"To what do we owe the pleasure?" Kairin asked as he settled into the cushions, appearing rather content.

"You're the one who seems pleased to see me, not the other way around," I growled.

"Yes, we are!" He confirmed. "Though, I'd like to assess your intentions before we proceed. Please, tell us what we can do for you, Demi-Goddess."

Clenching my jaw, I stared down at the man and spoke quietly, "Where is your father?"

Kairin's grin grew.

"What do you want with him?"

"I need information, and I mean to extract it by any means necessary."

Bryalyn moved from her seat, bringing us nose to nose.

"Is it easy for you to kill?" She asked.

The close proximity made me shift uncomfortably. They were getting me out of sorts, and that could not happen.

Cian rumbled an animalistic growl, gripping the back of the chair so tightly it began to crack.

Her eyes flicked to the vampire before remarking, "I'm surprised at your present company, after what you have endured at the hands of his kind."

I stood abruptly, sending the woman tumbling backwards.

"He is not like those beasts. He loved the people who were murdered, just as I did."

Kairin lifted his sister from the floor, whispering something in her ear that I could not discern. I looked to my companion, wondering if his enhanced hearing had picked up their hushed words. Cian's face looked hollow.

"She was your blood?" He asked the pair.

Bryalyn nodded, "Maygen's mother was Cammina Rosewick, half-breed daughter of our late uncle, Halwyn."

My blood chilled. The Elvish grandfather Maygen had told me about once before was of a noble line, and I had found their kin. I cursed myself for not inquiring about her heritage further. How was I supposed to dispose of them now?

"Our father had turned Maygen away when her family was slain, and she was just a child. There are a great many terrible things that man has done, but we haven't forgiven him for that. We never saw her again. We didn't receive an invitation to your engagement ball, but feared the worst when we heard what had transpired there." Kairin hesitated. "Did she not survive?"

Struggling against his tears, the vampire lowered his eyes, pressing his lips together to stifle his emotions.

"Were you her lover? I can see the heartbreak in your eyes."

The Elvish woman pushed past me to embrace Cian, startling him. He did not return the gesture, wary of the strangers.

"She never spoke of you," he returned.

"We had barely been given a chance to know Maygen when our father made his decision based on her lineage alone. There has never been a time where we possessed the power to go against him." Kairin looked at me and said, "Until now."

"You mean to use me against your father?" Laughing, I bared my teeth in a snarl. "How do I know you're not lying? I should torture the information about Greilor from you and then kill you all."

Red illuminated the small space.

The siblings reeled, stumbling away from me, unable to get their bearings due to intoxication.

I could use a drink right now.

"The kingdoms remain backwards and cruel due to those in power, where old Fae and Elvish lords have ruled for far too long," the man insisted. "Our father is a despicable man. Let us work together. We can get you any information you desire in exchange for your services."

"I assassinate him so you can replace him? You expect me to be swayed by claims of seeking justice for those mistreated under outdated rule?" I hissed.

"Yes," he confirmed, resolute.

"Celessa," Cian murmured. "If we play this right, we could get the information and resources we need, while potentially gaining an ally. If Harmyn was responsible for *any* of Maygen's suffering, then he deserves to die."

I considered for a moment, watching the trembling Elves. There was no fucking way I'd trust them, but I *did* trust Cian's judgement.

"Fine."

The bloody tendrils returned to dormancy.

"Let's get this over with."

The golden-skinned Elvish lord tumbled across the floor, tossed like a ragdoll by Cian's hand. He hissed and grunted in pain, too subdued by the influence of some drug slipped by one of his children to fight back. It seemed unfair, since he had no chance in the first place; but muting his physical abilities with a mild paralytic? Dirty.

"Forbidden scum," he spat at my feet, turning his head to Cian. "Filthy half-breed."

My companion bristled at the insult, clenching his jaw so tightly I thought the tendons might burst from his throat. The comment was so backwards and unnecessary. Why anger those who have the power to end your life, rather than beg for mercy?

"Who dwells within Greilor?" I asked again.

"Vampires, damn it! Everyone knows the vampires hide within the wasteland, you evil bitch!" Harmyn shouted, lunging for my legs but failing.

I kicked him away lazily, growing bored of this game.

"I'm going to need you to be more specific, my lord."

Sighing, I crouched down to look him in the eyes.

"You and I both know it's more than just wayward, rogue vampires running about a vast nothingness," I continued.

Baring his teeth, the lord moved toward me again; this time, I struck him in the face, flattening him to the floor. My power swelled, pooling at the surface to coat my arms - my protective, red second skin. This was pathetic. He knew he would die anyway, so why withhold the information? Who was he trying to protect?

"Please, no! Spare my father!" A new voice cried.

Lord Kairin had snagged a small, pale-haired woman and was restraining her by the arms.

"I would give you anything - I beg you!"

This woman was lighter in complexion than the others — Kairin, Bryalyn, and the youngest sister Gilwyn that had joined them shortly after we arrived. She bore some of the same features, ones derived from the man that was crumpled at my feet.

"If anyone is aware of what my father knows, it's her," Bryalyn grumbled, "The eldest and favored child."

"Yes, *favored*, her mother served me well and was of prestigious blood. She will always be held in a higher regard than you lot!" Harmyn grimaced at his children, spitting blood to the marble beneath him.

"Give me the information I desire," I demanded, glaring at the hysterical woman.

"Anything!" She agreed.

"You will say nothing, Raelyn, I forbid you!" Harmyn hissed.

A swift kick to the head should shut him up, I thought.

Before I could rear back, Raelyn was at my feet, cradling her father's head. She looked up at me with glassy green eyes.

"If you hurt him, I will say nothing, and your efforts will be wasted!"

Her brows furrowed in a show of resolution.

Scoffing at the audacity, I lifted her from the floor by her arm.

"Who dwells within Greilor?" I was really, really tired of repeating myself.

"Vampires: The Lukard family."

Finally, we're getting somewhere.

She continued, "The country is not barren as rumored, but rather it is lush and fruitful. It is a bustling city that lies beyond the mountain barrier, a great kingdom: centered in Kilvaul City."

A kingdom of vampires and outcasts, how great could it be?

"How do they access the Three Kingdoms? How is it that they have found their way into the courts and homes of nobles? Left unchecked to slaughter and destroy!"

I yelled into the woman's face, unable to contain my rage.

"To whom do their soldiers answer?" I demanded.

Tears spilled from Raelyn's eyes as she spoke, "The royal family, the court of nobility, and the council."

"How many?"

"My lady?" Her eyes were unsure.

"How many fucking vampires will I have to slaughter when I get there?"

My tone had deepened, nearly a growl.

"The Lukard family, King Kain and his queen, Morianne." She swallowed roughly before clarifying, "They have three sons and two daughters."

"Who else?"

"There is a large court, and many vampires answer to the royal family. There are many of mixed blood too, for they don't view them as lowly in their kingdom."

Raelyn glanced at her father, who scowled not at his daughter, but at *me*.

"The population within the country easily rivals that of Euros and Adristan combined."

That's impossible. It was unlikely the courts would allow something like this to go unheard of, let alone unchecked. How could this truth be hidden from the kingdoms? How could they leave their people in the dark?

"You lie," I hissed.

"No! No, I wouldn't!" She insisted, clutching my arm.

"How do we enter Greilor? How do its informants make passage to conspire with the tyrants?"

"It isn't like that, t-they're mostly g-good. Life there is m-much different, most of the people prosper, and it is beautiful!" She whimpered, "It is *our* home that is shrouded in darkness, rooted in evil. The Gods-"

"Do not speak to me of the Gods."

I released her to fall back in place with her father.

"I asked you a question, Lady Raelyn. How do we enter?"

"Death is better, my child. Do not jeopardize all we have worked for, all that is yet to come," Harmyn whispered to his daughter, though it seemed she was not as eager to accept such an end.

"Traitor's Pass, it breaks straight through the mountains. You need only a reinforced ship to sail the waters, as they are infested much like Serpent's Bay."

She clutched her father's arm, desperate to lift him from the floor.

Looking to Cian, I nodded toward the trembling woman.

"Remove her," I commanded.

The vampire obliged, reaching for and lifting Raelyn to carry her away. She battered against his shoulders, flailing wildly, screaming for mercy. Locking eyes with Lord Harmyn, I had one more question for him.

"Did you pass the information of my engagement celebration to the vampires?"

He forced himself up onto his knees, craning his head but never breaking eye contact. Harmyn sneered, attempting to hide the brief shadow of fear that passed over his features.

"Answer, my lord. Your fate is sealed. You should know it has been at the behest of mistreated children, who deserved better than what you gave them."

"I gave them everything!" He hissed.

"Answer," I demanded.

Harmyn swallowed, "Yes, it was I who passed the information to Greilor. Do your worst, *creature*."

With that, I bared my curse.

Angry, twisting streams of crimson birthed from my body, with wide gashes opening along my arms to release the essence. There was no pain, nor agony, just rage. Wrath.

This man deserved to die. I had been robbed of too many acts of vengeance, so I would not let this one slip through my fingers. The mist snaked along Harmyn's body, but he held his resolve; he held it until tendrils forced their way into his mouth, nose, and ears.

Gut wrenching screams filled the corridor as I ripped him apart from the inside out. Raelyn's cries grew louder until they stopped, as she had fainted in Cian's arms. Kairin watched mindfully, seeming to enjoy the spectacle. The remaining sisters held each other, taking in the demise of the man who had spawned them.

It seemed to be a recurring theme in the courts of the Three Kingdoms, that many immortal families were so prone to cruelty.

Oftentimes, the ones who suffered at their hands were those closest to them.

What was once Lord Harmyn fell, his body reducing to nothing more than a mess on the floor.

My gift retreated, refueled and writhing with the life it had consumed. Elves had magic, though faint, and my body was singing with it.

"Now," I turned to face Kairin fully, "You will take us to Ossarion and procure our passage to the traitor's realm. As the new lord of Rosenshire, you will be expected to take up all of your father's duties. You are now the direct line to Greilor, and if smugglers dwell within the city, they will answer to you."

"I have one condition, if I may, my lady."

The lord grinned carefully, gauging my reaction. I raised a brow.

"You must take my sisters with you, Bryalyn and Gilwyn. We have long suspected our father's indiscretions and have some scores of our own to settle with the vampires of Greilor. I have become indisposed due to my newfound position, so I will remain with Raelyn after your departure, to extract further information from her."

"Done," I agreed.

We traveled to Ossarion by carriage, making quick work of the commute.

Having departed in the morning, it was barely evening when we arrived in the coastal Elvish city. The horses pulled us along surprisingly smooth paths that were not bumpy and troublesome, like the cobbled and dirt roads of Teskaria and Euros. Peering from the window of the tiny room on wheels, it appeared the streets were almost pressed, like thousands of miniscule stones had been forced to fit together so perfectly that the surface was seamless.

Inside of our transport sat Cian, myself, and the two sisters meant to travel with us to Greilor. In the carriage just ahead were Kairin and Raelyn.

I'd had a great many thoughts during the trip, often interrupted by a pair of eyes fixated on me. Gilwyn's eyes. The Elvish woman's gaze was suspicious, making me squirm with discomfort.

I'd had quite enough of it.

"Is there something you would like to ask me, my lady?" I snapped, apparently a bit too harshly, as Cian jabbed me with an elbow.

"Yes." She shrugged, flicking her gaze between myself and my companion. "Do you know many vampires?"

Taken aback, I couldn't stop from scrunching my nose at the question.

"You could say that."

"I'm the only one she tolerates," Cian huffed, an attempt at humor, though we found ourselves unable to laugh.

Nodding my agreement, I turned my head away, hoping she was somewhat satisfied in her curiosity.

She wasn't.

"Have you ever killed one?"

Sighing, "Yes, a woman. Would have killed another if Fate had been on my side."

"Have you ever been with one?"

Every hair rose on my arms.

"I'm not sure what you mean."

"Romantically, of course. We're about to enter the land of vampires. I'm curious about your predisposition towards the afflicted." Gilwyn grinned. "They make excellent lovers," she continued before clenching her jaw, "Until they get bored and disappear to leave you wallowing in heartbreak."

I scoffed, knowing that feeling all too well. Aklys had abandoned me, and I wasn't sure if I could forgive him for it, if I ever saw him again. He's in Greilor, but where?

"I feel nothing but hatred for all of them, save Cian."

My vampire friend smirked slightly.

"They deserve everything that's coming."

Kairin used his sister to his advantage, as she had often joined their father in his indiscretions; the smugglers recognized her immediately. She was a fragile thing, consumed by the shock of her loved one's death, and now at the mercy of siblings who despised her.

I almost felt bad. Pity and guilt were stopped in their tracks by the waves of rage, ruin, and violence that crashed into each other, drowning all the once-good parts of me.

The Elvish lord made our arrangements to sail to the outlying shores of the mountain barrier, where the ship would leave us with a smaller, reinforced boat to take Traitor's Pass into Greilor. The reinforcements would protect us from potential underwater attacks and a thick, cage-like structure would guard us from above, as Basilisks were relentless in their assaults. Despite being a terrifying monster with spear-like teeth and razorblade scales, the thing you had to worry about most was their venom — even a graze was a death sentence.

Our Captain's name was Bronach - a surly, dark-skinned man, whose breath smelled of smoke and alcohol. The reminder of my vices made my toes curl, ever craving the relief they offered. I envied him, having no reason to pull himself from comfort, slurring his words as he spoke.

"The monsters only dwell where saltwater meets fresh, after that you'll be moving against the current to make your way from sea to city."

His accent was rich, reminding me of the way Calaeya spoke; an accent that was common along the Crimson Bay of Adristan.

"There is a fork in the river after the mountains have cleared; you must follow the one that leads north. The city is concealed by the densest forest known to the realm - the darkness acts as a shield to outsiders. Do not leave the water, and you will reach the riverport."

He showed us a very vague map, one that didn't reveal the city's true location or size.

"What happens if we leave the water?" I asked, raising a brow.

"They will see you as a threat. Their welcomed visitors know better," the man stared me down with deep-brown eyes, stressing every word.

"Well," Kairin sighed, slapping his palms against his thighs before standing, "it has been a pleasure, and I cannot thank you enough for your assistance, my lady."

He grinned at me, reaching out a hand.

Glancing at the gesture, I disregarded him, moving aside to allow Cian to make contact with the man instead. The vampire shook his arm abruptly, making unfaltering eye contact which the lord shrunk beneath.

"Thank you for your aid," he grumbled in response.

"My dear sisters." Lord Rosewick kissed each of the women on the forehead before embracing them together. "I pray to the Gods for success in all of your endeavors. Know I remain your loyal supporter, and you always have a home with me."

His words made little sense, perhaps he expected his sisters would not return, that they would perish in the cesspool of vampires. Perhaps, he was reassuring them that should they fail in whatever their task was, he would still welcome them home with open arms.

I did not know their business with the vampires, but it seemed clear that they were no friends of theirs; so, I did not care. Nothing mattered to me, but avenging Maygen and uncovering what became of the rest of our loved ones.

Nothing mattered, except ending every last one of them.

Chapter Twenty-Three

A Court Of Gods & Vampires

I'd taken the mysterious medicine that quells seasickness before allowing it to grasp me in its miserable clutches. With the tide and wind on our side, the voyage wasn't expected to be a long one.

Anticipation made it difficult to relax, and sobriety made it difficult to cope. I often smelled alcohol on the wind, as much of the small crew seemed to frequently feel the need to drown their own sorrows; my skin itched with craving.

It had proven difficult to find silence and freedom from the gaze of Gilwyn and her uncomfortable questions. Something about the woman didn't sit well with me; of all the Rosewick siblings, I was most wary of the almost *too* stereotypically beautiful lady. She floated about with the effortless grace of a Nymph, yet looked upon others with the cold, piercing stare of a demon.

I listened to Bronach shout demands at his men, often losing focus amidst his drunkenness to trail after the equally stunning Bryalyn, like she was a thick steak and he was a starving dog.

She had been focused on Cian, who avoided her at all costs, quickly moving on any time he caught sight of her approaching. It was like watching a pathetic game of 'dog-chases-cat-chases-mouse'. The woman was visibly frustrated, and I imagined that ladies who looked this way did not often face rejection. Though, I was surprised at her interest, considering he was half-vampire, and the sisters claimed they had scores to settle with the afflicted.

Returning from thought, I realized my fingers had been rubbing together absentmindedly. I was twirling the rings I wore on each hand. On the left, the purplish-blue gem atop a leaf-decorated band, my engagement ring: a promise of love and commitment from a man who wanted me... a man who had disappeared.

Three men have been lost to me: one by death, one by choice, and one by accident. As lost in redemption and misery as I was, I did think of Erelim, worry for him — I even missed him.

On my right ring finger was the gem made of how I imagined starlight, glowing white with depth and mystery untold. My mother had written to specify it was a key, which was nonsensical, as rings couldn't be keys. Perhaps, that meaning was better left buried, maybe I should have left it in Briobar.

Sensing a presence, I turned to see Gilwyn's attention fixed on me again, and I groaned internally.

"How are you faring, Lady Celessa?" She chirped.

"Fine. No need for formalities," I grumbled.

Gilwyn snickered, and the sound made me bristle, hairs rising on the back of my neck in response.

I turned my head and gripped the wooden railing tightly, looking out over the Glistening Sea, named for its sparkling blue waters. It was hard to believe that what lies beyond such beauty was the death of all good things. What awaited us was a land teeming with vampires and monsters.

"Are you anxious or nervous?" She tried again.

I pondered for a moment before answering, "Neither. Both. I don't know."

"You really mean to kill them all?"

My lips pressed together, and I lifted my hand to pinch the bridge of my nose.

"Yes."

"With your power?" The woman hummed, lowering her head in an attempt to meet my eyes.

I shrunk away from the close proximity.

"Yes."

Perhaps, if I was short with her, she would fuck off.

A small giggled passed her lips as she reached into the pocket of her fitted jacket, buttoned just underneath her bust to reveal the tops of breasts, which peeked over a too-tight corset.

Eyeing her suspiciously, I watched as she produced what appeared to be a flask. My body went rigid, mouthwatering. Averting my gaze, I hoped she would take a quick sip and return it to its hiding place. Instead, I found it hovering in my line of vision. My biggest temptation, my demise, lingered before me; it was mine to take if I wanted it.

"Care for some? To take the edge off?" She smiled.

My stomach twisted, throat bobbing. A cool sweat began to form on my brow as I stared down the spirits in her hand. Eyes darting, I searched for Cian so he might not bear witness to my weakness, my shame.

What harm would a few sips do? I could control myself, and I deserved some relief before committing mass murder.

I took the warm liquid from her hand and tipped the canister to my lips, scalding my throat and warming my belly. Every tense muscle relaxed and a relieved breath pushed from my lungs.

"Have as much as you like," she insisted. "There's more with my luggage."

Luggage. I almost hadn't noticed the stuffed case she'd hauled on board, full of clothes and all the comforts a lady might require during her travels. Why she needed so much, I didn't know. Surely our time in the country would be brief, as I planned to wipe out the vampire population and return my focus to other persons who had incurred my wrath — Asuras and my divine father.

There was nothing holding me back now, and there was no reason to settle into peace.

The Elvish woman began to float away, skipping along the deck, unaffected by the shifting of the boat rocking against gentle waves. All of the men were taken by the sight of her, in awe of how she twirled about, as she offered winks and smiles to several members of the crew.

I wondered if she'd take one to bed before we departed; she struck me as that kind of woman, which was incidentally a woman I'd been, it would seem. I followed along lazily, hesitant in my footing, with no desire to attract the attention of any strangers. I pulled my cloak around myself tightly.

Gilwyn proved to be fruitful, offering me another small container and inviting me into her quarters to indulge. The part of me that had been hesitant was quickly smothered by intoxication. We lounged comfortably on a surprisingly plush bed, one fit for nobility.

Her mouth ran in circles, filling my ears with words that I didn't absorb. Nothing concerned me but the reprieve from my misery. I didn't know how long she talked for, but rather only that I'd finished three of the containers before I began to falter.

Heavily under the influence, my eyes began to flutter.

"You seem tired, my lady. Would you like something comfortable to sleep in? You're welcome to stay here with me if you're not feeling up to finding your room," Gilwyn offered, holding out a mostly sheer shift for me to slip on.

Eyeing the garment and the woman, I debated my choices. I could stumble back to the cramped quarters Cian and I had been given to share, to sleep in dirty clothes, or I could accept her offer and sleep comfortably. Reluctantly accepting the clothing, I sat up, searching for a place of privacy to change.

There was none.

The Elvish woman must have sensed my dilemma, smiling with reassurance.

"Have you never undressed around someone other than your help? Nothing to be embarrassed of, my lady."

She moved to undo the ties of my shirt, and I flinched.

"I'll be gentle," she promised.

"I'm uncomfortable," I muttered, swatting her hands away. "I don't want *anyone* seeing me undressed."

"Oh, please, Celessa. It's just a body."

Gilwyn stripped away her jacket to quickly undo her corset, exposing her shoulders and bare chest, then forced her dress to her ankles.

My eyes bulged. I'd seen naked women before, but this was unexpected.

Her skin was perfect, without a blemish or scar, golden and glowing, like there was candlelight that danced beneath the surface. She was petite, yet somehow still had wide hips, giving her an hourglass figure. Small breasts sat upon her chest, with nipples peaked against the chill of late autumn. How was she so hairless? When was the last time I'd cared to do any hair removal on my body? I couldn't remember.

My cheeks flushed with embarrassment. I couldn't remember the last time I'd cared for myself, aside from the quickest and most basic bathing. I rarely brush my hair, instead I simply tie it into a messy knot behind my head — to keep the bothersome strands out of my face. Brushing my teeth was a chore, and when I do, my gums bleed.

The woman tried again, releasing me from my coat and pulling my rumpled shirt over my head. She hummed happily at the sight of my exposed upper body; an innocent sound that was made to cover something more animalistic. My head was spinning as she beckoned me flat with her hand. Fingers snaked across my body to untie my breeches and pull them down to be discarded. She was hovering, inspecting my body, reaching a hand up to touch her fingertips against my brand.

"What is this for?" She asked.

"I was told it is a God's mark," I slurred.

I had nearly forgotten about the tattoo due to always keeping it covered since the night we lost everything.

"Vampires branded me with it. It won't go away."

"So, you're the property of one of the deities?"

"I don't know," the words had to be forced out.

Why did I feel so damn sluggish? Something was wrong with me.

"I don't feel right."

"You just need to rest; you must be exhausted."

Gilwyn climbed into the bed, lifting the blankets and gesturing for me to join her. She beckoned me the way one might tease their lover.

What was happening?

She was alluring, so against my better judgment, I obliged her. Hours before, I'd seen this girl as nothing more than an inconvenience to endure. It seemed all of my reason was gone, that I wasn't in control of myself. My vision was blurring. I'd been drunk many times, yet had never lost control of myself like this before. I could barely move my limbs as she only covered my body partially, taking the opportunity to explore my chest.

"P-please," I barely mumbled. "Don't do that."

"You are lovely, Celessa. How many lovers have you taken?" She asked.

Why did she want to know that? Why did it matter?

I could barely force the words up my throat.

"Three."

"All men?" The woman asked, touching her lips to mine.

I couldn't even move to flinch, though I wanted to.

Numb, I was numb, and my body couldn't do *anything*. The room was spinning, my breathing labored, and I couldn't fight her. My power refused to come out. Alcohol had affected it before, but never to this degree. Everything was going wrong.

Her hand trailed along my abdomen, lowering until she was parting my most intimate area against my will, touching me in ways I did not want.

"Have you ever thought of experiencing a woman?"

"No," I pressed, praying she would stop.

Instead, Gilwyn circled my nerve endings, putting pressure on them in a way that would've made me jump if I could move my body. Lowering her head, she took my breast into her mouth, grazing my nipple with her teeth.

I didn't want this, so why was she doing it?

"Who was your favorite lover, my lady?" She pushed her tongue between my teeth and her fingers inside of my body.

I could barely breathe, as there was no feeling left in my extremities; I had no use of my arms or legs. I wished I couldn't feel how she was touching me elsewhere, that drunkenness would take me into sleep and free me from her clutches.

"Tell me who you truly want, Celessa."

The world was fading out, and the last word I remembered leaving my lips was, "Aklys."

The labyrinth was waterlogged, and I was knee deep in swirling blackness. Damp air made breathing feel more taxing, more difficult; it was thick in my lungs. I was lost. My limbs were heavy, weighed down by some invisible force that was trying to hold me back. Stopping was not an option, as I had to find her.

Find who?

Where am I? How did I get here?

Nothing about this made sense — but I pushed on, turning corners and trudging through the dark.

Everything was wet, the walls that grazed my fingertips left behind damp residue on my skin. If only I had some light, then maybe I could find her? Whoever *she* was.

My brain struggled to make sense of the situation, to figure out who was so important that I would brave this treacherous maze. Perhaps, I was unknowingly looking for those who might still be alive after the massacre? Erelim, Aithen, Daevian, and Chessane.

That didn't feel right either, for I was looking for *her*: a woman who matters to me.

Aloise? That didn't make sense, as she was safe in Evelia with her infant.

A Goddess, maybe? No, they mattered little to me.

This was a dream, I realized.

If I was seeking someone out, then they need not still breathe. I must be in pursuit of Maygen, for it was the only logical explanation. I pushed harder, feeling more desperate; I was desperate to look into her eyes, to see her smile, to hold her in my arms.

Please, don't wake up, I begged myself, *not until I find her.*

The water was getting deeper and colder, steadily rising to my chest.

"Keep going," a voice sounded.

It was both nearby and faraway, a foreign yet familiar presence.

I didn't question it, and simply forced myself onward.

"I need help!" I told the voice.

Forced to swim as the water grew deeper, I was quickly growing tired.

"Keep going," It demanded.

My body was so heavy, how could I possibly make it through? I'd drown first.

This is a dream, I reminded myself, *you can't get hurt, you won't die.*

I let my head slip beneath the surface, just to relax for a moment.

Below, an eerie light filtered in the gloomy waters. Not one, but many, strangely-shaped lights started to rise up through the depths. They were getting closer, nearly at my feet.

They grabbed me.

These were not lights; they were ghostly, glowing hands. I kicked and struggled as they pulled at my ankles, climbing my legs. There was no air to fuel my assault; I was trapped underwater, tired and cold.

Don't touch me, my conscience pleaded, *please don't touch me.*

The fingers squeezed my skin, invading every part of my body. I wanted to cry, but I could not. What choice did I have but to submit?

I was helpless.

"Don't give up," the voice was in my ear now, so close, but when I turned my head — there was nothing, no one.

Kicking and thrashing, I propelled myself toward the surface, a last effort to escape.

Breaking the water, sweet air inflated my burning lungs. The floor was beneath my feet again, the murky pool returning to its place lapping against my calves. Shrinking to the ground, with my back sliding against the wall, I sobbed. Holding my knees to my chest and pressing my face against them, I let everything out until there was nothing left but ragged, hiccupping breaths.

I knew I had been drunk before sleeping, but one of the welcome reprieves of drinking was that it spared me from nightmares. Why was I dreaming now?

"You were poisoned," the presence informed me.

My mind conjured images of Lord Harmyn struggling against what appeared to be a paralytic, making him sluggish and taking all the fight from within the man. The drug was given to him by his children.

His children.

Gilwyn.

I recoiled at the thought: she had drugged me and taken advantage of me in my vulnerable state. Why?

I felt dirty, awash in disbelief that the woman had assaulted me in such a way. I'd kill her for what she's done, to take something like my reason, my ability to say no, away from me.

What had she done when I was fully unconscious?

I rubbed my skin, failing to push away the feeling of her hands on my body. My stomach twisted, nauseated. Cursing my power for not protecting me, I attempted to summon it. I could at least use its glow to guide me through this place — but there was nothing. I couldn't even feel its usual presence lurking beneath my skin. It was gone.

I panicked.

What was I without the most formidable piece of myself? The thing that people feared, that gave me strength: my curse, my weapon. I'd become so reliant on it to protect me, but it had failed against Gilwyn and her drugs. It had failed to save Thibault, Isonei, and Maygen. It had failed to protect the people of Lysenna's estate. So many times, the only thing I had to fall back on proved to be as much of a failure as I was, and now it was gone.

What did that mean?

"You're almost there, Celessa, keep going."

"I can't. I don't want to," I whimpered. "I'm nothing now. I have no family, no friends, no power."

"As is the way of mortality. It is to lose, to fail, and to suffer. It is also to rebuild, to heal, and to move on. It is natural to part from those you love, as is the way of immortality. You are meant to endure when all else shall perish."

My head lifted slightly, eyes catching the flicker of what appeared to be torchlight just around the bend.

"Is this the way out?" I asked, looking toward the faint orange glow.

"Keep going."

Rising from the water, I steadied myself with a hand against the wall. I'll follow the light and escape the darkness. One step at a time, stride by stride. The promise of escape kept moving away, leading me further down the never-ending corridors.

When I thought I'd had enough, a break appeared. Ahead of me was the end, but labyrinths were never that simple. There was a choice to be made: two paths. One was consumed by daunting darkness, delving ever down. The other way, the floor ascended to the light I had thought was my salvation.

"The light, Celessa. Follow the light."

I moved forward, trying to obey the command.

Underfoot, the water's current picked up, pulling me toward the shadows. The voice began screaming, demanding I follow the light, choose the light. It shouted that I must fight it, fight against the darkness, fight against myself. I must be good; I had no choice.

Angry waves crashed against my legs, trying to sweep my feet out from under my body and carry me away.

"I have a choice!" I screamed back.

Silence.

There was no voice, no current.

Everything went still, silent.

"I have a choice."

Reassuring myself out loud felt necessary, that the forces at work around me had to hear my resolution.

Closing my eyes, I breathed in. My heart thumped loudly, the sound filling my ears.

Slow, slow your breathing, I thought.

No one gets to choose for me, for I control my own Fate.

My hands extended outwards, and I let my instincts guide me to where I was meant to be, to who I was meant to be. I kept walking, my senses driving me on; my path felt as if it was moving upward, then down, again and again.

When I opened myself up again, I met a shocking sight.

A woman stood before me, the woman I'd been looking for. We were alone together, surrounded by endless shadow, with nothing but an eerie white glow coming from below to illuminate us.

She was scared, yet brave; she was wounded, but healing. She was powerful because she embraced her weaknesses, beautiful in appearance and in heart. She was good, and she was bad; she was the neutral ground of the world's views, true to herself and to her purpose.

This woman radiated warmth, but when I reached to touch our fingertips together, she was cold. Her hand had met mine in perfect synchrony, in mimicry. I tilted my head, surprised when she moved to follow suit. We opened our mouths and scrunched our noses, harmonized in every movement.

"Who are you?" We asked, the sound of the voices echoing throughout vast nothingness.

I've seen her before.

"Is this me?" Unified words.

She flickered, changing appearances: One, a small girl with all of the world's hope shining in her eyes; Two, a teenager who felt confused about her place, about herself; Three, a woman who was broken and afraid; Four, a woman who felt loved and then scorned; Five, a woman who embraced herself and all she felt; Six, a woman who was drowning in loss after loss, unable to beat back the pain that plagued her; Seven... she was a monster.

Her eyes were black, her expression twisted and painted in blood.

"Turn around," she hissed, sending me reeling. "Turn around!" She screamed.

I turned, and she was everywhere. She was *everything*.

Her head flickered, taking the shapes of faces I had known: my parents, my sisters, my lovers, my friends, my enemies.

They all screamed.

"This is just a dream!" I told myself, covering my ears.

"Turn around!" The voices demanded, each one different, yet each one familiar.

"I can't!" I cried.

It stopped after what felt like an eternity, and the woman took my face in her hands.

"Turn around," she whispered.

When I did, I saw her again.

A mirror, it was a mirror, and I was holding myself.

"Wake up."

It's still dark. Why is it always fucking dark? Why is my mouth dry? What is in my mouth?

There were bars above me, dimly illuminated; nothing was in the sky, save for a thin sliver of the pale moon. Orange bounced off the grayish hue of the cage.

Turning my head, I realized our party was on the small transport barge. Cian sat upon a bench, tucked against the wall, facing away from me. Two blonde-haired women navigated the reinforced boat.

Realization struck me that we were making our way into Greilor. Somehow, I had been taken from the ship and placed into the secondary means of travel. I would have thought Cian had carried me in my drunken slumber, but that was not possible.

He was chained to the wall of the boat.

I was gagged.

A muffled sound left me as I struggled against metal restraints, and I called forth my blood mist, bidding it to waste away the cuffs and links. Once I was loose, I would kill the Rosewick women, and I would free Cian.

Except, I was powerless.

My dream had become reality, and I was weak.

Gilwyn padded over to me, kissing my parted lips and the tightly pulled cloth between them.

"Thank you for a lovely evening, Celessa. I won't soon forget it." She grinned. "What's wrong? Stuck?"

I growled past the fabric.

"There will be no more appearances made by that pesky power you possess, I'm afraid," she chuckled, touching the chains around my body, "You see, what choice did we have but to bring you to receive judgment? After you murdered our dear father, we feared for our own lives. We had to take whatever measures necessary to procure you, and your alcoholism made it all too easy...

"I even went to your bed after you threatened me with your power, in hopes I might be able to subdue you. It was awful, being ravaged against my will, after having just endured your wrath being unleashed upon my only remaining parent!"

She whimpered, feigning despair and wiping away imaginary tears.

This woman was flipping the script, rewriting recent events to play in her favor. She had done something unforgivable to me, and then she was disgusting enough to place the blame elsewhere, putting herself in my position with her words.

They had been in league with Greilor all along, and it seemed the Rosewick children were power hungry above all else. They used me to dispose of their father so that they could gain control of their court, so that they would be the ones to deliver me to the vampires.

They were monsters.

"How lucky we are that father had been given chains of God's Ore - meant specifically to capture you for the king. Kairin was so distraught, losing his father and being forced to assume the lordship; the task of delivering you fell to us."

Gilwyn gestured to Bryalyn, who met my stare with a wicked sneer.

"In case you weren't aware, God's Ore is silver imbued with the magic of the divine pantheon. Crafted by the Gods' own hands. It's the only thing in the realm that can imprison deities or filthy Amalgams like yourself. It represses their powers and the influence of their blood. There is no escape, so you may as well just lie there. You're good at that."

The Elvish woman bit her lip as she eyed me.

They must have known they'd have the means to capture me, that their father possessed such an item. How was it that he had come to be the bearer of something so powerful? The Gods were elusive and secretive, and they feared their own potential mortality so much that they murdered their Amalgam children because they rivaled them.

Only the magic of divine blood can take the life of a deity, and as far as I knew, I was their one remaining adversary.

As she turned away, I had thought to attempt wriggling free, but Gilwyn spun back to face me again.

"Might I say how disappointed I was when you divulged information to me of your past lovers. How is it that you hate vampires so much, yet have allowed one to touch your body? Why was the name of a vampire the one you called out rather than your intended husband, Celessa?"

She squeezed my face roughly, baring her teeth in snarl.

I remembered saying his name. If she knew it belonged to a vampire, that meant she knows who Aklys is. How?

"You've had your fun, so leave it alone before you end up killing her. You'll ruin our chances if she arrives dead," Bryalyn hissed. "The Gods' generosity only goes so far, and they want her for themselves."

Gilwyn released me, leaving the skin of my face sore.

"One more thing."

She reared back and struck me in the head.

Someone was kicking me in the leg, not once or twice, but again and again. I kicked back, hearing a muffled grunt in return.

Morning light assaulted my eyes, robbing my vision of the ability to process my surroundings. I was kicked again. Upon focusing, I met the angry and frightened expression of my friend, Cian. He was wrapped in chains and gagged as I was. Lifting his chin, he gestured for me to look ahead, to what was coming. I struggled to turn, arms and ankles wrapped tightly in the magic restraints.

What would I see when I faced the other way? What lies in wait beyond my field of vision?

Civilization — the largest city I'd ever seen, with a fortress castle that bested Licourt's in both height and size. We'd arrived in the heart of rebel territory.

I hadn't believed Raelyn, nor had I thought it possible for the rumored barren hellscape to find any semblance of sophistication; yet, there it stood. It was full of life, and surrounded by lush wilderness that passed by a beautiful, rapid current river which our boat sailed against. It was not a waste, but a prosperous and thriving country.

This was Kilvaul City, the very heart of the kingdom of vampires.

"Welcome, my *friends*." Gilwyn grinned, holding her arms out as if to embrace the scenery. "To the great forbidden kingdom, filled with those who have been biding their time as they await retribution."

What the fuck was she on about, now?

I'd love nothing more than to rip her tongue from her mouth. I gagged against the fabric between my teeth as I fought against it. Anger surged through me; I felt the slightest wisp of power tickle my bones.

It was not enough.

"You will answer for your crimes, Celessa," Bryalyn snarled, "For the murders of the nobles in Autumnmoor."

No, that was a lie; a horrible, twisted lie.

She continued, "For the murder of my father, beloved nobleman and Greilorian council member, trusted informant of the king. He was their most valued rebel and saboteur, an irreplaceable spy."

Shit, I would never escape that; these were Harmyn's daughters, so no one would believe that they'd set me up.

"And for the rape of my sister, you filthy cunt."

Screams of protest and pain erupted behind the gag. I thrashed wildly, tears stinging my eyes.

"I remember every bit of your body, Celessa. You're much more powerful than I, so what was I to do? No one will believe you," my abuser spat.

"You stand to be judged by King Kain Lukard and his council, overseen by their divine God."

The deities used to govern the kingdoms, long before the wars. They had meant to leave their children to their affairs, to name their own nobility and arrange systems of government, but that didn't matter to me.

She said God. Not deity, not Goddess, but God.

A man.

Which fucking one?

"Syades, God of Chaos, the great grasp in which Greilor is held."

My chest hollowed. Too many times, I had thought of myself as a product of chaos, that my power could be a product of nothing else. My curse absorbed and destroyed without restraint, which left behind little in its wake; it drained the life out of anything it touched.

Was he the one? Was this my divine father?

The snake tattoo itched, and my skin burned.

I would be left to beg for mercy from a court of Gods and vampires.

There was no hope for me now.

Chapter Twenty-Four

Cursed Royalty

Cries of outrage and disgust erupted from the crowds lining the cobbled streets. Onlookers gathered to bear witness and spew insults at the captured monster: the Amalgam. A feared, forbidden creature of myth, made reality — a physical being of flesh and blood.

The Rosewick sisters had taken my shoes. I wore only chains and the shift Gilwyn had offered me before the horrific experience I had endured at her hands; though, now, it was tattered and filthy. My feet ached as they paraded me through the city like some sick prize, a spoil of war.

Cian had been taken from me. A group of three vampire soldiers had met the women at the dock to exchange their prisoner. Though pointless, he'd fought not to leave me, struggling against the captors.

I'd recognized one, and he had recognized me. The man named Euric was one of those who had arrived in Teskaria to take Aklys away.

The man's lip curled in disgust and exasperation; deception apparent on his face. My lover had concealed me for the majority of the interaction with those strange men, covering my brand with my hair, shielding me with his body. Euric saw all of me now. He knew who I was, what I was.

Bryalyn and Gilwyn each sat atop a quarter horse, provided by the men who had welcomed them. Bryalyn held the rope that connected to the chains wrapped around my wrists and waist, dragging me along behind the animals.

I remained gagged, unable to voice any defense against the curses being shouted. My feet ached, and I stumbled often, as they were assaulted by sharp pebbles. The skin on my arms was raw, red from the friction of the metal cuffs and links.

Stray tears fell against my cheeks, not from pain, but shame. I cried from embarrassment. Rotten food was thrown at me to follow the foul words of passersby.

Monstrous whore, they said.

Abomination, they screamed.

They were relentless, merciless, and cut me with the sharpness of a thousand blades.

My identity was no secretive, elusive thing here. Here, it wasn't something that had attempted to be normalized and accepted by respected, kind persons of nobility. There was no safety of a warm keep, no protection of a loving lady, and no respect for being a lord's betrothed. To these strangers, in this strange land, I was a monster... Nothing more.

My mind fought to silence the voices of those berating me, to focus on something to keep me sane as I was made to walk to the looming castle ahead. I squinted against the foul-smelling produce that was tossed at my face and body.

Someone had decided to take it a step further, hurling a rock that struck me in the back of the leg. Pain blinded me for a moment, and I lost my footing, crumbling to the ground. My knees cracked against stone, leaving them scraped and bloodied.

Bryalyn hissed at the slight tug against the lead she held, and in return, she pulled it roughly. The action forced my arms forward, bringing my body flat against the ground, and my chin connected with the road.

My less-than-healed wound burned, and I realized the jerking of my arms likely reopened the puncture left by a dagger's blade. The warm dampening on the bit of cloth that caressed it confirmed that the delicate flesh had, in fact, been torn.

People laughed.

My eyes closed.

I remembered for a moment how I'd felt torturing Niall, how I'd relished in it — and I could not blame them for enjoying the spectacle, for finding amusement in my pain.

They knew nothing of the *person* I was. They cared not for my trauma, my pain, or my suffering. My existence was nothing more than a threat to them, something to be subdued and ended, for the safety of the realm. In their eyes, it was for the safety of their Gods.

I had magic, divine magic. Mages did not face persecution for their gifts unless it became twisted and dark. Mine was already perceived as such, and I had no chance to prove otherwise. There was no one here to protect me, no one to save me.

Bryalyn pulled again and shouted, "Get up, we don't have all day!"

Trembling, I pushed myself up. I struggled on toward my Fate, towards my end. Every decision I have ever made has led me here.

Was this inevitable?

The moment Aklys left me, I had wanted to follow. Every path taken in pursuit of him would have ended in this place. My lust for vengeance would have concluded the same, delivering me into the hands of my enemies.

Fool, you're a fool, I thought.

I signed my own death sentence by wanting to love a man I never should have met, and wished now that I hadn't. I sealed it in stone the moment I vowed to avenge my fallen friend, allowing myself to be overcome by grief and rage.

Curse vampires. Curse the Gods. Curse Fate, the wicked bitch.

A massive wall separated the castle from the city, fortified and gated. The doors were opened at our arrival, with armed guards holding back the angry citizens who had followed.

I fell again upon entering, tired and weak. There was no food in my system to give me energy, nor water offered to hydrate me. In fact, the last thing that had entered my body was wicked poison and alcohol: not the best things to fuel one's resolve.

My body folded into itself as I waited to be pulled or hurt again, but no one moved.

Several people approached, all dressed in the finery of nobility, of royalty. A towering man cast a shadow over me with his large body, his frame rivaling depictions of the deities.

He was pale with long black hair tied behind his head, the length of it resting over his shoulder. Atop the dark locks sat a gilded crown, twisted and unusual in appearance.

This person was the king of vampires.

"At last," he breathed, his voice was deep and chilling, rattling my bones.

A woman stood at his side; she was fragile in appearance, but exuded power unlike anything I'd ever experienced. Her parted lips revealed sharp fangs, with a face framed in unruly brown hair. She was his queen, I surmised.

"We must summon Syades immediately, as there is no time to delay!" She hissed; wide eyes fixed on my pathetic state.

"No need to fear, your Grace. We have utilized the chains gifted to our late father. God's Ore will hold her for as long as you require."

Bryalyn offered a tight-lipped, sure smile.

"Late father?" The king snapped, as his focus trained now on the Elvish woman.

Gilwyn, ever the actress, burst into an uncontrollable sob.

"The Amalgam, my king!" She wailed. "It murdered our father, one of many of the heinous crimes committed against your loyal servants!"

"You will both enlighten me to the deeds done by this creature."

He cast his eyes over me, silently summoning his men.

"Secure this in the Great Hall, and we will pass judgment once I have convened with our God."

Strength having left my limbs, I was limp.

Two men hoisted me from the ground, dragging my feet as they carried me away by my arms. The guards were visibly exasperated by the weight of my hanging body, as well as the heavy chains that hung from my wrists and midsection.

Safely out of earshot, they vocalized their discontent.

"How is it so damned heavy?"

It, he called me, as apparently I was not worthy of being humanized.

"It's the fucking chains - there's no way she weighs this much," the other grumbled in return.

"Wouldn't it be easier for one of us to carry it in our arms?" The first suggested, huffing.

"Do *you* want to touch it like that? I sure as hell don't."

My head hung, bobbing with their steps as they sauntered along. My field of vision was obscured by matted hair that fell over my face, concealing the world around me — hiding my tears.

This was it, the last of my resolve leaving me. Robbed of my life not once, but twice. All those I have loved have been stolen from me. My dignity, my pride, my sense of self, my consent, everything was stripped away; I was left bare and broken.

After what felt like an eternity, I was dropped to the floor.

My restraints were linked to a slab that sat in the center of a large, echoing room. I lifted my gaze slightly, just enough to look ahead. Two great thrones sat atop a dais a few meters away, one slightly bigger than the other. They were flanked by less-grand seating, mock thrones of a sort. To the left of the larger seat were three of the smaller chairs, and to the right of the other were two.

I remembered the details of Greilor royalty, the king and queen had three sons and two daughters.

Secured to what I imagined would be the place of my final stand in this life, the guards scurried a short distance away, glad to be rid of me.

Raising my chin, I looked upon the faces of the two men.

"Not what I expected," one remarked.

The man who spoke was slimmer than I'd realized, with tanned skin and dusty hair. He nudged his comrade — a tall, dark mortal with piercing green eyes and hair that was braided closely to his head.

"This is the thing laying waste to immortals? It bleeds red just like anything else I've seen. Doesn't *look* like God-spawn to me, shouldn't it be more intimidating?"

Emerald orbs scanned the bloodied injuries to my chin and knees.

"The things they've been saying had me believing it might have hooked claws or black eyes."

"Don't underestimate it! I've heard about the magic it uses."

The first man grabbed the elbow of his companion to halt his advance.

Jerking away, the guard with the carob complexion crouched to inspect me closer. He reached out a hand, angling in a way that I assumed meant he intended to touch my mark.

I bit down on the cloth that dried my tongue and lurched forward. My chains rattled, and I felt the slightest hint of satisfaction as he stumbled backwards, startled. They were treating me like an elusive animal forced into captivity, so I may as well act like one.

"Let's get out of here before someone realizes we've lingered. I have no interest in being labeled a sympathizer while you quell your curiosity."

Picking up his comrade, the guards made their leave. Loud, echoing steps faded away, followed by the slamming of great wooden doors closing behind them.

I had little range to move within my restraints, but thankfully, I had enough to curl into the fetal position. The hard surface beneath me was cold. No movement shifted the air, nor could a breeze be felt, nothing to stir the stagnation. The weight of defeat pooled in my chest, flowing from my eyes to drip to the floor.

My fingers rubbed together; I was grateful that, for all that had been stolen from me, I still had my rings. They were a small comfort.

Time crawled by; hours and hours passed.

Wake up.

Why?

He's here.

Who is here?

Turn around.

I can't.

Turn around.

I can't move.

TURN AROUND!

My eyes popped open.

I was still laying chained to the floor, curled into myself pitifully. I heard a sound, faint and cautious.

Step, step, step.

The sounds were slow, so slow. Anticipation pricked my skin, combining a mixture of fear and discomfort to settle in the pit of my stomach. Another step, I listened to the painfully drawn-out approach.

The sentience beneath my skin attempted to stir, stifled, imprisoned; it struggled.

Please, I thought, *please help me.*

The mysterious intruder stopped, stilling — watching.

I couldn't turn, couldn't confront this person, whoever they were. I'm not a fucking circus attraction, nor a trophy on display. I didn't want anyone hovering or keeping an eye on me. Where would I go? What could I do? I was useless, powerless. I was trapped.

My breathing was deep, forcibly steadied. I wouldn't give this stranger the satisfaction of knowing that I was unsettled. Frozen in place, I waited. There was no more sound as the seconds turned into minutes.

For a long time, I focused on my heartbeat. My eyes burned as I forced them to stay open as long as they could stand it, unwilling to miss even a second if someone appeared. Fists clenched, holding fast. Still, there was nothing. I couldn't take much more suspense.

Go away, I wanted to scream.

The steps came again, more hurried now, shuffling. The feet were in front of me, covered by leather shoes: fresh and still smelling of oil. Legs bent; the person was lowering themselves. My body tensed, ready to lash out again — but then, the gag was pulled from my mouth.

I looked into eyes that were strikingly familiar: Green and gold.

Aklys.

"What have you done, milady?"

Shock overtook my senses, "You!" I hissed. "What the fuck!"

His large hand clamped over my mouth, and he hushed me fervently. This was a man I knew yet did not. He was clean, tidy, proper; his typically windswept hair was neat, and he was wearing clothes that were well-fitted and decorated in finery. His face had been shaved, something he had done while I'd known him, but never as closely as it was now. He looked like a gentleman, not some wandering rogue vampire.

"Why are you here? Do you have any idea what you've done?" He whispered, frustrated.

He was frustrated? How dare he! I bit his hand, and he gasped, pulling it away.

"Why?" He grumbled. "I told you that you could not come here."

"A year!" Was all I could manage.

His face fell, frowning.

"You left me, and it's been a fucking year."

It was all I could do not to whimper.

"I had no choice."

"There is *always* a choice!" I retorted.

"Fine, then I chose to keep you safe!" He snapped. "Yet here you are, throwing it all away!"

I scoffed, "I made the choice to pursue vengeance, to take retribution at any cost."

"Against me? I hardly think-"

I cut him off.

"Against the vampires that murdered the only person in this world who I loved, and then some!"

Forcing myself up onto burning knees, I faced him fully.

"Your people took everything from me!"

Aklys looked stunned, clueless.

I felt insulted, struck with disbelief. How could he not know? This was from where vampires came, so surely they did not act on their own? He himself had been ordered from this place to procure the elusive Amalgam, only changing his mind *after* meeting me.

"I haven't been allowed to see them," he said.

The vampire's voice was small, pathetic.

I stilled before asking, "Who?"

Aklys looked at me with a solemn expression.

"The Vargens and their companions."

The air pushed from my lungs, a breath of both exasperation and relief.

"They're here?"

"Chessane Clearwater is of Greilor," his eyebrows pulled together as he spoke. "She had pulled as many from the massacre as she could. I never expected... I'm so... so sorry."

"Lysenna is dead," I choked out, struggling to continue, "The vampires we faced in Briobar brought me Isonei's severed head."

His cheeks flamed with anger, denial.

"Maygen," I whispered.

A hand moved to caress my face, to comfort me, but it was stopped in its tracks by a new presence.

"*Get away from her!*" A woman shouted, exploding with rage.

Gilwyn.

Aklys stood abruptly, facing her.

"Leave," he demanded.

"I will not! How dare you offer comfort to the woman who assaulted me, who murdered my father!" She growled.

"I know what kind of person you are, and better than most, Gilwyn. Your lies may work on the king and council, but I have not fallen for your schemes," the vampire hissed back.

She gave him a wicked grin in return.

"I will not have my future husband showing mercy to the creature that has wreaked havoc across the realm, spreading her *filth*."

Future husband?

"Our engagement ended years ago, and I want nothing to do with your barbarism," Aklys retorted.

Her future husband, the words bounced around my skull.

"Oh, but you enjoyed it once, and you enjoyed me," she insisted, reaching for him, "I enjoyed you too; I've missed you."

Aklys shoved her away, eliciting a frustrated grunt from the woman.

"Your father has reinstated our engagement! You have no choice in the matter! I will be a member of the royal family, and I will have power!"

She screamed, stomping her foot down like a toddler having a tantrum.

What did she mean? The royal family? He couldn't possibly...

My eyes darted between the two: my abuser and the man who had broken my heart.

"Ah!" She smiled, full of delight. "She doesn't know."

"Don't," he demanded, shaking his head.

"Scorned lover, kept in the dark, abandoned," Gilwyn giggled. "Don't I know the feeling all too well."

The Elvish woman tucked her pale locks behind an elongated ear.

"He has a habit of running away once he gets bored, so don't take it too personally."

Aklys' stare fixed on me, while panic and shame filled his eyes.

"What don't I know?" I whispered.

"The man you so desire is vampire royalty, Lady Celessa," she went on, causing my heartbeat to thunder in my ears. "You kneel before Prince Aklys Lukard, third son of Greilor's king."

I burned hotter than the sun.

"Tell me that isn't true."

Unblinking, he parted his fanged jaws, meaning to speak.

Traitor.

Gilwyn cackled as the throne room doors swung wide open, beating off of stone walls. The sound shocked me out of the stupor caused by truths revealed.

A flowing line of nobles poured into the room, accumulating persons of many races: Vampires, mortals, and Elves alike, but no

Fae to be seen. Under different circumstances, that might strike me as odd.

"There's no saving her now, my love," she purred to Aklys, who still looked down at me with a sorrowful expression. "Her judgment has come."

Just as the crowd settled, the sea of faces began to part, making way for something else.

Rather, they were making way for some*one* else.

In deafening silence, a man entered. He was a man of fire and smoke, shadows of endless darkness, split only by lightning. His power crackled across his skin, and his eyes glowed amber. This man's face greatly resembled the king's, bearing resemblance even to the vampire who had been standing before me. Behind him, two others followed.

They were deities: two Gods and a Goddess who had arrived to determine my sentence for the crimes I had committed.

The first deity's male companion radiated righteousness, and he looked upon those around the room with a scrutinizing, knowing gaze, as if judging each of them individually. He had the strongest, most intimidating build I'd ever seen — paired with deep bronze skin and long black hair that fell in tight, thick locks over his shoulders and across his chest.

The woman was tall and shockingly thin, her complexion sun tanned, with high cheekbones beneath narrow, deep-set eyes. Her warm brown hair was braided around her head in semblance of a crown, and an unearthly glow surrounded her, dancing across her skin. The Goddess did not observe the room; she only looked at me.

Every person, mortal and immortal alike, bowed in the presence of divinity. I could see them only by turning my shoulders and head as far as my restraints would allow. I held their gazes, my scabbed chin raised high.

A smile broke the stone expression of the pale God.

"Blood of my enemy," he sighed, his voice ethereal and chilling.

Court proceedings were torturous. I would take battling another Chimera over this bullshit.

All those attending were left to stand, save for the divine beings who took the thrones typically reserved for the royal family. Only the king joined them. Four pairs of eyes were trained on my face as the eldest prince, named Hadeon, read out the proper nonsense. After painfully long introductions, I now knew the names of the beings before me.

Arendiel, God of Wisdom, was the deep toned, warrior-looking man. Evette, Goddess of Justice, was the glowing woman. Syades, God of Chaos, was the supreme being, who was honored and worshiped by all who dwelled within Greilor.

I had thought myself to be of chaos, but after the words he used to address me, I feared that was not the case. There was no resemblance between myself and the deity, though my power mimicked his own in potency.

Blood of his enemy, it was possible he had many; the lore only spoke of one, though: Odric, God of War.

I must truly be a weapon after all.

If I made it out of here, I'd turn his own weapon against him.

"Will the court allow the calling of witnesses?" Hadeon asked his deities and king.

Syades smiled at me, a toothy grin that was nothing less than malicious, and fire danced in his golden eyes.

"Do you have any whom you would like to bring forth, my son?" Syades uttered as he turned to the king.

Son?

I was going to be sick at the realization.

Aklys was royalty, son of the king, and his father was the once-mortal offspring of a God. How had they become vampires? I had thought only Odric's children were cursed.

Aklys told me he suffered from a mimic curse, but I still didn't really know what that meant. There were many afflicted present, so surely not *all* of them were the product of Syades? Was the lore wrong? Had lies been spread throughout the realm?

"We will call forth Bryalyn and Gilwyn Rosewick, noble daughters of our late informant, Lord Harmyn Rosewick — allegedly murdered by the prisoner." King Kain Lukard held out his hand to gesture at me.

Murmurs of disgust rippled through the crowd. The nobility parted to let the Elvish women pass so that they could stand adjacent to my place on the floor.

Though Aklys had removed my gag, and no one attempted to replace it, I remained silent. The urge to cry out and fight back overtook me at the sight of the women's distraught appearances. They painted themselves as victims.

Liars, deceivers, villains: That's what they truly were. Saddened faces beheld them, pitying them, bearing sympathy for the pair. There was none for me, not a trace.

"Give an honest testimony and account of your experiences regarding the Amalgam, Celessa Umbraeon," Prince Hadeon demanded.

Bryalyn puffed her chest, preparing to deliver her statement, when Gilwyn covered her face and feigned sobs. The elder sister looked mildly irritated at her sibling's dramatics, quickly recomposing herself under the gazes of those passing judgment. She took her sister into her arms, mock comfort for a fabricated story.

"Beloved deities, your Grace, what we witnessed in Rosenshire were the actions of one who can be considered nothing less than a monster," she started, and I huffed in exasperation. "Celessa Umbraeon hunted us, you see, tracking my brother and I to an establishment we frequent. She threatened us without hesitation, ruining our previously enjoyable outing. Intimidated, but not without consideration, we invited her into our home."

My jaw clenched at her words.

"We meant to discreetly deliver her to my father under the guise of friendship and well-meaning. The Amalgam had other plans, though, because the moment he arrived in the chamber, she set her power upon him."

Bryalyn forced herself to choke up as she spun her web of lies.

I thought about how she looked with intrigue at her father's immobilized state, how she smiled as he was reduced to nothing.

"We begged mercy, and offered her everything we had, if she would only spare him. She wouldn't hear it. I've never seen someone so fueled by hatred, and for a man she had never met! When it was over, she offered us the same fate if we would not deliver her to your shores."

The woman lowered her head, appearing ashamed.

"Smuggling the God's Ore chains onboard the vessel, we prayed to Fate and to you, our divine rulers, that we might seize an opportunity to subdue her. The entire crew was fearful for their lives."

Lies, lies, lies.

"I was most concerned when she turned her attention to my poor sister."

Gilwyn continued to force herself to tears, clinging to Bryalyn's sleeve. My throat tightened at the display, panic rising into my chest as I shoved away the memories of what she had done to me - the truth of it being flipped onto its head.

"She suffered horribly at this demon's hands. Celessa forced Gilwyn to bed, assaulting her in the most atrocious of ways, committing a heinous crime. My sister, ever the devoted soldier, bore it as best as she could, waiting for the opportune moment to strike. When the Amalgam slept, we secured her in the chains, achieving our victory. We had no other thought but to deliver her to justice, to you."

Bryalyn brushed away nonexistent moisture from her eyes with her fingers.

Voices rose ever so slightly in hushed conversation. The few words I caught were 'disgusting', 'despicable', 'menace', and 'monster'. Amid those were others who whispered their hopes for my sentencing — my execution.

"Did the Amalgam act alone?" The king asked.

"Yes," Bryalyn answered.

"What?"

Sound finally escaped my lips.

All eyes were on me.

"Lady Celessa, you may not speak unless called upon by the court," Hadeon spoke to me for the first time; his eyes were soft, and it seemed he did not speak from a place of contempt.

I wondered if he had heard of me from his brother, if any of them were aware of the truth of my humanity. What information was given when he returned? What did they know?

"Where did this woman come across the information to connect your family to Greilor?" Arendiel asked, an eyebrow raised at the woman's concluded testimony.

Bryalyn fumbled for a brief moment, clearing her throat before attempting to answer, "We learned she had stolen information from the family who had generously offered her sanctuary, the Vargen family."

"And where are they?" He inquired, turning his attention to me.

"They're here." I met his eyes, unwavering. "What's left of them."

Arendiel and Evette turned to the king, who had become red in the face. They had not expected this, as it seemed I wasn't supposed to know. The tiny piece of information Aklys had given me could be my salvation, but where was he now?

"As is my companion, Cian," I continued, earning a sharp look from Hadeon, "A half-vampire man."

Bryalyn bared her teeth at me.

Murmurs broke out, sounds of concern and curiosity.

"Is this true?" Arendiel questioned Kain.

Clenching his jaw, "Yes," he confirmed.

"Will we be calling for their testimony?" Evette's voice was not at all what I'd expected, low and smooth.

"They are aware of the Amalgam's transgressions, and they are also here by *my* grace, despite harboring a forbidden creature. Their intentions have yet to be assessed, so they are in holding. I do not think we will find their testimony reliable or valuable, as they have been struck with tragedy and bewitched by this *thing*," the vampire king responded, looking to his divine father for approval.

Syades never stopped watching me. He didn't look away to hear Bryalyn's sob story, and he didn't entertain his son's questions - the deity simply stared, wearing a mask of indifference in an attempt to conceal curiosity and disdain, but I could see it in his eyes.

"Did this companion aid you in your crimes?" The God of Wisdom asked.

Yes, I thought.

Cian had known about the informants of Greilor, and he had helped me every step of the way, but I knew better. I would not condemn him. I must protect him, my friend, for Maygen.

"No," I decided. "He was not present for the murder of Lord Harmyn."

Forced to listen to several fabricated witness accounts, I simply waited. None of them stuck out to me, as I could recall none from memory. Information had been systematically planted in an effort to condemn me, and it was working.

What could I say? What could I do?

I could do nothing.

"Does the prisoner have *any* who are willing to testify on her behalf?" Arendiel inquired, eyes scanning the shifting crowd.

I braced myself. Without a witness, they would soon deliberate, reaching a conclusion to this madness. They would surely sentence me to death.

"Yes!" A woman's voice rang out.

My head whipped around, searching for the source of the sound.

"Yes, she has a witness!"

To my surprise, a woman whom I'd never seen before emerged from the seemingly unending rows of faces.

She was short, golden-skinned, with ringlets of brown hair framing her face. The woman was dressed in a way that mirrored the royal family, proper and decorated in gold, but her features did not match theirs. Also, she was *very* pregnant.

I gaped at the stranger, unsure if this was a good thing or the final condemnation of my existence. She wore a stern expression, staring down the king with unbridled ferocity.

"Your wife is connected to the Amalgam?" Kain hissed at his son, Hadeon.

She was a member of the royal family, indeed. A princess by marriage had come forth to defend me, but *why?*

I studied her further, inspecting her delicate, feminine features. The freckles across her nose and the green of her eyes reminded me of someone, someone who soon followed to stand by her side.

"My sister will testify on behalf of Lady Celessa."

Chessane.

It never ceases to amaze me how little of which I'm aware, how much has been hidden from me. The woman who was engaged to own my fiancé's brother, who had shared a home with us, was directly tied to Greilorian royalty. I couldn't fathom why the woman who presented her sibling was so willing to put herself and her family at risk of being labeled as sympathizers. What did they stand to gain?

"Loren-" Hadeon started, but the small woman raised her hand to silence her husband, and he obeyed.

"I have earned respect and good standing in this court, and my sister has served you loyally for years. You removed her from our home as a *child*, placing her with the Vargen family as an informant. She has fulfilled her duty a hundred times over, submitting to your will. Everything she has done has been for the good of the kingdom, despite having little choice. You will hear her!" Loren demanded.

Chessane looked me over, horrified at my condition. Her eyes simmered with sadness. She had always been kind to me, and I had always adored her for her compassion and beauty, inside and out. She knew me, everything I truly was.

The God of Wisdom smiled, beckoning her forward. His gaze met mine for a brief moment, revealing something akin to pity and understanding. Could he see through the lies that have been told by the grace of his gifts? Would I find mercy at his hand? Could he overrule the things that have been spoken? Could he stand against Syades and his kin? Would he? My mind was racing, heartbeat following suit.

"You have information regarding the Amalgam?" Evette hummed.

"I have a testimony regarding the humanity of *Celessa*," Chessane snapped, "a woman who has a name."

Tears welled, cascading down my cheeks in warm rivers of gratitude.

"This noble lady that you have deigned to treat as little more than an animal, is a person. She breathes and bleeds as any other being of this realm. She loves and hates, as is her right as a bearer of consciousness. The misled path she has taken has only been in the name of retribution. Many pursue vengeance in honor of those they have loved and lost; are they condemned so harshly as she has been?" The Mage argued, fists clenched and shoulders squared.

I'll admit to being surprised by her tenacity, having only ever witnessed her as soft and agreeable.

"If you have only come forth to speak from a place of emotional attachment, then your account is useless in these proceedings."

Evette sighed, waving a hand in dismissal.

"Would you have me speak from a place other than my heart, when the mind is capable of such dishonesty?" Chessane challenged.

"I would have you share factual accounts that prove guilt or innocence on behalf of the accused. We have received several testimonies that have condemned the Amalgam for her crimes against the realm and this court!" The Goddess shot back, straightening in her chair.

"The *fact* is that Celessa has acted from a place of love and of heartbreak. It does not erase what has happened, but it at least gives some insight. My *account* is that she is kind, and she is decent! She has suffered brutalities and untold trials; she is set back in her healing by tragedy after tragedy. I lived with her for the better part of a year. I woke with her each morning and bid her a good night at the end of each day. I watched her treat those around her with kindness, and I witnessed her love Maygen Vargen as fiercely as my own sister loves me."

Chessane looked at my reddened, wet cheeks, losing hold on tears of her own. She loved Maygen, too.

"Her loss has given your court the perfect excuse to condemn her, simply because you fear her capabilities. It is well-known how the Gods dealt with the first Amalgams, how you murdered your own children in the name of self-preservation. If it is not a crime to dispose of your own flesh and blood, how dare you demonize her for an act of love!"

At that, Evette shifted uncomfortably, swallowing down words that would surely besmirch her character. She embodied justice, and there was no justice in the slaughter of innocents. It was an important lesson to be learned, one I still needed to figure out for myself.

Clapping erupted: slow, loud, and dramatic.

Syades stood, bringing his hands together in mock commendation.

Stepping off the dais, smoke and flickers of chaotic magic danced around his feet, rolling off his body like storm clouds. Both Loren and Chessane shrunk away from his approach, clutching one another. The crowd lingering nearby even seemed to retract at his presence.

These people feared him, kept in order by chaos, and what an absolute fucking contradiction that was.

"Excellent delivery. It was touching, moving, and I dare say it has appealed to several faces who have turned to expressions of sympathy for your dear friend."

Syades touched my battered chin, lifting it with his fingers as he continued, "I know too well the humanity that resides in the blood of Amalgams. They are half-mortal, like many of you."

He spoke to the crowd when he said, "I am also aware of the mayhem which they are capable of: unpredictable, uncontrollable."

Pulling away his touch, he took another step toward the spectating nobility.

"The very reason for the extermination of demigod children was not based on empty accusations. It was because they proved that they were our enemies, harbingers of destruction.

"You see, our pantheon was once *broader*. Several deities beyond your knowledge existed in this realm before we made our gravest mistake in mingling with those without divine blood. At first, it seemed a blessing, a miracle that such children had been brought into existence. We'd been hopeful in spreading our gifts over the lands, gracing the kingdoms with divine beings who could sympathize with them, aid them, and coexist with them, all while answering to their deities.

"It could have been a beautiful bridge, built to connect those of mortality and those of divinity. However, power births madness, doesn't it? Mortals are not capable of properly wielding divine power. The Amalgams' mixed blood proved to be their undoing, allowing their own gifts and potential to twist their minds. *They* wanted to be the Gods, to answer to none. That is not possible when beings greater than themselves exist."

Syades's body swiveled.

"Self-preservation," he quoted, staring daggers at Chessane, "Is necessary to ensure the order of *everything*. Without your deities, this realm would shatter and collapse. After the divine murders committed by our half-breed children, this world was left in shambles. We who remained were left to rectify it, to rebuild. Forbidding the creation of any creatures capable of such destruction was necessary, for the good of all."

He pointed an angry finger at me.

"Our enemy, the thief of divinity and the death of all things just, has broken our most absolute law. The very existence of this creature threatens not only the lives of your Gods, but the lives of every living being. Odric's spawn has proven herself to be dangerous and merciless."

He turned back to Chessane and lowered his voice, "The woman of whom you speak likely died with her friend, as she has displayed no sense of humanity since, committing crimes of murder, rape, and treasonous intent. She even traveled here to enact her revenge on innocents."

"Your vampires murdered people I love!" I shouted, breaking my silence once more.

The wicked man smiled.

"Odric's vampires are responsible for their fates. Several of them reside here; it is true. Your family, they are, and my rebels too."

He gestured to a small group of afflicted persons standing together.

There stood two women and two men, one I had seen twice before. I recognized the vampire sent to retrieve Aklys, the same one who received the Rosewick women: Euric.

Odric's children - my alleged siblings - serve the one who cursed them, according to lore. How was that so? Was there any truth to the legends?

My temples throbbed.

"His own children know he is a foul God, and those who remain with him are brainwashed and have been in murderous pursuit of *you*. You are just like them, hellspawn. Would the masses be willing to allow such a beast to roam freely in their lands? Would they allow it to threaten their lives and the safety of all they hold dear?"

Several cries of outrage broke from the previously quiet crowd.

My breaths were ragged.

"Are we willing to risk everything again for the sake of one life that should have never been?" Syades asked his divine companions.

Evette grimaced, lifting her head in agreement with chaos. Arendiel frowned, looking me over once more before bowing his chin in submission.

This is it.

Syades threw his head back, and crackling power rippled over the surface of his skin. He was breathing in the friction of the air, and it fueled him.

"Have we reached a decision?" King Kain asked no one in particular.

Roars and cries filled the corridor, bouncing off the walls, drowning out any shred of sense or reason.

I panicked, my mouth was dry, though my eyes were not. It felt like I was choking on the words of masses of strangers, swayed by the proclamation of a man who held immense power and standing.

Chessane's account meant nothing to these people. I meant nothing.

"So we have," Syades hissed.

The king stood, and the deities followed suit.

"Celessa Umbraeon, daughter of Odric, God of War," Kain continued, "Your very existence is a crime against the realm, made more potent by your own actions. You are found guilty of treason, conspiracy, rape, and murder."

My breathing stopped altogether.

"You are sentenced to die."

Chapter Twenty-Five

With The Setting Sun

I'm going to die.

It felt surreal — the cheering as my execution was announced, the horror painted on Chessane's face, the air that refused to enter my lungs. I couldn't hear much; the sounds of the rowdy crowd were drowning out the words being spoken as the gods demanded order. My focus locked on to the king's face for a moment, and he smiled at my terror; I knew it was apparent on my face by my widened eyes and gaping jaws.

Did I really deserve this, to meet an end so abrupt, with no story worth telling to leave behind? I had never gotten the chance to see the world at peace, where I could smile out over the ocean or breathe in a high mountain's air. I wasted it.

I have been so motivated by all the wrong things, though they hadn't seemed wrong at the time. There have been few moments I haven't considered my existence to be cursed, wrong, and miserable. I didn't allow myself to accept a second chance. I didn't see that it was a gift.

It was a gift given to me by Maygen, who had stayed by my side every step of the way to see it through and to help me find peace. I had denied her that in my actions, with my words. Failure has consistently been the way of things, endlessly plaguing me. I'd thought I had failed her in losing my chance at vengeance; I hadn't. I had failed her by refusing to live.

Now it's over... I have no chance to fix it.

I have dishonored my best friend.

She's gone, and I'll never have the opportunity to live for us both, to make her sacrifices worthwhile, or to make sure that all she'd done for me had meant *something*.

I fucked up.

Would I be able to say goodbye? To embrace Chessane, to see Erelim's face, to tell Cian how sorry I am? Does an abomination deserve such pity? Does an Amalgam deserve to be blessed with such a kindness?

"What means would you have her ended by?" Kain asked Syades.

The God of Chaos circled me, shadows following suit, cloaking us.

"How would I have you die?" He hummed, sniffing the air — breathing in my fear. Syades groaned, "Your divinity is potent, Amalgam. Were you a true goddess, you may have found the potential to become the most powerful of us. It's a pity about your paternity."

"Remove my chains, and I'll show you how powerful I am!" I hissed.

Throaty laughter erupted, moving closer as he pressed his lips to my ear.

"Had I any mercy in me, it would have been possible to come to a more favorable arrangement. Had your father been another God, you may have stirred some sympathy from the rabble," Syades whispered.

"No one has any more right to hate him than I!" My head whipped to the side to face him.

"You?" Nose to nose with the God, he snarled. "He *stole* her from me! She was *mine*!"

Knowing he meant Astera, Goddess of the Stars, I found I didn't understand what he meant; she had chosen Odric, hadn't she? Syades cursed their children because of it, to make them suffer. Odric should hate *him* for committing such atrocities against his sons and daughters, as chaos had achieved its revenge.

"She chose him."

Syades hissed, the black cloud that swirled around us thickened, crackling with lightning.

"You mortal scum think you possess vast knowledge, but it's all lies! Your homeland is in his clutches, squeezed by the claws of malice and deceit! Astera's son stands before you - my son, king! Born before Odric committed his crimes, forcing her to exile! She is lost because of him, because of your father!"

I let the information settle within me for a moment, trying to rewrite all I had learned. Though, how did I know his account was the truth? How did I know it wasn't his own lie, crafted to control a great mass of people, to pit them against his enemies?

"You would condemn me for bearing his blood?" I scoffed, squinting against the dark wisps of magic.

"Any creature born of him will find no mercy. The few that dwell here only receive my grace for the sake of their defection and my love for their mother."

He smiled again.

"You have not betrayed him, and Astera is not your mother."

The shadowy storm fell, dissipating into the floor, revealing a mostly empty room. Noble persons and spectators had been cleared away, leaving only the royalty, the deities — and my sympathizers. My breathing hitched, and tears welled that obscured my vision. Before me were those I had feared lost: Erelim and Aithen Vargen, Cian and Daevian, and though I had already confirmed her safety with my own eyes, I was grateful Chessane still remained.

Arendiel cleared his throat, commanding my attention as he spoke, "I believe it wise to achieve closure for yourself and those you hold dear before you face your sentencing, my lady."

It was a small kindness for him to allow such a thing. It was another kindness to be addressed with my formal title when his companions dehumanized me so contemptuously.

My fiancé dropped to his knees, taking my face into his hands.

"I know they're lying; I know you didn't do the things they've accused you of."

"Tread lightly, boy," Syades hissed.

Erelim glared at the God, unafraid of chaos itself. I wish I'd admired him more when I had the opportunity, and I wish I'd seen him for the man he is: bold, brave, strong, selfless, and kind. My selfishness hadn't allowed it — but I could see him now.

I was too late.

"I'm sorry," I said, pulling his attention back to me. "I'm not a rapist, Erelim, but I am a murderer. I killed Harmyn Rosewick. I am a traitor, because I came here with the intention of killing all of *them*."

His brows furrowed, taking in my confession.

"I don't care! I know you and I know why you have chosen retribution. *We* know that you are good."

Offering him a forced smile of little reassurance I continued, "I'm sorry, Erelim, it would seem that I'm not. I am a monster born of a great calamity."

"Lord Altan Umbraeon was your father, not Odric the defiler!" Another low voice hissed, shouldering their way past the king.

He came back.

Erelim stiffened at Aklys' presence. I wondered if he knew what this man meant to me, who he was to me.

"She has never known the God of War, and she didn't even know he was her father until *you* told her! Few of you deigned to divulge such information, failing to enlighten even me as I was sent to procure her for you!"

The vampire pointed an accusing finger at his divine grandfather.

"She was raised a mortal lady of her house, then trapped and tortured by an agent of chaos. What she has become is your doing!" He shouted challengingly.

An agent of chaos? Were Asuras' atrocities committed at the behest of Greilor's command? Why did he keep me in Sanctuary, the secluded prison of the Three Kingdoms? Why was I kept alive and not handed over to this court? Why was Aklys sent to find me?

I was plagued with unanswered questions, questions that didn't matter anymore.

"It does not help that you lied." Syades grinned, making Aklys bristle as he spoke, "You are lucky to be of my blood, or you would be facing the same fate for your treasonous actions."

The God of Chaos flicked his hand, sending shadows scrambling for the throne room doors. The wooden barrier flew open, revealing Euric, waiting and standing just beyond the threshold. Moving toward our group, it was only a few breaths before he was face to face with the vampire prince.

"You told us she was a mere mortal, a plaything you'd picked up along the way. We could have procured the Amalgam a year ago when she escaped the Mage, had you not deceived us!" The blonde-haired man hissed.

Aklys snarled, snatching his adversary's collar. He'd moved to discard Euric, to throw him away from us, but he was halted by his father and brother. The king and Prince Hadeon grabbed his arms, pulling him away from the man, despite the violent thrashing against their efforts.

Struggling against their hold, he ground out, "She is your sister!"

Euric glanced at me from the corner of his eye, denying me his full attention.

"My blood by chance and circumstance, I have a choice in claiming her. We have no pity for the agents of Odric."

My shoulders fell a bit at his declaration.

Did I really harbor hope that he would have any affection for a stranger? Sibling or not, he doesn't know me; he only sees me as the hell spawn of a father he has forsaken. Not so long ago, I had wondered if I'd had other Amalgam siblings, but it would seem I did not; my family consisted of vampires that wished me dead.

"An agent has a clear mission, a purpose; they serve," I whispered, all eyes on me. "I've never known my purpose, as I have never known Odric."

The God of Chaos puffed his chest, exasperated.

"It matters little. An Amalgam is a threat no matter their parentage. You feed off of the destruction you cause, and I won't wait for it to find me."

He narrowed his eyes at Arendiel, who turned away.

"You may have your *closure*," Syades sneered, summoning his son and fellow deities.

Evette stood fast, watching me crumble under the weight of defeat as she murmured, "There is no justice in this." I looked up at her, a mixture of despair and rage boiling in the pit of my stomach as she finished, "But there is a necessity."

The alleged embodiment of justice whisked away, her glowing aura encircling her and trailing along as if she were running through morning mist. I watched her take her leave in dismay, what good did it do to tell me that my death was wrongfully sentenced?

Syades made it clear there was no choice, no escape — so why say such a thing?

Erelim pressed his lips to my forehead.

"I'll get you out of this," he swore.

I shook away the affection, denying him.

"You can't... they will return."

Cian and Chessane sat next to me on the floor. The woman to my left took my hand, holding it reassuringly in her own, stroking the skin with her fingers. The vampire to my right wrapped an arm around my shoulders, an act I hadn't expected, but one for which I was grateful.

I was consumed by a feeling that I had long denied: love.

Through the last year, I'd only allowed myself to truly love Maygen, convincing myself she was the only one who had deserved it, especially after the heartbreak I had faced. That was wrong of me, because my friends deserved it too. They were genuine, like a family. Even Aithen and Daevian, who stood idly by, watching us all in silence.

Erelim stood to challenge the vampire who still lingered after condemning me.

"How could you partake in the murder of your own family?" He spat at Euric.

When he looked at me, I noticed that Euric's eyes were a deep blue - so incredibly dark, yet not black, like the evening sky just before giving way to night. We looked nothing alike, as there were no subtle similarities you'd expect to see in siblings; though, I did heavily resemble my mother. I wondered if he looks like Odric.

The man watched me lean heavily into the comfort of my companions, an expression akin to confusion and disbelief painted over his features.

"Are you not ashamed?" Euric asked, pulling his eyes back to Erelim. "To have promised yourself to such a creature?"

Aklys had been lingering nearby, watching but not approaching, even after his family had left us. His head whipped to search between the looks being exchanged, before his attention flickered to my shackled hands — seeing something he hadn't before. A ring bearing a gem of purple and blue. His eyebrows pulled together.

"You could use this to save her."

His words chilled the blood in my veins.

"What?" Erelim turned to face Aklys.

The vampire grew unreasonably frustrated, outstretching his arm to gesture toward my hand.

"You're set to marry her?"

Only a subtle nod was offered in answer.

"Mages bind themselves to their spouses all the time. They do it with mortals to prolong their lifespan, and they do it with immortals to share their magic between two bodies - to offer a taste of immortality, but also to share their power."

Aklys looked at me with his magical eyes of green and gold.

"Convince them that you can mute her power by taking some of it into your body after your marriage, and bind yourself to her!" He demanded.

Euric let out a disgusted sound, to which Aklys responded aggressively, "She deserves to live! This woman has committed far less atrocities than any vampire that exists in this cesspool of a realm!"

"And if she decides to retaliate for what has been done? If she somehow manages to summon the power to end Syades or any of the other deities?" My 'brother' challenged.

"Good fucking riddance!" Aklys hissed.

Would he have me tear apart the realms?

One thing Syades was right about, was that I have shown my true colors. If I am truly as formidable as they fear, if there was any truth to the ramblings about Amalgams murdering deities and undoing creation - what was I capable of? There was no stopping me in the name of vengeance. I was too susceptible to impulsivity, fueled by rage, because I am a product of war. What do you do with a weapon that has the ability to collapse the world?

There's only one answer.

You do everything in your power to stop it.

There's only one way to preserve life, to keep these people before me safe. There is but one way to make sure I can't destroy everything the Gods have built.

I have to die.

"No."

"What?" Cian whispered, releasing his hold slightly.

Looking between the friends at my sides and back to the men in front of me, I stifled my fear and pain. Inhaling deeply, I summoned every shred of courage I had left.

"I won't be bound. There is no saving me."

Exhaling roughly, my declaration settled into the space between us all.

"Celessa, if there is a way we can spare you from death, we must! You don't deserve to die! It isn't right!" Chessane protested, running slender fingers through her bouncy ringlets of hair. "Maygen would fight for you, and she would want us to fight for you!"

My heart ached.

Counting her freckles, I wanted to commit the memories of their faces to the deepest recesses of my soul, so I might carry them with me into the Hereafter. I hope I never forget them. Twenty-seven freckles crawled across her cheekbones and the bridge of her nose, slightly darker than her beautiful sepia skin tone. She had the most vibrant green eyes I've ever seen, with long eyelashes, topped by neatly kept brows.

Turning to Cian, I frowned a bit.

We'd upheld each other through the hell that has been this past month, struggling and fighting together. It was a passing thought, that I would miss his comforting presence, his strength and surety. But how could I? I'll be dead. No one knows what happens in the afterlife, only that Dameniel waits for us all. For now, I breathed in his scent and fell further into the warm embrace of my most trusted friend.

Erelim settled into his place before me; he didn't try to touch me, nor did he try to speak.

He deserved better - he deserved a woman who was invested, not one that had been so preoccupied in her wayward, spurned affections, and the misery that resulted. He breathed heavily, failing to withhold the sob he struggled against. His head shook vigorously, gaze falling to look upon the ground.

"I'm sorry," I whispered, not just to him, but to all of them.

Lifting my shackled hand from Chessane's, moving as far as the restraints allow, I offered an extended finger to Erelim — a silent request for him to reclaim what he had given to me. He withdrew slightly, offended.

"You don't want it?" He huffed.

"I am not worthy of it," I amended, and I meant it. "I wish I was. You still have life ahead of you to try again."

Erelim wiped tears from his cheek before taking my hand into his own, folding his fingers around my fist to close it.

"No one is more worthy than you, Celessa. If you must venture to the afterlife, keep this and wait for me so that we might try again."

With my peripheral vision, I watched Aklys turn his back to us. Unable to stop my heart's intrusion into my thoughts, I wondered if he meant to conceal sadness, jealousy, or something else.

We lingered in silence for a long time, exchanging embraces and short offerings of reassurance. I absorbed every passing second, held onto every moment, and prayed that they would last.

So many times I had wished to die, foolishly wishing my life away. I had triumphed against death and beaten many odds. I'd been told that my heart's desire would be my undoing, and a Goddesses' warning rang true. Those who bathe in blood have done nothing but break me, in one way or another.

Heralds of chaos and war indeed — I had never expected vampires to be sired by both Syades and Odric, locked in a timeless feud; one I found myself at the very center of.

Why was Fate cruel? Why did the primordial beings allow their creations to carry on like this? What was the point?

Euric swiveled to face the door, the scratching of his shoes against the floor made me cringe; a soldier standing at attention.

They were coming.

Hysteric sobs threatened to shake me, but I fought to swallow them down, to be brave. How does one face their end with courage, with faith that there is something to be found after? What if the afterlife is merely a myth? There is no guarantee that death offers peace, so it could just be nothing. My mind raced, fearing the worst; what if it was like my torturous sleep? Would I be left flailing for the things I've done, the rules I've broken, and the crimes I've committed? What if what I find is true hell?

"Oh gods," I whispered shakily as the doors opened.

Aklys was on me in an instant, pushing Erelim away, grabbing at my restraints.

"You're not fucking dying! I won't let you!" He growled, his muscles straining and his face turning red as he pulled at the locked chains of God's Ore.

We watched him struggle, holding fast as the entourage of Gods and vampires approached. There were more of them this time: the entire royal family, those that had been standing with Euric during the trial, and several others.

"Return our guests to their accommodations. I don't want any interruptions as the sentence is carried out," the king demanded, sending forth armored men.

My friends fought back against the guards, calling out my name, and it all seemed to happen in a haze. It felt like I wasn't a part of it all, like it wasn't real. I saw obscured visuals, like watching through a warped glass pane. I heard muffled sounds; the way noise is filtered by cupping your hands over your ears.

They dragged them away, kicking and screaming in protest.

I would never see them again... those moments hadn't lasted long enough.

Kain had set his other sons on Aklys to subdue their brother. I could tell that Hadeon was trying to reason with him, while the other nameless prince became aggressive in his efforts. An eternity passed waiting for him to disappear from my sight, his last words to me falling on deaf ears.

If Fate had any mercy at all, my death would be quick.

"Have you decided?" Arendiel asked Syades in a hushed tone as they loomed over me.

"I think death by hanging would be the most suitable, given your fancy artwork."

Syades grinned, gesturing to the snake tattoo that wraps around my neck. It burned in protest.

I gave no indication of agreement or otherwise, did they want me to care? Death is death, and my final moments are upon me. The manner in which it was carried out made no real difference.

Euric and another vampire unlocked the God's Ore chains and lifted me from the floor.

My legs felt heavy, full of metal and stone.

Syades' kin left first, followed by Arendiel and Evette, and then the rest of the group that had entered the hall with them. My escorts waited a handful of minutes before continuing onward in pursuit of them.

"Keep your head up. Face this with dignity, and Dameniel will reward you in the Hereafter," Euric whispered, speaking of the God of Death.

That he deigned to speak to me at all after he'd been so cold was a surprise. My sense of reason faltered, so panic gripped me like a vice, and unfiltered words began to spew out.

"I wish I'd had the power to change things," I confessed. "I wish I'd been born different."

A flicker of empathy sparked in the vampire's dark eyes. It was almost as if he couldn't believe I was capable of regret, hopelessness, and instead of fighting, I was spinning fantasies to bring myself comfort.

"I loved my family more than anything," I went on, not caring if they wished to hear me or not. "I loved Maygen so much, and I thought she was the last of my family. I would have given anything for her life, even my own. The things I have done cannot be excused or forgiven, I know that. I will never regret the decisions I made in her name, though I have failed her."

The sun touched my skin. We'd left the confines of the castle walls, so there were no more cold floors, no more great empty halls. The brightness assaulted my vision, making my eyes water as I squinted against it — the last fading light to shine upon my face.

Blades of grass licked my bare feet, raw and cracked, and I welcomed the gentle caress from nature. I imagined it as a kiss goodbye.

My wrists stung, my joints ached, and my knees were weak and wobbly. I was forced to rely heavily on the men at my sides.

I thought about Isonei, with her skin the greenish hue of sweetgrass, hair like a summer's wildflower field, and eyes as clear as the noon sky. I looked upon the evening sky, sun low and leaving the expanse above a beautiful shade of deep blue, like Maygen's eyes. I gazed at the sunset as it glowed red and orange, reminiscent of Thibault's fiery hair.

Those I have loved and lost were waiting for me. I struggled to find peace in knowing that I would join them soon.

Across an open courtyard flanked by hedges and obscured by onlookers, stood the gallows. The fixture sported but a single noose, neatly tied, hanging as still as the bodies that watched me pass by.

All were unmoving save for the ever-watchful Gilwyn, who stood beside her sister, swaying excitedly with a grin plastered on her *perfect* face. The roaring of blood thundered in my ears, as my pulse began racing frantically at the sight of her.

Three deities stood atop the platform that long wooden stairs ascended to from the ground below, waiting for me.

What a fucking waste, all those years kept asleep, and then the long months of fighting to survive. Every stolen moment of a passion I had spent with a man who didn't belong to me and with another who might have truly loved me. Every fight lost and won, all the shared laughter with my friends, and every life taken unfairly proved there was no point, no rhyme or reason. It was all for nothing.

My life had meant nothing, served no purpose, and now it was ending at the foot of a staircase that leads to a rope.

One step at a time, I climbed. Eight, nine - the passing seconds felt like hours - thirteen, fourteen, fifteen wooden boards to the top. Every breath that escaped was more ragged than the last; my legs trembled and my hands shook the links binding them together.

I was ready, but I was not. I was afraid, but I still prayed for peace. I am realizing that I do not want to die, but it is far beyond choice or chance now.

Syades moved to lower the noose around my neck, and I flinched.

"Do not fucking touch me."

A fire roiled in my gut, fueled by fear and spite.

The God simply smiled, gesturing for Euric to collect the honor of securing the rope. With unsteady fingers, the vampire tightened the loop. His hands rested on my shoulders, most unexpectedly, and he squeezed me gently.

"With the setting sun, look to the sky and see the stars," he murmured.

The stars.

I imagined them — every speck of light Aklys had spun tales about, plastering the memory of my parent's painting against the darkening sky.

I loosed a frightened breath, grasping at strings of relief from the images I conjured, and I waited.

"Celessa Umbraeon, you have been found guilty of murder, treason, rape, and conspiracy. The Greilorian council and the presiding deities have sentenced you to death by hanging. Do you have any final words?"

The king's voice was so distant, so foreign, unimportant.

"I hope you all find your peace. I won't leave this realm alone."

It was a small token to a sad, familiar song; one that I felt more deeply now than ever before in these last moments of my life.

My body braced. I couldn't hear what the king spoke to his father, and I couldn't make sense of the world around me. My head spun, growing delirious with terror.

I don't want to die.

I almost considered praying to my divine father, though he'd never been anywhere for me before. He didn't care about my life, so he surely wouldn't care about my death, either. I wanted my *real* father, Lord Altan, and I wanted my mother. As I imagined them, I hummed the most sorrowful melody, a song of sinking low.

Smiling at the memory of their faces, I watched the darkening sky, and I laughed.

I'll be with my family again.

Shouting erupted from the crowd before the towering gallows, the masses parting, and people started screaming. Explosions of light sent bodies scattering, as several armored men were thrown great distances — Erelim Vargen, Aklys Lukard, and Chessane Clearwater made their way toward me. Cian, my closest remaining friend, held off the advance behind them with two swords in his clutches. To even further surprise, he was flanked by Daevian and Aithen.

A spectacle that I had not anticipated was unfolding just below.

They were fighting for me.

Despite battling valiantly, their progress was stopped short. They were outnumbered and overpowered, and they had angered their Gods.

Syades' booming voice carried across the yard, filling the air, angrily cursing the rebellious act as he summoned his forces of chaos.

Rolling smoke and ash came forth from his body in pursuit of the aggressors. There was blood on their hands, and they had incurred a wrath that they could not face alone.

They fought so hard that their faces were red, sweating and crying out on my behalf. I wanted to tell them to look away, to close their eyes, and that they shouldn't have come. I wanted to tell them that I would be okay because I would hold those I'd lost once again.

Before my words could be given life, the floor fell out from under my feet, and my body began its descent. I gasped as the world shifted in slow motion — the eyes of those left in this world who still cared for me widened with horror.

Aklys screamed so fiercely that it surely rattled the realm.

Until suddenly, there was nothing left.

There was nothing at all.

Chapter Twenty-Six

Look To The Sky & See The Stars

W*here am I?*

"Hello little one," an unfamiliar voice cooed softly.

Turning from the clear stream, I met a most exciting sight; a woman with green skin and big blue eyes smiled down at me. Mother had told me tales of these mystical people, along with stories of magic, the beginning of time, and of pure children born from deities: the Nymphs.

I was too awestruck to speak, with fascination crackling under my skin like the fire in our sitting room hearth. Warmth spread throughout my body as we gazed at each other, and she seemed as equally taken with me as I was with her.

Maybe she had never seen a mortal child before?

That was silly, of course she has - Nymphs love children.

"What's your name?" She asked with a voice like birdsong.

"I'm Lady Celessa Umbraeon. Who are you?"

The mystical woman chuckled at my formality, "I am Isonei, meadow Nymph and daughter of the Goddess Melissae."

"Your mother is a Goddess?" I chirped.

"She is!" Isonei smiled. "Are you familiar with Goddesses, sweet girl?"

I nodded excitedly, my hair tickling my cheeks.

"Would you like to meet her?"

A pale-green hand extended toward me, warm and welcoming. I reached to take it without a thought at first, but then hesitated.

"Will we be gone long?" I asked her.

A small frown played on the woman's lips as she thought.

"I think we would be away for quite a while, yes. My Goddess mother lives very far from here, in a very secret place where only special people may travel."

My hand fell back to my side, disappointment flipping my smile.

"I don't think Mother would be very happy with me if I was gone for a long time. I don't want my sisters to miss me. If I'm away, Father will have no one to sing his tunes with him. My sisters don't like his music, you see, and they say ladies shouldn't sing silly songs."

I noticed my fingers had been fidgeting with the fabric of my skirts and brushed them down quickly to smooth away the wrinkles.

"You are very thoughtful, Lady Celessa, but I think it is important for you to come with me. I'm sure your family will understand that you've been called by a Goddess. You wouldn't deny the summons of a deity, would you?"

The Nymph lowered herself to meet me at eye-level, and her smile now seemed forced.

"Maybe your mother could ask my mother if my family could bring me to visit? So I do not have to be away from them. I think I would be very sad without my family," I sighed. "My friends would miss me, too."

"I bet you have many friends, little one."

Isonei fell to her knees and patted the ground, offering me a seat next to her in the grass.

Grinning again, I joined her. This was nice enough, wasn't it? Being friends here at my home. I don't want to go away to secret places.

"I only have one *best* friend, and his name is Thibault."

"A boy? Here I thought you would have lines of little ladies at your door waiting to play dress up," she chuckled.

I wrinkled my nose at her and giggled.

"I really like Thibault. He taught me how to climb trees properly and how to catch minnows from the stream with my bare hands!"

"Tell me more, sweet lady," Isonei murmured, relaxing her posture fully to listen to my stories.

Hours passed with the Nymph as dusk painted the sky hues of violet and magenta, with the setting sun spitfire orange on the horizon. I had never been happier, for my dream of befriending a magical being had been fulfilled; I never wanted this to end. It was my own fairytale.

"Thank you for sharing so much with me, Celessa. I'll be sure to pass your stories along to my mother, so that she might know how lovely you are, as well. I'm afraid I must go now."

She rose from the ground.

"Will I see you again soon?"

I snatched her hand without warning, squeezing her fingers with my own.

Isonei freed her hand from mine gently, turning it over to expose my palm, where she placed a vibrant blue flower.

"Under one condition." She pointed at the blossom she'd given me and said, "You must steep this little flower like tea and drink it tonight before you rest your head."

Nodding my agreement, I found myself swept up in the Nymph's thin arms.

"Promise me, Celessa."

"Will it give me magical powers?"

"Something like that," she sighed into my hair as we embraced our goodbyes.

Our eyes met, and I saw my reflection in her glassy gaze.

"Until we meet again."

All at once, the Nymph vanished into flower petals, blue like the ones in my small hand. The petals fluttered and swirled with a wayward breeze that carried them into the forest and out of sight.

Squeezing my little gift tightly, I hurried back to the estate, eager to discover what the special tea might bestow upon me. I hoped it would be something I could use for good.

Who am I?

Worried about his intentions, my footing became less sure.

"We can't risk this! If we're found out, who knows what might happen? What about your father?" I pleaded, clutching onto the shirt of my best friend, my would-be lover.

"You are worth the risk."

He turned to look down into my eyes, cupping my face with his palms.

"We have waited all of our lives for the day we might be together, and we know now that will never happen if we leave it in the hands of the nobles. I've been deemed unworthy of you, and while that may be true, still I cannot live without you."

"You know the High Court has inquired for me! If my father does not let me go, it would bring ill-favor upon my house. While I do not wish to accept the offer, I cannot put that on my family; it's selfish," I insisted.

"Are *they* not selfish? What about what *you* want? Do you not want me? Do you not love me?"

Tears welled in his eyes; his beautiful green eyes that embodied the very depths of pine covered mountains.

"I do! You know I do!" I whimpered, touching my forehead to his lips.

"If your virtue is tarnished, if you give yourself to me, then the High Court will not want you. You could be *my wife*, and we could be together for as long as you will have me."

I was taken aback by the bluntness of his suggestion.

"You would have me dishonor and forsake my family?"

"Am I not worth it? Are *we* not worth it? We have been in love since we were children!"

The man pulled away from me, exasperated, but he tried again.

"If you truly loved me, you would risk this. I would risk never seeing my father again if it meant being with you, so why are you not willing to do the same?"

"Thibault, please," I begged, "I am. I will. I'm sorry."

My half-Fae desire forced me into an embrace, crushing his lips against my own.

I was afraid. I was afraid of the consequences, afraid of what life would be like if we followed-through, and afraid of losing my family. What if I never saw them again? What if we were banished to such cruel conditions that we're never able to make a good life for ourselves?

I had to prove my love and my loyalty to him so that we could be together. If Father might relent to the nobility, if he sent me to Licourt, I would never see Thibault again. He was right... This was a risk we had to take together.

Perhaps my family would see reason and allow us to remain in Briobar. We could find a small home in the city, marry, and have children. Thibault could find work in the market selling crops from his father's farm. Maybe everything would be okay.

Maybe.

Returning his embrace, I felt his hand slip underneath my shift, and panic set my skin ablaze. I threaded my fingers into his fiery locks of hair to steady myself, losing my breath with every stroke of his skin against my own. I don't know if I'm ready for this.

Our bodies felt as if they were fusing together, and Thibault had undone the ties of his breeches, shoving them down to expose his most intimate parts and pressing himself against me. My arms and legs trembled, and I was sure that I wasn't ready.

We should be married and in our newlywed bed, not committing adultery in his father's stables. Rough hands forced up my skirts - I wanted to change my mind, this wasn't right.

A small cry burst forth from my lips as he made a failed attempt into my body.

The stable doors flew open, with torchlight illuminating the musty building, revealing our indiscretions. Several guards in my father's employ rounded on Thibault, grabbing the man and prying him away from me. My clothes had fallen back into place to cover my legs, but my disheveled appearance was enough to elicit a cry of outrage from my father, who had followed behind his men.

Father struck Thibault with the back of his hand, and the sound of the connection reverberated through the small space.

I lashed out in protest, grabbing his arm.

"What have you done?" He demanded, turning back to deliver another blow to my lover.

"No, please, we didn't!" I cried.

Withdrawing, Father grabbed my wrist to lead me away. He had never laid a hand on me in such a manner before.

"Put him below," Lord Altan commanded the guards to place Thibault in the dungeon beneath the keep that was our home.

"Father, please, he didn't take my virtue! Don't punish him!" I begged.

"Do you know what you would have cost yourself had I not intervened, what you would have cost the family?" He snapped. "I turned a blind eye to your childish romance for too long, it seems. I had hoped you possessed the sense to end things before it got this far, Celessa. You have forced my hand. It did not have to be this way."

"What will you do?"

Hot tears washed away the sweat from my flushed cheeks.

"He will be punished. He cannot stay in Briobar. He cannot stay in Teskaria."

Exile.

Father was going to punish him by banishing him to one of the neighboring kingdoms.

My chest felt as though it had been caved in by a mallet, my breath stolen from me. We made a choice, and it was the wrong one. Now, Thibault would pay for it for the rest of his life, and I would truly never see him again, with no chance for redemption and no chance for a future together.

They chained his body to the whipping post: a thick stump of wood hammered deep into the ground. A barbaric punishment would be delivered to Thibault, one I'd only seen inflicted once before in my lifetime and still felt nauseated by the gruesome memory.

I'd begged and pleaded, beseeching my father to find reason and simply send him away, to spare him from this. Lord Altan insisted an example be made due to the number of witnesses to our indiscretions in his personal guard.

"Men talk," Father had said, "they need to know what happens to those who would dare attempt to defile a lady."

Truthfully, I do not think he wanted to hurt Thibault, and he was simply abiding by the laws laid down in the kingdoms generations ago. It was his duty as a lord to punish those who would defy the laws, and it was his duty as a father to protect his daughter.

Grigori wept for his son and for himself, knowing he would die before Thibault could return to the country, for he was a mortal man. The lashes would heal, the exile would pass, but never seeing your only family again was a particularly cruel and painful punishment all its own. His half-Fae son would live on for some time, outlasting many who stood here today, including myself.

"I am so sorry, Grigori. It's all my fault!" I cried, clutching the man's sleeve.

He patted my curled-up fists gently.

"Do not blame yourself, my dear. He knew better; we both know that to be true. My boy rarely considers reason before acting. He is always driven by impulse, with no sense. I daresay he got that from his mother." Grigori's voice cracked as he said, "Now he will face a fate similar to her own."

Lord Altan Umbraeon delivered a short address to the handful of bystanders who watched as the chosen guard approached a shirtless and bound Thibault - lash in hand.

I fought against the cry of protest rising up my throat, my heart beating wildly in my chest, like a startled bird trapped in a too small cage. I couldn't bear this, I couldn't allow it, because he hadn't followed through. He didn't deserve this.

The first crack of the whip exploded through the courtyard and into my body, as if I'd been struck by lightning. Thibault screamed and my arms reached out in answer to his cry and call for mercy.

Kind hands tugged me back, holding fast to prevent me from putting myself before the next blow.

"No, lady, you mustn't interfere."

Grigori frowned, restraining himself as much as he was me, obviously wishing to rescue his son from this unfair pain.

Another lash, another cry, and my breathing was beyond labored. My skin itched and burned, and heat pulsed through my veins more violently than ever before.

The guard reared up to strike him again, but I could take no more.

"That is enough!" I screamed.

The guard scowled at me, staying his swing for only a moment before responding, "He will receive five lashes, as is the law."

He hit him again.

Three lashes had left muscle exposed in the gaping wounds on Thibault's shoulders, blood soaked the ground and his breeches; his body began to falter. No mortal would survive this punishment, though I fear that may be the point of it. This man was half-mortal, so who knows how much could his body take.

Another blow would reveal bone, and enough is enough.

Breaking free of Grigori's hold, I leapt forward to advance against the guard. If he does not drop the whip, I will take it from him. Only a pace from the bastard, I was caught, and the guard smirked at me as the other men in my father's employ prevented me from following through.

He received another fucking lash.

I unleashed a scream so horrifying that the Gods would surely cower in their hiding, for fear of what had been borne of this atrocity. I had become so monstrous that the bodies at my sides had fled, and the assailant before me lay dead on the ground, rotting away into a pile of nothing.

All I could see was red.

What have I done?

His caress was tender, seductive, and so promising.

This time I was sure I would be married and live the life my family had wanted for me, the life they'd convinced me I wanted. How perfect a suitor he was, and I could hope for nothing more. His dark hair was long, cascading past his shoulders and dancing in the wind, glossy and as beautiful as the night. This man was magical, mysterious, and he radiated power and authority.

Though I was mortal, a Mage could extend the youth and life of his lover, so that they may live through long lasting days together — until the end.

How incredibly romantic.

What a perfect man, I was so lucky.

Sometimes my sense would filter back in, and I would remember the man I loved. I would remember Thibault, and I would yearn for him. My tongue would sour at the presence of the Mage who had begun courting me only a few weeks after my lover's exile.

What was wrong with me? How dare I indulge in the affections of another after all that had transpired, after all that I had done, and considering all that I had lost?

My father has hardly looked at me since that horrible, fateful day. I killed a man. I hadn't meant to, and I was barely able to recollect the incident, but I knew something had come forth from me that was terrifying and painful.

All I could remember clearly was the color red, the death, and the screams. I had fainted when it was over. Waking revealed that my actions had made no difference, and Thibault was gone forever.

When my mind fell into itself like this, I understood what was happening, that I was being entranced by my own gullible and vulnerable nature.

Asuras whispered into my ear, "Come back to me, my dear."

Fog, dark and wispy, swirled into my consciousness.

I turned to the man next to me, and noticed he looked especially handsome today. Was it a special occasion?

"What were we talking about?" I giggled, tucking myself under his arm.

"You were going to show me something, something *special*," he purred seductively, tracing his fingers along my jawline down toward my neck, trailing along the fabric that covered my chest.

"Anything for you, my lord. What would you like to see?" I nearly slurred my words, drunk on his intoxicating charm.

"Come, sweet Celessa. Let us go somewhere more private."

The man winked before he stood, offering his hand.

Happily, I accepted the gesture and allowed him to lead me toward the treeline near the edge of the estate property. My parents wouldn't approve of my being alone with him like this, but I was sure he would be my husband one day. He was a noble Mage, so surely Father would offer us his blessing.

Come to think of it, I wasn't sure which family he hailed from.

Does it matter?

Of course it doesn't matter; he is perfect.

Tucked away in the shadow of the forest, with the keep merely a smudge in the distance, I looked into the eyes of my suitor. My skin hummed and my heart fluttered; I was dizzy and warm.

I'd felt this way once before, when my sisters and I had snuck into the wine cellar and swiped a few loose bottles of aged red. We'd polished off several, becoming wildly intoxicated, and this felt the same. Perhaps I had just been drinking, so I must have forgotten.

"My lord-", I started, but Asuras pressed a finger to my lips, stalling my words.

"You will give me anything, won't you, Celessa?"

He grinned.

I nodded and said, "Anything."

Strong hands tore away the fabric of my bodice, exposing my bare breasts. I had never been seen in such a state by any man before, not even that boy I had fancied. What was his name again?

My fingers fumbled, trying to piece back together the garment.

"Don't cover up!" The man growled.

Immediately my hands dropped to my sides, frozen. I watched him and waited.

He began searching my skin, rotating my limbs in his hands, pulling at what was left of my clothing. I gasped, my body tensing to flee, but I stayed.

This was okay, and he could do whatever he wanted.

"Turn around," he demanded.

I obeyed.

The Mage ripped away my damaged dress, leaving only my sheer slip that also had been torn in the front, leaving me all but nude. Fabric slid across my skin, he was lifting the slip away from my thighs and rear. A whimper of protest stalled in my throat, and I remained still.

"Where the fuck is your mark?" He hissed.

What mark?

Asuras growled in frustration, pushing my body around before throwing me to the ground.

This was okay, he could do whatever he wanted.

His hand cupped my chin, squeezing my jaw to the point of pain.

"How obedient will you be, Celessa? You'll give me whatever I want?"

"Yes."

The answer was not my own.

"You'll let me do whatever I please, won't you?"

"Yes."

I was scared and I hated this. Why couldn't I escape?

"I'm going to take your life if you aren't compliant, do you understand?"

"Yes."

Trembling took hold as he lifted me from the ground, and the Mage forced me against a tree.

How did it come to this? Why am I here?

Please don't, I wanted to say. I wanted to cry and scream.

Asuras pressed his lips to my ear and whispered, "Give me your power."

Something roared to life inside of me in answer, like a hidden entity buried deep down, awakening at the call of its name: *Power*.

The stupor vanished as the magical hold lifted, leaving me sober and aware.

Ripping my body away, I lashed out with something that wasn't a part of me, but somehow it was. A red explosion filled the space between us as I whirled to fend off my attacker. My limbs went rigid with pain, nausea squeezing my gut at the release of this foreign presence.

You will not yield to the likes of him.

There was a voice inside of me, and I asked, "Who are you?"

I am you, and I am not. Fight for us.

Terrified of Asuras and of myself, I ran.

"You cannot escape me!" Asuras roared.

My feet carried me across the grasses between the forest and my home. I cried out, screaming for help. A force was behind me, upon me; I could sense it.

Slowing...

I was slowing down, burdened by exhaustion. My body was giving up. I cried out again. Turning toward the direction I'd fled, I could see him standing with his hands out, unveiling a wide wing span.

From his being, a rolling black cloud was birthed, and it had been sent after me; crashing against the ground in furious pursuit.

I knew I would not escape this.

You cannot escape a Dark Mage. He had hidden his affliction and bewitched me to take what I possessed, whatever *it* was.

My body could no longer keep up, and I was failing.

Someone please help me.

There was a voice calling my name, a voice that was so familiar; someone was coming to save me.

Collapsing to the ground, I was enveloped by the rolling smoke: thick, dark, and suffocating. Amidst the haze, the image of a person heading for me was obscured through wisps of black magic, they were frantic and weeping.

Hands were outstretched, desperate to reach me. Not just someone, though, but a couple of someones reached for me — my parents.

"I'm sorry," I whispered.

Everything disappeared.

I was falling into nothingness, with only my mind. I lingered, waiting for something, yet expecting nothing.

How has it come to this?

Every step I had taken, every decision I had made and fallen prey to, has led me here.

Why did this happen to me?

Divine blood was a marker for a twisted existence, unpredictable and yet set in stone.

Did I deserve such misery?

Did anyone deserve to be miserable? Why was life so cruel?

Was I dead?

I remembered falling, breaking, and dying.

My eyes opened, something unexpected in itself — I had true consciousness. I was awake.

I remembered my death. I had felt my soul depart from my physical being, my broken body. It had traveled somewhere far away, somewhere unknown and yet all too familiar to the realm of the living.

I should be stunned at that fact, as I laid here in this mysterious place, not entirely dead but certainly not alive. However, I couldn't bring myself to care about anything but the sight above me - the deep, dark, never-ending expanse.

A vast sky... full of stars.

This was the most impossible and mesmerizing thing I'd ever laid my eyes upon. How was this happening? To where had my soul been transported?

It wasn't possible that the stars have been in the Hereafter this entire time, was it? The most inexplicable and profound mystery of our realm was concealed by death itself.

I could not pull my eyes from the twinkling lights above, the mysterious specks of luminance, the *stars*. I'm looking at the fucking stars. Even the whispers growing louder all around me in the darkness could not sway my focus, my awareness of them only a vague and swiftly passing realization.

I had already experienced death, so there was nothing left for me to fear.

Beneath my sprawled figure was a bed of moss, and I registered the familiar sensation under my palms and against my fingertips. My toes curled up against nature's pillow, the faint tickle was pleasant enough to twist my lips into a grin. Soft fabric wrapped my body: a dress of old, fashioned from silk. My lungs filled with sweetly cool air, but my skin felt no chill. This was the most perfect, pleasant place in existence.

I would never leave; if this was meant to be my afterlife, then I was content.

Something finally captured my attention, a burning so cold it scorched and froze my skin all at once - the ring on my finger was beaming with starlight. The mysterious gift my mother had given me to hide away as a child, the same one I had recovered in

Briobar, glowed brightly. Lifting my hand above my face, I beheld it silhouetted against the sky, watching the gem mimic the beauty that glittered beyond. It blazed with ancient magic, but what I felt was not pain, it was euphoria.

We had ended up right where we were meant to be.

"Please tell me that this is a cruel hallucination and not the truth, tell me that you still live."

A hollow and ghostly voice carried into my consciousness, like whispering winds that twist between long grasses in open fields.

Had I truly heard someone, or was my mind playing tricks on me?

A large hand fell from the sky, it seemed, grasping my gown and pulling me from my bed on the forest floor. The world around me whirled, spinning violently at the sudden assault, the way it twists and contorts after you've consumed too much drink. My eyes fought to keep pace with the chaos, flinching away from the orange hues of fire.

Not fire... hair.

Cowering, I found myself looking up at the devastated face of a person I'd once known. A half-Fae man, tall and handsome, someone I had loved.

I was looking at the face of a dead man.

Thibault.

He shook me slightly, gripping my shoulders enough to register awareness but not to inflict pain. It's him: scarred lips and evergreen eyes, pale skin and hair of flames. Tears obscured the already difficult-to-register image of my first friend and my first love.

I had watched him die, and we were dead.

"Celessa, please." He wept, "Tell me this is not real."

"I-I'm sorry, I failed you all," I stammered with weepy eyes. He crushed me in a tight embrace, squeezing the sadness from my body with his scent, which exuded the smell of comfort and home.

Thibault sobbed into my hair, smoothing it down with one hand while the other clutched my waist.

I had hoped to find him here, but hadn't expected to find this man I cherished, mourned, and missed terribly. It was a dream and a nightmare in one, being here with him in spirit, but without our lives.

"It isn't usually like this," he whispered. "We often can't feel each other. We can't always see."

His grip tightened as he continued, "We can't always hear familiar voices or find the comfort of friends and those we love."

Thibault moved his hands to hold my face, angling my eyes toward his own.

"This is one of the greatest gifts I could have received in my afterlife, but at what cost? You should not be here."

There were so many things I wanted to tell him, for there was so much he had missed. Where to begin? Despite our teary-eyed reunion, the emotion of it all, my mind was still preoccupied.

"Thibault, the stars," I breathed, looking to the sky.

His hold faltered, confusion painting his features.

"Stars?"

"Look at them! How can you think of anything else?"

Releasing me fully, he brought my face down with gentle fingers, his eyes looking above then returning to meet my own.

"There are no stars, Celessa."

Chapter Twenty-Seven

Hereafter We Wander

Twinkling lights reflected in his eyes, but he could not see them. The entire expanse of magic glimmered in orbs of deep green, but he was blind to it.

How was that possible?

The stars were there, plain as day, glittering as brightly inside of us as above us. I couldn't understand how something supposedly hidden was so very apparent as he looked back at me, confused and uncertain. I am the first to see them since Astera's disappearance. The stars shone in the sky, and I couldn't even share the joy of it with Thibault.

Words escaped me, as I was unsure of how to explain what I was seeing.

His expression was already so expressively sad and burdened, only for me to begin spewing what he perceived as madness. How could I tell him that my mind was intact, that I wasn't crazy? Had my conjured illusions before my death followed my soul into the Hereafter? Had my brutal death shattered my grasp on what was real and what was not?

It seemed entirely possible.

That I had retained any sense of reason, after all I'd endured while I was alive, was a miracle in itself. Perhaps I *had* lost it, or perhaps it had become obscured, leaving my rationality shielded by rose-colored protection. I am fragile, wounded, and broken.

One thing I know for certain: I am dead.

This place is undoubtedly the Hereafter, where my afterlife has begun. What would that entail? Thibault's broken words offered little comfort, confessing he couldn't often find others, that he couldn't always hear them.

Death was told to offer peace, but it would seem we had been deceived.

"Thibault, have you found my family? Do you know where their souls are?"

I'd always been told that Dameniel, the God of Death, waits for all. If that was true, would this place not be overflowing with souls? How would Thibault have been able to find mine amidst so many others? Where was the elusive deity who controls such a place? Was I meant to be here or did I belong somewhere more... sinister?

For all I had done, I don't think I truly deserved peace or to rest.

"No, Celessa, I'm sorry..."

His expression was solemn, but pained, for he was miserable.

"Have you found your father?" I whispered.

Thibault had been dead for over a year, and to imagine him alone for all of that time made my heart ache.

"I see him sometimes, briefly. It isn't like being alive, Celessa. We're little more than wisps of shadows, adrift in this endless forest of lost, wandering souls."

His response was not what I had hoped for, but it was everything I had feared. This feels like a punishment. How long would I have with him before he disappears?

"How long do we have?"

I shivered, afraid of losing him again. What if I couldn't find him after this? What if my punishment is to be greeted by one I love, offering mere threads of hope to grasp for, and then left to suffer in solitude?

"I don't know," he confessed.

Thibault skimmed his hands across my arms, and they didn't feel quite right; they were not quite a touch, but more like the promise of one.

"W-wait, I have to tell you so much! Maygen, s-she died, and I need to know if she's here!"

"She died?"

He choked, and that was all he needed to say for me to understand that he hadn't come in contact with her soul. What if she was alone too?

There were so many things he needed to know, and I had more questions for him, but it seemed we were running out of time. One pressing thought took precedence over all else.

"You're a father!" I exclaimed, clinging to him.

His brows pulled together, again likely questioning my sanity. He looked at me with skepticism, as if he assumed I was referring to myself as the one who had bore his child. That wasn't possible, as our interaction had been entirely too *brief*.

"After you died, we fled from Briobar. In our travels, we met Isonei."

"The Nymph? The one who gave you the flower?"

I nodded, "Yes. She revealed that Aloise was pregnant with your child, your daughter. Her sickness - it was pregnancy."

Thibault swallowed roughly, tears glossing his eyes. He opened his mouth to speak, but it was becoming muted. My friend's soul was filtering away.

"No. No, no! Please don't go!" I begged, grasping at what was left of the fading figure. "I love you," I cried, "I'm sorry."

I was sorry — sorry that I had failed him, sorry that I didn't save him, sorry that I couldn't keep him with me. I was sorry for every moment we had lost, and every second I had wasted on blaming him, on hating him. I was sorry for not loving him better as the friend he needed.

All I could do was watch helplessly as he vanished into nothing, the weight of my loneliness and despair crushing me like a mountain had formed overhead, using its mighty body and the force of gravity to push me to the ground. I couldn't cry, couldn't move, couldn't breathe; I was consumed by despair.

No one deserved to be alone for all eternity.

My enemies had won.

They succeeded at torturing me, condemning me, and even murdering me. Did I not, at the very least, deserve some semblance of peace in death when so little had been found during my life?

My intentions had been mostly good, as I only sought out revenge where it was warranted: against those who deserved it. If I had lived without the many atrocities I'd faced, perhaps I would have been good. If only I had been mortal, I might have been better.

There were no distant voices now, and there were no wayward souls watching me from their hiding places; if they still saw me, they kept silent. There was no company save for the stars above, my one comfort — Astera's creation, her magic. It was visible to no one but me, it seemed.

My ring of starlight, the mysterious white gem: it still burns. It's happy in this place, among its likeness. It was my mother's gift, our secret.

The key.

"Leave this place," someone whispered.

In death I need not fear, so I paid no mind to the voice and its hushed words.

"You should not be here."

It grew louder.

If I closed my eyes, hopefully it would go away.

"I command you to leave this place!"

I opened my eyes.

In death, there is nothing I need to fear...
Except death himself.
Sterling gray eyes stared down, swirling with rage and disbelief.
Dameniel had found me.

He was nothing like I'd expected. I imagine none knew what he looked like, except for those dearly departed and the deities with whom he shared creation. His hair was short, barely protruding from his scalp, and his face appeared soft, without a trace of facial hair. With a thin body, short in stature, he reminded me of a teenage boy who had not quite reached maturity.

The God of Death angled a weapon at me: a long, misshapen sword that glowed white. The image was strange, as he'd always been depicted by mortals as a terrifying, grown man wielding a scythe. The longer I looked at him, the angrier he became, pressing the tip of the blade to my neck.

"Unless you wish to meet your true death, I suggest you do as I bid," he threatened. "No divinity is welcome in my realm, so return from whence you came."

"But I died," I whispered.

"Naturally," he hissed. "Otherwise, you would not be here, but it is time for you to go."

"How am I supposed to leave the Hereafter when I am *dead*?"

My voice boomed throughout the quiet emptiness as I rose from the ground.

He looked even smaller now, shorter than I by an inch or two, and much more nimble. The sword remained against my throat as I stood, and he didn't falter, but there was fear etched into his features; he was losing his composure. Why would a deity fear a dead Amalgam?

"I will not hesitate to defend my creation and those that dwell within!"

The threat sounded weak, but the power he exuded felt differently.

"What does it matter?" I laughed, and his position shifted at my demeanor.

"Do you wish to meet your true death?" He asked.

I bared my neck to him, pressing my flesh to the glowing weapon.

Dameniel stumbled, pulling away from me, and I raised a questioning brow.

"Y-you shouldn't be here."

The God of Death stutters when he's nervous?

"Tell that to the bastards who murdered me."

His sword fell to his side as he straightened his posture and said, "The vampire king."

I nodded and continued, "And his divine bastard of a father."

"Which of them ended your life? What was the means?"

Shouldn't *he* already know that, and wasn't that *his* purpose? Did he not deal with all manners of death and know the tragedy of the souls he harvested? Although, he did look rather surprised by my presence, like he didn't expect me to be here.

"They hung me with a rope. A vampire secured it. Does it matter?"

"Yes."

The word echoed, seeming to bounce off of the trees as it carried away.

My lips tugged down into a frown as I asked, "Why?"

"Why, indeed," he grumbled, turning to walk away.

Baffled, I trailed after the man with unsure footsteps, as he was surprisingly fast for someone with such short legs.

"Wait!" I called after him, hurrying along to meet his pace.

He continued on for some time before I felt winded and fed up. How was I even out of breath? How could I *breathe*? I'm dead.

"Please," I panted.

I nearly had to sprint to keep up with Dameniel as he ventured through the realm of his own design to who-knows-where.

Questions plagued me, as there were many things I wanted to ask the God: about Maygen, Isonei, and my family. I wanted to know where Thibault had vanished and why he couldn't stay with me. I needed to know why he asked me about the manner of my death.

Did he know my divine father?

"Odric," I stated loudly.

Dameniel froze, but he did not turn to face me.

"Do you know why he created me?"

"What?"

His shoulders tensed, recoiling at my question.

"Why did Odric create an Amalgam?" I clarified.

The God of Death shifted then, cleaving the very air before me with his white sword. I reeled from the attack, bracing myself for what he referred to as true death. My body fell to the ground, but as I pushed myself up onto my elbows, I saw the image of a person inside what seemed to be a rift between realms. A magical opening, that could lightly be described as a window, rippled above. Amid a frozen prison, decorated with ice and glittering snow, stood a man.

His breath fogged the air, damp heat clashing with bitter cold in a small cloud as he exhaled. Light brown hair dusted his forehead, with a short beard that matched in color crawling from chin to ear. Deep-blue eyes scanned the wintered wasteland, filled with what could only be perceived as deep, impenetrable sadness. Hopelessness. Curled along his neck was something that made me recoil, guts twisting with nausea; the tattoo of a serpent.

Dameniel, somehow, was showing me the God of War - my father.

I rose to my knees, peering into the portal at the man who damned me to a life of misery.

"Odric has been imprisoned for exactly one hundred sixty-three years. Shortly after your birth, to be precise."

The deity's face peered around the opening, scanning the imagery within.

"By whom?"

My fingertips pressed against the magical tear, and it was like touching glass.

"Several deities of the pantheon."

"For creating an Amalgam?" I asked.

I felt I already knew the answer to that question, for it was obvious, and I was the evidence.

"He did not create an Amalgam."

Blood drained from my face. That didn't make any sense.

Syades had confirmed that I was, in fact, Odric's child based solely on the brand I received. Was it a ruse? The snake tattoo had been a telltale of my paternity. I looked down at the mark, but it was gone. My skin was as clear as it had been before the vampires had delivered the god's design unto me. Someone else must be my father, and Odric had taken the fall for it.

Why?

I watched for a few more moments as the God of War rested his forehead against what appeared to be a magical barrier; it reminded me of how Aklys and I had once been separated, pressed against an invisible wall, desperate to reach each other. Odric was desperate to be released.

A woman appeared at his side, with the same blue eyes, and the same miserable frown. She spoke to him, though I could not hear what was said.

"Who is she?" I asked Dameniel.

Her hair was short, cut just below her ears, and she was very frail and malnourished, like she'd been starved. As her mouth moved, I caught the sight of fangs between her lips. She's a vampire. The woman faltered, caught by Odric who offered her his wrist. I was startled when she bit into his flesh, draining blood from the wound.

"Liatris, a daughter of Odric and Astera: she was condemned with her father for aiding him, along with several of her siblings. They are dying. His blood replenishes them, but it is barely enough to keep the five imprisoned children fed in their exile."

"Aiding him with what?" I whispered, feelings of pity stirring for the woman who clung desperately to her father's arm.

"Fulfilling the prophecy."

Dameniel closed the rift, returning us to the gloom.

To my surprise, the God offered me his hand, pulling my body up from the forest floor. He looked me over with his eyes of steel, wearing an expression caught somewhere between fear and intrigue. The sword was sheathed at his side, but he kept his hand gripped around the hilt.

"You said you would deliver my true death, does that mean I'm not really dead?"

My fingers fidgeted with the silk wrapped around my hips.

"They hung me at the gallows, and I know I died. I felt it."

I shook my head a bit, internally ridiculing myself for asking such a ridiculous question.

"You died a mortal death, and that is why you are here," he said as he looked at my hand that was still held in his own, inspecting the ring on my finger.

"How have you come to possess the key?"

It *is* a key, but is it a key to the stars?

"My mother told me to hide it when I was young. When I woke from my sleep, I went back for it," I mumbled.

"Can you see them then?" Dameniel's eyes lifted toward the sky.

"Yes. I can see them," I breathed, taking the glittering beauty once again. "I can see the stars."

Refocusing on the small man, a new question reached the tip of my tongue.

"What really happened to Astera?"

Straightening, he took in a lungful of air, steadying himself.

"Her exile has taken her far away from this realm, Celessa. She does not want to be found." A thin finger raised to point at my gemstone. "I do not know how your mother came to possess this ring, but it is the key to the magic Astera left behind. It is a gift from the Goddess herself."

I have the key to the fucking stars.

"What prophecy did Odric fulfill?"

Dameniel smirked, one corner of his lip twitching up.

"*Now* you are asking the right questions."

He beckoned me forward to lead me further into his darkness.

I held my questions in, and the potency of them made my tongue dry and my mouth sour. I needed to spit them out, but I waited, following this strange deity to the opening of what appeared to be a large cave.

"What is this place?" I whispered, intrigued by the mysterious formation.

It reminded me of a great mouth, with rocks jutting from the top and bottom like jagged teeth, swallowing the night with its untold depth.

"It is from where we emerged."

He lifted a hand, gesturing for me to enter.

Into the darkness we delved, deep into the mouth of the realm, toward the beginning of our world's creation. We continued down, down, down into the void.

Fear pimpled my skin, like a cold breeze had swept over me, a natural response to the ominous unknown. The last time I had ventured into such a mysterious place had been in a dream, in the labyrinth where I was met with a twisted and terrifying image of myself.

Throughout the duration of our descent, I let my thoughts wander in an attempt to piece together the information Dameniel had offered.

Odric was assumed to be my father, but it was not the truth, meaning another God must be responsible for my creation; I wasn't necessarily a *weapon*. The God of War was imprisoned for fulfilling a prophecy, and condemned after my birth, but what did that prophecy entail?

Astera did not want to be found, but left behind her magic for someone or *something* to find, concealing the stars within the depths of death itself. My ring was the key to her magic, but what did that mean, and how could I release it? What did it all mean, and what did it have to do with me?

I was cursed to forever have more questions than answers.

There was a faint glow ahead of a strange color, or rather several colors; I saw shades of orange, red, blue and purple. The different hues cast long rays against the walls as we approached, and my advance became slower and more hesitant.

"Is it safe?"

I turned to Dameniel, who was close behind.

Tipping his chin, he nodded slightly.

"For our kind, yes."

Our kind, surely meant bearers of divinity.

Large stone pillars filled with strange lights stood ahead, covered in symbols and words; some were easily discernible in their stories, where others were a mystery. Strange gemstones jutted from the rocks. Amidst the messy scriptures, two symbols caught my attention — a serpent and a star.

I brushed my fingers against the glowing engravings and asked, "Odric and Astera?"

"Yes," Dameniel responded, pointing to a jagged image that seemed to be a cross between a scythe and a sword. "This is me."

There had to be more than thirty of these strange symbols. If the ones I could name represented deities, then were they *all* connected to divine beings? Our realm only knows twelve Gods and Goddesses.

The God of Death continued along, signaling out those which I would be able to connect to faces: Calaeya, the beauty of the rose, Melissae, the rains of the seasons, Arendiel, the owl of wisdom, Evette, the scales of justice, and Syades, the flames of chaos.

Though there were many others, it seemed Dameniel knew those with whom I had come in contact. He pointed to another one, one that didn't make sense for the members of the pantheon I had learned about in my first life.

He directed my attention to a strange, winged beast of many colors, of fire and ash.

"In the beginning," Dameniel took his hand away from the picture to give me his full attention, his silver eyes glowing in the shadows, "We were many. Crafted from forces beyond comprehension, and they were one: unified."

He widened his arms, as if indicating that the many symbols did, in fact, refer to more deities.

"Fate came first, and despite the misconception, is not the parent of the first beings, but instead their sibling. It warned its brother and sister that dividing their power would be their undoing, but still they persisted. With each divine creation, their power lessened, and they were reduced to their most basic forms, one of light and one of dark; the balance on which Fate rested."

"The primordial beings?"

No one knew much about the 'first beings' aside from their creation of our deities, who then created our realm.

"Yes, Celessa, those responsible for all that has come to pass," he continued, turning to face the pillars.

"The light and the dark were responsible for spinning Fate with their magic, for without it, they would simply cease to be. Though weakened, they still bore enough power to turn the wheel, but they could no longer do it alone. The deities took up this great task, using our magic to influence the continuation, but we grew restless.

"Curiosity blesses and it damns, which we had to learn of our own merit, so we went on to engage in unions that would create our children."

I couldn't fathom Dameniel having children, appearing so young and innocent.

"Our children could not survive, as the watering down of magic was not conducive to life in the Nothingness."

The Nothingness, a place I had fallen so many times and feared was a product of my madness, was real.

"We had to find a way to preserve them, as we were plunged into the first misery with the continuous losses, and so we created the realms. The life within our creation resulted in a different kind of magic, the magic of new life and the birth of destiny. It fueled Fate, giving it power from the forces within, and the wheel began to spin on its own. We were free.

"It was not without steep cost, as our children were doomed to die, martyred as the first mortals. For the second time, despite all our efforts, we experienced loss and suffering. While some of us came to accept it, others could not; in time, with our blessings, the first immortal children were born. However, with power comes madness. Our offspring, mortal and immortal alike, suffered many afflictions that began to affect us as well: lust, greed, gluttony, envy, and wrath, to name a few.

"With these new comings, our magic shifted - giving each of us a purpose to serve the creation that spins Fate, to serve the very realm we had crafted. We could not choose how our power changed, forced to discern our abilities through trial and error, often failing and condemning the realms to chaos and ruin. It took centuries for us to learn that, without such failure, there was no evolution, and so we grew — we changed."

"You became the God of Death without a choice in the matter?"

I couldn't imagine the burden that came with such power, with such a daunting task.

"There is always a choice. We chose how our power was used, what came from it, our legacy, and what it meant to the realms."

He offered me a half-reassuring smile, like he wanted to believe his own words as he spoke them.

Dameniel approached the pillar to the far-left, and it glowed brighter in his presence as he skimmed his fingers over an inscription in the stone.

"Our creators are cryptic, as only they can commune directly with Fate in discerning the future. When we chose our own path to preserve our children, not so different from what they had chosen for themselves, they turned away from us. When they did, they turned against each other, as well.

"It was felt in all the realms, the *shift*. They'd been corrupted by our creation, and what forces affected us had extended to them, as well.

"Cemrin, the light, delivered to us a prophecy from Fate. It was foretold that the final deity would be born to remake the realms in magic, blessing us with an end to the discord, and then used their singular magic to create Astera, who gifted us the stars — drastically changing our creation with their beauty."

"But then the stars disappeared because she left?" I asked.

The silver orbs penetrated my very soul.

"Astera was not the one foretold; though, her symbol appeared all the same. She was created, not born."

An unsettling feeling bubbled up into my chest as I waited on bated breath for him to elaborate.

"The only beings *born* with divine magic are Amalgam children, but their births never marked symbols upon the pillars, until you," Dameniel continued, gesturing to the strange animal engraving he had pointed out before. "We feared their divinity would be the undoing of all we had made. The Amalgams did not relent without a fight, you see, they fought back when we sought to eradicate them to preserve our creation. Several deities perished forever, and many others fled."

"*That* is why Syades wanted me dead; he said Amalgams were a great calamity."

The small god hissed in anger, "*We* were the calamity! Those souls did not deserve the ends they met for our selfishness and ignorance. I separated from the others to create this place for them, the Hereafter, to harbor worthy souls so that they might find some semblance of peace. The pantheon was wrong, an Amalgam would not fulfill the prophecy. It was explicitly stated that a deity would be born."

"Deities aren't born... they're created. You said that yourself."

The truth was looming right in front of me, though my mind could not grasp it.

"Merok, the darkness, knew better than Cemrin. They resented their counterpart for attempting to fulfill the prophecy by creating a deity alone, something that had never been done before. With their greater understanding, Odric was called upon to deliver the essence of divine magic unto a mortal host. He was vulnerable, having lost Astera and several of his children, so he obliged Merok in fulfilling this task."

My breathing was ragged, painful, and distressed.

"Odric is not your father, Celessa. You have no father."

Dameniel grabbed my shoulders gently.

"The divinity delivered to your mortal mother was bound to a mortal body, and you were born. You were never an Amalgam — you are the Goddess born to remake the realms."

He pulled me close to the symbol that marked my existence and said, "A dragon was a creature of our early designs, a harbinger of destruction, as you must be the Goddess of Destruction; the only one with the power to undo all that has been done."

"I-I don't understand," I stammered.

Dameniel looked slightly flustered by my insecurity in his proclamation, but it didn't feel real.

I had believed myself cursed, believed myself to be an Amalgam, and even told as much by other deities. How could this be true? I didn't *feel* like a Goddess, though the power I bore was terrible and ever-changing.

"Every instance in which you used your magic, it grew stronger, yes?"

I nodded slightly.

"Your divinity was shedding its mortal prison each time it was released, revealing your truth. Over time, it would have fallen away completely, no longer restrained. When you died a mortal death, it finalized the transformation, freed from its bonds."

I'm not dead.

"You will return to the realm as you were always meant to be, Goddess."

Goddess.

"I'm the Goddess of Destruction?"

The sound of my voice was barely audible.

"That remains to be seen, as it is merely my interpretation. You must uncover your purpose as we all once did," Dameniel sighed. "I beseech you to free Odric - only he knows Merok's intentions."

I reeled at his request to unleash the God who I'd believed damned me. Even if he hadn't, he still branded me, tormented me, and sent his vampiric children to upset my entire life. His intentions destroyed me entirely, and I lost everything because of him.

My nightmares flashed in my mind, of the threats he delivered, of every life lost because of him. With a cruel twist of Fate, he is the only one in the realm who knows the truth, and I have no choice but to face him.

Once I uncover the truth, I will find the opportunity to claim his death.

My body felt like it was… slipping.

"Where is my family, Dameniel? Where are my parents? My sisters?"

I wouldn't leave without seeing them, without knowing if they found peace.

"Some things, Celessa, are better left buried."

"No!"

I reached for him, tried to grab him, to demand that he take me to them.

My hands filtered right through his body.

"None may retain physical form in this realm, but me," he declared.

My vision shifted, reality becoming splintered, shifting.

"Farewell, Goddess," Dameniel bid.

"No!" I tried again, but it was too late.

I've been here before, and I know this place.

This place was somewhere in between, somewhere where you couldn't really see or feel.

You could only hear and think.

Somewhere in the middle of life and death was a journey I had made before.

It didn't last long, this in between, just a few moments.

I have a choice, a purpose: destroy, rebuild, transform.

I must begin anew.

Against every odd, in spite of all those who have condemned me, and despite death itself, I returned.

Breathe.

I opened my eyes.

Chapter Twenty-Eight

Poorly Mistaken

Maygen

Some strange voice had been plaguing me, a whisper that only I could hear. Day after day, night after night, it persisted. Beckoning, as if carried by a lifeless phantom breeze, it called me.

I busied myself more than usual, trying to escape the constant gnawing at my mind. I didn't know what it was, or who it was, but I was afraid of it.

I was afraid of what it meant.

It had taken me a long time to fall into place, to find a sense of normalcy in a world without my grandfather. I didn't remember my parents much, since I'd been so young when they died. Halwyn, though, my mother's father - I missed him.

One couldn't tell by looking at me that I had Elvish blood - a blessing - it was easy to hide my heritage. I also bore watered down Mage blood from my father, muted by the mixing of many bloodlines, for I had no magical gifts. There was no need for me to live on the run, but my grandfather had been discovered to have created a family with a mortal woman.

He paid for it; they all did.

Thankfully, I was not alone. I had my father's family and all of those whom Lysenna had welcomed over the years. I had Cian.

I was too afraid to tell them about the distant call, something trying to pull me away from home. It started when I learned my family history, the darkness that had been swept away and buried over one hundred years ago.

A member of my ancestry was an Amalgam, something dangerous and forbidden. It was said that her power was great and terrible, and that she'd been disposed of by a great Mage, to save us all from her wrath.

The whisper says that the history is a lie, and that it has been rewritten.

"Maygen?" A familiar voice sliced through the fog, snagging my attention. "You cut yourself."

Looking down, I realized that a long gash had opened on the palm of my hand, probably from a knife in the dish basin.

Everything I did was absent-minded, as I was absorbed by cryptic words and strange feelings.

"Shit," I mumbled, wrapping it in a dingy cloth from the countertop.

"What's going on with you lately?"

Erelim, my cousin a few years older than I, grabbed my hand to put pressure on the wound.

"Don't say 'nothing'. We both know it's a lie. Talk to me," he insisted.

My molars pressed against the gummy flesh of my cheek, biting down to stop any confessions from flowing out. I trusted Erelim, but I wasn't sure he was the first person with whom I wanted to reveal my apparent insanity.

"What do you think about the last Amalgam?" I tried.

He raised a questioning brow, "The one from Teskaria? Your blood?"

I nodded.

"I think she was likely a victim. I mean, who wouldn't fight back against a death sentence? She didn't get to choose her parents, you know?"

Erelim sighed, rubbing the back of his neck, as he asked, "Is that what has been bothering you? I could talk to my mother-"

"No, no! Don't do that. I just..." My feet shuffled, as I was unsure of what to say next.

"I just don't feel right about it, you know? Something tells me that what we have learned is wrong, that she's still out there."

He hummed thoughtfully while his eyes darted around the room.

"There may be somewhere we can find answers. Mother has contraband from Greilor, and it's the one place where the Gods regularly commune with the people of the realm. Maybe there's more information about it in one of the books? It hasn't been *that* long since she was supposedly destroyed, right?"

It was forbidden to have any contact with the rebel country. Lysenna tried to keep her treasonous 'activities' secret from the rest of the house, but Erelim was the eldest son and her heir. She had no choice but to tell him a great many things, things he often relayed to me without her knowledge. She had to divulge to him just who or what she was communicating with in the rumored wastelands. However, what was known to *me* is that any who dwell there are enemies of the Three Kingdoms.

Erelim and I spent the better half of the night holed up in his room flipping through the books, reading illegal accounts from people who may be long dead by now. I had wanted to give up, as nothing seemed to hold the information we were searching for, until Erelim sprung up from his place on the bed and plopped some parchment on top of the opened book in my lap.

"Look at this!" He quietly exclaimed. "This references the deity responsible for creating the Amalgam: a harbinger of the darkness."

Finally, *something* that might satisfy the hushed voices invading my subconscious.

"It's a God, though it doesn't say which one. The deities forbid the creation of Amalgams due to their deadly nature and the havoc they wreaked upon the realms in the early ages. When his indiscretion was discovered, they imprisoned him."

"Does it say where?" I asked.

The language scrawled on the paper fluctuated between the common tongue and the old language of the gods, with which I was unfamiliar.

Erelim inspected it further, sounding out the foreign words until unveiling a favorable answer, "The far north, where nothing thrives."

The northern border of Euros cut off our country from a desolate winter land, frozen and uninhabitable. It would make sense that they would place a villain there, where no living being dared venture. However, it was only a few short days from our home in Autumnmoor to reach the closest settlement to the territory; Stillfrost Outpost. As far as I knew, the outpost stood abandoned.

"Are you going to tell Cian?"

My cousin's words cleaved my train of thought in two.

"What would I say? That I'm going crazy, hearing voices, and I think the only way to make it stop is to find answers about an *Amalgam*?"

I squeezed my head between sweaty palms.

"You're hearing voices?" Erelim asked.

I shuddered.

Shit.

"People don't just hear voices, Maygen. Either you're losing your mind..." He nudged me with an elbow. "Or something is summoning you through means of magic. Neither of which should be taken lightly."

"If it doesn't go away, I *will* lose my mind. Cian would never let me go searching for anything magic-related, and it could be dangerous."

A heavy sigh caved my chest inward, and the level of exasperation I felt was beyond comprehension.

The ghostly presence made itself known again, seemingly pleased with the information I had uncovered. Every hair on my body rose as it breathed purpose into my subconscious, sewing seeds of intention and truth in the crevices of my brain.

It needed her. *I* needed her.

Celessa, it whispered.

Groaning, I pushed two fingers against each temple as if I were trying to relieve a migraine. Did I have any choice in this matter? Why did it have to be me? Was it because I shared her blood?

I was afraid, and I felt alone.

"Maygen," Erelim's voice had softened with concern and affection.

"We have to tell Cian."

I nodded.

"And my mother," he added.

My aunt would not take this well. She feared the forces at work in the world and had always kept us safe from them at the estate. What would she think, and how would she react?

Erelim offered a hand to guide me from our workspace on the bed; I gripped it tightly, and he squeezed my fingers back to offer reassurance that we were making the right decision.

My limbs were tingling, my head humming with anticipation and dread. Though my steps were unsure, we arrived outside Lysenna's door all the same. It was late, and with every passing second, I was becoming more anxious.

I tapped against the wood lightly, secretly hoping that I wouldn't wake her, but in less than a moment the latch popped and the door opened. Lysenna's disheveled appearance did not indicate that she had been asleep, and she looked more distressed than anything, like she'd been plagued by nightmares or insomnia.

She stared at me with her strange purplish eyes, with brows furrowed and her jaw clenched.

"Have you heard it? That name?" The woman whispered.

Erelim nudged me inside before retreating back to the hallway.

"I'll get Cian," he murmured.

Lysenna gripped my shoulders, steering my attention back toward her.

"The name, child."

My breaths were ragged, and even my tongue seemed to tremble as I forced out the answer, "Celessa."

"No!" Cian growled.

Lysenna huffed in exasperation, pacing the length of her bedroom as we all watched from plush chairs sat against the far wall.

After Erelim and I had laid out the information we uncovered, as well as being urged to finally reveal the magic that plagued me, and apparently Lysenna as well, Cian was disinterested in hearing any more. He knew what I meant to do and what I had already decided. I didn't blame him for being wary, as any rational person would be, but the sentience that invaded my consciousness offered no other choice.

"You could die. Why waste your life for something that may not exist? Why risk everything for a vague mystery at best?" He shouted, rising from his resting place as sweat began beading against his forehead.

"I'm going mad, Cian. Mad. Every passing day it gets worse, and it feels like it's physically pulling me toward this, whatever it is. I have to do *something*," I murmured, my voice low.

"So, we could start at the source?" Erelim suggested, gathering our attention. "It said the God who created the Amalgam is imprisoned in the far north, and if that's true, what if we find them?"

"And incur the wrath of a deity scorned? You're out of your damn mind!" Cian spat.

"If they are imprisoned, it is doubtful that physical magics would be able to escape the barrier in which they are kept. Otherwise, it would be too easy to seek a way out," my cousin argued, his comment was followed by muttered curses that passed between the two men.

"Yes," I whispered, quieting the room.

"No!" Cian reiterated.

I stood, approaching the man I love, taking his hands in my own.

"Though I need you by my side, if you will not come with me, I will go alone."

Invisible claws scraped my mind, pushing me further.

"I have no choice."

A lone tear rolled down my cheek at the thundering headache the assault left behind.

"It *hurts*, Cian," my lip quivered as I uttered the words.

Strong fingers squeezed my shoulder from behind.

"I will go with you, Maygen. We will go as far as we need to, to fix this," Erelim reaffirmed, directing his attention to Cian. "Are you with us?"

My lover's fangs pressed into his bottom lip as his dark brows furrowed and loving eyes trained on my face; I searched for something in his frustration.

A long silence passed between us before he finally answered.

"I'm with you."

We traveled by carriage, overloaded with provisions. Though hesitant, Lysenna gave us her blessing in our travels, paying the hired help double their normal wages to ensure we'd have everything we needed for our excursion and then some extra, a lot extra. She made us swear to stay a safe distance away from the God if we found him, to get whatever information we could and then flee.

As expected, Stillfrost Outpost was, in fact, abandoned. It was quiet, and snow tumbled across the ground, forced from its resting place by strong winter winds. Only a handful of buildings still remained erect, where several others had fallen prey to the relentless assault of time and unforgiving weather, tattered and crumbling. This place felt like death.

It had only taken the three of us two days to reach this desolate place, just south of the border to a forbidden mystery, a place none dared to wander. I was curious if it had always been this way, or if the Gods made it so. It was a perfect location for their prisoners, as it was unsurvivable, unless, of course, that prisoner happened to be a deity - forever lost in their own misery.

"Make sure you layer up. The carriage won't be able to make it through the pass, we'll be going on foot," Erelim commanded, tossing me a heavy, fur-lined coat.

"The horses?" Cian inquired.

"I'm sure they'd do their best, but I'm not sure it's worth the risk," Erelim sighed, frowning, as he skimmed the document from Greilor. "This needs to happen as quickly as possible. Based on the descriptions in these readings, it's directly north of the border past the outpost, so we aren't far off."

I shrugged on several articles of clothing before finishing with the coat. Cian knelt at my feet, lacing up the heavy boots I'd pulled over thick wool socks.

"You know, I can still reach even with all of this junk on," I offered lightheartedly.

Cian sighed, "I feel helpless, Maygen. You felt like you had to struggle on your own all this time, and it led us somewhere we could potentially *die*."

He looked up from his place on the ground, locking our eyes.

"We've barely lived. We deserve a peaceful life after all we have been through."

He was right.

We were both orphans, our parents claimed by the cruelty of the world. Life before then hadn't been easy, though we didn't remember it much. Being noble children of mixed lineage, we were born with targets on our backs. Our very existence was frowned upon, and for many in the Three Kingdoms, it was a death sentence.

It was sickening to think how persons of nobility would cast out their family members for those they chose to love, for having children that weren't 'pure blooded'. They would order them to be hunted down, seeking to punish them, or worse.

It was more bearable for people who were without noble blood, for there were less expectations, less rules. To find commoners of mixed race wasn't unusual, though they were treated worse than their counterparts. It's harder for them to find work, to secure legal marriages, and to even be treated fairly by society. I dreamed of a different world, a better one, where our parents still lived, and we were openly accepted by family and acquaintances alike.

"I haven't had a chance to..." Cian trailed off.

Erelim cast us a sidelong glance and scurried away, busying himself with loading provisions into our packs.

"To what?" I inquired, cocking a brow at Erelim's sudden strange behavior.

Cian's expression turned serious, but he remained on his knees, gazing up at me.

"Oh," I breathed, my muscles all tensing in unison.

"The ring is at the estate," he started, "But I don't want this to wait any longer, just in case."

Nodding slowly, I waited for him to continue, excited and nervous all at once. I love Cian, but what he was about to propose frightened me, and it always has. Despite the stories of love and marriage told to me of my parents, of Lysenna and her late husband, I had never found matrimony appealing. I didn't need a title to ensure my enduring love, but I think I was already beginning to feel differently.

"I know of your reservations about this but-"

I cut him off with a gentle finger against his lips.

"How I feel about you goes beyond my own foolishness."

I smiled.

His lip quivered at my confession, and he continued, "I love you, Maygen. I want to love you forever, in every way. I want everyone to know how much I love you, through every expression. I would be honored if you would become my wife."

If I cry, it'll probably just freeze to my cheeks, so a sob-stifled-laugh took the place of my tears of joy.

"Yes."

Cian rose to embrace me, bathing me in his warmth. Another wave of heat hit me, as Erelim crushed us with affection of his own.

"Damn it," my now-fiancé sighed.

Erelim's chest bounced as he hiccupped a sob, crying as he squeezed us. He'd always been very open with his love for us all, never one to shy away from physical displays or vocal expressions of his feelings. It was funny and heartwarming. Cian was blessed to have a loyal best friend, and I was blessed to have a great cousin.

"I've never been so happy! I thought it was never going to happen!" He sniffled.

"You're ridiculous," Cian grumbled.

I can see you, the voice whispered, prompting me to rip myself away from the two men — whirling, startled, I searched for the source.

"Where are you?" I called out to something, to someone.

Erelim and Cian went silent, watching as I frantically searched amidst a vast expanse of white for the God, and seeing nothing at all.

Closer, it insisted.

I trembled, a shiver caused not by the bitter cold, but by fear.

I know who you are, Maygen, the magic hissed.

My breathing became ragged, terrified, and I wanted to go home. I couldn't. My feet were rooted to that spot, unwilling to let me go anywhere but forward, toward this mystery that may be my undoing. This place, this purpose, could very well sign my death sentence.

I wanted nothing to do with Gods and monsters, with their curses and their legends; I just wanted to live. Deep down, I knew I had no choice and that my life would never truly be my own again.

One step at a time, I moved forward, sure that I would find it. I *felt* it. My hand reached out ahead of my body, and disappeared before my eyes from the wrist down.

I gasped, pulling it back.

Strong hands gripped my waist from behind, and Cian's breath in my ear was hot and as unsteady as my own.

"I don't like this."

He turned to look at Erelim and asked, "What is it?"

"A barrier, it seems, one of illusion."

My cousin attempted to push through as I had done, but was stopped as if he had pressed against a reflectionless mirror.

"Do they have to let you in?" I asked.

He frowned slightly and confessed, "I don't know."

Erelim's eyes flicked to Cian, tilting his head to gesture that he should try as well.

One spot of warmth left my body as he raised a hand away from my hip to touch the magic, and slowly, his fingers disappeared behind the veil.

"Shit," Erelim hissed. "I can't use my magic to protect you two if I can't get through."

The winter winds stilled for a moment, leaving little more than a breeze that caressed my face, almost as if to reassure or encourage me.

"I think..." I took a deep breath. "I think we'll be safe. Whoever it is, doesn't want to hurt me. Maybe I should go alone?"

Cian bristled at the suggestion, exclaiming, "Over my dead body! If I can pass through, then there is no damn reason for you to do this by yourself. I am with you, Maygen, now and always."

I was so blessed to be loved by this man.

Pressing my fingers into my lover's hand and offering a small smile to my cousin, I turned toward the obstacle in our way, and we pushed through. It was like moving through the thickest fog, slightly blurring my vision and making my chest feel heavy, like my lungs had filled with moisture. The magic left us in a slight daze, reminding me of the head high you get when smoking the special flowers that Aithen hides from Lysenna.

The burning in my neck and the scream that tore up my throat signified the sudden assault of what I *thought* might be a person. Instantaneously reverting into defense-mode swept away that strange feeling and replaced it with pain and terror. I flailed and fought against my attacker, kicking and pulling at anything with which I could make contact.

My head was beginning to feel light because I was losing blood.

"Cian!" I screamed, but no help came.

A handful of seconds in this place, and I was going to die.

If I was still clinging to life, then it was in a dream-state, obscured and surreal. Perhaps I was floating? It seemed I was drifting over the icy ground as I looked up at an overcast sky, with sad gray clouds aglow in sunlight which couldn't break through.

Snowflakes seemed to flutter in slow motion, kissing my cheeks, clinging to my eyelashes, and obstructing my vision for only a moment until I blinked them away. The cold was seeping through the layers of my clothing, creeping down into my bones and gripping my heart, slowing the rhythmic beats.

Was this what death felt like? Was it reminiscent of soaring along beautiful terrain, the last place you see before it claims you — wondering if you truly met your end, or if anything was real?

Breath was still inflating my lungs, pushing my ribs against my skin as they stretched. I *felt* alive, so what had happened to me? I was freezing and shivering, but holding onto something, some*one*.

In fact, I was being carried by someone.

My eyes flicked away from the glittering precipitation, looking for my savior, looking for Cian.

Who I found was a man, but someone whom I'd never seen before. His hair was a soft shade of brown, and his eyes were so deeply blue, like the bottomless depths of a frozen sea. Underneath his beard I was sure he had a nice jawline, as you could tell by the high cheekbones and lips that were just full enough to pull his features together in an attractive way.

He noticed that I was looking at him, that I was alive. I was cradled in his arms as he continued to walk along, not saying a word, but I could still hear him.

Maygen, the voice was his, and it caressed my mind gently, reassuringly.

"It's you," I croaked.

He was the one who summoned me, the imprisoned one — the God.

Acknowledgement was given with the slightest nod before he ducked into the doorway of a small, crudely-built shelter. There was a fire in the center of the one-room building, surrounded by a few beds with tattered blankets on the ground. Though, the fire must have been fueled by magic, as there were no branches beneath to keep it lit.

The deity set me down on one of the makeshift beds before sitting beside me, a look of poorly-concealed defeat and solemnity painted over his features.

"Who are you?" I asked, fighting against the dizziness that plagued me.

"I am Odric," the man replied, steadying me with his hands as I faltered.

"The God of War?"

"Yes, Maygen, and I have called upon you to fulfill a great purpose."

I wasn't sure I was built for such things, for greatness or for carrying out the tasks of a divine being.

Not knowing exactly what he expected from me made me uneasy. How was I meant to understand what he needed from me when I couldn't focus? My neck throbbed, sore and stiff. Someone had attacked me, I remembered, touching the wound gingerly with my fingertips.

"I am sorry about that," Odric sighed, brushing my injury with his palm.

Relief washed over me at the site of his touch, clearing away the physical pain, but doing little to quell the effects of blood loss.

"You must understand, my dear, I can only do so much for them," he whispered. "They're starving."

I turned my head to scan the room, but saw no one.

"Who?"

"My children," he amended.

I remembered the lore taught to the peoples of the realm, how Odric and Astera's children came to be cursed — how they became vampires. A startling realization washed over me, something I knew but didn't think of often. Cian was half-vampire; he was fathered by one of the first vampires, a son of Odric.

This God is his grandfather.

"Cian-" I started.

"Is safe," the deity interrupted, "and being profusely apologized to by the aunts and uncles he has just met."

Speechless, I waited on bated breath for the man to elaborate. He offered a small smile, one that was forced and wary, drained.

"Five of my children have been victims of this unforgiving punishment; loyal to the end, they are."

Odric huffed what could almost be considered a laugh.

"My eldest girl, Liatris, was the one who mistakenly attacked you."

"Why?" I managed to ask.

"As I said, they're starving. We have been trapped here for well over a hundred years."

A century with no heat, no food, and no civilization. One hundred years alone in exile with no way to escape, with no aid, nor hope.

I couldn't believe how cruel that was, until I remembered the information his magic forced me to uncover; he had been punished for creating something that could undo life as we knew it, a being who could shatter reality and break apart the realms. He created an Amalgam.

"Why have you summoned me? What could I possibly do to help you?"

I quickly felt exasperated, my fear of the unknown resurfacing.

Odric looked deeply into my eyes, penetrating my being with his magic, which in turn began erasing much of my doubt and worry. My concerns of what lay ahead were all but wiped away, replaced with a sense of purpose and an unyielding desire to succeed in whatever he might ask of me. I would do what he needed, and I would try to not be afraid.

"I need you to release Celessa Umbraeon. The time has come for the realms to be remade, and no one will accomplish bringing her to her destiny but you, Maygen."

"Why me?" I whispered.

"Because she will love you, and you will love her. There is no greater driving force in this world, for there is nothing more unshakeable than true connection between friends, between *family*."

He said that word in such a strange way that something in me felt like it was a lie, but it was quickly pushed away, smothered.

She was my family, and I must save her.

"Her power is unlike anything that has ever been, and she is the key to righting the wrongs to create something better. She is destruction, and she is salvation. Fate cannot continue on without her."

"And if I fail?"

Odric paused for a moment and showed me something I hadn't thought was possible, fear in a God.

"Then, everything will end. That cannot happen, not when it has all come so far."

When we emerged from the shelter, I was stunned at just how warm the seemingly frigid shack was compared to the winds that ravaged the wasteland.

Cian stood nearby, showing his family how he was able to pass through the barrier by pushing his fingers through and watching them disappear. There were three women and two men, who all looked as if they were on the brink of death, with emaciated figures and hollow eyes.

Seeing them like this made me notice that there didn't appear to be any resemblance between my fiancé and his kin; I wondered if they might look more alike when they're healthy. I found myself curious about what Cian's father had looked like, because I knew he heavily resembled his mother with her dark skin and hair.

Perhaps Cian and Daevian's appearances had helped in hiding their lineage from the courts, for the vampires who stood before me were incredibly, sickly pale; whereas, the men I cared for were rich in tone and glowing with beauty.

I looked to Odric, unsure of how to proceed, unsure of what would come next and where to go from here.

"What happens now? How do I find her?" I asked him.

The God's eyes glimmered, penetrating my mind with his gaze. I worried in that moment that he would be able to sense my lingering hesitance, my wariness, that hint of resistance.

If I could escape this task, then I would. Perhaps if I ran, his magic could not reach me. Maybe it had only worked because we had been so close nearby, as this man was clearly bereft of strength and barely clung on to what he had left to keep his children alive.

Unexpectedly, he gripped my neck, and it happened faster than I could register. Cian cried out in anger at the sight and charged at him, but was quickly subdued in the same manner.

Some strange magic was flooding into us, pooling his commands into our chests as if it were the air in our lungs or the blood in our veins.

"You will be left on the shores of Desmoterion *alone*, you will slay all who get in your way, and you will free Celessa Umbraeon."

His head turned to Cian as he continued, "You will leave her there, and you will wait for her in Dawn's End."

There was no escape, no release from his clutches as he refocused his gaze to meet my own.

"She must be delivered to Briobar, and then swiftly brought to Euros. You will open your home and care for her. You must give her purpose, friendship, and comfort - and then you must die."

Die?

I didn't want to die.

"But why?" I managed to squeak past the tightening grip.

His silence was prolonged, thoughtful and calculated.

"Because she must unleash her wrath, and there is no better way to coerce it than to lose that which she loves most."

Odric turned us, forcing our bodies toward the barrier. The closer he got to the magic, the angrier his skin became, turning red against our throats and heating up to a nearly scalding temperature; we did not scream, and we did not fight.

We could only obey.

"I will not let her die," Cian stated in absolute resolution.

A small, barely audible laugh escaped one of the bodies from somewhere behind us, telltale of the truth: there was nothing he could do to stop it.

"You will have no choice, boy, as this is bigger than any of you," Odric growled.

"I'm afraid," I whispered.

"Fear not, for you won't remember a thing. You will know nothing except for what it is you are meant to do, and who you are meant to be for our Goddess."

Startled, I tried to turn my head to look at him again.

"I thought she was an Amalgam?"

Odric grinned.

"No, my dear, she's just a helpless mortal," he whispered, then shoved Cian and I through the wall.

"Maygen?" A muffled voice called.

It was frigid; every part of me was cold, frozen, unmoving. I could see her face, her brown hair, and her hazel eyes. She was beautiful. I could see her, asleep on a stone table — she was so thin, her skin was dull, and she looked lifeless.

She was my family, so I had to do something; I had to save her.

My eyes opened to Erelim's worried expression, checking me over, with a blinding white sky above him. Would he understand what I'd decided, and would he support me in my endeavors? What would he think when I told him what I meant to do, what I *had* to do, for her?

"What happened in there?" My cousin asked, concern etched deeply into the lines of his frown.

What *did* happen in there?

"I don't think we found anything," I sighed as I struggled to remember. "The magic obscured everything; it even made the voice go away."

"It's gone? Are you feeling better?"

Erelim's shoulders relaxed slightly at my declaration, and he pulled my body from the ground to guide me to the carriage.

The journey home was quiet, but not in an uncomfortable way.

I needed to decide how to get to Sanctuary because I think that's where Celessa is located. It was the most untouchable place in the Three Kingdoms. Only mortals could enter through the magic placed by the Dark Mage, as many without immortality served him because they could never challenge him.

Cian was still asleep in the back of the carriage, and while I didn't remember either of us fainting, I surmised that the magic must have taken too much of a toll when we passed through. The details were foggy, and I couldn't remember much aside from the snowy expanse and a small shelter with empty beds. I could recall a strange fire with no wood.

What had happened to Cian and I?

"Erelim," I whispered, almost too wary to commit fully in requesting his attention.

"Yeah?" He returned, raising an eyebrow at my withdrawn state.

"When we return to the keep, I have to go."

"Go?" He huffed, "Go where?"

I waited a moment before responding, unsure of exactly what I wanted or needed to say.

"I am going to save Celessa."

Acknowledgments

I'd like first to thank my family, the ones I hold closest to me; without seeing your faces day and night, I would not have the motivation or drive to continue growing as a person and pushing towards my goals.

Keira, Jeremy, and Lyanna: your smiles, laughs, hugs, and never-ending love give me strength. You make me want to be better, *do* better, and make things that are wondrous. I want nothing more than for you three to be proud of me and to always follow your own dreams. Ben: for encouraging me each and every day, ensuring I always have everything I need to succeed, and giving me the reassurance I need to make it through, I am eternally grateful and indebted to you. None of this would have been possible without your kindness and generosity. Without you, I would not be where I am or who I am. Thank you for all that you do. I love you all endlessly.

Frank and Vern, without your consistent kindness and consideration, I would surely lose my mind. You two have stepped up in more ways than I could've asked, and you have had a large hand in shaping me into the woman who I am today. You showed me the level of stability and security I wanted to achieve in my life, and with every venture into something new, you have always supported me. You have been my voices of reason and truth, keeping me aware and focused, but never letting me fall after I've stumbled. Thank you for picking me back up, no matter what.

To my mom: any time I have an emergency or a mental breakdown, you're the one whom I call; I'm forever grateful we have the relationship that we do today. Also, I fully blame you for my smutty book addiction, and now I'm the one writing it. See what you did? I'm grateful, though, for you kindled the spark of my interest in reading, which grew into a roaring flame. From entertaining my short stories as a kid, to groaning all the way to the bookstore every time a new *Warriors* book was released (that I absolutely *had* to have and would stay up all night reading at nine years old), all the way to reading the *Fifty Shades* books together, thank you for always making sure if I wanted to read something, I had it in my hand. Now, I'm an author, and that wouldn't have been possible without you.

To my dad: you have been the creative voice in my head since I was a child. I may not have become an artist or a musician, but I have found my way in the creative world, and I can attribute that to wanting to be like you. Even though I have strayed from several of the paths you'd hoped I would take, I genuinely hope you are proud of me. Having a voice is something that has always been extremely important to me, and that voice being heard even more so. You have instilled in me that importance throughout this life. Without your guidance, I fear I may not have any of the confidence or tenacity I have worked tooth-and-nail to build, to become the woman I am today. Every creative endeavor I have ever pursued has been supported and encouraged by you, and I will forever be grateful.

For my siblings Christian Moretti, Daylynn Enriquez, and Isabella Franey: you have all shaped me into the person I've become. Early in life, I was compelled to be the best version of myself I could be, if only to make you proud. Although I was handed an early parenting role for the sake of ensuring you all were cared for, I truly believe it was for the better, for all of us. The love we share has kept me afloat in even the darkest of times, and I can't imagine life without any of you. I am thankful to be your big sister and, even more so, your friend.

A monumental amount of thanks is deserved for my wonderful editor, Madison Ennis. I simply could not have done this without you. I am so thankful to have been connected with someone so honest, kind, encouraging, and efficient as you. Your comments and reactions with regards to my writing as we worked through this project together helped me find a sense of confidence in my creative abilities. Being sure I was able to afford your services in such a trying time for me financially has been more of a blessing than I can express, and I am so grateful for you. I cannot wait to see what the future holds for our professional relationship and friendship.

For my devoted beta readers, I am more appreciative than I can express for you all: Miranda Brownawell, Frances Martin, Hannah Gerard, Courtney Stemmler, Jessica Brown, Desiree Franey, and Kellie Kauffman. You maintained meeting my deadlines, tolerating my incessant bothering, and giving me the honest feedback I so craved. Without your support, I would have continued to second-guess everything I had done thus far. You have eased my doubt with your words of encouragement. Furthermore, I am grateful to have friends in my life who were so willing to be a part of a dream I have spent my entire life hoping to achieve; I would not have made it to publishing without you all.

Miranda, *specifically* you have been a rock and voice of reason for me throughout it all. Thank you for listening to every idea, entertaining every manic rant about my characters (no matter how deranged), and supporting every single decision I've made. I couldn't imagine pursuing creativity without you.

Franny and Jess: I couldn't ask for better fantasy dweebs with whom to bounce ideas. I'm grateful to have been able to share my story with you, and to be allowed to peer into your creative minds and read your own work, as well. I can't wait to see us all grow as readers and writers, and I am manifesting your success in your creative endeavors; I hope I will have the opportunity to be a part of it.

Courtney and Desiree: having two avid readers and well-read critics on my project has given me an insurmountable amount of anxiety, but if anyone has reassured me that my work is worth reading, it has been you two. Your honesty and grace throughout this process has humbled me and encouraged me to keep pushing through.

Hannah and Kellie, though we have not known each other long, your willingness to participate in this endeavor has warmed my dark, little heart. It was refreshing to have people on the project who stand to risk nothing through their honesty, and it was incredibly helpful to me as I prepared for publishing. Thank you for taking this plunge with me.

Finally, thank you to my readers who made it through the book, and especially if you checked my acknowledgements out of curiosity to see my progression. I look forward to sharing more of my ideas and fantasies with you in the future, and I am excited to see what the future holds for us all.

World Map courtesy of features available on Inkarnate.com
Cover design courtesy of Chris Moretti
Finalized cover design courtesy of Pandora_halk on Fiverr.com

Inspirational Acknowledgments

I would like to thank various creators for the inspiration that they have unknowingly provided to an adoring fan, which pushed and guided me through the process of writing this novel. Without these valuable strangers, my story would not be what it is today. I am deeply grateful for the art released by these individuals, and the comfort and creativity it has offered me throughout my own journey of finding myself and pursuing my dreams.

Lyrical & Instrumental

Bad Omens
Noah Sebastian, Joakim Karlsson, Nicholas Ruffilo, & Nick Folio

Your music has become deeply engraved within my creative being, and I often find myself reading your lyrics and playing through your songs in times where I struggle to find my voice. The emotion within your words, while enhanced by incredible instrumental scores, often helped to ignite my imagination and encouraged me to keep pushing forward. It's guided me throughout my creative process to achieve my dream of becoming a published author. I feel that throughout my year-long journey of writing my first novel, your words have inspired me the most. From the bottom of my heart, thank you.

Lindsey Stirling

This music is some of the most fantastical, fantasy-esque melodies to have ever graced my ears. In times where I was struggling to visualize a scene, your instrumentals opened up a place within me where beauty resides, gracefully transferring it onto the pages of this story. I am deeply appreciative of the enchanting and alluring melodies you have shared with our world. For me personally, it has offered genuine peace and clarity. Thank you.

Caskets
Chris McIntosh, Benji Wilson, Matt Flood, Craig Robinson, & James Lazenby

Hidden parts of myself were exposed through indulging in your music; thanks to your lyrics, emotions which have otherwise been repressed were allowed to surface and contribute to the writing of my novel. In times where my characters felt great sorrow, the beauty of your words helped me to find my own, so that I might convey such intense emotions as harmoniously as you have. Thank you greatly for the inspiration you have offered.

Halsey
Ashley Frangipane

The empowerment, especially for a woman such as myself, that comes from your music greatly influenced my storyline, especially where female characters are concerned. These women, who come from my mind, face many hardships and rampant oppression, and they must fight to have their own identity and overcome these hardships - much like us. I look forward to having your music to guide me throughout this series, as they step into their power the way you have. Thank you for being a beacon of strength.

About the Author

Jordyn A Moretti is a small business owner, hobby artist, and author of the new novel *Cursed Is The Blood*.

Growing up in western Pennsylvania, Jordyn enjoyed escaping the reality of small town life through the adventures inside of her favorite novels. Beginning at a young age, she was an avid writer and reader, and found herself drawn to fantasy works such as Lord of the Rings, Game of Thrones, and her favorite childhood series, Warriors. A fantasy enthusiast; she is also passionate about her crystal business, women's rights, and her journey through motherhood.

Jordyn loves to hear from her readers!
You can email her at authorjmoretti@gmail.com
Find her on:
Facebook Author Jordyn A Moretti
Instagram @authorjamoretti
Tiktok @realjamoretti
Twitter @realJAMoretti
Find the World Map for Cursed Is The Blood on her social media pages

Printed in Great Britain
by Amazon